Robert Louis Stevenson (13 November 1850 – 3 December 1894) was a Scottish novelist and travel writer, most noted for Treasure Island, Kidnapped, Strange Case of Dr Jekyll and Mr Hyde, and A Child's Garden of Verses. Born and educated in Edinburgh, Stevenson suffered from serious bronchial trouble for much of his life, but continued to write prolifically and travel widely, in defiance of his poor health. As a young man, he mixed in London literary circles, receiving encouragement from Andrew Lang, Edmund Gosse, Leslie Stephen and W. E. Henley, the last of whom may have provided the model for Long John Silver in Treasure Island. His travels took him to France, America and Australia, before he finally settled in Samoa, where he died. A celebrity in his lifetime, Stevenson attracted a more negative critical response for much of the 20th century, though his reputation has been largely restored. He is currently ranked as the 26th most translated author in the world.(Source: Wikipedia)

Literary works:
The Hair Trunk or The Ideal Commonwealth (1877)
Unfinished and unpublished.
Treasure Island (1883)
Prince Otto (1885)
Strange Case of Dr Jekyll and Mr Hyde (1886),
Kidnapped (1886)
The Black Arrow: A Tale of the Two Roses (1888)
The Master of Ballantrae: A Winter's Tale (1889),
The Wrong Box (1889)
The Wrecker (1892); co-written with Lloyd Osbourne.
Catriona (1893)
The Ebb-Tide (1894); co-written with Lloyd Osbourne.
Weir of Hermiston (1896)

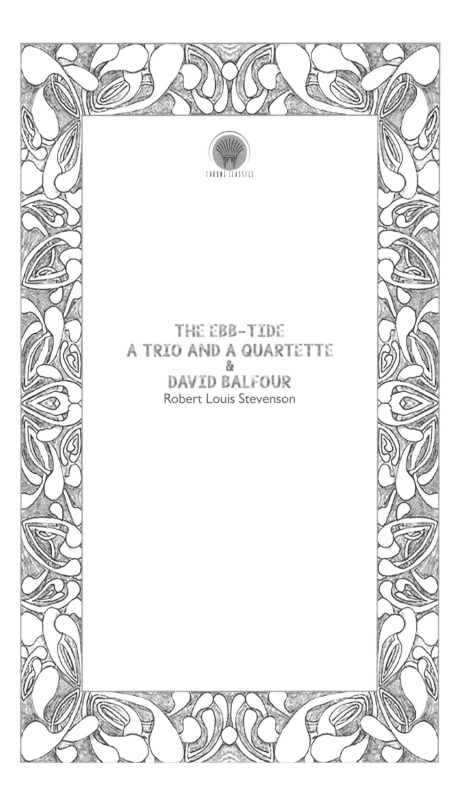

THRONE CLASSICS

THE EBB-TIDE
A TRIO AND A QUARTETTE
&
DAVID BALFOUR
Robert Louis Stevenson

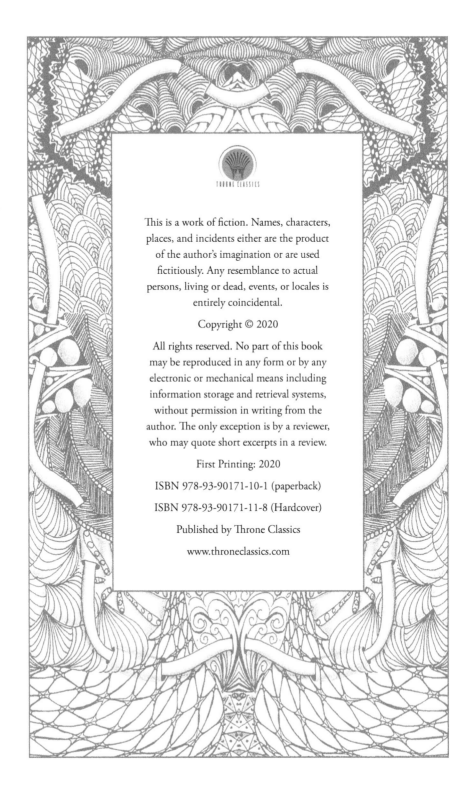

THRONE CLASSICS

First Printing: 2020

ISBN 978-93-90171-10-1 (paperback)

ISBN 978-93-90171-11-8 (Hardcover)

Published by Throne Classics

www.throneclassics.com

Contents

THE EBB-TIDE
A TRIO AND A QUARTETTE
&
DAVID BALFOUR

THE EBB-TIDE. A TRIO AND A QUARTETTE

PART I. THE TRIO

Chapter 1. NIGHT ON THE BEACH

Throughout the island world of the Pacific, scattered men of many European races and from almost every grade of society carry activity and disseminate disease. Some prosper, some vegetate. Some have mounted the steps of thrones and owned islands and navies. Others again must marry for a livelihood; a strapping, merry, chocolate-coloured dame supports them in sheer idleness; and, dressed like natives, but still retaining some foreign element of gait or attitude, still perhaps with some relic (such as a single eye-glass) of the officer and gentleman, they sprawl in palm-leaf verandahs and entertain an island audience with memoirs of the music-hall. And there are still others, less pliable, less capable, less fortunate, perhaps less base, who continue, even in these isles of plenty, to lack bread.

At the far end of the town of Papeete, three such men were seated on the beach under a purao tree.

It was late. Long ago the band had broken up and marched musically home, a motley troop of men and women, merchant clerks and navy officers, dancing in its wake, arms about waist and crowned with garlands. Long ago darkness and silence had gone from house to house about the tiny pagan city. Only the street lamps shone on, making a glow-worm halo in the umbrageous alleys or drawing a tremulous image on the waters of the port. A sound of snoring ran among the piles of lumber by the Government pier. It was wafted ashore from the graceful clipper-bottomed schooners, where they lay moored close in like dinghies, and their crews were stretched upon the deck under the open sky or huddled in a rude tent amidst the disorder of merchandise.

But the men under the purao had no thought of sleep. The same temperature in England would have passed without remark in summer; but it was bitter cold for the South Seas. Inanimate nature knew it, and the bottle of cocoanut oil stood frozen in every bird-cage house about the island; and the men knew it, and shivered. They wore flimsy cotton clothes, the same they had sweated in by day and run the gauntlet of the tropic showers; and to complete their evil case, they had no breakfast to mention, less dinner, and no supper at all.

In the telling South Sea phrase, these three men were ON THE BEACH. Common calamity had brought them acquainted, as the three most miserable English-speaking creatures in Tahiti; and beyond their misery, they knew next to nothing of each other, not even their true names. For each had made a long apprenticeship in going downward; and each, at some stage of the descent, had been shamed into the adoption of an alias. And yet not one of them had figured in a court of justice; two were men of kindly virtues; and one, as he sat and shivered under the purao, had a tattered Virgil in his pocket.

Certainly, if money could have been raised upon the book, Robert Herrick would long ago have sacrificed that last possession; but the demand for literature, which is so marked a feature in some parts of the South Seas, extends not so far as the dead tongues; and the Virgil, which he could not exchange against a meal, had often consoled him in his hunger. He would study it, as he lay with tightened belt on the floor of the old calaboose, seeking favourite passages and finding new ones only less beautiful because they lacked the consecration of remembrance. Or he would pause on random country walks; sit on the path side, gazing over the sea on the mountains of Eimeo; and dip into the Aeneid, seeking sortes. And if the oracle (as is the way of oracles) replied with no very certain nor encouraging voice, visions of England at least would throng upon the exile's memory: the busy schoolroom, the green playing-fields, holidays at home, and the perennial roar of London, and the fireside, and the white head of his father. For it is the destiny of those grave, restrained and classic writers, with whom we make enforced and often painful acquaintanceship at school, to pass into the blood and become native in the memory; so that a phrase of Virgil speaks not so much of Mantua or Augustus, but of English places and the student's own irrevocable youth.

Robert Herrick was the son of an intelligent, active, and ambitious man, small partner in a considerable London house. Hopes were conceived of the boy; he was sent to a good school, gained there an Oxford scholarship, and proceeded in course to the Western University. With all his talent and taste (and he had much of both) Robert was deficient in consistency and intellectual manhood, wandered in bypaths of study, worked at music or at metaphysics when he should have been at Greek, and took at last a paltry degree. Almost at the same time, the London house was disastrously wound up; Mr Herrick must begin the world again as a clerk in a strange office, and Robert relinquish his ambitions and accept with gratitude a career that he detested and despised. He had no head for figures, no interest in affairs, detested the constraint of hours, and despised the aims and the success of merchants. To grow rich was none of his ambitions; rather to do well. A worse or a more bold young man would have refused the destiny; perhaps tried his future with his pen; perhaps enlisted. Robert, more prudent, possibly more timid, consented to embrace that way of life in which he could most readily assist his family. But he did so with a mind divided; fled the neighbourhood of former comrades; and chose, out of several positions placed at his disposal, a clerkship in New York.

His career thenceforth was one of unbroken shame. He did not drink, he was exactly honest, he was never rude to his employers, yet was everywhere discharged. Bringing no interest to his duties, he brought no attention; his day was a tissue of things neglected and things done amiss; and from place to place and from town to town, he carried the character of one thoroughly incompetent. No man can bear the word applied to him without some flush of colour, as indeed there is none other that so emphatically slams in a man's face the door of self-respect. And to Herrick, who was conscious of talents and acquirements, who looked down upon those humble duties in which he was found wanting, the pain was the more exquisite. Early in his fall, he had ceased to be able to make remittances; shortly after, having nothing but failure to communicate, he ceased writing home; and about a year before this tale begins, turned suddenly upon the streets of San Francisco by a vulgar and infuriated German Jew, he had broken the last bonds of self-respect, and upon a sudden impulse, changed his name and invested his last dollar in a passage on the mail brigantine, the City of Papeete. With what expectation he had trimmed his flight for the South Seas, Herrick perhaps scarcely knew. Doubtless there were fortunes to be made in pearl and copra; doubtless others not more gifted than himself had climbed in the island world to be queen's consorts and king's ministers. But if Herrick had gone there with any manful purpose, he would have kept his father's name; the alias betrayed his moral bankruptcy; he had struck his flag; he entertained no hope to reinstate himself or help his straitened family; and he came to the islands (where he knew the climate to be soft, bread cheap, and manners easy) a skulker from life's battle and his own immediate duty. Failure, he had said, was his portion; let it be a pleasant failure.

It is fortunately not enough to say 'I will be base.' Herrick continued in the islands his career of failure; but in the new scene and under the new name, he suffered no less sharply than before. A place was got, it was lost in the old style; from the long-suffering of the keepers of restaurants he fell to more open charity upon the wayside; as time went on, good nature became weary, and after a repulse or two, Herrick became shy. There were women enough who would have supported a far worse and a far uglier man; Herrick never met or never knew them: or if he did both, some manlier feeling would revolt, and he preferred starvation. Drenched with rains, broiling by day, shivering by night, a disused and ruinous prison for a bedroom, his diet begged or pilfered out of rubbish heaps, his associates two creatures equally outcast with himself, he had drained for months the cup of penitence. He had known what it was to be resigned, what it was to break forth in a childish fury of rebellion against fate, and what it was to sink into the coma of despair. The time had changed him. He told himself no longer tales of an easy and perhaps agreeable declension; he read his nature otherwise; he had proved himself incapable of rising, and he now learned by experience that he could not stoop to fall. Something that was scarcely pride or strength, that was perhaps only refinement, withheld him from capitulation; but he looked on upon his own misfortune with a growing rage, and sometimes wondered at his patience.

It was now the fourth month completed, and still there was no change or sign of change. The moon, racing through a world of flying clouds of every size and shape and density, some black as ink stains, some delicate as lawn,

14

threw the marvel of her Southern brightness over the same lovely and detested scene: the island mountains crowned with the perennial island cloud, the embowered city studded with rare lamps, the masts in the harbour, the smooth mirror of the lagoon, and the mole of the barrier reef on which the breakers whitened. The moon shone too, with bull's-eye sweeps, on his companions; on the stalwart frame of the American who called himself Brown, and was known to be a master mariner in some disgrace; and on the dwarfish person, the pale eyes and toothless smile of a vulgar and bad-hearted cockney clerk. Here was society for Robert Herrick! The Yankee skipper was a man at least: he had sterling qualities of tenderness and resolution; he was one whose hand you could take without a blush. But there was no redeeming grace about the other, who called himself sometimes Hay and sometimes Tomkins, and laughed at the discrepancy; who had been employed in every store in Papeete, for the creature was able in his way; who had been discharged from each in turn, for he was wholly vile; who had alienated all his old employers so that they passed him in the street as if he were a dog, and all his old comrades so that they shunned him as they would a creditor.

Not long before, a ship from Peru had brought an influenza, and it now raged in the island, and particularly in Papeete. From all round the purao arose and fell a dismal sound of men coughing, and strangling as they coughed. The sick natives, with the islander's impatience of a touch of fever, had crawled from their houses to be cool and, squatting on the shore or on the beached canoes, painfully expected the new day. Even as the crowing of cocks goes about the country in the night from farm to farm, accesses of coughing arose, and spread, and died in the distance, and sprang up again. Each miserable shiverer caught the suggestion from his neighbour, was torn for some minutes by that cruel ecstasy, and left spent and without voice or courage when it passed. If a man had pity to spend, Papeete beach, in that cold night and in that infected season, was a place to spend it on. And of all the sufferers, perhaps the least deserving, but surely the most pitiable, was the London clerk. He was used to another life, to houses, beds, nursing, and the dainties of the sickroom; he lay there now, in the cold open, exposed to the gusting of the wind, and with an empty belly. He was besides infirm; the disease shook him to the vitals; and his companions watched his endurance

15

with surprise. A profound commiseration filled them, and contended with and conquered their abhorrence. The disgust attendant on so ugly a sickness magnified this dislike; at the same time, and with more than compensating strength, shame for a sentiment so inhuman bound them the more straitly to his service; and even the evil they knew of him swelled their solicitude, for the thought of death is always the least supportable when it draws near to the merely sensual and selfish. Sometimes they held him up; sometimes, with mistaken helpfulness, they beat him between the shoulders; and when the poor wretch lay back ghastly and spent after a paroxysm of coughing, they would sometimes peer into his face, doubtfully exploring it for any mark of life. There is no one but has some virtue: that of the clerk was courage; and he would make haste to reassure them in a pleasantry not always decent.

'I'm all right, pals,' he gasped once: 'this is the thing to strengthen the muscles of the larynx.'

'Well, you take the cake!' cried the captain.

'O, I'm good plucked enough,' pursued the sufferer with a broken utterance. 'But it do seem bloomin' hard to me, that I should be the only party down with this form of vice, and the only one to do the funny business. I think one of you other parties might wake up. Tell a fellow something.'

'The trouble is we've nothing to tell, my son,' returned the captain.

'I'll tell you, if you like, what I was thinking,' said Herrick.

'Tell us anything,' said the clerk, 'I only want to be reminded that I ain't dead.'

Herrick took up his parable, lying on his face and speaking slowly and scarce above his breath, not like a man who has anything to say, but like one talking against time.

'Well, I was thinking this,' he began: 'I was thinking I lay on Papeete beach one night—all moon and squalls and fellows coughing—and I was cold and hungry, and down in the mouth, and was about ninety years of age, and had spent two hundred and twenty of them on Papeete beach. And I was thinking I wished I had a ring to rub, or had a fairy godmother, or could raise Beelzebub. And I was trying to remember how you did it. I knew you made a ring of skulls, for I had seen that in the Freischutz: and that you took off your coat and turned up your sleeves, for I had seen Formes do that when he was playing Kaspar, and you could see (by the way he went about it) it was a business he had studied; and that you ought to have something to kick up a smoke and a bad smell, I dare say a cigar might do, and that you ought to say the Lord's Prayer backwards. Well, I wondered if I could do that; it seemed rather a feat, you see. And then I wondered if I would say it forward, and I thought I did. Well, no sooner had I got to WORLD WITHOUT END, than I saw a man in a pariu, and with a mat under his arm, come along the beach from the town. He was rather a hard-favoured old party, and he limped and crippled, and all the time he kept coughing. At first I didn't cotton to his looks, I thought, and then I got sorry for the old soul because he coughed so hard. I remembered that we had some of that cough mixture the American consul gave the captain for Hay. It never did Hay a ha'porth of service, but I thought it might do the old gentleman's business for him, and stood up. "Yorana!" says I. "Yorana!" says he. "Look here," I said, "I've got some first-rate stuff in a bottle; it'll fix your cough, savvy? Haere mai and I'll measure you a tablespoonful in the palm of my hand, for all our plate is at the bankers." So I thought the old party came up, and the nearer he came, the less I took to him. But I had passed my word, you see.'

'Wot is this bloomin' drivel?' interrupted the clerk. 'It's like the rot there is in tracts.'

'It's a story; I used to tell them to the kids at home,' said Herrick. 'If it bores you, I'll drop it.'

'O, cut along!' returned the sick man, irritably. 'It's better than nothing.'

'Well,' continued Herrick, 'I had no sooner given him the cough mixture than he seemed to straighten up and change, and I saw he wasn't a Tahitian after all, but some kind of Arab, and had a long beard on his chin. "One good turn deserves another," says he. "I am a magician out of the Arabian Nights, and this mat that I have under my arm is the original carpet of Mohammed

Ben Somebody-or-other. Say the word, and you can have a cruise upon the carpet." "You don't mean to say this is the Travelling Carpet?" I cried. "You bet I do," said he. "You've been to America since last I read the Arabian Nights," said I, a little suspicious. "I should think so," said he. "Been everywhere. A man with a carpet like this isn't going to moulder in a semi-detached villa." Well, that struck me as reasonable. "All right," I said; "and do you mean to tell me I can get on that carpet and go straight to London, England?" I said, "London, England," captain, because he seemed to have been so long in your part of the world. "In the crack of a whip," said he. I figured up the time. What is the difference between Papeete and London, captain?'

'Taking Greenwich and Point Venus, nine hours, odd minutes and seconds,' replied the mariner.

'Well, that's about what I made it,' resumed Herrick, 'about nine hours. Calling this three in the morning, I made out I would drop into London about noon; and the idea tickled me immensely. "There's only one bother," I said, "I haven't a copper cent. It would be a pity to go to London and not buy the morning Standard." "O!" said he, "you don't realise the conveniences of this carpet. You see this pocket? you've only got to stick your hand in, and you pull it out filled with sovereigns."

'Double-eagles, wasn't if' inquired the captain.

'That was what it was!' cried Herrick. 'I thought they seemed unusually big, and I remember now I had to go to the money-changers at Charing Cross and get English silver.'

'O, you went there?' said the clerk. 'Wot did you do? Bet you had a B. and S.!'

'Well, you see, it was just as the old boy said—like the cut of a whip,' said Herrick. 'The one minute I was here on the beach at three in the morning, the next I was in front of the Golden Cross at midday. At first I was dazzled, and covered my eyes, and there didn't seem the smallest change; the roar of the Strand and the roar of the reef were like the same: hark to it now, and you can hear the cabs and buses rolling and the streets resound! And then at last I could look about, and there was the old place, and no mistake! With the statues in the square, and St Martin's-in-the-Fields, and the bobbies, and the sparrows, and the hacks; and I can't tell you what I felt like. I felt like crying, I believe, or dancing, or jumping clean over the Nelson Column. I was like a fellow caught up out of Hell and flung down into the dandiest part of Heaven. Then I spotted for a hansom with a spanking horse. "A shilling for yourself, if you're there in twenty minutes!" said I to the jarvey. He went a good pace, though of course it was a trifle to the carpet; and in nineteen minutes and a half I was at the door.'

'What door?' asked the captain.

'Oh, a house I know of,' returned Herrick.

'But it was a public-house!' cried the clerk—only these were not his words. 'And w'y didn't you take the carpet there instead of trundling in a growler?'

'I didn't want to startle a quiet street,' said the narrator.

'Bad form. And besides, it was a hansom.'

'Well, and what did you do next?' inquired the captain.

'Oh, I went in,' said Herrick.

'The old folks?' asked the captain.

'That's about it,' said the other, chewing a grass.

'Well, I think you are about the poorest 'and at a yarn!' cried the clerk. 'Crikey, it's like Ministering Children! I can tell you there would be more beer and skittles about my little jaunt. I would go and have a B. and S. for luck. Then I would get a big ulster with astrakhan fur, and take my cane and do the la-de-la down Piccadilly. Then I would go to a slap-up restaurant, and have green peas, and a bottle of fizz, and a chump chop—Oh! and I forgot, I'd 'ave some devilled whitebait first—and green gooseberry tart, and 'ot coffee, and some of that form of vice in big bottles with a seal—Benedictine—that's the bloomin' nyme! Then I'd drop into a theatre, and pal on with some chappies, and do the dancing rooms and bars, and that, and wouldn't go 'ome till morning, till daylight doth appear. And the next day I'd have water-cresses, 'am, muffin, and fresh butter; wouldn't I just, O my!'

The clerk was interrupted by a fresh attack of coughing.

'Well, now, I'll tell you what I would do,' said the captain: 'I would have none of your fancy rigs with the man driving from the mizzen cross-trees, but a plain fore-and-aft hack cab of the highest registered tonnage. First of all, I would bring up at the market and get a turkey and a sucking-pig. Then I'd go to a wine merchant's and get a dozen of champagne, and a dozen of some sweet wine, rich and sticky and strong, something in the port or madeira line, the best in the store. Then I'd bear up for a toy-store, and lay out twenty dollars in assorted toys for the piccaninnies; and then to a confectioner's and take in cakes and pies and fancy bread, and that stuff with the plums in it; and then to a news-agency and buy all the papers, all the picture ones for the kids, and all the story papers for the old girl about the Earl discovering himself to Anna-Mariar and the escape of the Lady Maude from the private madhouse; and then I'd tell the fellow to drive home.'

'There ought to be some syrup for the kids,' suggested Herrick; 'they like syrup.'

'Yes, syrup for the kids, red syrup at that!' said the captain. 'And those things they pull at, and go pop, and have measly poetry inside. And then I tell you we'd have a thanksgiving day and Christmas tree combined. Great Scott, but I would like to see the kids! I guess they would light right out of the house, when they saw daddy driving up. My little Adar—'

The captain stopped sharply.

'Well, keep it up!' said the clerk.

'The damned thing is, I don't know if they ain't starving!' cried the captain.

'They can't be worse off than we are, and that's one comfort,' returned the clerk. 'I defy the devil to make me worse off.'

It seemed as if the devil heard him. The light of the moon had been some time cut off and they had talked in darkness. Now there was heard a roar, which drew impetuously nearer; the face of the lagoon was seen to whiten; and before they had staggered to their feet, a squall burst in rain upon the outcasts. The rage and volume of that avalanche one must have lived in the tropics to conceive; a man panted in its assault, as he might pant under a shower-bath; and the world seemed whelmed in night and water.

They fled, groping for their usual shelter—it might be almost called their home—in the old calaboose; came drenched into its empty chambers; and lay down, three sops of humanity on the cold coral floors, and presently, when the squall was overpast, the others could hear in the darkness the chattering of the clerk's teeth.

'I say, you fellows,' he walled, 'for God's sake, lie up and try to warm me. I'm blymed if I don't think I'll die else!'

So the three crept together into one wet mass, and lay until day came, shivering and dozing off, and continually re-awakened to wretchedness by the coughing of the clerk.

Chapter 2. MORNING ON THE BEACH—THE THREE LETTERS

The clouds were all fled, the beauty of the tropic day was spread upon Papeete; and the wall of breaking seas upon the reef, and the palms upon the islet, already trembled in the heat. A French man-of-war was going out, homeward bound; she lay in the middle distance of the port, an ant heap for activity. In the night a schooner had come in, and now lay far out, hard by the passage; and the yellow flag, the emblem of pestilence, flew on her. From up the coast, a long procession of canoes headed round the point and towards the market, bright as a scarf with the many-coloured clothing of the natives and the piles of fruit. But not even the beauty and the welcome warmth of the morning, not even these naval movements, so interesting to sailors and to idlers, could engage the attention of the outcasts. They were still cold at heart, their mouths sour from the want of steep, their steps rambling from the lack of food; and they strung like lame geese along the beach in a disheartened silence. It was towards the town they moved; towards the town whence smoke arose, where happier folk were breakfasting; and as they went, their hungry eyes were upon all sides, but they were only scouting for a meal.

A small and dingy schooner lay snug against the quay, with which it was connected by a plank. On the forward deck, under a spot of awning, five Kanakas who made up the crew, were squatted round a basin of fried feis, and drinking coffee from tin mugs.

'Eight bells: knock off for breakfast!' cried the captain with a miserable heartiness. 'Never tried this craft before; positively my first appearance; guess I'll draw a bumper house.'

He came close up to where the plank rested on the grassy quay; turned his back upon the schooner, and began to whistle that lively air, 'The Irish Washerwoman.' It caught the ears of the Kanaka seamen like a preconcerted signal; with one accord they looked up from their meal and crowded to the ship's side, fei in hand and munching as they looked. Even as a poor brown Pyrenean bear dances in the streets of English towns under his master's baton;

even so, but with how much more of spirit and precision, the captain footed it in time to his own whistling, and his long morning shadow capered beyond him on the grass. The Kanakas smiled on the performance; Herrick looked on heavy-eyed, hunger for the moment conquering all sense of shame; and a little farther off, but still hard by, the clerk was torn by the seven devils of the influenza.

The captain stopped suddenly, appeared to perceive his audience for the first time, and represented the part of a man surprised in his private hour of pleasure.

'Hello!' said he.

The Kanakas clapped hands and called upon him to go on.

'No, SIR!' said the captain. 'No eat, no dance. Savvy?'

'Poor old man!' returned one of the crew. 'Him no eat?'

'Lord, no!' said the captain. 'Like-um too much eat. No got.'

'All right. Me got,' said the sailor; 'you tome here. Plenty toffee, plenty fei. Nutha man him tome too.'

'I guess we'll drop right in,' observed the captain; and he and his companions hastened up the plank. They were welcomed on board with the shaking of hands; place was made for them about the basin; a sticky demijohn of molasses was added to the feast in honour of company, and an accordion brought from the forecastle and significantly laid by the performer's side.

'Ariana,' said he lightly, touching the instrument as he spoke; and he fell to on a long savoury fei, made an end of it, raised his mug of coffee, and nodded across at the spokesman of the crew. 'Here's your health, old man; you're a credit to the South Pacific,' said he.

With the unsightly greed of hounds they glutted themselves with the hot food and coffee; and even the clerk revived and the colour deepened in his eyes. The kettle was drained, the basin cleaned; their entertainers, who had waited on their wants throughout with the pleased hospitality of Polynesians, made haste to bring forward a dessert of island tobacco and rolls of pandanus leaf to serve as paper; and presently all sat about the dishes puffing like Indian Sachems.

'When a man 'as breakfast every day, he don't know what it is,' observed the clerk.

'The next point is dinner,' said Herrick; and then with a passionate utterance: 'I wish to God I was a Kanaka!'

'There's one thing sure,' said the captain. 'I'm about desperate, I'd rather hang than rot here much longer.' And with the word he took the accordion and struck up. 'Home, sweet home.'

'O, drop that!' cried Herrick, 'I can't stand that.'

'No more can I,' said the captain. 'I've got to play something though: got to pay the shot, my son.' And he struck up 'John Brown's Body' in a fine sweet baritone: 'Dandy Jim of Carolina,' came next; 'Rorin the Bold,' 'Swing low, Sweet Chariot,' and 'The Beautiful Land' followed. The captain was paying his shot with usury, as he had done many a time before; many a meal had he bought with the same currency from the melodious-minded natives, always, as now, to their delight.

He was in the middle of 'Fifteen Dollars in the Inside Pocket,' singing with dogged energy, for the task went sore against the grain, when a sensation was suddenly to be observed among the crew.

'Tapena Tom harry my,' said the spokesman, pointing.

And the three beachcombers, following his indication, saw the figure of a man in pyjama trousers and a white jumper approaching briskly from the town.

'Captain Tom is coming.'

'That's Tapena Tom, is it?' said the captain, pausing in his music. 'I don't seem to place the brute.'

'We'd better cut,' said the clerk. ''E's no good.'

'Well,' said the musician deliberately, 'one can't most generally always tell. I'll try it on, I guess. Music has charms to soothe the savage Tapena, boys. We might strike it rich; it might amount to iced punch in the cabin.'

'Hiced punch? O my!' said the clerk. 'Give him something 'ot, captain. "Way down the Swannee River"; try that.'

'No, sir! Looks Scotch,' said the captain; and he struck, for his life, into 'Auld Lang Syne.'

Captain Tom continued to approach with the same business-like alacrity; no change was to be perceived in his bearded face as he came swinging up the plank: he did not even turn his eyes on the performer.

'*We twa hae paidled in the burn*

Frae morning tide till dine,'

went the song.

Captain Tom had a parcel under his arm, which he laid on the house roof, and then turning suddenly to the strangers: 'Here, you!' he bellowed, 'be off out of that!'

The clerk and Herrick stood not on the order of their going, but fled incontinently by the plank. The performer, on the other hand, flung down the instrument and rose to his full height slowly.

'What's that you say?' he said. 'I've half a mind to give you a lesson in civility.'

'You set up any more of your gab to me,' returned the Scotsman, 'and I'll show ye the wrong side of a jyle. I've heard tell of the three of ye. Ye're not long for here, I can tell ye that. The Government has their eyes upon ye. They make short work of damned beachcombers, I'll say that for the French.'

'You wait till I catch you off your ship!' cried the captain: and then, turning to the crew, 'Good-bye, you fellows!' he said. 'You're gentlemen, anyway! The worst nigger among you would look better upon a quarter-deck than that filthy Scotchman.'

Captain Tom scorned to reply; he watched with a hard smile the departure of his guests; and as soon as the last foot was off the plank; turned to the hands to work cargo.

The beachcombers beat their inglorious retreat along the shore; Herrick first, his face dark with blood, his knees trembling under him with the hysteria of rage. Presently, under the same purao where they had shivered the night before, he cast himself down, and groaned aloud, and ground his face into the sand.

'Don't speak to me, don't speak to me. I can't stand it,' broke from him.

The other two stood over him perplexed.

'Wot can't he stand now?' said the clerk. ''Asn't he 'ad a meal? I'M lickin' my lips.'

Herrick reared up his wild eyes and burning face. 'I can't beg!' he screamed, and again threw himself prone.

'This thing's got to come to an end,' said the captain with an intake of the breath.

'Looks like signs of an end, don't it?' sneered the clerk.

'He's not so far from it, and don't you deceive yourself,' replied the captain. 'Well,' he added in a livelier voice, 'you fellows hang on here, and I'll go and interview my representative.'

Whereupon he turned on his heel, and set off at a swinging sailor's walk towards Papeete.

It was some half hour later when he returned. The clerk was dozing with his back against the tree: Herrick still lay where he had flung himself; nothing showed whether he slept or waked.

'See, boys!' cried the captain, with that artificial heartiness of his which was at times so painful, 'here's a new idea.' And he produced note paper, stamped envelopes, and pencils, three of each. 'We can all write home by the mail brigantine; the consul says I can come over to his place and ink up the

26

addresses.'

'Well, that's a start, too,' said the clerk. 'I never thought of that.'

'It was that yarning last night about going home that put me up to it,' said the captain.

'Well, 'and over,' said the clerk. 'I'll 'ave a shy,' and he retired a little distance to the shade of a canoe.

The others remained under the purao. Now they would write a word or two, now scribble it out; now they would sit biting at the pencil end and staring seaward; now their eyes would rest on the clerk, where he sat propped on the canoe, leering and coughing, his pencil racing glibly on the paper.

'I can't do it,' said Herrick suddenly. 'I haven't got the heart.'

'See here,' said the captain, speaking with unwonted gravity; 'it may be hard to write, and to write lies at that; and God knows it is; but it's the square thing. It don't cost anything to say you're well and happy, and sorry you can't make a remittance this mail; and if you don't, I'll tell you what I think it is—I think it's about the high-water mark of being a brute beast.'

'It's easy to talk,' said Herrick. 'You don't seem to have written much yourself, I notice.'

'What do you bring in me for?' broke from the captain. His voice was indeed scarce raised above a whisper, but emotion clanged in it. 'What do you know about me? If you had commanded the finest barque that ever sailed from Portland; if you had been drunk in your berth when she struck the breakers in Fourteen Island Group, and hadn't had the wit to stay there and drown, but came on deck, and given drunken orders, and lost six lives—I could understand your talking then! There,' he said more quietly, 'that's my yarn, and now you know it. It's a pretty one for the father of a family. Five men and a woman murdered. Yes, there was a woman on board, and hadn't no business to be either. Guess I sent her to Hell, if there is such a place. I never dared go home again; and the wife and the little ones went to England to her father's place. I don't know what's come to them,' he added, with a bitter shrug.

'Thank you, captain,' said Herrick. 'I never liked you better.'

They shook hands, short and hard, with eyes averted, tenderness swelling in their bosoms.

'Now, boys! to work again at lying!' said the captain.

'I'll give my father up,' returned Herrick with a writhen smile. 'I'll try my sweetheart instead for a change of evils.'

And here is what he wrote:

'Emma, I have scratched out the beginning to my father, for I think I can write more easily to you. This is my last farewell to all, the last you will ever hear or see of an unworthy friend and son. I have failed in life; I am quite broken down and disgraced. I pass under a false name; you will have to tell my father that with all your kindness. It is my own fault. I know, had I chosen, that I might have done well; and yet I swear to you I tried to choose. I could not bear that you should think I did not try. For I loved you all; you must never doubt me in that, you least of all. I have always unceasingly loved, but what was my love worth? and what was I worth? I had not the manhood of a common clerk, I could not work to earn you; I have lost you now, and for your sake I could be glad of it. When you first came to my father's house—do you remember those days? I want you to—you saw the best of me then, all that was good in me. Do you remember the day I took your hand and would not let it go—and the day on Battersea Bridge, when we were looking at a barge, and I began to tell you one of my silly stories, and broke off to say I loved you? That was the beginning, and now here is the end. When you have read this letter, you will go round and kiss them all good-bye, my father and mother, and the children, one by one, and poor uncle; And tell them all to forget me, and forget me yourself. Turn the key in the door; let no thought of me return; be done with the poor ghost that pretended he was a man and stole your love. Scorn of myself grinds in me as I write. I should tell you I am well and happy, and want for nothing. I do not exactly make money, or I should send a remittance; but I am well cared for, have friends, live in a beautiful place and climate, such as we have dreamed of together, and no pity need be wasted on me. In such places, you understand, it is easy to live, and live well, but often hard to make sixpence in money. Explain this to my father, he will understand. I have no more to say; only linger, going out, like an unwilling guest. God in heaven bless you. Think of me to the last, here, on a bright beach, the sky and sea immoderately blue, and the great breakers roaring outside on a barrier reef, where a little isle sits green with palms. I am well and strong. It is a more pleasant way to die than if you were crowding about me on a sick-bed. And yet I am dying. This is my last kiss. Forgive, forget the unworthy.'

So far he had written, his paper was all filled, when there returned a memory of evenings at the piano, and that song, the masterpiece of love, in which so many have found the expression of their dearest thoughts. 'Einst, O wunder!' he added. More was not required; he knew that in his love's heart the context would spring up, escorted with fair images and harmony; of how all through life her name should tremble in his ears, her name be everywhere repeated in the sounds of nature; and when death came, and he lay dissolved, her memory lingered and thrilled among his elements.

'Once, O wonder! once from the ashes of my heart

Arose a blossom—'

Herrick and the captain finished their letters about the same time; each was breathing deep, and their eyes met and were averted as they closed the envelopes.

'Sorry I write so big,' said the captain gruffly. 'Came all of a rush, when it did come.'

'Same here,' said Herrick. 'I could have done with a ream when I got started; but it's long enough for all the good I had to say.'

They were still at the addresses when the clerk strolled up, smirking and twirling his envelope, like a man well pleased. He looked over Herrick's shoulder.

'Hullo,' he said, 'you ain't writing 'ome.'

'I am, though,' said Herrick; 'she lives with my father. Oh, I see what you mean,' he added. 'My real name is Herrick. No more Hay'—they had both used the same alias—'no more Hay than yours, I dare say.'

'Clean bowled in the middle stump!' laughed the clerk. 'My name's 'Uish if you want to know. Everybody has a false nyme in the Pacific. Lay you five to three the captain 'as.'

'So I have too,' replied the captain; 'and I've never told my own since the day I tore the title page out of my Bowditch and flung the damned thing into the sea. But I'll tell it to you, boys. John Davis is my name. I'm Davis of the Sea Ranger.'

'Dooce you are!' said Hush. 'And what was she? a pirate or a slyver?'

'She was the fastest barque out of Portland, Maine,' replied the captain; 'and for the way I lost her, I might as well have bored a hole in her side with an auger.'

'Oh, you lost her, did you?' said the clerk. ''Ope she was insured?'

No answer being returned to this sally, Huish, still brimming over with vanity and conversation, struck into another subject.

'I've a good mind to read you my letter,' said he. 'I've a good fist with a pen when I choose, and this is a prime lark. She was a barmaid I ran across in Northampton; she was a spanking fine piece, no end of style; and we cottoned at first sight like parties in the play. I suppose I spent the chynge of a fiver on that girl. Well, I 'appened to remember her nyme, so I wrote to her, and told her 'ow I had got rich, and married a queen in the Hislands, and lived in a blooming palace. Such a sight of crammers! I must read you one bit about my opening the nigger parliament in a cocked 'at. It's really prime.'

The captain jumped to his feet. 'That's what you did with the paper that I went and begged for you?' he roared.

It was perhaps lucky for Huish—it was surely in the end unfortunate for all—that he was seized just then by one of his prostrating accesses of cough; his comrades would have else deserted him, so bitter was their resentment.

When the fit had passed, the clerk reached out his hand, picked up the letter, which had fallen to the earth, and tore it into fragments, stamp and all.

'Does that satisfy you?' he asked sullenly.

'We'll say no more about it,' replied Davis.

Chapter 3. THE OLD CALABOOSE—DESTINY AT THE DOOR

The old calaboose, in which the waifs had so long harboured, is a low, rectangular enclosure of building at the corner of a shady western avenue and a little townward of the British consulate. Within was a grassy court, littered with wreckage and the traces of vagrant occupation. Six or seven cells opened from the court: the doors, that had once been locked on mutinous whalermen, rotting before them in the grass. No mark remained of their old destination, except the rusty bars upon the windows.

The floor of one of the cells had been a little cleared; a bucket (the last remaining piece of furniture of the three caitiffs) stood full of water by the door, a half cocoanut shell beside it for a drinking cup; and on some ragged ends of mat Huish sprawled asleep, his mouth open, his face deathly. The glow of the tropic afternoon, the green of sunbright foliage, stared into that shady place through door and window; and Herrick, pacing to and fro on the coral floor, sometimes paused and laved his face and neck with tepid water from the bucket. His long arrears of suffering, the night's vigil, the insults of the morning, and the harrowing business of the letter, had strung him to that point when pain is almost pleasure, time shrinks to a mere point, and death and life appear indifferent. To and fro he paced like a caged brute; his mind whirling through the universe of thought and memory; his eyes, as he went, skimming the legends on the wall. The crumbling whitewash was all full of them: Tahitian names, and French, and English, and rude sketches of ships under sail and men at fisticuffs.

It came to him of a sudden that he too must leave upon these walls the memorial of his passage. He paused before a clean space, took the pencil out, and pondered. Vanity, so hard to dislodge, awoke in him. We call it vanity at least; perhaps unjustly. Rather it was the bare sense of his existence prompted him; the sense of his life, the one thing wonderful, to which he scarce clung with a finger. From his jarred nerves there came a strong sentiment of coming change; whether good or ill he could not say: change, he knew no more—

change, with inscrutable veiled face, approaching noiseless. With the feeling, came the vision of a concert room, the rich hues of instruments, the silent audience, and the loud voice of the symphony. 'Destiny knocking at the door,' he thought; drew a stave on the plaster, and wrote in the famous phrase from the Fifth Symphony. 'So,' thought he, 'they will know that I loved music and had classical tastes. They? He, I suppose: the unknown, kindred spirit that shall come some day and read my memor querela. Ha, he shall have Latin too!' And he added: terque quaterque beati Queis ante ora patrum.

He turned again to his uneasy pacing, but now with an irrational and supporting sense of duty done. He had dug his grave that morning; now he had carved his epitaph; the folds of the toga were composed, why should he delay the insignificant trifle that remained to do? He paused and looked long in the face of the sleeping Huish, drinking disenchantment and distaste of life. He nauseated himself with that vile countenance. Could the thing continue? What bound him now? Had he no rights?—only the obligation to go on, without discharge or furlough, bearing the unbearable? Ich trage unertragliches, the quotation rose in his mind; he repeated the whole piece, one of the most perfect of the most perfect of poets; and a phrase struck him like a blow: Du, stolzes Herz, A hast es ja gewolit. Where was the pride of his heart? And he raged against himself, as a man bites on a sore tooth, in a heady sensuality of scorn. 'I have no pride, I have no heart, no manhood,' he thought, 'or why should I prolong a life more shameful than the gallows? Or why should I have fallen to it? No pride, no capacity, no force. Not even a bandit! and to be starving here with worse than banditti—with this trivial hell-hound!' His rage against his comrade rose and flooded him, and he shook a trembling fist at the sleeper.

A swift step was audible. The captain appeared upon the threshold of the cell, panting and flushed, and with a foolish face of happiness. In his arms he carried a loaf of bread and bottles of beer; the pockets of his coat were bulging with cigars.

He rolled his treasures on the floor, grasped Herrick by both hands, and crowed with laughter.

'Broach the beer!' he shouted. 'Broach the beer, and glory hallelujah!'

'Beer?' repeated Huish, struggling to his feet. 'Beer it is!' cried Davis. 'Beer and plenty of it. Any number of persons can use it (like Lyon's tooth-tablet) with perfect propriety and neatness. Who's to officiate?'

'Leave me alone for that,' said the clerk. He knocked the necks off with a lump of coral, and each drank in succession from the shell.

'Have a weed,' said Davis. 'It's all in the bill.'

'What is up?' asked Herrick.

The captain fell suddenly grave. 'I'm coming to that,' said he. 'I want to speak with Herrick here. You, Hay—or Huish, or whatever your name is—you take a weed and the other bottle, and go and see how the wind is down by the purao. I'll call you when you're wanted!'

'Hay? Secrets? That ain't the ticket,' said Huish.

'Look here, my son,' said the captain, 'this is business, and don't you make any mistake about it. If you're going to make trouble, you can have it your own way and stop right here. Only get the thing right: if Herrick and I go, we take the beer. Savvy?'

'Oh, I don't want to shove my oar in,' returned Huish. 'I'll cut right enough. Give me the swipes. You can jaw till you're blue in the face for what I care. I don't think it's the friendly touch: that's all.' And he shambled grumbling out of the cell into the staring sun.

The captain watched him clear of the courtyard; then turned to Herrick.

'What is it?' asked Herrick thickly.

'I'll tell you,' said Davis. 'I want to consult you. It's a chance we've got. What's that?' he cried, pointing to the music on the wall.

'What?' said the other. 'Oh, that! It's music; it's a phrase of Beethoven's I was writing up. It means Destiny knocking at the door.'

'Does it?' said the captain, rather low; and he went near and studied the inscription; 'and this French?' he asked, pointing to the Latin.

'O, it just means I should have been luckier if I had died at horne,' returned Herrick impatiently. 'What is this business?'

'Destiny knocking at the door,' repeated the captain; and then, looking over his shoulder. 'Well, Mr Herrick, that's about what it comes to,' he added.

'What do you mean? Explain yourself,' said Herrick.

But the captain was again staring at the music. 'About how long ago since you wrote up this truck?' he asked.

'What does it matter?' exclaimed Herrick. 'I dare say half an hour.'

'My God, it's strange!' cried Davis. 'There's some men would call that accidental: not me. That—' and he drew his thick finger under the music— 'that's what I call Providence.'

'You said we had a chance,' said Herrick.

'Yes, SIR!' said the captain, wheeling suddenly face to face with his companion. 'I did so. If you're the man I take you for, we have a chance.'

'I don't know what you take me for,' was the reply. 'You can scarce take me too low.'

'Shake hands, Mr Herrick,' said the captain. 'I know you. You're a gentleman and a man of spirit. I didn't want to speak before that bummer there; you'll see why. But to you I'll rip it right out. I got a ship.'

'A ship?' cried Herrick. 'What ship?'

'That schooner we saw this morning off the passage.'

'The schooner with the hospital flag?'

'That's the hooker,' said Davis. 'She's the Farallone, hundred and sixty tons register, out of 'Frisco for Sydney, in California champagne. Captain, mate, and one hand all died of the smallpox, same as they had round in the Paumotus, I guess. Captain and mate were the only white men; all the hands Kanakas; seems a queer kind of outfit from a Christian port. Three of them left and a cook; didn't know where they were; I can't think where they were either, if you come to that; Wiseman must have been on the booze, I guess, to sail the course he did. However, there HE was, dead; and here are the Kanakas as good as lost. They bummed around at sea like the babes in the wood; and tumbled end-on upon Tahiti. The consul here took charge. He offered the berth to Williams; Williams had never had the smallpox and backed down. That was when I came in for the letter paper; I thought there was something up when the consul asked me to look in again; but I never let on to you fellows, so's you'd not be disappointed. Consul tried M'Neil; scared of smallpox. He tried Capirati, that Corsican and Leblue, or whatever his name is, wouldn't lay a hand on it; all too fond of their sweet lives. Last of all, when there wasn't nobody else left to offer it to, he offers it to me. "Brown, will you ship captain and take her to Sydney?" says he. "Let me choose my own mate and another white hand," says I, "for I don't hold with this Kanaka crew racket; give us all two months' advance to get our clothes and instruments out of pawn, and I'll take stock tonight, fill up stores, and get to sea tomorrow before dark!" That's what I said. "That's good enough," says the consul, "and you can count yourself damned lucky, Brown," says he. And he said it pretty meaningful-appearing, too. However, that's all one now. I'll ship Huish before the mast—of course I'll let him berth aft—and I'll ship you mate at seventy-five dollars and two months' advance.'

'Me mate? Why, I'm a landsman!' cried Herrick.

'Guess you've got to learn,' said the captain. 'You don't fancy I'm going to skip and leave you rotting on the beach perhaps? I'm not that sort, old man. And you're handy anyway; I've been shipmates with worse.'

'God knows I can't refuse,' said Herrick. 'God knows I thank you from my heart.'

'That's all right,' said the captain. 'But it ain't all.' He turned aside to light a cigar.

'What else is there?' asked the other, with a pang of undefinable alarm.

'I'm coming to that,' said Davis, and then paused a little. 'See here,' he began, holding out his cigar between his finger and thumb, 'suppose you figure up what this'll amount to. You don't catch on? Well, we get two months' advance; we can't get away from Papeete—our creditors wouldn't let us go—for less; it'll take us along about two months to get to Sydney; and when we get there, I just want to put it to you squarely: What the better are we?'

'We're off the beach at least,' said Herrick.

'I guess there's a beach at Sydney,' returned the captain; 'and I'll tell you one thing, Mr Herrick—I don't mean to try. No, SIR! Sydney will never see me.'

'Speak out plain,' said Herrick.

'Plain Dutch,' replied the captain. 'I'm going to own that schooner. It's nothing new; it's done every year in the Pacific. Stephens stole a schooner the other day, didn't he? Hayes and Pease stole vessels all the time. And it's the making of the crowd of us. See here—you think of that cargo. Champagne! why, it's like as if it was put up on purpose. In Peru we'll sell that liquor off at the pier-head, and the schooner after it, if we can find a fool to buy her; and then light out for the mines. If you'll back me up, I stake my life I carry it through.'

'Captain,' said Herrick, with a quailing voice, 'don't do it!'

'I'm desperate,' returned Davis. 'I've got a chance; I may never get another. Herrick, say the word; back me up; I think we've starved together long enough for that.'

'I can't do it. I'm sorry. I can't do it. I've not fallen as low as that,' said Herrick, deadly pale.

'What did you say this morning?' said Davis. 'That you couldn't beg? It's the one thing or the other, my son.'

'Ah, but this is the jail!' cried Herrick. 'Don't tempt me. It's the jail.'

'Did you hear what the skipper said on board that schooner?' pursued the captain. 'Well, I tell you he talked straight. The French have let us alone for a long time; It can't last longer; they've got their eye on us; and as sure as you live, in three weeks you'll be in jail whatever you do. I read it in the consul's face.'

'You forget, captain,' said the young man. 'There is another way. I can die; and to say truth, I think I should have died three years ago.'

The captain folded his arms and looked the other in the face. 'Yes,' said he, 'yes, you can cut your throat; that's a frozen fact; much good may it do you! And where do I come in?'

The light of a strange excitement came in Herrick's face. 'Both of us,' said he, 'both of us together. It's not possible you can enjoy this business. Come,' and he reached out a timid hand, 'a few strokes in the lagoon—and rest!'

'I tell you, Herrick, I'm 'most tempted to answer you the way the man does in the Bible, and say, "Get thee behind me, Satan!"' said the captain. 'What! you think I would go drown myself, and I got children starving? Enjoy it? No, by God, I do not enjoy it! but it's the row I've got to hoe, and I'll hoe it till I drop right here. I have three of them, you see, two boys and the one girl, Adar. The trouble is that you are not a parent yourself. I tell you, Herrick, I love you,' the man broke out; 'I didn't take to you at first, you were so anglified and tony, but I love you now; it's a man that loves you stands here and wrestles with you. I can't go to sea with the bummer alone; it's not possible. Go drown yourself, and there goes my last chance—the last chance of a poor miserable beast, earning a crust to feed his family. I can't do nothing but sail ships, and I've no papers. And here I get a chance, and you go back on me! Ah, you've no family, and that's where the trouble is!'

'I have indeed,' said Herrick.

'Yes, I know,' said the captain, 'you think so. But no man's got a family till he's got children. It's only the kids count. There's something about the little shavers... I can't talk of them. And if you thought a cent about this father that I hear you talk of, or that sweetheart you were writing to this morning, you would feel like me. You would say, What matters laws, and God, and that? My folks are hard up, I belong to them, I'll get them bread, or, by God!

I'll get them wealth, if I have to burn down London for it. That's what you would say. And I'll tell you more: your heart is saying so this living minute. I can see it in your face. You're thinking, Here's poor friendship for the man I've starved along of, and as for the girl that I set up to be in love with, here's a mighty limp kind of a love that won't carry me as far as 'most any man would go for a demijohn of whisky. There's not much ROmance to that love, anyway; it's not the kind they carry on about in songbooks. But what's the good of my carrying on talking, when it's all in your inside as plain as print? I put the question to you once for all. Are you going to desert me in my hour of need?—you know if I've deserted you—or will you give me your hand, and try a fresh deal, and go home (as like as not) a millionaire? Say no, and God pity me! Say yes, and I'll make the little ones pray for you every night on their bended knees. "God bless Mr Herrick!" that's what they'll say, one after the other, the old girl sitting there holding stakes at the foot of the bed, and the damned little innocents... He broke off. 'I don't often rip out about the kids,' he said; 'but when I do, there's something fetches loose.'

'Captain,' said Herrick faintly, 'is there nothing else?'

'I'll prophesy if you like,' said the captain with renewed vigour. 'Refuse this, because you think yourself too honest, and before a month's out you'll be jailed for a sneak-thief. I give you the word fair. I can see it, Herrick, if you can't; you're breaking down. Don't think, if you refuse this chance, that you'll go on doing the evangelical; you're about through with your stock; and before you know where you are, you'll be right out on the other side. No, it's either this for you; or else it's Caledonia. I bet you never were there, and saw those white, shaved men, in their dust clothes and straw hats, prowling around in gangs in the lamplight at Noumea; they look like wolves, and they look like preachers, and they look like the sick; Hulsh is a daisy to the best of them. Well, there's your company. They're waiting for you, Herrick, and you got to go; and that's a prophecy.'

And as the man stood and shook through his great stature, he seemed indeed like one in whom the spirit of divination worked and might utter oracles. Herrick looked at him, and looked away; It seemed not decent to spy upon such agitation; and the young man's courage sank.

39

'You talk of going home,' he objected. 'We could never do that.'

'WE could,' said the other. 'Captain Brown couldn't, nor Mr Hay, that shipped mate with him couldn't. But what's that to do with Captain Davis or Mr Herrick, you galoot?'

'But Hayes had these wild islands where he used to call,' came the next fainter objection.

'We have the wild islands of Peru,' retorted Davis. 'They were wild enough for Stephens, no longer agone than just last year. I guess they'll be wild enough for us.'

'And the crew?'

'All Kanakas. Come, I see you're right, old man. I see you'll stand by.' And the captain once more offered his hand.

'Have it your own way then,' said Herrick. 'I'll do it: a strange thing for my father's son. But I'll do it. I'll stand by you, man, for good or evil.'

'God bless you!' cried the captain, and stood silent. 'Herrick,' he added with a smile, 'I believe I'd have died in my tracks, if you'd said, No!'

And Herrick, looking at the man, half believed so also.

'And now we'll go break it to the bummer,' said Davis.

'I wonder how he'll take it,' said Herrick.

'Him? Jump at it!' was the reply.

Chapter 4. THE YELLOW FLAG

The schooner Farallone lay well out in the jaws of the pass, where the terrified pilot had made haste to bring her to her moorings and escape. Seen from the beach through the thin line of shipping, two objects stood conspicuous to seaward: the little isle, on the one hand, with its palms and the guns and batteries raised forty years before in defence of Queen Pomare's capital; the outcast Farallone, upon the other, banished to the threshold of the port, rolling there to her scuppers, and flaunting the plague-flag as she rolled. A few sea birds screamed and cried about the ship; and within easy range, a man-of-war guard boat hung off and on and glittered with the weapons of marines. The exuberant daylight and the blinding heaven of the tropics picked out and framed the pictures.

A neat boat, manned by natives in uniform, and steered by the doctor of the port, put from shore towards three of the afternoon, and pulled smartly for the schooner. The fore-sheets were heaped with sacks of flour, onions, and potatoes, perched among which was Huish dressed as a foremast hand; a heap of chests and cases impeded the action of the oarsmen; and in the stern, by the left hand of the doctor, sat Herrick, dressed in a fresh rig of slops, his brown beard trimmed to a point, a pile of paper novels on his lap, and nursing the while between his feet a chronometer, for which they had exchanged that of the Farallone, long since run down and the rate lost.

They passed the guard boat, exchanging hails with the boat-swain's mate in charge, and drew near at last to the forbidden ship. Not a cat stirred, there was no speech of man; and the sea being exceeding high outside, and the reef close to where the schooner lay, the clamour of the surf hung round her like the sound of battle.

'Ohe la goelette!' sang out the doctor, with his best voice.

Instantly, from the house where they had been stowing away stores, first Davis, and then the ragamuffin, swarthy crew made their appearance.

'Hullo, Hay, that you?' said the captain, leaning on the rail. 'Tell the old man to lay her alongside, as if she was eggs. There's a hell of a run of sea here, and his boat's brittle.'

The movement of the schooner was at that time more than usually violent. Now she heaved her side as high as a deep sea steamer's, and showed the flashing of her copper; now she swung swiftly toward the boat until her scuppers gurgled.

'I hope you have sea legs,' observed the doctor. 'You will require them.'

Indeed, to board the Farallone, in that exposed position where she lay, was an affair of some dexterity. The less precious goods were hoisted roughly in; the chronometer, after repeated failures, was passed gently and successfully from hand to hand; and there remained only the more difficult business of embarking Huish. Even that piece of dead weight (shipped A.B. at eighteen dollars, and described by the captain to the consul as an invaluable man) was at last hauled on board without mishap; and the doctor, with civil salutations, took his leave.

The three co-adventurers looked at each other, and Davis heaved a breath of relief.

'Now let's get this chronometer fixed,' said he, and led the way into the house. It was a fairly spacious place; two staterooms and a good-sized pantry opened from the main cabin; the bulkheads were painted white, the floor laid with waxcloth. No litter, no sign of life remained; for the effects of the dead men had been disinfected and conveyed on shore. Only on the table, in a saucer, some sulphur burned, and the fumes set them coughing as they entered. The captain peered into the starboard stateroom, where the bed-clothes still lay tumbled in the bunk, the blanket flung back as they had flung it back from the disfigured corpse before its burial.

'Now, I told these niggers to tumble that truck overboard,' grumbled Davis. 'Guess they were afraid to lay hands on it. Well, they've hosed the place out; that's as much as can be expected, I suppose. Huish, lay on to these blankets.'

42

'See you blooming well far enough first,' said Huish, drawing back.

'What's that?' snapped the captain. 'I'll tell you, my young friend, I think you make a mistake. I'm captain here.'

'Fat lot I care,' returned the clerk.

'That so?' said Davis. 'Then you'll berth forward with the niggers! Walk right out of this cabin.'

'Oh, I dessay!' said Huish. 'See any green in my eye? A lark's a lark.'

'Well, now, I'll explain this business, and you'll see (once for all) just precisely how much lark there is to it,' said Davis. 'I'm captain, and I'm going to be it. One thing of three. First, you take my orders here as cabin steward, in which case you mess with us. Or second, you refuse, and I pack you forward—and you get as quick as the word's said. Or, third and last, I'll signal that man-of-war and send you ashore under arrest for mutiny.'

'And, of course, I wouldn't blow the gaff? O no!' replied the jeering Huish.

'And who's to believe you, my son?' inquired the captain. 'No, sir! There ain't no lark about my captainising. Enough said. Up with these blankets.'

Huish was no fool, he knew when he was beaten; and he was no coward either, for he stepped to the bunk, took the infected bed-clothes fairly in his arms, and carried them out of the house without a check or tremor.

'I was waiting for the chance,' said Davis to Herrick. 'I needn't do the same with you, because you understand it for yourself.'

'Are you going to berth here?' asked Herrick, following the captain into the stateroom, where he began to adjust the chronometer in its place at the bed-head.

'Not much!' replied he. 'I guess I'll berth on deck. I don't know as I'm afraid, but I've no immediate use for confluent smallpox.'

'I don't know that I'm afraid either,' said Herrick. 'But the thought of these two men sticks in my throat; that captain and mate dying here, one opposite to the other. It's grim. I wonder what they said last?'

'Wiseman and Wishart?' said the captain. 'Probably mighty small potatoes. That's a thing a fellow figures out for himself one way, and the real business goes quite another. Perhaps Wiseman said, "Here old man, fetch up the gin, I'm feeling powerful rocky." And perhaps Wishart said, "Oh, hell!"'

'Well, that's grim enough,' said Herrick.

'And so it is,' said Davis. 'There; there's that chronometer fixed. And now it's about time to up anchor and clear out.'

He lit a cigar and stepped on deck.

'Here, you! What's YOUR name?' he cried to one of the hands, a lean-flanked, clean-built fellow from some far western island, and of a darkness almost approaching to the African.

'Sally Day,' replied the man.

'Devil it is,' said the captain. 'Didn't know we had ladies on board. Well, Sally, oblige me by hauling down that rag there. I'll do the same for you another time.' He watched the yellow bunting as it was eased past the cross-trees and handed down on deck. 'You'll float no more on this ship,' he observed. 'Muster the people aft, Mr Hay,' he added, speaking unnecessarily loud, 'I've a word to say to them.'

It was with a singular sensation that Herrick prepared for the first time to address a crew. He thanked his stars indeed, that they were natives. But even natives, he reflected, might be critics too quick for such a novice as himself; they might perceive some lapse from that precise and cut-and-dry English which prevails on board a ship; it was even possible they understood no other; and he racked his brain, and overhauled his reminiscences of sea romance for some appropriate words.

'Here, men! tumble aft!' he said. 'Lively now! All hands aft!'

They crowded in the alleyway like sheep.

44

'Here they are, sir,' said Herrick.

For some time the captain continued to face the stern; then turned with ferocious suddenness on the crew, and seemed to enjoy their shrinking.

'Now,' he said, twisting his cigar in his mouth and toying with the spokes of the wheel, 'I'm Captain Brown. I command this ship. This is Mr Hay, first officer. The other white man is cabin steward, but he'll stand watch and do his trick. My orders shall be obeyed smartly. You savvy, "smartly"? There shall be no growling about the kaikai, which will be above allowance. You'll put a handle to the mate's name, and tack on "sir" to every order I give you. If you're smart and quick, I'll make this ship comfortable for all hands.' He took the cigar out of his mouth. 'If you're not,' he added, in a roaring voice, 'I'll make it a floating hell. Now, Mr Hay, we'll pick watches, if you please.'

'All right,' said Herrick.

'You will please use "sir" when you address me, Mr Hay,' said the captain. 'I'll take the lady. Step to starboard, Sally.' And then he whispered in Herrick's ear: 'take the old man.'

'I'll take you, there,' said Herrick.

'What's your name?' said the captain. 'What's that you say? Oh, that's no English; I'll have none of your highway gibberish on my ship. We'll call you old Uncle Ned, because you've got no wool on the top of your head, just the place where the wool ought to grow. Step to port, Uncle. Don't you hear Mr Hay has picked you? Then I'll take the white man. White Man, step to starboard. Now which of you two is the cook? You? Then Mr Hay takes your friend in the blue dungaree. Step to port, Dungaree. There, we know who we all are: Dungaree, Uncle Ned, Sally Day, White Man, and Cook. All F.F.V.'s I guess. And now, Mr Hay, we'll up anchor, if you please.'

'For Heaven's sake, tell me some of the words,' whispered Herrick.

An hour later, the Farallone was under all plain sail, the rudder hard a-port, and the cheerfully clanking windlass had brought the anchor home.

'All clear, sir,' cried Herrick from the bow.

45

The captain met her with the wheel, as she bounded like a stag from her repose, trembling and bending to the puffs. The guard boat gave a parting hail, the wake whitened and ran out; the Farallone was under weigh.

Her berth had been close to the pass. Even as she forged ahead Davis slewed her for the channel between the pier ends of the reef, the breakers sounding and whitening to either hand. Straight through the narrow band of blue, she shot to seaward: and the captain's heart exulted as he felt her tremble underfoot, and (looking back over the taffrail) beheld the roofs of Papeete changing position on the shore and the island mountains rearing higher in the wake.

But they were not yet done with the shore and the horror of the yellow flag. About midway of the pass, there was a cry and a scurry, a man was seen to leap upon the rail, and, throwing his arms over his head, to stoop and plunge into the sea.

'Steady as she goes,' the captain cried, relinquishing the wheel to Huish.

The next moment he was forward in the midst of the Kanakas, belaying pin in hand.

'Anybody else for shore?' he cried, and the savage trumpeting of his voice, no less than the ready weapon in his hand, struck fear in all. Stupidly they stared after their escaped companion, whose black head was visible upon the water, steering for the land. And the schooner meanwhile slipt like a racer through the pass, and met the long sea of the open ocean with a souse of spray.

'Fool that I was, not to have a pistol ready!' exclaimed Davis. 'Well, we go to sea short-handed, we can't help that. You have a lame watch of it, Mr Hay.'

'I don't see how we are to get along,' said Herrick.

'Got to,' said the captain. 'No more Tahiti for me.'

Both turned instinctively and looked astern. The fair island was unfolding mountain top on mountain top; Eimeo, on the port board, lifted her splintered pinnacles; and still the schooner raced to the open sea.

'Think!' cried the captain with a gesture, 'yesterday morning I danced for my breakfast like a poodle dog.'

Chapter 5. THE CARGO OF CHAMPAGNE

The ship's head was laid to clear Eimeo to the north, and the captain sat down in the cabin, with a chart, a ruler, and an epitome.

'East a half no'the,' said he, raising his face from his labours. 'Mr Hay, you'll have to watch your dead reckoning; I want every yard she makes on every hair's-breadth of a course. I'm going to knock a hole right straight through the Paumotus, and that's always a near touch. Now, if this South East Trade ever blew out of the S.E., which it don't, we might hope to lie within half a point of our course. Say we lie within a point of it. That'll just about weather Fakarava. Yes, sir, that's what we've got to do, if we tack for it. Brings us through this slush of little islands in the cleanest place: see?' And he showed where his ruler intersected the wide-lying labyrinth of the Dangerous Archipelago. 'I wish it was night, and I could put her about right now; we're losing time and easting. Well, we'll do our best. And if we don't fetch Peru, we'll bring up to Ecuador. All one, I guess. Depreciated dollars down, and no questions asked. A remarkable fine institootion, the South American don.'

Tahiti was already some way astern, the Diadem rising from among broken mountains—Eimeo was already close aboard, and stood black and strange against the golden splendour of the west—when the captain took his departure from the two islands, and the patent log was set.

Some twenty minutes later, Sally Day, who was continually leaving the wheel to peer in at the cabin clock, announced in a shrill cry 'Fo'bell,' and the cook was to be seen carrying the soup into the cabin.

'I guess I'll sit down and have a pick with you,' said Davis to Herrick. 'By the time I've done, it'll be dark, and we'll clap the hooker on the wind for South America.'

In the cabin at one corner of the table, immediately below the lamp, and on the lee side of a bottle of champagne, sat Huish. 'What's this? Where did that come from?' asked the captain.

'It's fizz, and it came from the after-'old, if you want to know,' said Huish, and drained his mug.

'This'll never do,' exclaimed Davis, the merchant seaman's horror of breaking into cargo showing incongruously forth on board that stolen ship. 'There was never any good came of games like that.'

'You byby!' said Huish. 'A fellow would think (to 'ear him) we were on the square! And look 'ere, you've put this job up 'ansomely for me, 'aven't you? I'm to go on deck and steer while you two sit and guzzle, and I'm to go by nickname, and got to call you "sir" and "mister." Well, you look here, my bloke: I'll have fizz ad lib., or it won't wash. I tell you that. And you know mighty well, you ain't got any man-of-war to signal now.'

Davis was staggered. 'I'd give fifty dollars this had never happened,' he said weakly.

'Well, it 'as 'appened, you see,' returned Huish. 'Try some; it's devilish good.'

The Rubicon was crossed without another struggle. The captain filled a mug and drank.

'I wish it was beer,' he said with a sigh. 'But there's no denying it's the genuine stuff and cheap at the money. Now, Huish, you clear out and take your wheel.'

The little wretch had gained a point, and he was gay. 'Ay, ay, sir,' said he, and left the others to their meal.

'Pea soup!' exclaimed the captain. 'Blamed if I thought I should taste pea soup again!'

Herrick sat inert and silent. It was impossible after these months of hopeless want to smell the rough, high-spiced sea victuals without lust, and his mouth watered with desire of the champagne. It was no less impossible to have assisted at the scene between Huish and the captain, and not to perceive, with sudden bluntness, the gulf where he had fallen. He was a thief among thieves. He said it to himself. He could not touch the soup. If he had moved at all, it must have been to leave the table, throw himself overboard, and drown—an honest man.

'Here,' said the captain, 'you look sick, old man; have a drop of this.'

The champagne creamed and bubbled in the mug; its bright colour, its lively effervescence, seized his eye. 'It is too late to hesitate,' he thought; his hand took the mug instinctively; he drank, with unquenchable pleasure and desire of more; drained the vessel dry, and set it down with sparkling eyes.

'There is something in life after all!' he cried. 'I had forgot what it was like. Yes, even this is worth while. Wine, food, dry clothes—why, they're worth dying, worth hanging, for! Captain, tell me one thing: why aren't all the poor folk foot-pads?'

'Give it up,' said the captain.

'They must be damned good,' cried Herrick. 'There's something here beyond me. Think of that calaboose! Suppose we were sent suddenly back.' He shuddered as though stung by a convulsion, and buried his face in his clutching hands.

'Here, what's wrong with you?' cried the captain. There was no reply; only Herrick's shoulders heaved, so that the table was shaken. 'Take some more of this. Here, drink this. I order you to. Don't start crying when you're out of the wood.'

'I'm not crying,' said Herrick, raising his face and showing his dry eyes. 'It's worse than crying. It's the horror of that grave that we've escaped from.'

'Come now, you tackle your soup; that'll fix you,' said Davis kindly. 'I told you-you were all broken up. You couldn't have stood out another week.'

'That's the dreadful part of it!' cried Herrick. 'Another week and I'd have murdered someone for a dollar! God! and I know that? And I'm still living? It's some beastly dream.'

'Quietly, quietly! Quietly does it, my son. Take your pea soup. Food, that's what you want,' said Davis.

The soup strengthened and quieted Herrick's nerves; another glass of wine, and a piece of pickled pork and fried banana completed what the soup began; and he was able once more to look the captain in the face.

'I didn't know I was so much run down,' he said.

'Well,' said Davis, 'you were as steady as a rock all day: now you've had a little lunch, you'll be as steady as a rock again.'

'Yes,' was the reply, 'I'm steady enough now, but I'm a queer kind of a first officer.'

'Shucks!' cried the captain. 'You've only got to mind the ship's course, and keep your slate to half a point. A babby could do that, let alone a college graduate like you. There ain't nothing TO sailoring, when you come to look it in the face. And now we'll go and put her about. Bring the slate; we'll have to start our dead reckoning right away.'

The distance run since the departure was read off the log by the binnacle light and entered on the slate.

'Ready about,' said the captain. 'Give me the wheel, White Man, and you stand by the mainsheet. Boom tackle, Mr Hay, please, and then you can jump forward and attend head sails.'

'Ay, ay, sir,' responded Herrick.

'All clear forward?' asked Davis.

'All clear, sir.'

'Hard a-lee!' cried the captain. 'Haul in your slack as she comes,' he called to Huish. 'Haul in your slack, put your back into it; keep your feet out of the coils.' A sudden blow sent Huish flat along the deck, and the captain was in his place. 'Pick yourself up and keep the wheel hard over!' he roared. 'You wooden fool, you wanted to get killed, I guess. Draw the jib,' he cried a moment later; and then to Huish, 'Give me the wheel again, and see if you can coil that sheet.'

But Huish stood and looked at Davis with an evil countenance. 'Do you know you struck me?' said he.

'Do you know I saved your life?' returned the other, not deigning to look at him, his eyes travelling instead between the compass and the sails. 'Where would you have been, if that boom had swung out and you bundled in the clack? No, SIR, we'll have no more of you at the mainsheet. Seaport towns are full of mainsheet-men; they hop upon one leg, my son, what's left of them, and the rest are dead. (Set your boom tackle, Mr Hay.) Struck you, did I? Lucky for you I did.'

'Well,' said Huish slowly, 'I daresay there may be somethink in that. 'Ope there is.' He turned his back elaborately on the captain, and entered the house, where the speedy explosion of a champagne cork showed he was attending to his comfort.

Herrick came aft to the captain. 'How is she doing now?' he asked.

'East and by no'the a half no'the,' said Davis. 'It's about as good as I expected.'

'What'll the hands think of it?' said Herrick.

'Oh, they don't think. They ain't paid to,' says the captain.

'There was something wrong, was there not? between you and—' Herrick paused.

'That's a nasty little beast, that's a biter,' replied the captain, shaking his head. 'But so long as you and me hang in, it don't matter.'

Herrick lay down in the weather alleyway; the night was cloudless, the movement of the ship cradled him, he was oppressed besides by the first generous meal after so long a time of famine; and he was recalled from deep sleep by the voice of Davis singing out: 'Eight bells!'

He rose stupidly, and staggered aft, where the captain gave him the wheel.

'By the wind,' said the captain. 'It comes a little puffy; when you get a heavy puff, steal all you can to windward, but keep her a good full.'

He stepped towards the house, paused and hailed the forecastle.

'Got such a thing as a concertina forward?' said he. 'Bully for you, Uncle Ned. Fetch it aft, will you?'

The schooner steered very easy; and Herrick, watching the moon-whitened sails, was overpowered by drowsiness. A sharp report from the cabin startled him; a third bottle had been opened; and Herrick remembered the Sea Ranger and Fourteen Island Group. Presently the notes of the accordion sounded, and then the captain's voice:

> 'O honey, with our pockets full of money,
>
> We will trip, trip, trip, we will trip it on the quay,
>
> And I will dance with Kate, and Tom will dance with Sall,
>
> When we're all back from South Amerikee.'

So it went to its quaint air; and the watch below lingered and listened by the forward door, and Uncle Ned was to be seen in the moonlight nodding time; and Herrick smiled at the wheel, his anxieties a while forgotten. Song followed song; another cork exploded; there were voices raised, as though the pair in the cabin were in disagreement; and presently it seemed the breach was healed; for it was now the voice of Huish that struck up, to the captain's accompaniment—

> 'Up in a balloon, boys,
>
> Up in a balloon,
>
> All among the little stars
>
> And round about the moon.'

A wave of nausea overcame Herrick at the wheel. He wondered why the air, the words (which were yet written with a certain knack), and the voice and accent of the singer, should all jar his spirit like a file on a man's teeth. He sickened at the thought of his two comrades drinking away their reason upon stolen wine, quarrelling and hiccupping and waking up, while the doors of the prison yawned for them in the near future. 'Shall I have sold my honour for nothing?' he thought; and a heat of rage and resolution glowed in his bosom—rage against his comrades—resolution to carry through this business if it might be carried; pluck profit out of shame, since the shame at least was now inevitable; and come home, home from South America—how did the song go?—'with his pockets full of money':

'O honey, with our pockets full of money,

We will trip, trip, trip, we will trip it on the quay:'

so the words ran in his head; and the honey took on visible form, the quay rose before him and he knew it for the lamplit Embankment, and he saw the lights of Battersea bridge bestride the sullen river. All through the remainder of his trick, he stood entranced, reviewing the past. He had been always true to his love, but not always sedulous to recall her. In the growing calamity of his life, she had swum more distant, like the moon in mist. The letter of farewell, the dishonourable hope that had surprised and corrupted him in his distress, the changed scene, the sea, the night and the music—all stirred him to the roots of manhood. 'I WILL win her,' he thought, and ground his teeth. 'Fair or foul, what matters if I win her?'

'Fo' bell, matey. I think um fo' bell'—he was suddenly recalled by these words in the voice of Uncle Ned.

'Look in at the clock, Uncle,' said he. He would not look himself, from horror of the tipplers.

'Him past, matey,' repeated the Hawaiian.

'So much the better for you, Uncle,' he replied; and he gave up the wheel, repeating the directions as he had received them.

He took two steps forward and remembered his dead reckoning. 'How has she been heading?' he thought; and he flushed from head to foot. He had not observed or had forgotten; here was the old incompetence; the slate must be filled up by guess. 'Never again!' he vowed to himself in silent fury, 'never again. It shall be no fault of mine if this miscarry.' And for the remainder of his watch, he stood close by Uncle Ned, and read the face of the compass as perhaps he had never read a letter from his sweetheart.

All the time, and spurring him to the more attention, song, loud talk, fleering laughter and the occasional popping of a cork, reached his ears from the interior of the house; and when the port watch was relieved at midnight, Huish and the captain appeared upon the quarter-deck with flushed faces and uneven steps, the former laden with bottles, the latter with two tin mugs. Herrick silently passed them by. They hailed him in thick voices, he made no answer, they cursed him for a churl, he paid no heed although his belly quivered with disgust and rage. He closed-to the door of the house behind him, and cast himself on a locker in the cabin—not to sleep he thought— rather to think and to despair. Yet he had scarce turned twice on his uneasy bed, before a drunken voice hailed him in the ear, and he must go on deck again to stand the morning watch.

The first evening set the model for those that were to follow. Two cases of champagne scarce lasted the four-and-twenty hours, and almost the whole was drunk by Huish and the captain. Huish seemed to thrive on the excess; he was never sober, yet never wholly tipsy; the food and the sea air had soon healed him of his disease, and he began to lay on flesh. But with Davis things went worse. In the drooping, unbuttoned figure that sprawled all day upon the lockers, tippling and reading novels; in the fool who made of the evening watch a public carouse on the quarter-deck, it would have been hard to recognise the vigorous seaman of Papeete roads. He kept himself reasonably well in hand till he had taken the sun and yawned and blotted through his calculations; but from the moment he rolled up the chart, his hours were passed in slavish self-indulgence or in hoggish slumber. Every other branch of his duty was neglected, except maintaining a stern discipline about the dinner table. Again and again Herrick would hear the cook called aft, and see him running with fresh tins, or carrying away again a meal that had been totally condemned. And the more the captain became sunk in drunkenness, the more delicate his palate showed itself. Once, in the forenoon, he had a bo'sun's chair rigged over the rail, stripped to his trousers, and went overboard with a pot of paint. 'I don't like the way this schooner's painted,' said he, 'and

I've taken a down upon her name.' But he tired of it in half an hour, and the schooner went on her way with an incongruous patch of colour on the stern, and the word Farallone part obliterated and part looking through. He refused to stand either the middle or the morning watch. It was fine-weather sailing, he said; and asked, with a laugh, 'Who ever heard of the old man standing watch himself?' To the dead reckoning which Herrick still tried to keep, he would pay not the least attention nor afford the least assistance.

'What do we want of dead reckoning?' he asked. 'We get the sun all right, don't we?'

'We mayn't get it always though,' objected Herrick. 'And you told me yourself you weren't sure of the chronometer.'

'Oh, there ain't no flies in the chronometer!' cried Davis.

'Oblige me so far, captain,' said Herrick stiffly. 'I am anxious to keep this reckoning, which is a part of my duty; I do not know what to allow for current, nor how to allow for it. I am too inexperienced; and I beg of you to help me.'

'Never discourage zealous officer,' said the captain, unrolling the chart again, for Herrick had taken him over his day's work and while he was still partly sober. 'Here it is: look for yourself; anything from west to west no'the-west, and anyways from five to twenty-five miles. That's what the A'm'ralty chart says; I guess you don't expect to get on ahead of your own Britishers?'

'I am trying to do my duty, Captain Brown,' said Herrick, with a dark flush, 'and I have the honour to inform you that I don't enjoy being trifled with.'

'What in thunder do you want?' roared Davis. 'Go and look at the blamed wake. If you're trying to do your duty, why don't you go and do it? I guess it's no business of mine to go and stick my head over the ship's rump? I guess it's yours. And I'll tell you what it is, my fine fellow, I'll trouble you not to come the dude over me. You're insolent, that's what's wrong with you. Don't you crowd me, Mr Herrick, Esquire.'

Herrick tore up his papers, threw them on the floor, and left the cabin.

'He's turned a bloomin' swot, ain't he?' sneered Huish.

'He thinks himself too good for his company, that's what ails Herrick, Esquire,' raged the captain. 'He thinks I don't understand when he comes the heavy swell. Won't sit down with us, won't he? won't say a civil word? I'll serve the son of a gun as he deserves. By God, Huish, I'll show him whether he's too good for John Davis!'

'Easy with the names, cap',' said Huish, who was always the more sober. 'Easy over the stones, my boy!'

'All right, I will. You're a good sort, Huish. I didn't take to you at first, but I guess you're right enough. Let's open another bottle,' said the captain; and that day, perhaps because he was excited by the quarrel, he drank more recklessly, and by four o'clock was stretched insensible upon the locker.

Herrick and Huish supped alone, one after the other, opposite his flushed and snorting body. And if the sight killed Herrick's hunger, the isolation weighed so heavily on the clerk's spirit, that he was scarce risen from table ere he was currying favour with his former comrade.

Herrick was at the wheel when he approached, and Huish leaned confidentially across the binnacle.

'I say, old chappie,' he said, 'you and me don't seem to be such pals somehow.'

Herrick gave her a spoke or two in silence; his eye, as it skirted from the needle to the luff of the foresail, passed the man by without speculation. But Huish was really dull, a thing he could support with difficulty, having no resources of his own. The idea of a private talk with Herrick, at this stage of their relations, held out particular inducements to a person of his character. Drink besides, as it renders some men hyper-sensitive, made Huish callous. And it would almost have required a blow to make him quit his purpose.

'Pretty business, ain't it?' he continued; 'Dyvis on the lush? Must say I thought you gave it 'im A1 today. He didn't like it a bit; took on hawful after you were gone.—"'Ere," says I, "'old on, easy on the lush," I says. "'Errick was

57

right, and you know it. Give 'im a chanst," I says.—"Uish," sezee, "don't you gimme no more of your jaw, or I'll knock your bloomin' eyes out." Well, wot can I do, 'Errick? But I tell you, I don't 'arf like it. It looks to me like the Sea Rynger over again.'

Still Herrick was silent.

'Do you hear me speak?' asked Huish sharply. 'You're pleasant, ain't you?'

'Stand away from that binnacle,' said Herrick.

The clerk looked at him, long and straight and black; his figure seemed to writhe like that of a snake about to strike; then he turned on his heel, went back to the cabin and opened a bottle of champagne. When eight bells were cried, he slept on the floor beside the captain on the locker; and of the whole starboard watch, only Sally Day appeared upon the summons. The mate proposed to stand the watch with him, and let Uncle Ned lie down; it would make twelve hours on deck, and probably sixteen, but in this fair-weather sailing, he might safely sleep between his tricks of wheel, leaving orders to be called on any sign of squalls. So far he could trust the men, between whom and himself a close relation had sprung up. With Uncle Ned he held long nocturnal conversations, and the old man told him his simple and hard story of exile, suffering, and injustice among cruel whites. The cook, when he found Herrick messed alone, produced for him unexpected and sometimes unpalatable dainties, of which he forced himself to eat. And one day, when he was forward, he was surprised to feel a caressing hand run down his shoulder, and to hear the voice of Sally Day crooning in his ear: 'You gootch man!' He turned, and, choking down a sob, shook hands with the negrito. They were kindly, cheery, childish souls. Upon the Sunday each brought forth his separate Bible—for they were all men of alien speech even to each other, and Sally Day communicated with his mates in English only, each read or made believe to read his chapter, Uncle Ned with spectacles on his nose; and they would all join together in the singing of missionary hymns. It was thus a cutting reproof to compare the islanders and the whites aboard the Farallone. Shame ran in Herrick's blood to remember what employment he was on, and to see these poor souls—and even Sally Day, the child of cannibals, in all likelihood a cannibal himself—so faithful to what they knew of good. The fact that he was held in grateful favour by these innocents served like blinders to his conscience, and there were times when he was inclined, with Sally Day, to call himself a good man. But the height of his favour was only now to appear. With one voice, the crew protested; ere Herrick knew what they were doing, the cook was aroused and came a willing volunteer; all hands clustered about their mate with expostulations and caresses; and he was bidden to lie down and take his customary rest without alarm.

'He tell you tlue,' said Uncle Ned. 'You sleep. Evely man hae he do all light. Evely man he like you too much.'

Herrick struggled, and gave way; choked upon some trivial words of gratitude; and walked to the side of the house, against which he leaned, struggling with emotion.

Uncle Ned presently followed him and begged him to lie down.

'It's no use, Uncle Ned,' he replied. 'I couldn't sleep. I'm knocked over with all your goodness.'

'Ah, no call me Uncle Ned no mo'!' cried the old man. 'No my name! My name Taveeta, all-e-same Taveeta King of Islael. Wat for he call that Hawaii? I think no savvy nothing—all-e-same Wise-a-mana.'

It was the first time the name of the late captain had been mentioned, and Herrick grasped the occasion. The reader shall be spared Uncle Ned's unwieldy dialect, and learn in less embarrassing English, the sum of what he now communicated. The ship had scarce cleared the Golden Gates before the captain and mate had entered on a career of drunkenness, which was scarcely interrupted by their malady and only closed by death. For days and weeks they had encountered neither land nor ship; and seeing themselves lost on the huge deep with their insane conductors, the natives had drunk deep of terror.

At length they made a low island, and went in; and Wiseman and Wishart landed in the boat.

There was a great village, a very fine village, and plenty Kanakas in

59

that place; but all mighty serious; and from every here and there in the back parts of the settlement, Taveeta heard the sounds of island lamentation. 'I no savvy TALK that island,' said he. 'I savvy hear um CLY. I think, Hum! too many people die here!' But upon Wiseman and Wishart the significance of that barbaric keening was lost. Full of bread and drink, they rollicked along unconcerned, embraced the girls who had scarce energy to repel them, took up and joined (with drunken voices) in the death wail, and at last (on what they took to be an invitation) entered under the roof of a house in which was a considerable concourse of people sitting silent. They stooped below the eaves, flushed and laughing; within a minute they came forth again with changed faces and silent tongues; and as the press severed to make way for them, Taveeta was able to perceive, in the deep shadow of the house, the sick man raising from his mat a head already defeatured by disease. The two tragic triflers fled without hesitation for their boat, screaming on Taveeta to make haste; they came aboard with all speed of oars, raised anchor and crowded sail upon the ship with blows and curses, and were at sea again—and again drunk—before sunset. A week after, and the last of the two had been committed to the deep. Herrick asked Taveeta where that island was, and he replied that, by what he gathered of folks' talk as they went up together from the beach, he supposed it must be one of the Paumotus. This was in itself probable enough, for the Dangerous Archipelago had been swept that year from east to west by devastating smallpox; but Herrick thought it a strange course to lie from Sydney. Then he remembered the drink.

'Were they not surprised when they made the island?' he asked.

'Wise-a-mana he say "dam! what this?"' was the reply.

'O, that's it then,' said Herrick. 'I don't believe they knew where they were.'

'I think so too,' said Uncle Ned. 'I think no savvy. This one mo' betta,' he added, pointing to the house where the drunken captain slumbered: 'Take-a-sun all-e-time.'

The implied last touch completed Herrick's picture of the life and death of his two predecessors; of their prolonged, sordid, sodden sensuality as they sailed, they knew not whither, on their last cruise. He held but a twinkling and unsure belief in any future state; the thought of one of punishment he derided; yet for him (as for all) there dwelt a horror about the end of the brutish man. Sickness fell upon him at the image thus called up; and when he compared it with the scene in which himself was acting, and considered the doom that seemed to brood upon the schooner, a horror that was almost superstitious fell upon him. And yet the strange thing was, he did not falter. He who had proved his incapacity in so many fields, being now falsely placed amid duties which he did not understand, without help, and it might be said without countenance, had hitherto surpassed expectation; and even the shameful misconduct and shocking disclosures of that night seemed but to nerve and strengthen him. He had sold his honour; he vowed it should not be in vain; 'it shall be no fault of mine if this miscarry,' he repeated. And in his heart he wondered at himself. Living rage no doubt supported him; no doubt also, the sense of the last cast, of the ships burned, of all doors closed but one, which is so strong a tonic to the merely weak, and so deadly a depressant to the merely cowardly.

For some time the voyage went otherwise well. They weathered Fakarava with one board; and the wind holding well to the southward and blowing fresh, they passed between Ranaka and Ratiu, and ran some days north-east by east-half-east under the lee of Takume and Honden, neither of which they made. In about 14 degrees South and between 134 and 135 degrees West, it fell a dead calm with rather a heavy sea. The captain refused to take in sail, the helm was lashed, no watch was set, and the Farallone rolled and banged for three days, according to observation, in almost the same place. The fourth morning, a little before day, a breeze sprang up and rapidly freshened. The captain had drunk hard the night before; he was far from sober when he was roused; and when he came on deck for the first time at half-past eight, it was plain he had already drunk deep again at breakfast. Herrick avoided his eye; and resigned the deck with indignation to a man more than half-seas over.

By the loud commands of the captain and the singing out of fellows at the ropes, he could judge from the house that sail was being crowded on the ship; relinquished his half-eaten breakfast; and came on deck again, to find the main and the jib topsails set, and both watches and the cook turned out to hand the staysail. The Farallone lay already far over; the sky was obscured with misty scud; and from the windward an ominous squall came flying up, broadening and blackening as it rose.

Fear thrilled in Herrick's vitals. He saw death hard by; and if not death, sure ruin. For if the Farallone lived through the coming squall, she must surely be dismasted. With that their enterprise was at an end, and they themselves bound prisoners to the very evidence of their crime. The greatness of the peril and his own alarm sufficed to silence him. Pride, wrath, and shame raged without issue in his mind; and he shut his teeth and folded his arms close.

The captain sat in the boat to windward, bellowing orders and insults, his eyes glazed, his face deeply congested; a bottle set between his knees, a glass in his hand half empty. His back was to the squall, and he was at first intent upon the setting of the sail. When that was done, and the great trapezium of canvas had begun to draw and to trail the lee-rail of the Farallone level with the foam, he laughed out an empty laugh, drained his glass, sprawled back among the lumber in the boat, and fetched out a crumpled novel.

Herrick watched him, and his indignation glowed red hot. He glanced to windward where the squall already whitened the near sea and heralded its coming with a singular and dismal sound. He glanced at the steersman, and saw him clinging to the spokes with a face of a sickly blue. He saw the crew were running to their stations without orders. And it seemed as if something broke in his brain; and the passion of anger, so long restrained, so long eaten in secret, burst suddenly loose and shook him like a sail. He stepped across to the captain and smote his hand heavily on the drunkard's shoulder.

'You brute,' he said, in a voice that tottered, 'look behind you!'

'Wha's that?' cried Davis, bounding in the boat and upsetting the champagne.

'You lost the Sea Ranger because you were a drunken sot,' said Herrick. 'Now you're going to lose the Farallone. You're going to drown here the same way as you drowned others, and be damned. And your daughter shall walk the streets, and your sons be thieves like their father.'

For the moment, the words struck the captain white and foolish. 'My God!' he cried, looking at Herrick as upon a ghost; 'my God, Herrick!'

'Look behind you, then!' reiterated the assailant.

The wretched man, already partly sobered, did as he was told, and in the same breath of time leaped to his feet. 'Down staysail!' he trumpeted. The hands were thrilling for the order, and the great sail came with a run, and fell half overboard among the racing foam. 'Jib topsail-halyards! Let the stays'l be,' he said again.

But before it was well uttered, the squall shouted aloud and fell, in a solid mass of wind and rain commingled, on the Farallone; and she stooped under the blow, and lay like a thing dead. From the mind of Herrick reason fled; he clung in the weather rigging, exulting; he was done with life, and he gloried in the release; he gloried in the wild noises of the wind and the choking onslaught of the rain; he gloried to die so, and now, amid this coil of the elements. And meanwhile, in the waist up to his knees in water—so low the schooner lay—the captain was hacking at the foresheet with a pocket knife. It was a question of seconds, for the Farallone drank deep of the encroaching seas. But the hand of the captain had the advance; the foresail boom tore apart the last strands of the sheet and crashed to leeward; the Farallone leaped up into the wind and righted; and the peak and throat halyards, which had long been let go, began to run at the same instant.

For some ten minutes more she careered under the impulse of the squall; but the captain was now master of himself and of his ship, and all danger at an end. And then, sudden as a trick change upon the stage, the squall blew by, the wind dropped into light airs, the sun beamed forth again upon the tattered schooner; and the captain, having secured the foresail boom and set a couple of hands to the pump, walked aft, sober, a little pale, and with the sodden end of a cigar still stuck between his teeth even as the squall had found it. Herrick followed him; he could scarce recall the violence of his late emotions, but he felt there was a scene to go through, and he was anxious and even eager to go through with it.

The captain, turning at the house end, met him face to face, and averted his eyes. 'We've lost the two tops'ls and the stays'l,' he gabbled. 'Good business, we didn't lose any sticks. I guess you think we're all the better without the kites.'

'That's not what I'm thinking,' said Herrick, in a voice strangely quiet, that yet echoed confusion in the captain's mind.

'I know that,' he cried, holding up his hand. 'I know what you're thinking. No use to say it now. I'm sober.'

'I have to say it, though,' returned Herrick.

'Hold on, Herrick; you've said enough,' said Davis. 'You've said what I would take from no man breathing but yourself; only I know it's true.'

'I have to tell you, Captain Brown,' pursued Herrick, 'that I resign my position as mate. You can put me in irons or shoot me, as you please; I will make no resistance—only, I decline in any way to help or to obey you; and I suggest you should put Mr Huish in my place. He will make a worthy first officer to your captain, sir.' He smiled, bowed, and turned to walk forward.

'Where are you going, Herrick?' cried the captain, detaining him by the shoulder.

'To berth forward with the men, sir,' replied Herrick, with the same hateful smile. 'I've been long enough aft here with you—gentlemen.'

'You're wrong there,' said Davis. 'Don't you be too quick with me; there ain't nothing wrong but the drink—it's the old story, man! Let me get sober once, and then you'll see,' he pleaded.

'Excuse me, I desire to see no more of you,' said Herrick.

The captain groaned aloud. 'You know what you said about my children?' he broke out.

'By rote. In case you wish me to say it you again?' asked Herrick.

'Don't!' cried the captain, clapping his hands to his ears. 'Don't make me kill a man I care for! Herrick, if you see me put glass to my lips again till we're ashore, I give you leave to put bullet through me; I beg you to do it! You're the only man aboard whose carcase is worth losing; do you think I don't know that? do you think I ever went back on you? I always knew you were in the right of it—drunk or sober, I knew that. What do you want?—an oath? Man, you're clever enough to see that this is sure-enough earnest.'

'Do you mean there shall be no more drinking?' asked Herrick, 'neither by you nor Huish? that you won't go on stealing my profits and drinking my champagne that I gave my honour for? and that you'll attend to your duties, and stand watch and watch, and bear your proper share of the ship's work, instead of leaving it all on the shoulders of a landsman, and making yourself the butt and scoff of native seamen? Is that what you mean? If it is, be so good as to say it categorically.'

'You put these things in a way hard for a gentleman to swallow,' said the captain. 'You wouldn't have me say I was ashamed of myself? Trust me this once; I'll do the square thing, and there's my hand on it.'

'Well, I'll try it once,' said Herrick. 'Fail me again...'

'No more now!' interrupted Davis. 'No more, old man! Enough said. You've a riling tongue when your back's up, Herrick. Just be glad we're friends again, the same as what I am; and go tender on the raws; I'll see as you don't repent it. We've been mighty near death this day—don't say whose fault it was!—pretty near hell, too, I guess. We're in a mighty bad line of life, us two, and ought to go easy with each other.'

He was maundering; yet it seemed as if he were maundering with some design, beating about the bush of some communication that he feared to make, or perhaps only talking against time in terror of what Herrick might say next. But Herrick had now spat his venom; his was a kindly nature, and, content with his triumph, he had now begun to pity. With a few soothing words, he sought to conclude the interview, and proposed that they should change their clothes.

'Not right yet,' said Davis. 'There's another thing I want to tell you first.

You know what you said about my children? I want to tell you why it hit me so hard; I kind of think you'll feel bad about it too. It's about my little Adar. You hadn't ought to have quite said that—but of course I know you didn't know. She—she's dead, you see.'

'Why, Davis!' cried Herrick. 'You've told me a dozen times she was alive! Clear your head, man! This must be the drink.'

'No, SIR,' said Davis. 'She's dead. Died of a bowel complaint. That was when I was away in the brig Oregon. She lies in Portland, Maine. "Adar, only daughter of Captain John Davis and Mariar his wife, aged five." I had a doll for her on board. I never took the paper off'n that doll, Herrick; it went down the way it was with the Sea Ranger, that day I was damned.'

The Captain's eyes were fixed on the horizon, he talked with an extraordinary softness but a complete composure; and Herrick looked upon him with something that was almost terror.

'Don't think I'm crazy neither,' resumed Davis. 'I've all the cold sense that I know what to do with. But I guess a man that's unhappy's like a child; and this is a kind of a child's game of mine. I never could act up to the plain-cut truth, you see; so I pretend. And I warn you square; as soon as we're through with this talk, I'll start in again with the pretending. Only, you see, she can't walk no streets,' added the captain, 'couldn't even make out to live and get that doll!'

Herrick laid a tremulous hand upon the captain's shoulder.

'Don't do that,' cried Davis, recoiling from the touch. 'Can't you see I'm all broken up the way it is? Come along, then; come along, old man; you can put your trust in me right through; come along and get dry clothes.'

They entered the cabin, and there was Huish on his knees prising open a case of champagne.

''Vast, there!' cried the captain. 'No more of that. No more drinking on this ship.'

'Turned teetotal, 'ave you?' inquired Hu'sh. 'I'm agreeable. About time, eh? Bloomin' nearly lost another ship, I fancy.' He took out a bottle and began calmly to burst the wire with the spike of a corkscrew.

'Do you hear me speak?' cried Davis.

'I suppose I do. You speak loud enough,' said Huish. 'The trouble is that I don't care.'

Herrick plucked the captain's sleeve. 'Let him free now,' he said. 'We've had all we want this morning.'

'Let him have it then,' said the captain. 'It's his last.'

By this time the wire was open, the string was cut, the head of glided paper was torn away; and Huish waited, mug in hand, expecting the usual explosion. It did not follow. He eased the cork with his thumb; still there was no result. At last he took the screw and drew it. It came out very easy and with scarce a sound.

''Illo!' said Huish. ''Ere's a bad bottle.'

He poured some of the wine into the mug; it was colourless and still. He smelt and tasted it.

'W'y, wot's this?' he said. 'It's water!'

If the voice of trumpets had suddenly sounded about the ship in the midst of the sea, the three men in the house could scarcely have been more stunned than by this incident. The mug passed round; each sipped, each smelt of it; each stared at the bottle in its glory of gold paper as Crusoe may have stared at the footprint; and their minds were swift to fix upon a common apprehension. The difference between a bottle of champagne and a bottle of water is not great; between a shipload of one or the other lay the whole scale from riches to ruin.

A second bottle was broached. There were two cases standing ready in a stateroom; these two were brought out, broken open, and tested. Still with the same result: the contents were still colourless and tasteless, and dead as the rain in a beached fishing-boat.

'Crikey!' said Huish.

'Here, let's sample the hold!' said the captain, mopping his brow with a back-handed sweep; and the three stalked out of the house, grim and heavy-footed.

All hands were turned out; two Kanakas were sent below, another stationed at a purchase; and Davis, axe in hand, took his place beside the coamings.

'Are you going to let the men know?' whispered Herrick.

'Damn the men!' said Davis. 'It's beyond that. We've got to know ourselves.'

Three cases were sent on deck and sampled in turn; from each bottle, as the captain smashed it with the axe, the champagne ran bubbling and creaming.

'Go deeper, can't you?' cried Davis to the Kanakas in the hold.

The command gave the signal for a disastrous change. Case after case came up, bottle after bottle was burst and bled mere water. Deeper yet, and they came upon a layer where there was scarcely so much as the intention to deceive; where the cases were no longer branded, the bottles no longer wired or papered, where the fraud was manifest and stared them in the face.

'Here's about enough of this foolery!' said Davis. 'Stow back the cases in the hold, Uncle, and get the broken crockery overboard. Come with me,' he added to his co-adventurers, and led the way back into the cabin.

Chapter 6. THE PARTNERS

Each took a side of the fixed table; it was the first time they had sat down at it together; but now all sense of incongruity, all memory of differences, was quite swept away by the presence of the common ruin.

'Gentlemen,' said the captain, after a pause, and with very much the air of a chairman opening a board-meeting, 'we're sold.'

Huish broke out in laughter. 'Well, if this ain't the 'ighest old rig!' he cried. 'And Dyvis, 'ere, who thought he had got up so bloomin' early in the mornin'! We've stolen a cargo of spring water! Oh, my crikey!' and he squirmed with mirth.

The captain managed to screw out a phantom smile.

'Here's Old Man Destiny again,' said he to Herrick, 'but this time I guess he's kicked the door right in.'

Herrick only shook his head.

'O Lord, it's rich!' laughed Huish. 'It would really be a scrumptious lark if it 'ad 'appened to somebody else! And wot are we to do next? Oh, my eye! with this bloomin' schooner, too?'

'That's the trouble,' said Davis. 'There's only one thing certain: it's no use carting this old glass and ballast to Peru. No, SIR, we're in a hole.'

'O my, and the merchand' cried Huish; 'the man that made this shipment! He'll get the news by the mail brigantine; and he'll think of course we're making straight for Sydney.'

'Yes, he'll be a sick merchant,' said the captain. 'One thing: this explains the Kanaka crew. If you're going to lose a ship, I would ask no better myself than a Kanaka crew. But there's one thing it don't explain; it don't explain why she came down Tahiti ways.'

'Wy, to lose her, you byby!' said Huish.

'A lot you know,' said the captain. 'Nobody wants to lose a schooner; they want to lose her ON HER COURSE, you skeericks! You seem to think underwriters haven't got enough sense to come in out of the rain.'

'Well,' said Herrick, 'I can tell you (I am afraid) why she came so far to the eastward. I had it of Uncle Ned. It seems these two unhappy devils, Wiseman and Wishart, were drunk on the champagne from the beginning—and died drunk at the end.'

The captain looked on the table.

'They lay in their two bunks, or sat here in this damned house,' he pursued, with rising agitation, 'filling their skins with the accursed stuff, till sickness took them. As they sickened and the fever rose, they drank the more. They lay here howling and groaning, drunk and dying, all in one. They didn't know where they were, they didn't care. They didn't even take the sun, it seems.'

'Not take the sun?' cried the captain, looking up. 'Sacred Billy! what a crowd!'

'Well, it don't matter to Joe!' said Huish. 'Wot are Wiseman and the t'other buffer to us?'

'A good deal, too,' says the captain. 'We're their heirs, I guess.'

'It is a great inheritance,' said Herrick.

'Well, I don't know about that,' returned Davis. 'Appears to me as if it might be worse. 'Tain't worth what the cargo would have been of course, at least not money down. But I'll tell you what it appears to figure up to. Appears to me as if it amounted to about the bottom dollar of the man in 'Frisco.'

''Old on,' said Huish. 'Give a fellow time; 'ow's this, umpire?'

'Well, my sons,' pursued the captain, who seemed to have recovered his assurance, 'Wiseman and Wishart were to be paid for casting away this old schooner and its cargo. We're going to cast away the schooner right enough;

70

and I'll make it my private business to see that we get paid. What were W. and W. to get? That's more'n I can tell. But W. and W. went into this business themselves, they were on the crook. Now WE'RE on the square, we only stumbled into it; and that merchant has just got to squeal, and I'm the man to see that he squeals good. No, sir! there's some stuffing to this Farallone racket after all.'

'Go it, cap!' cried Huish. 'Yoicks! Forrard! 'Old 'ard! There's your style for the money! Blow me if I don't prefer this to the hother.'

'I do not understand,' said Herrick. 'I have to ask you to excuse me; I do not understand.'

'Well now, see here, Herrick,' said Davis, 'I'm going to have a word with you anyway upon a different matter, and it's good that Huish should hear it too. We're done with this boozing business, and we ask your pardon for it right here and now. We have to thank you for all you did for us while we were making hogs of ourselves; you'll find me turn-to all right in future; and as for the wine, which I grant we stole from you, I'll take stock and see you paid for it. That's good enough, I believe. But what I want to point out to you is this. The old game was a risky game. The new game's as safe as running a Vienna Bakery. We just put this Farallone before the wind, and run till we're well to looard of our port of departure and reasonably well up with some other place, where they have an American Consul. Down goes the Farallone, and good-bye to her! A day or so in the boat; the consul packs us home, at Uncle Sam's expense, to 'Frisco; and if that merchant don't put the dollars down, you come to me!'

'But I thought,' began Herrick; and then broke out; 'oh, let's get on to Peru!'

'Well, if you're going to Peru for your health, I won't say no!' replied the captain. 'But for what other blame' shadow of a reason you should want to go there, gets me clear. We don't want to go there with this cargo; I don't know as old bottles is a lively article anywhere; leastways, I'll go my bottom cent, it ain't Peru. It was always a doubt if we could sell the schooner; I never rightly hoped to, and now I'm sure she ain't worth a hill of beans; what's wrong with her, I don't know; I only know it's something, or she wouldn't be here with this truck in her inside. Then again, if we lose her, and land in Peru, where are we? We can't declare the loss, or how did we get to Peru? In that case the merchant can't touch the insurance; most likely he'll go bust; and don't you think you see the three of us on the beach of Callao?'

'There's no extradition there,' said Herrick.

'Well, my son, and we want to be extraded,' said the captain.

'What's our point? We want to have a consul extrade us as far as San Francisco and that merchant's office door. My idea is that Samoa would be found an eligible business centre. It's dead before the wind; the States have a consul there, and 'Frisco steamers call, so's we could skip right back and interview the merchant.'

'Samoa?' said Herrick. 'It will take us for ever to get there.'

'Oh, with a fair wind!' said the captain.

'No trouble about the log, eh?' asked Huish.

'No, SIR,' said Davis. 'Light airs and baffling winds. Squalls and calms. D. R.: five miles. No obs. Pumps attended. And fill in the barometer and thermometer off of last year's trip.' 'Never saw such a voyage,' says you to the consul. 'Thought I was going to run short...' He stopped in mid career. 'Say,' he began again, and once more stopped. 'Beg your pardon, Herrick,' he added with undisguised humility, 'but did you keep the run of the stores?'

'Had I been told to do so, it should have been done, as the rest was done, to the best of my little ability,' said Herrick. 'As it was, the cook helped himself to what he pleased.'

Davis looked at the table.

'I drew it rather fine, you see,' he said at last. 'The great thing was to clear right out of Papeete before the consul could think better of it. Tell you what: I guess I'll take stock.'

And he rose from table and disappeared with a lamp in the lazarette.

''Ere's another screw loose,' observed Huish.

'My man,' said Herrick, with a sudden gleam of animosity, 'it is still your watch on deck, and surely your wheel also?'

'You come the 'eavy swell, don't you, ducky?' said Huish.

'Stand away from that binnacle. Surely your w'eel, my man. Yah.'

He lit a cigar ostentatiously, and strolled into the waist with his hands in his pockets.

In a surprisingly short time, the captain reappeared; he did not look at Herrick, but called Huish back and sat down.

'Well,' he began, 'I've taken stock—roughly.' He paused as if for somebody to help him out; and none doing so, both gazing on him instead with manifest anxiety, he yet more heavily resumed. 'Well, it won't fight. We can't do it; that's the bed rock. I'm as sorry as what you can be, and sorrier. We can't look near Samoa. I don't know as we could get to Peru.'

'Wot-ju mean?' asked Huish brutally.

'I can't 'most tell myself,' replied the captain. 'I drew it fine; I said I did; but what's been going on here gets me! Appears as if the devil had been around. That cook must be the holiest kind of fraud. Only twelve days, too! Seems like craziness. I'll own up square to one thing: I seem to have figured too fine upon the flour. But the rest—my land! I'll never understand it! There's been more waste on this twopenny ship than what there is to an Atlantic Liner.' He stole a glance at his companions; nothing good was to be gleaned from their dark faces; and he had recourse to rage. 'You wait till I interview that cook!' he roared and smote the table with his fist. 'I'll interview the son of a gun so's he's never been spoken to before. I'll put a bead upon the—'

'You will not lay a finger on the man,' said Herrick. 'The fault is yours and you know it. If you turn a savage loose in your store-room, you know what to expect. I will not allow the man to be molested.'

It is hard to say how Davis might have taken this defiance; but he was diverted to a fresh assailant.

'Well!' drawled Huish, 'you're a plummy captain, ain't you? You're a blooming captain! Don't you, set up any of your chat to me, John Dyvis: I know you now, you ain't any more use than a bloomin' dawl! Oh, you "don't know", don't you? Oh, it "gets you", do it? Oh, I dessay! W'y, we en't you 'owling for fresh tins every blessed day? 'Ow often 'ave I 'eard you send the 'ole bloomin' dinner off and tell the man to chuck it in the swill tub? And breakfast? Oh, my crikey! breakfast for ten, and you 'ollerin' for more! And now you "can't 'most tell"! Blow me, if it ain't enough to make a man write an insultin' letter to Gawd! You dror it mild, John Dyvis; don't 'andle me; I'm dyngerous.'

Davis sat like one bemused; it might even have been doubted if he heard, but the voice of the clerk rang about the cabin like that of a cormorant among the ledges of the cliff.

'That will do, Huish,' said Herrick.

'Oh, so you tyke his part, do you? you stuck-up sneerin' snob! Tyke it then. Come on, the pair of you. But as for John Dyvis, let him look out! He struck me the first night aboard, and I never took a blow yet but wot I gave as good. Let him knuckle down on his marrow bones and beg my pardon. That's my last word.'

'I stand by the Captain,' said Herrick. 'That makes us two to one, both good men; and the crew will all follow me. I hope I shall die very soon; but I have not the least objection to killing you before I go. I should prefer it so; I should do it with no more remorse than winking. Take care—take care, you little cad!'

The animosity with which these words were uttered was so marked in itself, and so remarkable in the man who uttered them that Huish stared, and even the humiliated Davis reared up his head and gazed at his defender. As for Herrick, the successive agitations and disappointments of the day had left him wholly reckless; he was conscious of a pleasant glow, an agreeable excitement; his head seemed empty, his eyeballs burned as he turned them, his throat was dry as a biscuit; the least dangerous man by nature, except in so far as the weak are always dangerous, at that moment he was ready to slay or to be slain with equal unconcern.

Here at least was the gage thrown down, and battle offered; he who should speak next would bring the matter to an issue there and then; all knew it to be so and hung back; and for many seconds by the cabin clock, the trio sat motionless and silent.

Then came an interruption, welcome as the flowers in May.

'Land ho!' sang out a voice on deck. 'Land a weatha bow!'

'Land!' cried Davis, springing to his feet. 'What's this? There ain't no land here.'

And as men may run from the chamber of a murdered corpse, the three ran forth out of the house and left their quarrel behind them, undecided.

The sky shaded down at the sea level to the white of opals; the sea itself, insolently, inkily blue, drew all about them the uncompromising wheel of the horizon. Search it as they pleased, not even the practisect eye of Captain Davis could descry the smallest interruption. A few filmy clouds were slowly melting overhead; and about the schooner, as around the only point of interest, a tropic bird, white as a snowflake, hung, and circled, and displayed, as it turned, the long vermilion feather of its tall. Save the sea and the heaven, that was all.

'Who sang out land?' asked Davis. 'If there's any boy playing funny dog with me, I'll teach him skylarking!'

But Uncle Ned contentedly pointed to a part of the horizon, where a greenish, filmy iridescence could be discerned floating like smoke on the pale heavens.

Davis applied his glass to it, and then looked at the Kanaka. 'Call that land?' said he. 'Well, it's more than I do.'

'One time long ago,' said Uncle Ned, 'I see Anaa all-e-same that, four five hours befo' we come up. Capena he say sun go down, sun go up again; he say lagoon all-e-same milla.'

'All-e-same WHAT?' asked Davis.

'Milla, sah,' said Uncle Ned.

'Oh, ah! mirror,' said Davis. 'I see; reflection from the lagoon. Well, you know, it is just possible, though it's strange I never heard of it. Here, let's look at the chart.'

They went back to the cabin, and found the position of the schooner well to windward of the archipelago in the midst of a white field of paper.

'There! you see for yourselves,' said Davis.

'And yet I don't know,' said Herrick, 'I somehow think there's something in it. I'll tell you one thing too, captain; that's all right about the reflection; I heard it in Papeete.'

'Fetch up that Findlay, then!' said Davis. 'I'll try it all ways. An island wouldn't come amiss, the way we're fixed.'

The bulky volume was handed up to him, broken-backed as is the way with Findlay; and he turned to the place and began to run over the text, muttering to himself and turning over the pages with a wetted finger.

'Hullo!' he exclaimed. 'How's this?' And he read aloud. 'New Island. According to M. Delille this island, which from private interests would remain unknown, lies, it is said, in lat. 12 degrees 49' 10" S. long. 113 degrees 6' W. In addition to the position above given Commander Matthews, H.M.S. Scorpion, states that an island exists in lat. 12 degrees 0' S. long. 13 degrees 16' W. This must be the same, if such an island exists, which is very doubtful, and totally disbelieved in by South Sea traders.'

'Golly!' said Huish.

'It's rather in the conditional mood,' said Herrick.

'It's anything you please,' cried Davis, 'only there it is! That's our place, and don't you make any mistake.'

'"Which from private interests would remain unknown,"' read Herrick, over his shoulder. 'What may that mean?'

'It should mean pearls,' said Davis. 'A pearling island the government don't know about? That sounds like real estate. Or suppose it don't mean anything. Suppose it's just an island; I guess we could fill up with fish, and cocoanuts, and native stuff, and carry out the Samoa scheme hand over fist. How long did he say it was before they raised Anaa? Five hours, I think?'

'Four or five,' said Herrick.

Davis stepped to the door. 'What breeze had you that time you made Anaa, Uncle Ned?' said he.

'Six or seven knots,' was the reply.

'Thirty or thirty-five miles,' said Davis. 'High time we were shortening sail, then. If it is an island, we don't want to be butting our head against it in the dark; and if it isn't an island, we can get through it just as well by daylight. Ready about!' he roared.

And the schooner's head was laid for that elusive glimmer in the sky, which began already to pale in lustre and diminish in size, as the stain of breath vanishes from a window pane. At the same time she was reefed close down.

PART II. THE QUARTETTE

Chapter 7. THE PEARL-FISHER

About four in the morning, as the captain and Herrick sat together on the rail, there arose from the midst of the night in front of them the voice of breakers. Each sprang to his feet and stared and listened. The sound was continuous, like the passing of a train; no rise or fall could be distinguished; minute by minute the ocean heaved with an equal potency against the invisible isle; and as time passed, and Herrick waited in vain for any vicissitude in the volume of that roaring, a sense of the eternal weighed upon his mind. To the expert eye the isle itself was to be inferred from a certain string of blots along the starry heaven. And the schooner was laid to and anxiously observed till daylight.

There was little or no morning bank. A brightening came in the east; then a wash of some ineffable, faint, nameless hue between crimson and silver; and then coals of fire. These glimmered a while on the sea line, and seemed to brighten and darken and spread out, and still the night and the stars reigned undisturbed; it was as though a spark should catch and glow and creep along the foot of some heavy and almost incombustible wall-hanging, and the room itself be scarce menaced. Yet a little after, and the whole east glowed with gold and scarlet, and the hollow of heaven was filled with the daylight.

The isle—the undiscovered, the scarce believed-in—now lay before them and close aboard; and Herrick thought that never in his dreams had he beheld anything more strange and delicate. The beach was excellently white, the continuous barrier of trees inimitably green; the land perhaps ten feet high, the trees thirty more. Every here and there, as the schooner coasted northward, the wood was intermitted; and he could see clear over the inconsiderable strip of land (as a man looks over a wall) to the lagoon within—and clear over that again to where the far side of the atoll prolonged its pencilling of trees against the morning sky. He tortured himself to find analogies. The isle was like the rim of a great vessel sunken in the waters; it was like the embankment of an annular railway grown upon with wood: so slender it seemed amidst the outrageous breakers, so frail and pretty, he would scarce have wondered to see it sink and disappear without a sound, and the waves close smoothly over its descent.

Meanwhile the captain was in the forecross-trees, glass in hand, his eyes in every quarter, spying for an entrance, spying for signs of tenancy. But the isle continued to unfold itself in joints, and to run out in indeterminate capes, and still there was neither house nor man, nor the smoke of fire. Here a multitude of sea-birds soared and twinkled, and fished in the blue waters; and there, and for miles together, the fringe of cocoa-palm and pandanus extended desolate, and made desirable green bowers for nobody to visit, and the silence of death was only broken by the throbbing of the sea.

The airs were very light, their speed was small; the heat intense. The decks were scorching underfoot, the sun flamed overhead, brazen, out of a brazen sky; the pitch bubbled in the seams, and the brains in the brain-pan. And all the while the excitement of the three adventurers glowed about their bones like a fever. They whispered, and nodded, and pointed, and put mouth to ear, with a singular instinct of secrecy, approaching that island underhand like eavesdroppers and thieves; and even Davis from the cross-trees gave his orders mostly by gestures. The hands shared in this mute strain, like dogs, without comprehending it; and through the roar of so many miles of breakers, it was a silent ship that approached an empty island.

At last they drew near to the break in that interminable gangway. A spur of coral sand stood forth on the one hand; on the other a high and thick tuft of trees cut off the view; between was the mouth of the huge laver. Twice a day the ocean crowded in that narrow entrance and was heaped between these frail walls; twice a day, with the return of the ebb, the mighty surplusage of water must struggle to escape. The hour in which the Farallone came there was the hour of flood. The sea turned (as with the instinct of the homing pigeon) for the vast receptacle, swept eddying through the gates, was transmuted, as it did so, into a wonder of watery and silken hues, and brimmed into the inland sea beyond. The schooner looked up close-hauled, and was caught and carried away by the influx like a toy. She skimmed; she flew; a momentary shadow touched her decks from the shore-side trees; the bottom of the channel showed up for a moment and was in a moment gone; the next, she floated on the bosom of the lagoon, and below, in the transparent chamber of waters, a myriad of many-coloured fishes were sporting, a myriad pale-flowers of coral diversified the floor.

Herrick stood transported. In the gratified lust of his eye, he forgot the past and the present; forgot that he was menaced by a prison on the one hand and starvation on the other; forgot that he was come to that island, desperately foraging, clutching at expedients. A drove of fishes, painted like the rainbow and billed like parrots, hovered up in the shadow of the schooner, and passed clear of it, and glinted in the submarine sun. They were beautiful, like birds, and their silent passage impressed him like a strain of song.

Meanwhile, to the eye of Davis in the cross-trees, the lagoon continued to expand its empty waters, and the long succession of the shore-side trees to be paid out like fishing line off a reel. And still there was no mark of habitation. The schooner, immediately on entering, had been kept away to the nor'ard where the water seemed to be the most deep; and she was now skimming past the tall grove of trees, which stood on that side of the channel and denied further view. Of the whole of the low shores of the island, only this bight remained to be revealed. And suddenly the curtain was raised; they began to open out a haven, snugly elbowed there, and beheld, with an astonishment beyond words, the roofs of men.

The appearance, thus 'instantaneously disclosed' to those on the deck of the Farallone, was not that of a city, rather of a substantial country farm with its attendant hamlet: a long line of sheds and store-houses; apart, upon the one side, a deep-verandah'ed dwelling-house; on the other, perhaps a dozen native huts; a building with a belfry and some rude offer at architectural features that might be thought to mark it out for a chapel; on the beach in front some heavy boats drawn up, and a pile of timber running forth into the burning shallows of the lagoon. From a flagstaff at the pierhead, the red ensign of England was displayed. Behind, about, and over, the same tall grove of palms, which had masked the settlement in the beginning, prolonged its root of tumultuous green fans, and turned and ruffled overhead, and sang its silver song all day in the wind. The place had the indescribable but unmistakable appearance of being in commission; yet there breathed from it a sense of desertion that was almost poignant, no human figure was to be observed going to and fro about the houses, and there was no sound of human industry or enjoyment. Only, on the top of the beach and hard by the flagstaff, a woman of exorbitant stature and as white as snow was to be seen beckoning with uplifted arm. The second glance identified her as a piece of naval sculpture, the figure-head of a ship that had long hovered and plunged into so many running billows, and was now brought ashore to be the ensign and presiding genius of that empty town.

The Farallone made a soldier's breeze of it; the wind, besides, was stronger inside than without under the lee of the land; and the stolen schooner opened out successive objects with the swiftness of a panorama, so that the adventurers stood speechless. The flag spoke for itself; it was no frayed and weathered trophy that had beaten itself to pieces on the post, flying over desolation; and to make assurance stronger, there was to be descried in the deep shade of the verandah, a glitter of crystal and the fluttering of white napery. If the figure-head at the pier end, with its perpetual gesture and its leprous whiteness, reigned alone in that hamlet as it seemed to do, it would not have reigned long. Men's hands had been busy, men's feet stirring there, within the circuit of the clock. The Farallones were sure of it; their eyes dug in the deep shadow of the palms for some one hiding; if intensity of looking might have prevailed, they would have pierced the walls of houses; and there came to them, in these pregnant seconds, a sense of being watched and played with, and of a blow impending, that was hardly bearable.

The extreme point of palms they had just passed enclosed a creek, which was thus hidden up to the last moment from the eyes of those on board; and from this, a boat put suddenly and briskly out, and a voice hailed.

'Schooner ahoy!' it cried. 'Stand in for the pier! In two cables' lengths you'll have twenty fathoms water and good holding ground.'

The boat was manned with a couple of brown oarsmen in scanty kilts of blue. The speaker, who was steering, wore white clothes, the full dress of the tropics; a wide hat shaded his face; but it could be seen that he was of stalwart size, and his voice sounded like a gentleman's. So much could be made out. It was plain, besides, that the Farallone had been descried some time before at sea, and the inhabitants were prepared for its reception.

Mechanically the orders were obeyed, and the ship berthed; and the three adventurers gathered aft beside the house and waited, with galloping pulses and a perfect vacancy of mind, the coming of the stranger who might mean so much to them. They had no plan, no story prepared; there was no time to make one; they were caught red-handed and must stand their chance. Yet this anxiety was chequered with hope. The island being undeclared, it was not possible the man could hold any office or be in a position to demand their papers. And beyond that, if there was any truth in Findlay, as it now seemed there should be, he was the representative of the 'private reasons,' he must see their coming with a profound disappointment; and perhaps (hope whispered) he would be willing and able to purchase their silence.

The boat was by that time forging alongside, and they were able at last to see what manner of man they had to do with. He was a huge fellow, six feet four in height, and of a build proportionately strong, but his sinews seemed to be dissolved in a listlessness that was more than languor. It was only the eye that corrected this impression; an eye of an unusual mingled brilliancy and softness, sombre as coal and with lights that outshone the topaz; an eye of unimpaired health and virility; an eye that bid you beware of the man's devastating anger. A complexion, naturally dark, had been tanned in the island to a hue hardly distinguishable from that of a Tahitian; only his manners and movements, and the living force that dwelt in him, like fire in flint, betrayed the European. He was dressed in white drill, exquisitely made; his scarf and tie were of tender-coloured silks; on the thwart beside him there leaned a Winchester rifle.

'Is the doctor on board?' he cried as he came up. 'Dr Symonds, I mean? You never heard of him? Nor yet of the Trinity Hall? Ah!'

He did not look surprised, seemed rather to affect it in politeness; but his eye rested on each of the three white men in succession with a sudden weight of curiosity that was almost savage. 'Ah, THEN!' said he, 'there is some small mistake, no doubt, and I must ask you to what I am indebted for this pleasure?'

He was by this time on the deck, but he had the art to be quite unapproachable; the friendliest vulgarian, three parts drunk, would have known better than take liberties; and not one of the adventurers so much as offered to shake hands.

'Well,' said Davis, 'I suppose you may call it an accident. We had heard of your island, and read that thing in the Directory about the PRIVATE REASONS, you see; so when we saw the lagoon reflected in the sky, we put her head for it at once, and so here we are.'

''Ope we don't intrude!' said Huish.

The stranger looked at Huish with an air of faint surprise, and looked pointedly away again. It was hard to be more offensive in dumb show.

'It may suit me, your coming here,' he said. 'My own schooner is overdue, and I may put something in your way in the meantime. Are you open to a charter?'

'Well, I guess so,' said Davis; 'it depends.'

'My name is Attwater,' continued the stranger. 'You, I presume, are the captain?'

'Yes, sir. I am the captain of this ship: Captain Brown,' was the reply.

'Well, see 'ere!' said Huish, 'better begin fair! 'E's skipper on deck right enough, but not below. Below, we're all equal, all got a lay in the adventure; when it comes to business, I'm as good as 'e; and what I say is, let's go into the 'ouse and have a lush, and talk it over among pals. We've some prime fizz,' he said, and winked.

The presence of the gentleman lighted up like a candle the vulgarity of the clerk; and Herrick instinctively, as one shields himself from pain, made haste to interrupt.

'My name is Hay,' said he, 'since introductions are going. We shall be very glad if you will step inside.'

Attwater leaned to him swiftly. 'University man?' said he.

'Yes, Merton,' said Herrick, and the next moment blushed scarlet at his indiscretion.

'I am of the other lot,' said Attwater: 'Trinity Hall, Cambridge. I called my schooner after the old shop. Well! this is a queer place and company for us to meet in, Mr Hay,' he pursued, with easy incivility to the others. 'But do you bear out ... I beg this gentleman's pardon, I really did not catch his name.'

'My name is 'Uish, sir,' returned the clerk, and blushed in turn.

'Ah!' said Attwater. And then turning again to Herrick, 'Do you bear out Mr Whish's description of your vintage? or was it only the unaffected poetry of his own nature bubbling up?'

Herrick was embarrassed; the silken brutality of their visitor made him blush; that he should be accepted as an equal, and the others thus pointedly ignored, pleased him in spite of himself, and then ran through his veins in a recoil of anger.

'I don't know,' he said. 'It's only California; it's good enough, I believe.'

Attwater seemed to make up his mind. 'Well then, I'll tell you what: you three gentlemen come ashore this evening and bring a basket of wine with you; I'll try and find the food,' he said. 'And by the by, here is a question I should have asked you when I come on board: have you had smallpox?'

'Personally, no,' said Herrick. 'But the schooner had it.'

'Deaths?' from Attwater.

'Two,' said Herrick.

'Well, it is a dreadful sickness,' said Attwater.

''Ad you any deaths?' asked Huish, ''ere on the island?'

'Twenty-nine,' said Attwater. 'Twenty-nine deaths and thirty-one cases, out of thirty-three souls upon the island.—That's a strange way to calculate, Mr Hay, is it not? Souls! I never say it but it startles me.'

'Oh, so that's why everything's deserted?' said Huish.

'That is why, Mr Whish,' said Attwater; 'that is why the house is empty and the graveyard full.'

'Twenty-nine out of thirty-three!' exclaimed Herrick, 'Why, when it came to burying—or did you bother burying?'

'Scarcely,' said Attwater; 'or there was one day at least when we gave up. There were five of the dead that morning, and thirteen of the dying, and no one able to go about except the sexton and myself. We held a council of war, took the... empty bottles... into the lagoon, and buried them.' He looked over his shoulder, back at the bright water. 'Well, so you'll come to dinner, then? Shall we say half-past six. So good of you!'

His voice, in uttering these conventional phrases, fell at once into the false measure of society; and Herrick unconsciously followed the example.

'I am sure we shall be very glad,' he said. 'At half-past six? Thank you

so very much.'

   "'For my voice has been tuned to the note of the gun

   That startles the deep when the combat's begun,"'

quoted Attwater, with a smile, which instantly gave way to an air of funereal solemnity. 'I shall particularly expect Mr Whish,' he continued. 'Mr Whish, I trust you understand the invitation?'

'I believe you, my boy!' replied the genial Huish.

'That is right then; and quite understood, is it not?' said Attwater. 'Mr Whish and Captain Brown at six-thirty without fault—and you, Hay, at four sharp.'

And he called his boat.

During all this talk, a load of thought or anxiety had weighed upon the captain. There was no part for which nature had so liberally endowed him as that of the genial ship captain. But today he was silent and abstracted. Those who knew him could see that he hearkened close to every syllable, and seemed to ponder and try it in balances. It would have been hard to say what look there was, cold, attentive, and sinister, as of a man maturing plans, which still brooded over the unconscious guest; it was here, it was there, it was nowhere; it was now so little that Herrick chid himself for an idle fancy; and anon it was so gross and palpable that you could say every hair on the man's head talked mischief.

He woke up now, as with a start. 'You were talking of a charter,' said he.

'Was I?' said Attwater. 'Well, let's talk of it no more at present.'

'Your own schooner is overdue, I understand?' continued the captain.

'You understand perfectly, Captain Brown,' said Attwater; 'thirty-three days overdue at noon today.'

'She comes and goes, eh? plies between here and...?' hinted the captain.

'Exactly; every four months; three trips in the year,' said Attwater.

'You go in her, ever?' asked Davis.

'No, one stops here,' said Attwater, 'one has plenty to attend to.'

'Stop here, do you?' cried Davis. 'Say, how long?'

'How long, O Lord,' said Attwater with perfect, stern gravity. 'But it does not seem so,' he added, with a smile.

'No, I dare say not,' said Davis. 'No, I suppose not. Not with all your gods about you, and in as snug a berth as this. For it is a pretty snug berth,' said he, with a sweeping look.

'The spot, as you are good enough to indicate, is not entirely intolerable,' was the reply.

'Shell, I suppose?' said Davis.

86

'Yes, there was shell,' said Attwater.

'This is a considerable big beast of a lagoon, sir,' said the captain. 'Was there a—was the fishing—would you call the fishing anyways GOOD?'

'I don't know that I would call it anyways anything,' said Attwater, 'if you put it to me direct.'

'There were pearls too?' said Davis.

'Pearls, too,' said Attwater.

'Well, I give out!' laughed Davis, and his laughter rang cracked like a false piece. 'If you're not going to tell, you're not going to tell, and there's an end to it.'

'There can be no reason why I should affect the least degree of secrecy about my island,' returned Attwater; 'that came wholly to an end with your arrival; and I am sure, at any rate, that gentlemen like you and Mr Whish, I should have always been charmed to make perfectly at home. The point on which we are now differing—if you can call it a difference—is one of times and seasons. I have some information which you think I might impart, and I think not. Well, we'll see tonight! By-by, Whish!' He stepped into his boat and shoved off. 'All understood, then?' said he. 'The captain and Mr Whish at six-thirty, and you, Hay, at four precise. You understand that, Hay? Mind, I take no denial. If you're not there by the time named, there will be no banquet; no song, no supper, Mr Whish!'

White birds whisked in the air above, a shoal of parti-coloured fishes in the scarce denser medium below; between, like Mahomet's coffin, the boat drew away briskly on the surface, and its shadow followed it over the glittering floor of the lagoon. Attwater looked steadily back over his shoulders as he sat; he did not once remove his eyes from the Farallone and the group on her quarter-deck beside the house, till his boat ground upon the pier. Thence, with an agile pace, he hurried ashore, and they saw his white clothes shining in the chequered dusk of the grove until the house received him.

The captain, with a gesture and a speaking countenance, called the

87

adventurers into the cabin.

'Well,' he said to Herrick, when they were seated, 'there's one good job at least. He's taken to you in earnest.'

'Why should that be a good job?' said Herrick.

'Oh, you'll see how it pans out presently,' returned Davis. 'You go ashore and stand in with him, that's all! You'll get lots of pointers; you can find out what he has, and what the charter is, and who's the fourth man—for there's four of them, and we're only three.'

'And suppose I do, what next?' cried Herrick. 'Answer me that!'

'So I will, Robert Herrick,' said the captain. 'But first, let's see all clear. I guess you know,' he said with an imperious solemnity, 'I guess you know the bottom is out of this Farallone speculation? I guess you know it's RIGHT out? and if this old island hadn't been turned up right when it did, I guess you know where you and I and Huish would have been?'

'Yes, I know that,' said Herrick. 'No matter who's to blame, I know it. And what next?'

'No matter who's to blame, you know it, right enough,' said the captain, 'and I'm obliged to you for the reminder. Now here's this Attwater: what do you think of him?'

'I do not know,' said Herrick. 'I am attracted and repelled. He was insufferably rude to you.'

'And you, Huish?' said the captain.

Huish sat cleaning a favourite briar root; he scarce looked up from that engrossing task. 'Don't ast me what I think of him!' he said. 'There's a day comin', I pray Gawd, when I can tell it im myself.'

'Huish means the same as what I do,' said Davis. 'When that man came stepping around, and saying "Look here, I'm Attwater"—and you knew it was so, by God!—I sized him right straight up. Here's the real article, I said, and I don't like it; here's the real, first-rate, copper-bottomed aristocrat. 'AW'

I DON'T KNOW YE, DO I? GOD DAMN YE, DID GOD MAKE YE?' No, that couldn't be nothing but genuine; a man got to be born to that, and notice! smart as champagne and hard as nails; no kind of a fool; no, SIR! not a pound of him! Well, what's he here upon this beastly island for? I said. HE'S not here collecting eggs. He's a palace at home, and powdered flunkies; and if he don't stay there, you bet he knows the reason why! Follow?'

'O yes, I 'ear you,' said Huish.

'He's been doing good business here, then,' continued the captain. 'For ten years, he's been doing a great business. It's pearl and shell, of course; there couldn't be nothing else in such a place, and no doubt the shell goes off regularly by this Trinity Hall, and the money for it straight into the bank, so that's no use to us. But what else is there? Is there nothing else he would be likely to keep here? Is there nothing else he would be bound to keep here? Yes, sir; the pearls! First, because they're too valuable to trust out of his hands. Second, because pearls want a lot of handling and matching; and the man who sells his pearls as they come in, one here, one there, instead of hanging back and holding up—well, that man's a fool, and it's not Attwater.'

'Likely,' said Huish, 'that's w'at it is; not proved, but likely.'

'It's proved,' said Davis bluntly.

'Suppose it was?' said Herrick. 'Suppose that was all so, and he had these pearls—a ten years' collection of them?—Suppose he had? There's my question.'

The captain drummed with his thick hands on the board in front of him; he looked steadily in Herrick's face, and Herrick as steadily looked upon the table and the pattering fingers; there was a gentle oscillation of the anchored ship, and a big patch of sunlight travelled to and fro between the one and the other.

'Hear me!' Herrick burst out suddenly.

'No, you better hear me first,' said Davis. 'Hear me and understand me. WE'VE got no use for that fellow, whatever you may have. He's your kind, he's not ours; he's took to you, and he's wiped his boots on me and Huish.

Save him if you can!'

'Save him?' repeated Herrick.

'Save him, if you're able!' reiterated Davis, with a blow of his clenched fist. 'Go ashore, and talk him smooth; and if you get him and his pearls aboard, I'll spare him. If you don't, there's going to be a funeral. Is that so, Huish? does that suit you?'

'I ain't a forgiving man,' said Huish, 'but I'm not the sort to spoil business neither. Bring the bloke on board and bring his pearls along with him, and you can have it your own way; maroon him where you like—I'm agreeable.'

'Well, and if I can't?' cried Herrick, while the sweat streamed upon his face. 'You talk to me as if I was God Almighty, to do this and that! But if I can't?'

'My son,' said the captain, 'you better do your level best, or you'll see sights!'

'O yes,' said Huish. 'O crikey, yes!' He looked across at Herrick with a toothless smile that was shocking in its savagery; and his ear caught apparently by the trivial expression he had used, broke into a piece of the chorus of a comic song which he must have heard twenty years before in London: meaningless gibberish that, in that hour and place, seemed hateful as a blasphemy: 'Hikey, pikey, crikey, fikey, chillingawallaba dory.'

The captain suffered him to finish; his face was unchanged.

'The way things are, there's many a man that wouldn't let you go ashore,' he resumed. 'But I'm not that kind. I know you'd never go back on me, Herrick! Or if you choose to—go, and do it, and be damned!' he cried, and rose abruptly from the table.

He walked out of the house; and as he reached the door, turned and called Huish, suddenly and violently, like the barking of a dog. Huish followed, and Herrick remained alone in the cabin.

'Now, see here!' whispered Davis. 'I know that man. If you open your mouth to him again, you'll ruin all.'

Chapter 8. BETTER ACQUAINTANCE

The boat was gone again, and already half-way to the Farallone, before Herrick turned and went unwillingly up the pier. From the crown of the beach, the figure-head confronted him with what seemed irony, her helmeted head tossed back, her formidable arm apparently hurling something, whether shell or missile, in the direction of the anchored schooner. She seemed a defiant deity from the island, coming forth to its threshold with a rush as of one about to fly, and perpetuated in that dashing attitude. Herrick looked up at her, where she towered above him head and shoulders, with singular feelings of curiosity and romance, and suffered his mind to travel to and fro in her life-history. So long she had been the blind conductress of a ship among the waves; so long she had stood here idle in the violent sun, that yet did not avail to blister her; and was even this the end of so many adventures? he wondered, or was more behind? And he could have found in his heart to regret that she was not a goddess, nor yet he a pagan, that he might have bowed down before her in that hour of difficulty.

When he now went forward, it was cool with the shadow of many well-grown palms; draughts of the dying breeze swung them together overhead; and on all sides, with a swiftness beyond dragon-flies or swallows, the spots of sunshine flitted, and hovered, and returned. Underfoot, the sand was fairly solid and quite level, and Herrick's steps fell there noiseless as in new-fallen snow. It bore the marks of having been once weeded like a garden alley at home; but the pestilence had done its work, and the weeds were returning. The buildings of the settlement showed here and there through the stems of the colonnade, fresh painted, trim and dandy, and all silent as the grave. Only, here and there in the crypt, there was a rustle and scurry and some crowing of poultry; and from behind the house with the verandahs, he saw smoke arise and heard the crackling of a fire.

The stone houses were nearest him upon his right. The first was locked; in the second, he could dimly perceive, through a window, a certain accumulation of pearl-shell piled in the far end; the third, which stood gaping open on the afternoon, seized on the mind of Herrick with its multiplicity and disorder of romantic things. Therein were cables, windlasses and blocks of every size and capacity; cabin windows and ladders; rusty tanks, a companion hutch; a binnacle with its brass mountings and its compass idly pointing, in the confusion and dusk of that shed, to a forgotten pole; ropes, anchors, harpoons, a blubber dipper of copper, green with years, a steering wheel, a tool chest with the vessel's name upon the top, the Asia: a whole curiosity-shop of sea curios, gross and solid, heavy to lift, ill to break, bound with brass and shod with iron. Two wrecks at the least must have contributed to this random heap of lumber; and as Herrick looked upon it, it seemed to him as if the two ships' companies were there on guard, and he heard the tread of feet and whisperings, and saw with the tail of his eye the commonplace ghosts of sailor men.

This was not merely the work of an aroused imagination, but had something sensible to go upon; sounds of a stealthy approach were no doubt audible; and while he still stood staring at the lumber, the voice of his host sounded suddenly, and with even more than the customary softness of enunciation, from behind.

'Junk,', it said, 'only old junk! And does Mr Hay find a parable?'

'I find at least a strong impression,' replied Herrick, turning quickly, lest he might be able to catch, on the face of the speaker, some commentary on the words.

Attwater stood in the doorway, which he almost wholly filled; his hands stretched above his head and grasping the architrave. He smiled when their eyes Met, but the expression was inscrutable.

'Yes, a powerful impression. You are like me; nothing so affecting as ships!' said he. 'The ruins of an empire would leave me frigid, when a bit of an old rail that an old shellback leaned on in the middle watch, would bring me up all standing. But come, let's see some more of the island. It's all sand and coral and palm trees; but there's a kind of a quaintness in the place.'

'I find it heavenly,' said Herrick, breathing deep, with head bared in the shadow.

'Ah, that's because you're new from sea,' said Attwater. 'I dare say, too, you can appreciate what one calls it. It's a lovely name. It has a flavour, it has a colour, it has a ring and fall to it; it's like its author—it's half Christian! Remember your first view of the island, and how it's only woods and water; and suppose you had asked somebody for the name, and he had answered— nemorosa Zacynthos!'

'Jam medio apparet fluctu!' exclaimed Herrick. 'Ye gods, yes, how good!'

'If it gets upon the chart, the skippers will make nice work of it,' said Attwater. 'But here, come and see the diving-shed.'

He opened a door, and Herrick saw a large display of apparatus neatly ordered: pumps and pipes, and the leaded boots, and the huge snouted helmets shining in rows along the wall; ten complete outfits.

'The whole eastern half of my lagoon is shallow, you must understand,' said Attwater; 'so we were able to get in the dress to great advantage. It paid beyond belief, and was a queer sight when they were at it, and these marine monsters'—tapping the nearest of the helmets—'kept appearing and reappearing in the midst of the lagoon. Fond of parables?' he asked abruptly.

'O yes!' said Herrick.

'Well, I saw these machines come up dripping and go down again, and come up dripping and go down again, and all the while the fellow inside as dry as toast!' said Attwater; 'and I thought we all wanted a dress to go down into the world in, and come up scatheless. What do you think the name was?' he inquired.

'Self-conceit,' said Herrick.

'Ah, but I mean seriously!' said Attwater.

'Call it self-respect, then!' corrected Herrick, with a laugh.

'And why not Grace? Why not God's Grace, Hay?' asked Attwater. 'Why not the grace of your Maker and Redeemer, He who died for you, He who

93

upholds you, He whom you daily crucify afresh? There is nothing here,'—striking on his bosom—'nothing there'—smiting the wall—'and nothing there'—stamping—'nothing but God's Grace! We walk upon it, we breathe it; we live and die by it; it makes the nails and axles of the universe; and a puppy in pyjamas prefers self-conceit!' The huge dark man stood over against Herrick by the line of the divers' helmets, and seemed to swell and glow; and the next moment the life had gone from him. 'I beg your pardon,' said he; 'I see you don't believe in God?'

'Not in your sense, I am afraid,' said Herrick.

'I never argue with young atheists or habitual drunkards,' said Attwater flippantly. 'Let us go across the island to the outer beach.'

It was but a little way, the greatest width of that island scarce exceeding a furlong, and they walked gently. Herrick was like one in a dream. He had come there with a mind divided; come prepared to study that ambiguous and sneering mask, drag out the essential man from underneath, and act accordingly; decision being till then postponed. Iron cruelty, an iron insensibility to the suffering of others, the uncompromising pursuit of his own interests, cold culture, manners without humanity; these he had looked for, these he still thought he saw. But to find the whole machine thus glow with the reverberation of religious zeal, surprised him beyond words; and he laboured in vain, as he walked, to piece together into any kind of whole his odds and ends of knowledge—to adjust again into any kind of focus with itself, his picture of the man beside him.

'What brought you here to the South Seas?' he asked presently.

'Many things,' said Attwater. 'Youth, curiosity, romance, the love of the sea, and (it will surprise you to hear) an interest in missions. That has a good deal declined, which will surprise you less. They go the wrong way to work; they are too parsonish, too much of the old wife, and even the old apple wife. CLOTHES, CLOTHES, are their idea; but clothes are not Christianity, any more than they are the sun in heaven, or could take the place of it! They think a parsonage with roses, and church bells, and nice old women bobbing in the lanes, are part and parcel of religion. But religion is a savage thing, like the

94

universe it illuminates; savage, cold, and bare, but infinitely strong.'

'And you found this island by an accident?' said Herrick.

'As you did!' said Attwater. 'And since then I have had a business, and a colony, and a mission of my own. I was a man of the world before I was a Christian; I'm a man of the world still, and I made my mission pay. No good ever came of coddling. A man has to stand up in God's sight and work up to his weight avoirdupois; then I'll talk to him, but not before. I gave these beggars what they wanted: a judge in Israel, the bearer of the sword and scourge; I was making a new people here; and behold, the angel of the Lord smote them and they were not!'

With the very uttering of the words, which were accompanied by a gesture, they came forth out of the porch of the palm wood by the margin of the sea and full in front of the sun which was near setting. Before them the surf broke slowly. All around, with an air of imperfect wooden things inspired with wicked activity, the crabs trundled and scuttled into holes. On the right, whither Attwater pointed and abruptly turned, was the cemetery of the island, a field of broken stones from the bigness of a child's hand to that of his head, diversified by many mounds of the same material, and walled by a rude rectangular enclosure. Nothing grew there but a shrub or two with some white flowers; nothing but the number of the mounds, and their disquieting shape, indicated the presence of the dead.

'The rude forefathers of the hamlet sleep!'

quoted Attwater as he entered by the open gateway into that unholy close. 'Coral to coral, pebbles to pebbles,' he said, 'this has been the main scene of my activity in the South Pacific. Some were good, and some bad, and the majority (of course and always) null. Here was a fellow, now, that used to frisk like a dog; if you had called him he came like an arrow from a bow; if you had not, and he came unbidden, you should have seen the deprecating eye and the little intricate dancing step. Well, his trouble is over now, he has lain down with kings and councillors; the rest of his acts, are they not written in the book of the chronicles? That fellow was from Penrhyn; like all the Penrhyn islanders he was ill to manage; heady, jealous, violent: the man with

95

the nose! He lies here quiet enough. And so they all lie.

"And darkness was the burier of the dead!"'

He stood, in the strong glow of the sunset, with bowed head; his voice sounded now sweet and now bitter with the varying sense.

'You loved these people?' cried Herrick, strangely touched.

'I?' said Attwater. 'Dear no! Don't think me a philanthropist. I dislike men, and hate women. If I like the islands at all, it is because you see them here plucked of their lendings, their dead birds and cocked hats, their petticoats and coloured hose. Here was one I liked though,' and he set his foot upon a mound. 'He was a fine savage fellow; he had a dark soul; yes, I liked this one. I am fanciful,' he added, looking hard at Herrick, 'and I take fads. I like you.'

Herrick turned swiftly and looked far away to where the clouds were beginning to troop together and amass themselves round the obsequies of day. 'No one can like me,' he said.

'You are wrong there,' said the other, 'as a man usually is about himself. You are attractive, very attractive.'

'It is not me,' said Herrick; 'no one can like me. If you knew how I despised myself—and why!' His voice rang out in the quiet graveyard.

'I knew that you despised yourself,' said Attwater. 'I saw the blood come into your face today when you remembered Oxford. And I could have blushed for you myself, to see a man, a gentleman, with these two vulgar wolves.'

Herrick faced him with a thrill. 'Wolves?' he repeated.

'I said wolves and vulgar wolves,' said Attwater. 'Do you know that today, when I came on board, I trembled?'

'You concealed it well,' stammered Herrick.

'A habit of mine,' said Attwater. 'But I was afraid, for all that: I was afraid of the two wolves.' He raised his hand slowly. 'And now, Hay, you poor lost puppy, what do you do with the two wolves?'

'What do I do? I don't do anything,' said Herrick. 'There is nothing wrong; all is above board; Captain Brown is a good soul; he is a... he is...' The phantom voice of Davis called in his ear: 'There's going to be a funeral' and the sweat burst forth and streamed on his brow. 'He is a family man,' he resumed again, swallowing; 'he has children at home—and a wife.'

'And a very nice man?' said Attwater. 'And so is Mr Whish, no doubt?'

'I won't go so far as that,' said Herrick. 'I do not like Huish. And yet... he has his merits too.'

'And, in short, take them for all in all, as good a ship's company as one would ask?' said Attwater.

'O yes,' said Herrick, 'quite.'

'So then we approach the other point of why you despise yourself?' said Attwater.

'Do we not all despise ourselves?' cried Herrick. 'Do not you?'

'Oh, I say I do. But do I?' said Attwater. 'One thing I know at least: I never gave a cry like yours. Hay! it came from a bad conscience! Ah, man, that poor diving dress of self-conceit is sadly tattered! Today, now, while the sun sets, and here in this burying place of brown innocents, fall on your knees and cast your sins and sorrows on the Redeemer. Hay—'

'Not Hay!' interrupted the other, strangling. 'Don't call me that! I mean... For God's sake, can't you see I'm on the rack?'

'I see it, I know it, I put and keep you there, my fingers are on the screws!' said Attwater. 'Please God, I will bring a penitent this night before His throne. Come, come to the mercy-seat! He waits to be gracious, man— waits to be gracious!'

He spread out his arms like a crucifix, his face shone with the brightness of a seraph's; in his voice, as it rose to the last word, the tears seemed ready.

Herrick made a vigorous call upon himself. 'Attwater,' he said, 'you push me beyond bearing. What am I to do? I do not believe. It is living truth to you; to me, upon my conscience, only folk-lore. I do not believe there is any form of words under heaven by which I can lift the burthen from my shoulders. I must stagger on to the end with the pack of my responsibility; I cannot shift it; do you suppose I would not, if I thought I could? I cannot—cannot—cannot—and let that suffice.'

The rapture was all gone from Artwater's countenance; the dark apostle had disappeared; and in his place there stood an easy, sneering gentleman, who took off his hat and bowed. It was pertly done, and the blood burned in Herrick's face.

'What do you mean by that?' he cried.

'Well, shall we go back to the house?' said Attwater. 'Our guests will soon be due.'

Herrick stood his ground a moment with clenched fists and teeth; and as he so stood, the fact of his errand there slowly swung clear in front of him, like the moon out of clouds. He had come to lure that man on board; he was failing, even if it could be said that he had tried; he was sure to fail now, and knew it, and knew it was better so. And what was to be next?

With a groan he turned to follow his host, who was standing with polite smile, and instantly and somewhat obsequiously led the way in the now darkened colonnade of palms. There they went in silence, the earth gave up richly of her perfume, the air tasted warm and aromatic in the nostrils; and from a great way forward in the wood, the brightness of lights and fire marked out the house of Attwater.

Herrick meanwhile resolved and resisted an immense temptation to go up, to touch him on the arm and breathe a word in his ear: 'Beware, they are going to murder you.' There would be one life saved; but what of the two others? The three lives went up and down before him like buckets in a well, or like the scales of balances. It had come to a choice, and one that must be speedy. For certain invaluable minutes, the wheels of life ran before him, and he could still divert them with a touch to the one side or the other, still choose who was to live and who was to die. He considered the men. Attwater intrigued, puzzled, dazzled, enchanted and revolted him; alive, he seemed but a doubtful good; and the thought of him lying dead was so unwelcome that it pursued him, like a vision, with every circumstance of colour and sound. Incessantly, he had before him the image of that great mass of man stricken down in varying attitudes and with varying wounds; fallen prone, fallen supine, fallen on his side; or clinging to a doorpost with the changing face and the relaxing fingers of the death-agony. He heard the click of the trigger, the thud of the ball, the cry of the victim; he saw the blood flow. And this building up of circumstance was like a consecration of the man, till he seemed to walk in sacrificial fillets. Next he considered Davis, with his thick-fingered, coarse-grained, oat-bread commonness of nature, his indomitable valour and mirth in the old days of their starvation, the endearing blend of his faults and virtues, the sudden shining forth of a tenderness that lay too deep for tears; his children, Adar and her bowel complaint, and Adar's doll. No, death could not be suffered to approach that head even in fancy; with a general heat and a bracing of his muscles, it was borne in on Herrick that Adar's father would find in him a son to the death. And even Huish showed a little in that sacredness; by the tacit adoption of daily life they were become brothers; there was an implied bond of loyalty in their cohabitation of the ship and their passed miseries, to which Herrick must be a little true or wholly dishonoured. Horror of sudden death for horror of sudden death, there was here no hesitation possible: it must be Attwater. And no sooner was the thought formed (which was a sentence) than his whole mind of man ran in a panic to the other side: and when he looked within himself, he was aware only of turbulence and inarticulate outcry.

In all this there was no thought of Robert Herrick. He had complied with the ebb-tide in man's affairs, and the tide had carried him away; he heard already the roaring of the maelstrom that must hurry him under. And in his bedevilled and dishonoured soul there was no thought of self.

For how long he walked silent by his companion Herrick had no guess. The clouds rolled suddenly away; the orgasm was over; he found himself placid with the placidity of despair; there returned to him the power of commonplace speech; and he heard with surprise his own voice say: 'What a lovely evening!'

'Is it not?' said Attwater. 'Yes, the evenings here would be very pleasant if one had anything to do. By day, of course, one can shoot.'

'You shoot?' asked Herrick.

'Yes, I am what you would call a fine shot,' said Attwater. 'It is faith; I believe my balls will go true; if I were to miss once, it would spoil me for nine months.'

'You never miss, then?' said Herrick.

'Not unless I mean to,' said Attwater. 'But to miss nicely is the art. There was an old king one knew in the western islands, who used to empty a Winchester all round a man, and stir his hair or nick a rag out of his clothes with every ball except the last; and that went plump between the eyes. It was pretty practice.'

'You could do that?' asked Herrick, with a sudden chill.

'Oh, I can do anything,' returned the other. 'You do not understand: what must be, must.'

They were now come near to the back part of the house. One of the men was engaged about the cooking fire, which burned with the clear, fierce, essential radiance of cocoanut shells. A fragrance of strange meats was in the air. All round in the verandahs lamps were lighted, so that the place shone abroad in the dusk of the trees with many complicated patterns of shadow.

'Come and wash your hands,' said Attwater, and led the way into a clean, matted room with a cot bed, a safe, or shelf or two of books in a glazed case, and an iron washing-stand. Presently he cried in the native, and there appeared for a moment in the doorway a plump and pretty young woman with a clean towel.

'Hullo!' cried Herrick, who now saw for the first time the fourth survivor of the pestilence, and was startled by the recollection of the captain's orders.

'Yes,' said Attwater, 'the whole colony lives about the house, what's left

100

of it. We are all afraid of devils, if you please! and Taniera and she sleep in the front parlour, and the other boy on the verandah.'

'She is pretty,' said Herrick.

'Too pretty,' said Attwater. 'That was why I had her married. A man never knows when he may be inclined to be a fool about women; so when we were left alone, I had the pair of them to the chapel and performed the ceremony. She made a lot of fuss. I do not take at all the romantic view of marriage,' he explained.

'And that strikes you as a safeguard?' asked Herrick with amazement.

'Certainly. I am a plain man and very literal. WHOM GOD HATH JOINED TOGETHER, are the words, I fancy. So one married them, and respects the marriage,' said Attwater.

'Ah!' said Herrick.

'You see, I may look to make an excellent marriage when I go home,' began Attwater, confidentially. 'I am rich. This safe alone'—laying his hand upon it—'will be a moderate fortune, when I have the time to place the pearls upon the market. Here are ten years' accumulation from a lagoon, where I have had as many as ten divers going all day long; and I went further than people usually do in these waters, for I rotted a lot of shell, and did splendidly. Would you like to see them?'

This confirmation of the captain's guess hit Herrick hard, and he contained himself with difficulty. 'No, thank you, I think not,' said he. 'I do not care for pearls. I am very indifferent to all these...'

'Gewgaws?' suggested Attwater. 'And yet I believe you ought to cast an eye on my collection, which is really unique, and which—oh! it is the case with all of us and everything about us!—hangs by a hair. Today it groweth up and flourisheth; tomorrow it is cut down and cast into the oven. Today it is here and together in this safe; tomorrow—tonight!—it may be scattered. Thou fool, this night thy soul shall be required of thee.'

'I do not understand you,' said Herrick.

'Not?' said Attwater.

'You seem to speak in riddles,' said Herrick, unsteadily. 'I do not understand what manner of man you are, nor what you are driving at.'

Attwater stood with his hands upon his hips, and his head bent forward. 'I am a fatalist,' he replied, 'and just now (if you insist on it) an experimentalist. Talking of which, by the bye, who painted out the schooner's name?' he said, with mocking softness, 'because, do you know? one thinks it should be done again. It can still be partly read; and whatever is worth doing, is surely worth doing well. You think with me? That is so nice! Well, shall we step on the verandah? I have a dry sherry that I would like your opinion of.'

Herrick followed him forth to where, under the light of the hanging lamps, the table shone with napery and crystal; followed him as the criminal goes with the hangman, or the sheep with the butcher; took the sherry mechanically, drank it, and spoke mechanical words of praise. The object of his terror had become suddenly inverted; till then he had seen Attwater trussed and gagged, a helpless victim, and had longed to run in and save him; he saw him now tower up mysterious and menacing, the angel of the Lord's wrath, armed with knowledge and threatening judgment. He set down his glass again, and was surprised to see it empty.

'You go always armed?' he said, and the next moment could have plucked his tongue out.

'Always,' said Attwater. 'I have been through a mutiny here; that was one of my incidents of missionary life.'

And just then the sound of voices reached them, and looking forth from the verandah they saw Huish and the captain drawing near.

Chapter 9. THE DINNER PARTY

They sat down to an island dinner, remarkable for its variety and excellence; turtle soup and steak, fish, fowls, a sucking pig, a cocoanut salad, and sprouting cocoanut roasted for dessert. Not a tin had been opened; and save for the oil and vinegar in the salad, and some green spears of onion which Attwater cultivated and plucked with his own hand, not even the condiments were European. Sherry, hock, and claret succeeded each other, and the Farallone champagne brought up the rear with the dessert.

It was plain that, like so many of the extremely religious in the days before teetotalism, Attwater had a dash of the epicure. For such characters it is softening to eat well; doubly so to have designed and had prepared an excellent meal for others; and the manners of their host were agreeably mollified in consequence.

A cat of huge growth sat on his shoulders purring, and occasionally, with a deft paw, capturing a morsel in the air. To a cat he might be likened himself, as he lolled at the head of his table, dealing out attentions and innuendoes, and using the velvet and the claw indifferently. And both Huish and the captain fell progressively under the charm of his hospitable freedom.

Over the third guest, the incidents of the dinner may be said to have passed for long unheeded. Herrick accepted all that was offered him, ate and drank without tasting, and heard without comprehension. His mind was singly occupied in contemplating the horror of the circumstances in which he sat. What Attwater knew, what the captain designed, from which side treachery was to be first expected, these were the ground of his thoughts. There were times when he longed to throw down the table and flee into the night. And even that was debarred him; to do anything, to say anything, to move at all, were only to precipitate the barbarous tragedy; and he sat spellbound, eating with white lips. Two of his companions observed him narrowly, Attwater with raking, sidelong glances that did not interrupt his talk, the captain with a heavy and anxious consideration.

'Well, I must say this sherry is a really prime article,' said Huish. ''Ow much does it stand you in, if it's a fair question?'

'A hundred and twelve shillings in London, and the freight to Valparaiso, and on again,' said Attwater. 'It strikes one as really not a bad fluid.'

'A 'undred and twelve!' murmured the clerk, relishing the wine and the figures in a common ecstasy: 'O my!'

'So glad you like it,' said Attwater. 'Help yourself, Mr Whish, and keep the bottle by you.'

'My friend's name is Huish and not Whish, sit,' said the captain with a flush.

'I beg your pardon, I am sure. Huish and not Whish, certainly,' said Attwater. 'I was about to say that I have still eight dozen,' he added, fixing the captain with his eye.

'Eight dozen what?' said Davis.

'Sherry,' was the reply. 'Eight dozen excellent sherry. Why, it seems almost worth it in itself; to a man fond of wine.'

The ambiguous words struck home to guilty consciences, and Huish and the captain sat up in their places and regarded him with a scare.

'Worth what?' said Davis.

'A hundred and twelve shillings,' replied Attwater.

The captain breathed hard for a moment. He reached out far and wide to find any coherency in these remarks; then, with a great effort, changed the subject.

'I allow we are about the first white men upon this island, sir,' said he.

Attwater followed him at once, and with entire gravity, to the new ground. 'Myself and Dr Symonds excepted, I should say the only ones,' he returned. 'And yet who can tell? In the course of the ages someone may have lived here, and we sometimes think that someone must. The cocoa palms grow all round the island, which is scarce like nature's planting. We found besides, when we landed, an unmistakable cairn upon the beach; use unknown; but probably erected in the hope of gratifying some mumbo jumbo whose very name is forgotten, by some thick-witted gentry whose very bones are lost. Then the island (witness the Directory) has been twice reported; and since my tenancy, we have had two wrecks, both derelict. The rest is conjecture.'

'Dr Symonds is your partner, I guess?' said Davis.

'A dear fellow, Symonds! How he would regret it, if he knew you had been here!' said Attwater.

''E's on the Trinity 'All, ain't he?' asked Huish.

'And if you could tell me where the Trinity 'All was, you would confer a favour, Mr Whish!' was the reply.

'I suppose she has a native crew?' said Davis.

'Since the secret has been kept ten years, one would suppose she had,' replied Attwater.

'Well, now, see 'ere!' said Huish. 'You have everything about you in no end style, and no mistake, but I tell you it wouldn't do for me. Too much of "the old rustic bridge by the mill"; too retired, by 'alf. Give me the sound of Bow Bells!'

'You must not think it was always so,' replied Attwater, 'This was once a busy shore, although now, hark! you can hear the solitude. I find it stimulating. And talking of the sound of bells, kindly follow a little experiment of mine in silence.' There was a silver bell at his right hand to call the servants; he made them a sign to stand still, struck the bell with force, and leaned eagerly forward. The note rose clear and strong; it rang out clear and far into the night and over the deserted island; it died into the distance until there only lingered in the porches of the ear a vibration that was sound no longer. 'Empty houses, empty sea, solitary beaches!' said Attwater. 'And yet God hears the bell! And yet we sit in this verandah on a lighted stage with all heaven for spectators! And you call that solitude?'

There followed a bar of silence, during which the captain sat mesmerised.

Then Attwater laughed softly. 'These are the diversions of a lonely, man,' he resumed, 'and possibly not in good taste. One tells oneself these little fairy tales for company. If there SHOULD happen to be anything in folk-lore, Mr Hay? But here comes the claret. One does not offer you Lafitte, captain, because I believe it is all sold to the railroad dining cars in your great country; but this Brine-Mouton is of a good year, and Mr Whish will give me news of it.'

'That's a queer idea of yours!' cried the captain, bursting with a sigh from the spell that had bound him. 'So you mean to tell me now, that you sit here evenings and ring up... well, ring on the angels... by yourself?'

'As a matter of historic fact, and since you put it directly, one does not,' said Attwater. 'Why ring a bell, when there flows out from oneself and everything about one a far more momentous silence? the least beat of my heart and the least thought in my mind echoing into eternity for ever and for ever and for ever.'

'O look 'ere,' said Huish, 'turn down the lights at once, and the Band of 'Ope will oblige! This ain't a spiritual seance.'

'No folk-lore about Mr Whish—I beg your pardon, captain: Huish not Whish, of course,' said Attwater.

As the boy was filling Huish's glass, the bottle escaped from his hand and was shattered, and the wine spilt on the verandah floor. Instant grimness as of death appeared on the face of Attwater; he smote the bell imperiously, and the two brown natives fell into the attitude of attention and stood mute and trembling. There was just a moment of silence and hard looks; then followed a few savage words in the native; and, upon a gesture of dismissal, the service proceeded as before.

None of the party had as yet observed upon the excellent bearing of the two men. They were dark, undersized, and well set up; stepped softly, waited deftly, brought on the wines and dishes at a look, and their eyes attended studiously on their master.

106

'Where do you get your labour from anyway?' asked Davis.

'Ah, where not?' answered Attwater.

'Not much of a soft job, I suppose?' said the captain.

'If you will tell me where getting labour is!' said Attwater with a shrug. 'And of course, in our case, as we could name no destination, we had to go far and wide and do the best we could. We have gone as far west as the Kingsmills and as far south as Rapa-iti. Pity Symonds isn't here! He is full of yarns. That was his part, to collect them. Then began mine, which was the educational.'

'You mean to run them?' said Davis.

'Ay! to run them,' said Attwater.

'Wait a bit,' said Davis, 'I'm out of my depth. How was this? Do you mean to say you did it single-handed?'

'One did it single-handed,' said Attwater, 'because there was nobody to help one.'

'By God, but you must be a holy terror!' cried the captain, in a glow of admiration.

'One does one's best,' said Attwater.

'Well, now!' said Davis, 'I have seen a lot of driving in my time and been counted a good driver myself; I fought my way, third mate, round the Cape Horn with a push of packet rats that would have turned the devil out of hell and shut the door on him; and I tell you, this racket of Mr Attwater's takes the cake. In a ship, why, there ain't nothing to it! You've got the law with you, that's what does it. But put me down on this blame' beach alone, with nothing but a whip and a mouthful of bad words, and ask me to... no, SIR! it's not good enough! I haven't got the sand for that!' cried Davis. 'It's the law behind,' he added; 'it's the law does it, every time!'

'The beak ain't as black as he's sometimes pynted,' observed Huish, humorously.

'Well, one got the law after a fashion,' said Attwater. 'One had to be a

107

number of things. It was sometimes rather a bore.'

'I should smile!' said Davis. 'Rather lively, I should think!'

'I dare say we mean the same thing,' said Attwater. 'However, one way or another, one got it knocked into their heads that they MUST work, and they DID... until the Lord took them!'

''Ope you made 'em jump,' said Huish.

'When it was necessary, Mr Whish, I made them jump,' said Attwater.

'You bet you did,' cried the captain. He was a good deal flushed, but not so much with wine as admiration; and his eyes drank in the huge proportions of the other with delight. 'You bet you did, and you bet that I can see you doing it! By God, you're a man, and you can say I said so.'

'Too good of you, I'm sure,' said Attwater.

'Did you—did you ever have crime here?' asked Herrick, breaking his silence with a pungent voice.

'Yes,' said Attwater, 'we did.'

'And how did you handle that, sir?' cried the eager captain.

'Well, you see, it was a queer case,' replied Attwater, 'it was a case that would have puzzled Solomon. Shall I tell it you? yes?'

The captain rapturously accepted.

'Well,' drawled Attwater, 'here is what it was. I dare say you know two types of natives, which may be called the obsequious and the sullen? Well, one had them, the types themselves, detected in the fact; and one had them together. Obsequiousness ran out of the first like wine out of a bottle, sullenness congested in the second. Obsequiousness was all smiles; he ran to catch your eye, he loved to gabble; and he had about a dozen words of beach English, and an eighth-of-an-inch veneer of Christianity. Sullens was industrious; a big down-looking bee. When he was spoken to, he answered with a black look and a shrug of one shoulder, but the thing would be done. I don't give him to you for a model of manners; there was nothing showy about Sullens; but he was strong and steady, and ungraciously obedient. Now Sullens got into trouble; no matter how; the regulations of the place were broken, and he was punished accordingly—without effect. So, the next day, and the next, and the day after, till I began to be weary of the business, and Sullens (I am afraid) particularly so. There came a day when he was in fault again, for the—oh, perhaps the thirtieth time; and he rolled a dull eye upon me, with a spark in it, and appeared to speak. Now the regulations of the place are formal upon one point: we allow no explanations; none are received, none allowed to be offered. So one stopped him instantly; but made a note of the circumstance. The next day, he was gone from the settlement. There could be nothing more annoying; if the labour took to running away, the fishery was wrecked. There are sixty miles of this island, you see, all in length like the Queen's Highway; the idea of pursuit in such a place was a piece of single-minded childishness, which one did not entertain. Two days later, I made a discovery; it came in upon me with a flash that Sullens had been unjustly punished from beginning to end, and the real culprit throughout had been Obsequiousness. The native who talks, like the woman who hesitates, is lost. You set him talking and lying; and he talks, and lies, and watches your face to see if he has pleased you; till at last, out comes the truth! It came out of Obsequiousness in the regular course. I said nothing to him; I dismissed him; and late as it was, for it was already night, set off to look for Sullens. I had not far to go: about two hundred yards up the island, the moon showed him to me. He was hanging in a cocoa palm—I'm not botanist enough to tell you how—but it's the way, in nine cases out of ten, these natives commit suicide. His tongue was out, poor devil, and the birds had got at him; I spare you details, he was an ugly sight! I gave the business six good hours of thinking in this verandah. My justice had been made a fool of; I don't suppose that I was ever angrier. Next day, I had the conch sounded and all hands out before sunrise. One took one's gun, and led the way, with Obsequiousness. He was very talkative; the beggar supposed that all was right now he had confessed; in the old schoolboy phrase, he was plainly 'sucking up' to me; full of protestations of goodwill and good behaviour; to which one answered one really can't remember what. Presently the tree came in sight, and the hanged man. They all burst out lamenting for their comrade in the island way, and Obsequiousness was the loudest of the mourners. He was quite genuine; a noxious creature, without any consciousness of guilt. Well, presently—to make a long story short—one told him to go up the tree. He stared a bit, looked at one with a trouble in his eye, and had rather a sickly smile; but went. He was obedient to the last; he had all the pretty virtues, but the truth was not in him. So soon as he was up, he looked down, and there was the rifle covering him; and at that he gave a whimper like a dog. You could bear a pin drop; no more keening now. There they all crouched upon the ground, with bulging eyes; there was he in the tree top, the colour of the lead; and between was the dead man, dancing a bit in the air. He was obedient to the last, recited his crime, recommended his soul to God. And then...'

Attwater paused, and Herrick, who had been listening attentively, made a convulsive movement which upset his glass.

'And then?' said the breathless captain.

'Shot,' said Attwater. 'They came to ground together.'

Herrick sprang to his feet with a shriek and an insensate gesture.

'It was a murder,' he screamed. 'A cold-hearted, bloody-minded murder! You monstrous being! Murderer and hypocrite—murderer and hypocrite— murderer and hypocrite—' he repeated, and his tongue stumbled among the words.

The captain was by him in a moment. 'Herrick!' he cried, 'behave yourself! Here, don't be a blame' fool!'

Herrick struggled in his embrace like a frantic child, and suddenly bowing his face in his hands, choked into a sob, the first of many, which now convulsed his body silently, and now jerked from him indescribable and meaningless sounds.

'Your friend appears over-excited,' remarked Attwater, sitting unmoved but all alert at table.

'It must be the wine,' replied the captain. 'He ain't no drinking man, you see. I—I think I'll take him away. A walk'll sober him up, I guess.'

He led him without resistance out of the verandah and into the night, in which they soon melted; but still for some time, as they drew away, his comfortable voice was to be heard soothing and remonstrating, and Herrick answering, at intervals, with the mechanical noises of hysteria.

''E's like a bloomin' poultry yard!' observed Huish, helping himself to wine (of which he spilled a good deal) with gentlemanly ease. 'A man should learn to beyave at table,' he added.

'Rather bad form, is it not?' said Attwater. 'Well, well, we are left tete-a-tete. A glass of wine with you, Mr Whish!'

Chapter 10. THE OPEN DOOR

The captain and Herrick meanwhile turned their back upon the lights in Attwater's verandah, and took a direction towards the pier and the beach of the lagoon.

The isle, at this hour, with its smooth floor of sand, the pillared roof overhead, and the prevalent illumination of the lamps, wore an air of unreality like a deserted theatre or a public garden at midnight. A man looked about him for the statues and tables. Not the least air of wind was stirring among the palms, and the silence was emphasised by the continuous clamour of the surf from the seashore, as it might be of traffic in the next street.

Still talking, still soothing him, the captain hurried his patient on, brought him at last to the lagoon-side, and leading him down the beach, laved his head and face with the tepid water. The paroxysm gradually subsided, the sobs became less convulsive and then ceased; by an odd but not quite unnatural conjunction, the captain's soothing current of talk died away at the same time and by proportional steps, and the pair remained sunk in silence. The lagoon broke at their feet in petty wavelets, and with a sound as delicate as a whisper; stars of all degrees looked down on their own images in that vast mirror; and the more angry colour of the Farallone's riding lamp burned in the middle distance. For long they continued to gaze on the scene before them, and hearken anxiously to the rustle and tinkle of that miniature surf, or the more distant and loud reverberations from the outer coast. For long speech was denied them; and when the words came at last, they came to both simultaneously. 'Say, Herrick...'the captain was beginning.

But Herrick, turning swiftly towards his companion, bent him down with the eager cry: 'Let's up anchor, captain, and to sea!'

'Where to, my son?' said the captain. 'Up anchor's easy saying. But where to?'

'To sea,' responded Herrick. 'The sea's big enough! To sea—away from this dreadful island and that, oh! that sinister man!'

'Oh, we'll see about that,' said Davis. 'You brace up, and we'll see about that. You're all run down, that's what's wrong with you; you're all nerves, like Jemimar; you've got to brace up good and be yourself again, and then we'll talk.'

'To sea,' reiterated Herrick, 'to sea tonight—now—this moment!'

'It can't be, my son,' replied the captain firmly. 'No ship of mine puts to sea without provisions, you can take that for settled.'

'You don't seem to understand,' said Herrick. 'The whole thing is over, I tell you. There is nothing to do here, when he knows all. That man there with the cat knows all; can't you take it in?'

'All what?' asked the captain, visibly discomposed. 'Why, he received us like a perfect gentleman and treated us real handsome, until you began with your foolery—and I must say I seen men shot for less, and nobody sorry! What more do you expect anyway?'

Herrick rocked to and fro upon the sand, shaking his head.

'Guying us,' he said, 'he was guying us—only guying us; it's all we're good for.'

'There was one queer thing, to be sure,' admitted the captain, with a misgiving of the voice; 'that about the sherry. Damned if I caught on to that. Say, Herrick, you didn't give me away?'

'Oh! give you away!' repeated Herrick with weary, querulous scorn. 'What was there to give away? We're transparent; we've got rascal branded on us: detected rascal—detected rascal! Why, before he came on board, there was the name painted out, and he saw the whole thing. He made sure we would kill him there and then, and stood guying you and Huish on the chance. He calls that being frightened! Next he had me ashore; a fine time I had! THE TWO WOLVES, he calls you and Huish.—WHAT IS THE PUPPY DOING WITH THE TWO WOLVES? he asked. He showed me his pearls; he said they might be dispersed before morning, and ALL HUNG BY A

HAIr—and smiled as he said it, such a smile! O, it's no use, I tell you! He knows all, he sees through all; we only make him laugh with our pretences—he looks at us and laughs like God!'

There was a silence. Davis stood with contorted brows, gazing into the night.

'The pearls?' he said suddenly. 'He showed them to you? he has them?'

'No, he didn't show them; I forgot: only the safe they were in,' said Herrick. 'But you'll never get them!'

'I've two words to say to that,' said the captain.

'Do you think he would have been so easy at table, unless he was prepared?' cried Herrick. 'The servants were both armed. He was armed himself; he always is; he told me. You will never deceive his vigilance. Davis, I know it! It's all up; all up. There's nothing for it, there's nothing to be done: all gone: life, honour, love. Oh, my God, my God, why was I born?'

Another pause followed upon this outburst.

The captain put his hands to his brow.

'Another thing!' he broke out. 'Why did he tell you all this? Seems like madness to me!'

Herrick shook his head with gloomy iteration. 'You wouldn't understand if I were to tell you,' said he.

'I guess I can understand any blame' thing that you can tell me,' said the captain.

'Well, then, he's a fatalist,' said Herrick.

'What's that, a fatalist?' said Davis.

'Oh, it's a fellow that believes a lot of things,' said Herrick, 'believes that his bullets go true; believes that all falls out as God chooses, do as you like to prevent it; and all that.'

'Why, I guess I believe right so myself,' said Davis.

'You do?' said Herrick.

'You bet I do!' says Davis.

Herrick shrugged his shoulders. 'Well, you must be a fool,' said he, and he leaned his head upon his knees.

The captain stood biting his hands.

'There's one thing sure,' he said at last. 'I must get Huish out of that. HE'S not fit to hold his end up with a man like you describe.'

And he turned to go away. The words had been quite simple; not so the tone; and the other was quick to catch it.

'Davis!' he cried, 'no! Don't do it. Spare ME, and don't do it—spare yourself, and leave it alone—for God's sake, for your children's sake!'

His voice rose to a passionate shrillness; another moment, and he might be overheard by their not distant victim. But Davis turned on him with a savage oath and gesture; and the miserable young man rolled over on his face on the sand, and lay speechless and helpless.

The captain meanwhile set out rapidly for Attwater's house. As he went, he considered with himself eagerly, his thoughts racing. The man had understood, he had mocked them from the beginning; he would teach him to make a mockery of John Davis! Herrick thought him a god; give him a second to aim in, and the god was overthrown. He chuckled as he felt the butt of his revolver. It should be done now, as he went in. From behind? It was difficult to get there. From across the table? No, the captain preferred to shoot standing, so as you could be sure to get your hand upon your gun. The best would be to summon Huish, and when Attwater stood up and turned—ah, then would be the moment. Wrapped in his ardent prefiguration of events, the captain posted towards the house with his head down.

'Hands up! Halt!' cried the voice of Attwater.

And the captain, before he knew what he was doing, had obeyed. The surprise was complete and irremediable. Coming on the top crest of his murderous intentions, he had walked straight into an ambuscade, and now stood, with his hands impotently lifted, staring at the verandah.

The party was now broken up. Attwater leaned on a post, and kept Davis covered with a Winchester. One of the servants was hard by with a second at the port arms, leaning a little forward, round-eyed with eager expectancy. In the open space at the head of the stair, Huish was partly supported by the other native; his face wreathed in meaningless smiles, his mind seemingly sunk in the contemplation of an unlighted cigar.

'Well,' said Attwater, 'you seem to me to be a very twopenny pirate!'

The captain uttered a sound in his throat for which we have no name; rage choked him.

'I am going to give you Mr Whish—or the wine-sop that remains of him,' continued Attwater. 'He talks a great deal when he drinks, Captain Davis of the Sea Ranger. But I have quite done with him—and return the article with thanks. Now,' he cried sharply. 'Another false movement like that, and your family will have to deplore the loss of an invaluable parent; keep strictly still, Davis.'

Attwater said a word in the native, his eye still undeviatingly fixed on the captain; and the servant thrust Huish smartly forward from the brink of the stair. With an extraordinary simultaneous dispersion of his members, that gentleman bounded forth into space, struck the earth, ricocheted, and brought up with his arms about a palm. His mind was quite a stranger to these events; the expression of anguish that deformed his countenance at the moment of the leap was probably mechanical; and he suffered these convulsions in silence; clung to the tree like an infant; and seemed, by his dips, to suppose himself engaged in the pastime of bobbing for apples. A more finely sympathetic mind or

116

a more observant eye might have remarked, a little in front of him on

the sand, and still quite beyond reach, the unlighted cigar.

'There is your Whitechapel carrion!' said Attwater. 'And now

you might very well ask me why I do not put a period to you at once, as

you deserve. I will tell you why, Davis. It is because I have nothing to

do with the Sea Ranger and the people you drowned, or the Farallone and

the champagne that you stole. That is your account with God, He keeps

it, and He will settle it when the clock strikes. In my own case, I have

nothing to go on but suspicion, and I do not kill on suspicion, not even

vermin like you. But understand! if ever I see any of you again, it is

another matter, and you shall eat a bullet. And now take yourself off.

March! and as you value what you call your life, keep your hands up as

you go!'

The captain remained as he was, his hands up, his mouth open: mesmerised with fury.

'March!' said Attwater. 'One—two—three!'

And Davis turned and passed slowly away. But even as he went, he was meditating a prompt, offensive return. In the twinkling of an eye, he had leaped behind a tree; and was crouching there, pistol in hand, peering from either side of his place of ambush with bared teeth; a serpent already poised to strike. And already he was too late. Attwater and his servants had disappeared; and only the lamps shone on the deserted table and the bright sand about the house, and threw into the night in all directions the strong and tall shadows of the palms.

Davis ground his teeth. Where were they gone, the cowards? to what hole had they retreated beyond reach? It was in vain he should try anything, he, single and with a second-hand revolver, against three persons, armed with Winchesters, and who did not show an ear out of any of the apertures of that lighted and silent house? Some of them might have already ducked below it from the rear, and be drawing a bead upon him at that moment from the low-browed crypt, the receptacle of empty bottles and broken crockery. No, there was nothing to be done but to bring away (if it were still possible) his shattered and demoralised forces.

'Huish,' he said, 'come along.'

''S lose my ciga',' said Huish, reaching vaguely forward.

The captain let out a rasping oath. 'Come right along here,' said he.

''S all righ'. Sleep here 'th Atty-Attwa. Go boar' t'morr',' replied the festive one.

'If you don't come, and come now, by the living God, I'll shoot you!' cried the captain.

It is not to be supposed that the sense of these words in any way penetrated to the mind of Hulsh; rather that, in a fresh attempt upon the cigar, he overbalanced himself and came flying erratically forward: a course which brought him within reach of Davis.

'Now you walk straight,' said the captain, clutching him, 'or I'll know why not!'

''S lose my ciga',' replied Huish.

The captain's contained fury blazed up for a moment. He twisted Huish round, grasped him by the neck of the coat, ran him in front of him to the pier end, and flung him savagely forward on his face.

'Look for your cigar then, you swine!' said he, and blew his boat call till the pea in it ceased to rattle.

An immediate activity responded on board the Farallone; far away voices, and soon the sound of oars, floated along the surface of the lagoon; and at the same time, from nearer hand, Herrick aroused himself and strolled languidly up. He bent over the insignificant figure of Huish, where it grovelled, apparently insensible, at the base of the figure-head.

'Dead?' he asked.

'No, he's not dead,' said Davis.

'And Attwater?' asked Herrick.

'Now you just shut your head!' replied Davis. 'You can do that, I fancy, and by God, I'll show you how! I'll stand no more of your drivel.'

They waited accordingly in silence till the boat bumped on the furthest piers; then raised Huish, head and heels, carried him down the gangway, and flung him summarily in the bottom. On the way out he was heard murmuring of the loss of his cigar; and after he had been handed up the side like baggage, and cast down in the alleyway to slumber, his last audible expression was: 'Splen'l fl' Attwa'!' This the expert construed into 'Splendid fellow, Attwater'; with so much innocence had this great spirit issued from the adventures of the evening.

The captain went and walked in the waist with brief, irate turns; Herrick leaned his arms on the taffrail; the crew had all turned in. The ship had a gentle, cradling motion; at times a block piped like a bird. On shore, through the colonnade of palm stems, Attwater's house was to be seen shining steadily with many lamps. And there was nothing else visible, whether in the heaven above or in the lagoon below, but the stars and their reflections. It might have been minutes or it might have been hours, that Herrick leaned there, looking in the glorified water and drinking peace. 'A bath of stars,' he was thinking; when a hand was laid at last on his shoulder.

'Herrick,' said the captain, 'I've been walking off my trouble.'

A sharp jar passed through the young man, but he neither answered nor so much as turned his head.

'I guess I spoke a little rough to you on shore,' pursued the captain; 'the fact is, I was real mad; but now it's over, and you and me have to turn to and think.'

'I will NOT think,' said Herrick.

'Here, old man!' said Davis, kindly; 'this won't fight, you know! You've got to brace up and help me get things straight. You're not going back on a friend? That's not like you, Herrick!'

'O yes, it is,' said Herrick.

'Come, come!' said the captain, and paused as if quite at a loss. 'Look here,' he cried, 'you have a glass of champagne. I won't touch it, so that'll show you if I'm in earnest. But it's just the pick-me-up for you; it'll put an edge on you at once.'

'O, you leave me alone!' said Herrick, and turned away.

The captain caught him by the sleeve; and he shook him off and turned on him, for the moment, like a demoniac.

'Go to hell in your own way!' he cried.

And he turned away again, this time unchecked, and stepped forward to where the boat rocked alongside and ground occasionally against the schooner. He looked about him. A corner of the house was interposed between the captain and himself; all was well; no eye must see him in that last act. He slid silently into the boat; thence, silently, into the starry water.

Instinctively he swam a little; it would be time enough to stop by and by.

The shock of the immersion brightened his mind immediately. The events of the ignoble day passed before him in a frieze of pictures, and he thanked 'whatever Gods there be' for that open door of suicide. In such a little while he would be done with it, the random business at an end, the prodigal son come home. A very bright planet shone before him and drew a trenchant wake along the water. He took that for his line and followed it. That was the last earthly thing that he should look upon; that radiant speck, which he had soon magnified into a City of Laputa, along whose terraces there walked men and women of awful and benignant features, who viewed him with distant commiseration. These imaginary spectators consoled him;

he told himself their talk, one to another; it was of himself and his sad destiny.

From such flights of fancy, he was aroused by the growing coldness of the water. Why should he delay? Here, where he was now, let him drop the curtain, let him seek the ineffable refuge, let him lie down with all races and generations of men in the house of sleep. It was easy to say, easy to do. To stop swimming: there was no mystery in that, if he could do it. Could he? And he could not. He knew it instantly. He was aware instantly of an opposition in his members, unanimous and invincible, clinging to life with a single and fixed resolve, finger by finger, sinew by sinew; something that was at once he and not he—at once within and without him;—the shutting of some miniature valve in his brain, which a single manly thought should suffice to open—and the grasp of an external fate ineluctable as gravity. To any man there may come at times a consciousness that there blows, through all the articulations of his body, the wind of a spirit not wholly his; that his mind rebels; that another girds him and carries him whither he would not. It came now to Herrick, with the authority of a revelation. There was no escape possible. The open door was closed in his recreant face. He must go back into the world and amongst men without illusion. He must stagger on to the end with the pack of his responsibility and his disgrace, until a cold, a blow, a merciful chance ball, or the more merciful hangman, should dismiss him from his infamy. There were men who could commit suicide; there were men who could not; and he was one who could not.

For perhaps a minute, there raged in his mind the coil of this discovery; then cheerless certitude followed; and, with an incredible simplicity of submission to ascertained fact, he turned round and struck out for shore. There was a courage in this which he could not appreciate; the ignobility of his cowardice wholly occupying him. A strong current set against him like a wind in his face; he contended with it heavily, wearily, without enthusiasm, but with substantial advantage; marking his progress the while, without pleasure, by the outline of the trees. Once he had a moment of hope. He heard to the southward of him, towards the centre of the lagoon, the wallowing of some great fish, doubtless a shark, and paused for a little, treading water. Might not this be the hangman? he thought. But the wallowing died away; mere silence succeeded; and Herrick pushed on again for the shore, raging as he went at his own nature. Ay, he would wait for the shark; but if he had heard him coming!... His smile was tragic. He could have spat upon himself.

About three in the morning, chance, and the set of the current, and the bias of his own right-handed body, so decided it between them that he came to shore upon the beach in front of Attwater's. There he sat down, and looked forth into a world without any of the lights of hope. The poor diving dress of self-conceit was sadly tattered! With the fairy tale of suicide, of a refuge always open to him, he had hitherto beguiled and supported himself in the trials of life; and behold! that also was only a fairy tale, that also was folk-lore. With the consequences of his acts he saw himself implacably confronted for the duration of life: stretched upon a cross, and nailed there with the iron bolts of his own cowardice. He had no tears; he told himself no stories. His disgust with himself was so complete that even the process of apologetic mythology had ceased. He was like a man cast down from a pillar, and every bone broken. He lay there, and admitted the facts, and did not attempt to rise.

Dawn began to break over the far side of the atoll, the sky brightened, the clouds became dyed with gorgeous colours, the shadows of the night lifted. And, suddenly, Herrick was aware that the lagoon and the trees wore again their daylight livery; and he saw, on board the Farallone, Davis extinguishing the lantern, and smoke rising from the galley.

Davis, without doubt, remarked and recognised the figure on the beach; or perhaps hesitated to recognise it; for after he had gazed a long while from under his hand, he went into the house and fetched a glass. It was very powerful; Herrick had often used it. With an instinct of shame, he hid his face in his hands.

'And what brings you here, Mr Herrick-Hay, or Mr Hay-Herrick?' asked the voice of Attwater. 'Your back view from my present position is remarkably fine, and I would continue to present it. We can get on very nicely as we are, and if you were to turn round, do you know? I think it would be awkward.'

Herrick slowly rose to his feet; his heart throbbed hard, a hideous excitement shook him, but he was master of himself. Slowly he turned, and faced Attwater and the muzzle of a pointed rifle. 'Why could I not do that last night?' he thought.

'Well, why don't you fire?' he said aloud, with a voice that trembled.

Attwater slowly put his gun under his arm, then his hands in his pockets.

'What brings you here?' he repeated.

'I don't know,' said Herrick; and then, with a cry: 'Can you do anything with me?'

'Are you armed?' said Attwater. 'I ask for the form's sake.'

'Armed? No!' said Herrick. 'O yes, I am, too!' And he flung upon the beach a dripping pistol.

'You are wet,' said Attwater.

'Yes, I am wet,' said Herrick. 'Can you do anything with me?'

Attwater read his face attentively.

'It would depend a good deal upon what you are,' said he.

'What I am? A coward!' said Herrick.

'There is very little to be done with that,' said Attwater. 'And yet the description hardly strikes one as exhaustive.'

'Oh, what does it matter?' cried Herrick. 'Here I am. I am broken crockery; I am a burst drum; the whole of my life is gone to water; I have nothing left that I believe in, except my living horror of myself. Why do I come to you? I don't know; you are cold, cruel, hateful; and I hate you, or I think I hate you. But you are an honest man, an honest gentleman. I put myself, helpless, in your hands. What must I do? If I can't do anything, be merciful and put a bullet through me; it's only a puppy with a broken leg!'

'If I were you, I would pick up that pistol, come up to the house, and put on some dry clothes,' said Attwater.

'If you really mean it?' said Herrick. 'You know they—we—they. .. But you know all.'

'I know quite enough,' said Attwater. 'Come up to the house.'

And the captain, from the deck of the Farallone, saw the two men pass together under the shadow of the grove.

Chapter 11. DAVID AND GOLIATH

Huish had bundled himself up from the glare of the day—his face to the house, his knees retracted. The frail bones in the thin tropical raiment seemed scarce more considerable than a fowl's; and Davis, sitting on the rail with his arm about a stay, contemplated him with gloom, wondering what manner of counsel that insignificant figure should contain. For since Herrick had thrown him off and deserted to the enemy, Huish, alone of mankind, remained to him to be a helper and oracle.

He considered their position with a sinking heart. The ship was a stolen ship; the stores, either from initial carelessness or ill administration during the voyage, were insufficient to carry them to any port except back to Papeete; and there retribution waited in the shape of a gendarme, a judge with a queer-shaped hat, and the horror of distant Noumea. Upon that side, there was no glimmer of hope. Here, at the island, the dragon was roused; Attwater with his men and his Winchesters watched and patrolled the house; let him who dare approach it. What else was then left but to sit there, inactive, pacing the decks—until the Trinity Hall arrived and they were cast into irons, or until the food came to an end, and the pangs of famine succeeded? For the Trinity Hall Davis was prepared; he would barricade the house, and die there defending it, like a rat in a crevice. But for the other? The cruise of the Farallone, into which he had plunged only a fortnight before, with such golden expectations, could this be the nightmare end of it? The ship rotting at anchor, the crew stumbling and dying in the scuppers? It seemed as if any extreme of hazard were to be preferred to so grisly a certainty; as if it would be better to up-anchor after all, put to sea at a venture, and, perhaps, perish at the hands of cannibals on one of the more obscure Paumotus. His eye roved swiftly over sea and sky in quest of any promise of wind, but the fountains of the Trade were empty. Where it had run yesterday and for weeks before, a roaring blue river charioting clouds, silence now reigned; and the whole height of the atmosphere stood balanced. On the endless ribbon of island that stretched out to either hand of him its array of golden and green and silvery palms, not the most volatile frond was to be seen stirring; they drooped to their stable images in the lagoon like things carved of metal, and already their long line began to reverberate heat. There was no escape possible that day, none probable on the morrow. And still the stores were running out!

Then came over Davis, from deep down in the roots of his being, or at least from far back among his memories of childhood and innocence, a wave of superstition. This run of ill luck was something beyond natural; the chances of the game were in themselves more various; it seemed as if the devil must serve the pieces. The devil? He heard again the clear note of Attwater's bell ringing abroad into the night, and dying away. How if God...?

Briskly, he averted his mind. Attwater: that was the point. Attwater had food and a treasure of pearls; escape made possible in the present, riches in the future. They must come to grips, with Attwater; the man must die. A smoky heat went over his face, as he recalled the impotent figure he had made last night and the contemptuous speeches he must bear in silence. Rage, shame, and the love of life, all pointed the one way; and only invention halted: how to reach him? had he strength enough? was there any help in that misbegotten packet of bones against the house?

His eyes dwelled upon him with a strange avidity, as though he would read into his soul; and presently the sleeper moved, stirred uneasily, turned suddenly round, and threw him a blinking look. Davis maintained the same dark stare, and Huish looked away again and sat up.

'Lord, I've an 'eadache on me!' said he. 'I believe I was a bit swipey last night. W'ere's that cry-byby 'Errick?'

'Gone,' said the captain.

'Ashore?' cried Huish. 'Oh, I say! I'd 'a gone too.'

'Would you?' said the captain.

'Yes, I would,' replied Huish. 'I like Attwater. 'E's all right; we got on like one o'clock when you were gone. And ain't his sherry in it, rather? It's like Spiers and Ponds' Amontillado! I wish I 'ad a drain of it now.' He sighed.

'Well, you'll never get no more of it—that's one thing,' said Davis, gravely.

''Ere! wot's wrong with you, Dyvis? Coppers 'ot? Well, look at me! I ain't grumpy,' said Huish; 'I'm as plyful as a canary-bird, I am.'

'Yes,' said Davis, 'you're playful; I own that; and you were playful last night, I believe, and a damned fine performance you made of it.'

''Allo!' said Huish. ''Ow's this? Wot performance?'

'Well, I'll tell you,' said the captain, getting slowly off the rail.

And he did: at full length, with every wounding epithet and absurd detail repeated and emphasised; he had his own vanity and Huish's upon the grill, and roasted them; and as he spoke, he inflicted and endured agonies of humiliation. It was a plain man's masterpiece of the sardonic.

'What do you think of it?' said he, when he had done, and looked down at Huish, flushed and serious, and yet jeering.

'I'll tell you wot it is,' was the reply, 'you and me cut a pretty dicky figure.'

'That's so,' said Davis, 'a pretty measly figure, by God! And, by God, I want to see that man at my knees.'

'Ah!' said Huish. ''Ow to get him there?'

'That's it!' cried Davis. 'How to get hold of him! They're four to two; though there's only one man among them to count, and that's Attwater. Get a bead on Attwater, and the others would cut and run and sing out like frightened poultry—and old man Herrick would come round with his hat for a share of the pearls. No, SIR! it's how to get hold of Attwater! And we daren't even go ashore; he would shoot us in the boat like dogs.'

'Are you particular about having him dead or alive?' asked Huish.

'I want to see him dead,' said the captain.

'Ah, well!' said Huish, 'then I believe I'll do a bit of breakfast.'

127

And he turned into the house.

The captain doggedly followed him.

'What's this?' he asked. 'What's your idea, anyway?'

'Oh, you let me alone, will you?' said Huish, opening a bottle of champagne. 'You'll 'ear my idea soon enough. Wyte till I pour some chain on my 'ot coppers.' He drank a glass off, and affected to listen. ''Ark!' said he, ''ear it fizz. Like 'am fryin', I declyre. 'Ave a glass, do, and look sociable.'

'No!' said the captain, with emphasis; 'no, I will not! there's business.'

'You p'ys your money and you tykes your choice, my little man,' returned Huish. 'Seems rather a shyme to me to spoil your breakfast for wot's really ancient 'istory.'

He finished three parts of a bottle of champagne, and nibbled a corner of biscuit, with extreme deliberation; the captain sitting opposite and champing the bit like an impatient horse. Then Huish leaned his arms on the table and looked Davis in the face.

'W'en you're ready!' said he.

'Well, now, what's your idea?' said Davis, with a sigh.

'Fair play!' said Huish. 'What's yours?'

'The trouble is that I've got none,' replied Davis; and wandered for some time in aimless discussion of the difficulties in their path, and useless explanations of his own fiasco.

'About done?' said Huish.

'I'll dry up right here,' replied Davis.

'Well, then,' said Huish, 'you give me your 'and across the table, and say, "Gawd strike me dead if I don't back you up."'

His voice was hardly raised, yet it thrilled the hearer. His face seemed the epitome of cunning, and the captain recoiled from it as from a blow.

128

'What for?' said he.

'Luck,' said Huish. 'Substantial guarantee demanded.'

And he continued to hold out his hand.

'I don't see the good of any such tomfoolery,' said the other.

'I do, though,' returned Huish. 'Gimme your 'and and say the words; then you'll 'ear my view of it. Don't, and you won't.'

The captain went through the required form, breathing short, and gazing on the clerk with anguish. What to fear, he knew not; yet he feared slavishly what was to fall from the pale lips.

'Now, if you'll excuse me 'alf a second,' said Huish, 'I'll go and fetch the byby.'

'The baby?' said Davis. 'What's that?'

'Fragile. With care. This side up,' replied the clerk with a wink, as he disappeared.

He returned, smiling to himself, and carrying in his hand a silk handkerchief. The long stupid wrinkles ran up Davis's brow, as he saw it. What should it contain? He could think of nothing more recondite than a revolver.

Huish resumed his seat.

'Now,' said he, 'are you man enough to take charge of 'Errick and the niggers? Because I'll take care of Hattwater.'

'How?' cried Davis. 'You can't!'

'Tut, tut!' said the clerk. 'You gimme time. Wot's the first point? The first point is that we can't get ashore, and I'll make you a present of that for a 'ard one. But 'ow about a flag of truce? Would that do the trick, d'ye think? or would Attwater simply blyze aw'y at us in the bloomin' boat like dawgs?'

'No,' said Davis, 'I don't believe he would.'

'No more do I,' said Huish; 'I don't believe he would either; and I'm sure I 'ope he won't! So then you can call us ashore. Next point is to get near the managin' direction. And for that I'm going to 'ave you write a letter, in w'ich you s'y you're ashamed to meet his eye, and that the bearer, Mr J. L. 'Uish, is empowered to represent you. Armed with w'ich seemin'ly simple expedient, Mr J. L. 'Uish will proceed to business.'

He paused, like one who had finished, but still held Davis with his eye.

'How?' said Davis. 'Why?'

'Well, you see, you're big,' returned Huish; ''e knows you 'ave a gun in your pocket, and anybody can see with 'alf an eye that you ain't the man to 'esitate about usin' it. So it's no go with you, and never was; you're out of the runnin', Dyvis. But he won't be afryde of me, I'm such a little un! I'm unarmed—no kid about that—and I'll hold my 'ands up right enough.' He paused. 'If I can manage to sneak up nearer to him as we talk,' he resumed, 'you look out and back me up smart. If I don't, we go aw'y again, and nothink to 'urt. See?'

The captain's face was contorted by the frenzied effort to comprehend.

'No, I don't see,' he cried, 'I can't see. What do you mean?'

'I mean to do for the Beast!' cried Huish, in a burst of venomous triumph. 'I'll bring the 'ulkin' bully to grass. He's 'ad his larks out of me; I'm goin' to 'ave my lark out of 'im, and a good lark too!'

'What is it?' said the captain, almost in a whisper.

'Sure you want to know?' asked Huish.

Davis rose and took a turn in the house.

'Yes, I want to know,' he said at last with an effort.

'We'n you're back's at the wall, you do the best you can, don't you?' began the clerk. 'I s'y that, because I 'appen to know there's a prejudice against it; it's considered vulgar, awf'ly vulgar.' He unrolled the handkerchief and showed a four-ounce jar. 'This 'ere's vitriol, this is,' said he.

130

The captain stared upon him with a whitening face.

'This is the stuff!' he pursued, holding it up. 'This'll burn to the bone; you'll see it smoke upon 'im like 'ell fire! One drop upon 'is bloomin' heyesight, and I'll trouble you for Attwater!'

'No, no, by God!' exclaimed the captain.

'Now, see 'ere, ducky,' said Huish, 'this is my bean feast, I believe? I'm goin' up to that man single-'anded, I am. 'E's about seven foot high, and I'm five foot one. 'E's a rifle in his 'and, 'e's on the look-out, 'e wasn't born yesterday. This is Dyvid and Goliar, I tell you! If I'd ast you to walk up and face the music I could understand. But I don't. I on'y ast you to stand by and spifflicate the niggers. It'll all come in quite natural; you'll see, else! Fust thing, you know, you'll see him running round and owling like a good un...'

'Don't!' said Davis. 'Don't talk of it!'

'Well, you ARE a juggins!' exclaimed Huish. 'What did you want? You wanted to kill him, and tried to last night. You wanted to kill the 'ole lot of them and tried to, and 'ere I show you 'ow; and because there's some medicine in a bottle you kick up this fuss!'

'I suppose that's so,' said Davis. 'It don't seem someways reasonable, only there it is.'

'It's the happlication of science, I suppose?' sneered Huish.

'I don't know what it is,' cried Davis, pacing the floor; 'it's there! I draw the line at it. I can't put a finger to no such piggishness. It's too damned hateful!'

'And I suppose it's all your fancy pynted it,' said Huish, 'w'en you take a pistol and a bit o' lead, and copse a man's brains all over him? No accountin' for tystes.'

'I'm not denying it,' said Davis, 'It's something here, inside of me. It's foolishness; I dare say it's dam foolishness. I don't argue, I just draw the line. Isn't there no other way?'

'Look for yourself,' said Huish. 'I ain't wedded to this, if you think I am; I ain't ambitious; I don't make a point of playin' the lead; I offer to, that's all, and if you can't show me better, by Gawd, I'm goin' to!'

'Then the risk!' cried Davis.

'If you ast me straight, I should say it was a case of seven to one and no takers,' said Huish. 'But that's my look-out, ducky, and I'm gyme, that's wot I am: gyme all through.'

The captain looked at him. Huish sat there, preening his sinister vanity, glorying in his precedency in evil; and the villainous courage and readiness of the creature shone out of him like a candle from a lantern. Dismay and a kind of respect seized hold on Davis in his own despite. Until that moment, he had seen the clerk always hanging back, always listless, uninterested, and openly grumbling at a word of anything to do; and now, by the touch of an enchanter's wand, he beheld him sitting girt and resolved, and his face radiant. He had raised the devil, he thought; and asked who was to control him? and his spirits quailed.

'Look as long as you like,' Huish was going on. 'You don't see any green in my eye! I ain't afryde of Attwater, I ain't afryde of you, and I ain't afryde of words. You want to kill people, that's wot YOU want; but you want to do it in kid gloves, and it can't be done that w'y. Murder ain't genteel, it ain't easy, it ain't safe, and it tykes a man to do it. 'Ere's the man.'

'Huish!' began the captain with energy; and then stopped, and remained staring at him with corrugated brows.

'Well, hout with it!' said Huish. ''Ave you anythink else to put up? Is there any other chanst to try?'

The captain held his peace.

'There you are then!' said Huish with a shrug.

Davis fell again to his pacing.

'Oh, you may do sentry-go till you're blue in the mug, you won't find anythink else,' said Huish.

There was a little silence; the captain, like a man launched on a swing, flying dizzily among extremes of conjecture and refusal.

'But see,' he said, suddenly pausing. 'Can you? Can the thing be done? It—it can't be easy.'

'If I get within twenty foot of 'im it'll be done; so you look out,' said Huish, and his tone of certainty was absolute.

'How can you know that?' broke from the captain in a choked cry. 'You beast, I believe you've done it before!'

'Oh, that's private affyres,' returned Huish, 'I ain't a talking man.'

A shock of repulsion struck and shook the captain; a scream rose almost to his lips; had he uttered it, he might have cast himself at the same moment on the body of Huish, might have picked him up, and flung him down, and wiped the cabin with him, in a frenzy of cruelty that seemed half moral. But the moment passed; and the abortive crisis left the man weaker. The stakes were so high—the pearls on the one hand—starvation and shame on the other. Ten years of pearls! The imagination of Davis translated them into a new, glorified existence for himself and his family. The seat of this new life must be in London; there were deadly reasons against Portland, Maine; and the pictures that came to him were of English manners. He saw his boys marching in the procession of a school, with gowns on, an usher marshalling them and reading as he walked in a great book. He was installed in a villa, semi-detached; the name, Rosemore, on the gateposts. In a chair on the gravel walk, he seemed to sit smoking a cigar, a blue ribbon in his buttonhole, victor over himself and circumstances, and the malignity of bankers. He saw the parlour with red curtains and shells on the mantelpiece—and with the fine inconsistency of visions, mixed a grog at the mahogany table ere he turned in. With that the Farallone gave one of the aimless and nameless movements which (even in an anchored ship and even in the most profound calm) remind one of the mobility of fluids; and he was back again under the cover of the house, the fierce daylight besieging it all round and glaring in the chinks, and the clerk in a rather airy attitude, awaiting his decision.

He began to walk again. He aspired after the realisation of these dreams, like a horse nickering for water; the lust of them burned in his inside. And the only obstacle was Attwater, who had insulted him from the first. He gave Herrick a full share of the pearls, he insisted on it; Huish opposed him, and he trod the opposition down; and praised himself exceedingly. He was not going to use vitriol himself; was he Huish's keeper? It was a pity he had asked, but after all!... he saw the boys again in the school procession, with the gowns he had thought to be so 'tony' long since... And at the same time the incomparable shame of the last evening blazed up in his mind.

'Have it your own way!' he said hoarsely.

'Oh, I knew you would walk up,' said Huish. 'Now for the letter. There's paper, pens and ink. Sit down and I'll dictyte.'

The captain took a seat and the pen, looked a while helplessly at the paper, then at Huish. The swing had gone the other way; there was a blur upon his eyes. 'It's a dreadful business,' he said, with a strong twitch of his shoulders.

'It's rather a start, no doubt,' said Huish. 'Tyke a dip of ink. That's it. William John Hattwater, Esq., Sir': he dictated.

'How do you know his name is William John?' asked Davis.

'Saw it on a packing case,' said Huish. 'Got that?'

'No,' said Davis. 'But there's another thing. What are we to write?'

'O my golly!' cried the exasperated Huish. 'Wot kind of man do YOU call yourself? I'M goin' to tell you wot to write; that's my pitch; if you'll just be so bloomin' condescendin' as to write it down! WILLIAM JOHN ATTWATER, ESQ., SIR': he reiterated. And the captain at last beginning half mechanically to move his pen, the dictation proceeded:

It is with feelings of shyme and 'artfelt contrition that I approach you after the yumiliatin' events of last night. Our Mr 'Errick has left the ship, and will have doubtless communicated to you the nature of our 'opes. Needless to s'y, these are no longer possible: Fate 'as declyred against us, and we bow the 'ead. Well awyre as I am of the just suspicions with w'ich I am regarded, I do not venture to solicit the fyvour of an interview for myself, but in order to put an end to a situytion w'ich must be equally pyneful to all, I 'ave deputed my friend and partner, Mr J. L. Huish, to l'y before you my proposals, and w'ich by their moderytion, Will, I trust, be found to merit your attention. Mr J. L. Huish is entirely unarmed, I swear to Gawd! and will 'old 'is 'ands over 'is 'ead from the moment he begins to approach you. I am your fytheful servant, John Davis.

Huish read the letter with the innocent joy of amateurs, chuckled gustfully to himself, and reopened it more than once after it was folded, to repeat the pleasure; Davis meanwhile sitting inert and heavily frowning.

Of a sudden he rose; he seemed all abroad. 'No!' he cried. 'No! it can't be! It's too much; it's damnation. God would never forgive it.'

'Well, and 'oo wants Him to?' returned Huish, shrill with fury. 'You were damned years ago for the Sea Rynger, and said so yourself. Well then, be damned for something else, and 'old your tongue.'

The captain looked at him mistily. 'No,' he pleaded, 'no, old man! don't do it.'

''Ere now,' said Huish, 'I'll give you my ultimytum. Go or st'y w'ere you are; I don't mind; I'm goin' to see that man and chuck this vitriol in his eyes. If you st'y I'll go alone; the niggers will likely knock me on the 'ead, and a fat lot you'll be the better! But there's one thing sure: I'll 'ear no more of your moonin', mullygrubbin' rot, and tyke it stryte.'

The captain took it with a blink and a gulp. Memory, with phantom voices, repeated in his cars something similar, something he had once said to Herrick—years ago it seemed.

'Now, gimme over your pistol,' said Huish. 'I 'ave to see all clear. Six shots, and mind you don't wyste them.'

The captain, like a man in a nightmare, laid down his revolver on the table, and Huish wiped the cartridges and oiled the works.

It was close on noon, there was no breath of wind, and the heat was scarce bearable, when the two men came on deck, had the boat manned, and passed down, one after another, into the stern-sheets. A white shirt at the end of an oar served as a flag of truce; and the men, by direction, and to give it the better chance to be observed, pulled with extreme slowness. The isle shook before them like a place incandescent; on the face of the lagoon blinding copper suns, no bigger than sixpences, danced and stabbed them in the eyeballs; there went up from sand and sea, and even from the boat, a glare of scathing brightness; and as they could only peer abroad from between closed lashes, the excess of light seemed to be changed into a sinister darkness, comparable to that of a thundercloud before it bursts.

The captain had come upon this errand for any one of a dozen reasons, the last of which was desire for its success. Superstition rules all men; semi-ignorant and gross natures, like that of Davis, it rules utterly. For murder he had been prepared; but this horror of the medicine in the bottle went beyond him, and he seemed to himself to be parting the last strands that united him to God. The boat carried him on to reprobation, to damnation; and he suffered himself to be carried passively consenting, silently bidding farewell to his better self and his hopes. Huish sat by his side in towering spirits that were not wholly genuine. Perhaps as brave a man as ever lived, brave as a weasel, he must still reassure himself with the tones of his own voice; he must play his part to exaggeration, he must out-Herod Herod, insult all that was respectable, and brave all that was formidable, in a kind of desperate wager with himself.

'Golly, but it's 'ot!' said he. 'Cruel 'ot, I call it. Nice d'y to get your gruel in! I s'y, you know, it must feel awf'ly peculiar to get bowled over on a d'y like this. I'd rather 'ave it on a cowld and frosty morning, wouldn't you? (Singing) "'Ere we go round the mulberry bush on a cowld and frosty mornin'." (Spoken) Give you my word, I 'aven't thought o' that in ten year; used to sing it at a hinfant school in 'Ackney, 'Ackney Wick it was. (Singing) "This is the way the tyler does, the tyler does." (Spoken) Bloomin' 'umbug. 'Ow are you off now, for the notion of a future styte? Do you cotton to the tea-fight views, or the old red 'ot boguey business?'

'Oh, dry up!' said the captain.

'No, but I want to know,' said Huish. 'It's within the sp'ere of practical politics for you and me, my boy; we may both be bowled over, one up, t'other down, within the next ten minutes. It would be rather a lark, now, if you only skipped across, came up smilin' t'other side, and a hangel met you with a B. and S. under his wing. 'Ullo, you'd s'y: come, I tyke this kind.'

The captain groaned. While Huish was thus airing and exercising his bravado, the man at his side was actually engaged in prayer. Prayer, what for? God knows. But out of his inconsistent, illogical, and agitated spirit, a stream of supplication was poured forth, inarticulate as himself, earnest as death and judgment.

'Thou Gawd seest me!' continued Huish. 'I remember I had that written in my Bible. I remember the Bible too, all about Abinadab and parties. Well, Gawd!' apostrophising the meridian, 'you're goin' to see a rum start presently, I promise you that!'

The captain bounded.

'I'll have no blasphemy!' he cried, 'no blasphemy in my boat.'

'All right, cap,' said Huish. 'Anythink to oblige. Any other topic you would like to sudgest, the rynegyge, the lightnin' rod, Shykespeare, or the musical glasses? 'Ere's conversation on a tap. Put a penny in the slot, and... 'ullo! 'ere they are!' he cried. 'Now or never is 'e goin' to shoot?'

And the little man straightened himself into an alert and dashing attitude, and looked steadily at the enemy. But the captain rose half up in the boat with eyes protruding.

'What's that?' he cried.

'Wot's wot?' said Huish.

'Those—blamed things,' said the captain.

And indeed it was something strange. Herrick and Attwater, both armed with Winchesters, had appeared out of the grove behind the figure-head; and to either hand of them, the sun glistened upon two metallic objects, locomotory like men, and occupying in the economy of these creatures the places of heads—only the heads were faceless. To Davis between wind and water, his mythology appeared to have come alive, and Tophet to be vomiting demons. But Huish was not mystified a moment.

'Divers' 'elmets, you ninny. Can't you see?' he said.

'So they are,' said Davis, with a gasp. 'And why? Oh, I see, it's for armour.'

'Wot did I tell you?' said Huish. 'Dyvid and Goliar all the w'y and back.'

The two natives (for they it was that were equipped in this unusual panoply of war) spread out to right and left, and at last lay down in the shade, on the extreme flank of the position. Even now that the mystery was explained, Davis was hatefully preoccupied, stared at the flame on their crests, and forgot, and then remembered with a smile, the explanation.

Attwater withdrew again into the grove, and Herrick, with his gun under his arm, came down the pier alone.

About half-way down he halted and hailed the boat.

'What do you want?' he cried.

'I'll tell that to Mr Attwater,' replied Huish, stepping briskly on the ladder. 'I don't tell it to you, because you played the trucklin' sneak. Here's a letter for him: tyke it, and give it, and be 'anged to you!'

'Davis, is this all right?' said Herrick.

Davis raised his chin, glanced swiftly at Herrick and away again, and held his peace. The glance was charged with some deep emotion, but whether of hatred or of fear, it was beyond Herrick to divine.

'Well,' he said, 'I'll give the letter.' He drew a score with his foot on the boards of the gangway. 'Till I bring the answer, don't move a step past this.'

And he returned to where Attwater leaned against a tree, and gave him the letter. Attwater glanced it through.

'What does that mean?' he asked, passing it to Herrick.

'Treachery?'

'Oh, I suppose so!' said Herrick.

'Well, tell him to come on,' said Attwater. 'One isn't a fatalist for nothing. Tell him to come on and to look out.'

Herrick returned to the figure-head. Half-way down the pier the clerk was waiting, with Davis by his side.

'You are to come along, Huish,' said Herrick. 'He bids you look out, no tricks.'

Huish walked briskly up the pier, and paused face to face with the young man.

'W'ere is 'e?' said he, and to Herrick's surprise, the low-bred, insignificant face before him flushed suddenly crimson and went white again.

'Right forward,' said Herrick, pointing. 'Now your hands above your head.'

The clerk turned away from him and towards the figure-head, as though he were about to address to it his devotions; he was seen to heave a deep breath; and raised his arms. In common with many men of his unhappy physical endowments, Huish's hands were disproportionately long and broad, and the palms in particular enormous; a four-ounce jar was nothing in that capacious fist. The next moment he was plodding steadily forward on his mission.

Herrick at first followed. Then a noise in his rear startled him, and he turned about to find Davis already advanced as far as the figure-head. He came, crouching and open-mouthed, as the mesmerised may follow the mesmeriser; all human considerations, and even the care of his own life, swallowed up in one abominable and burning curiosity.

'Halt!' cried Herrick, covering him with his rifle. 'Davis, what are you doing, man? YOU are not to come.'

Davis instinctively paused, and regarded him with a dreadful vacancy of eye.

'Put your back to that figure-head, do you hear me? and stand fast!' said Herrick.

The captain fetched a breath, stepped back against the figure-head, and instantly redirected his glances after Huish.

There was a hollow place of the sand in that part, and, as it were, a glade among the cocoa palms in which the direct noonday sun blazed intolerably. At the far end, in the shadow, the tall figure of Attwater was to be seen leaning on a tree; towards him, with his hands over his head, and his steps smothered in the sand, the clerk painfully waded. The surrounding glare threw out and exaggerated the man's smallness; it seemed no less perilous an enterprise, this that he was gone upon, than for a whelp to besiege a citadel.

'There, Mr Whish. That will do,' cried Attwater. 'From that distance, and keeping your hands up, like a good boy, you can very well put me in possession of the skipper's views.'

The interval betwixt them was perhaps forty feet; and Huish measured it with his eye, and breathed a curse. He was already distressed with labouring in the loose sand, and his arms ached bitterly from their unnatural position. In the palm of his right hand, the jar was ready; and his heart thrilled, and his voice choked as he began to speak.

'Mr Hattwater,' said he, 'I don't know if ever you 'ad a mother...'

'I can set your mind at rest: I had,' returned Attwater; 'and henceforth, if I might venture to suggest it, her name need not recur in our communications. I should perhaps tell you that I am not amenable to the pathetic.'

'I am sorry, sir, if I 'ave seemed to tresparse on your private feelin's,' said the clerk, cringing and stealing a step. 'At least, sir, you will never pe'suade me that you are not a perfec' gentleman; I know a gentleman when I see him; and as such, I 'ave no 'esitation in throwin' myself on your merciful consideration.

It IS 'ard lines, no doubt; it's 'ard lines to have to hown yourself beat; it's 'ard lines to 'ave to come and beg to you for charity.'

'When, if things had only gone right, the whole place was as good as your own?' suggested Attwater. 'I can understand the feeling.'

'You are judging me, Mr Attwater,' said the clerk, 'and God knows how unjustly! THOU GAWD SEEST ME, was the tex' I 'ad in my Bible, w'ich my father wrote it in with 'is own 'and upon the fly leaf.'

'I am sorry I have to beg your pardon once more,' said Attwater; 'but, do you know, you seem to me to be a trifle nearer, which is entirely outside of our bargain. And I would venture to suggest that you take one—two—three—steps back; and stay there.'

The devil, at this staggering disappointment, looked out of Huish's face, and Attwater was swift to suspect. He frowned, he stared on the little man, and considered. Why should he be creeping nearer? The next moment, his gun was at his shoulder.

'Kindly oblige me by opening your hands. Open your hands wide—let me see the fingers spread, you dog—throw down that thing you're holding!' he roared, his rage and certitude increasing together.

And then, at almost the same moment, the indomitable Huish decided to throw, and Attwater pulled the trigger. There was scarce the difference of a second between the two resolves, but it was in favour of the man with the rifle; and the jar had not yet left the clerk's hand, before the ball shattered both. For the twinkling of an eye the wretch was in hell's agonies, bathed in liquid flames, a screaming bedlamite; and then a second and more merciful bullet stretched him dead.

The whole thing was come and gone in a breath. Before Herrick could turn about, before Davis could complete his cry of horror, the clerk lay in the sand, sprawling and convulsed.

Attwater ran to the body; he stooped and viewed it; he put his finger in the vitriol, and his face whitened and hardened with anger.

141

Davis had not yet moved; he stood astonished, with his back to the figure-head, his hands clutching it behind him, his body inclined forward from the waist.

Attwater turned deliberately and covered him with his rifle.

'Davis,' he cried, in a voice like a trumpet, 'I give you sixty seconds to make your peace with God!'

Davis looked, and his mind awoke. He did not dream of self-defence, he did not reach for his pistol. He drew himself up instead to face death, with a quivering nostril.

'I guess I'll not trouble the Old Man,' he said; 'considering the job I was on, I guess it's better business to just shut my face.'

Attwater fired; there came a spasmodic movement of the victim, and immediately above the middle of his forehead, a black hole marred the whiteness of the figure-head. A dreadful pause; then again the report, and the solid sound and jar of the bullet in the wood; and this time the captain had felt the wind of it along his cheek. A third shot, and he was bleeding from one ear; and along the levelled rifle Attwater smiled like a Red Indian.

The cruel game of which he was the puppet was now clear to Davis; three times he had drunk of death, and he must look to drink of it seven times more before he was despatched. He held up his hand.

'Steady!' he cried; 'I'll take your sixty seconds.'

'Good!' said Attwater.

The captain shut his eyes tight like a child: he held his hands up at last with a tragic and ridiculous gesture.

'My God, for Christ's sake, look after my two kids,' he said; and then, after a pause and a falter, 'for Christ's sake, Amen.'

And he opened his eyes and looked down the rifle with a quivering mouth.

'But don't keep fooling me long!' he pleaded.

'That's all your prayer?' asked Attwater, with a singular ring in his voice.

'Guess so,' said Davis.

So?' said Attwater, resting the butt of his rifle on the ground, 'is that done? Is your peace made with Heaven? Because it is with me. Go, and sin no more, sinful father. And remember that whatever you do to others, God shall visit it again a thousand-fold upon your innocents.'

The wretched Davis came staggering forward from his place against the figure-head, fell upon his knees, and waved his hands, and fainted.

When he came to himself again, his head was on Attwater's arm, and close by stood one of the men in divers' helmets, holding a bucket of water, from which his late executioner now laved his face. The memory of that dreadful passage returned upon him in a clap; again he saw Huish lying dead, again he seemed to himself to totter on the brink of an unplumbed eternity. With trembling hands he seized hold of the man whom he had come to slay; and his voice broke from him like that of a child among the nightmares of fever: 'O! isn't there no mercy? O! what must I do to be saved?'

'Ah!' thought Attwater, 'here's the true penitent.'

Chapter 12. TAIL-PIECE

On a very bright, hot, lusty, strongly blowing noon, a fortnight after the events recorded, and a month since the curtain rose upon this episode, a man might have been spied, praying on the sand by the lagoon beach. A point of palm trees isolated him from the settlement; and from the place where he knelt, the only work of man's hand that interrupted the expanse, was the schooner Farallone, her berth quite changed, and rocking at anchor some two miles to windward in the midst of the lagoon. The noise of the Trade ran very boisterous in all parts of the island; the nearer palm trees crashed and whistled in the gusts, those farther off contributed a humming bass like the roar of cities; and yet, to any man less absorbed, there must have risen at times over this turmoil of the winds, the sharper note of the human voice from the settlement. There all was activity. Attwater, stripped to his trousers and lending a strong hand of help, was directing and encouraging five Kanakas; from his lively voice, and their more lively efforts, it was to be gathered that some sudden and joyful emergency had set them in this bustle; and the Union Jack floated once more on its staff. But the suppliant on the beach, unconscious of their voices, prayed on with instancy and fervour, and the sound of his voice rose and fell again, and his countenance brightened and was deformed with changing moods of piety and terror.

Before his closed eyes, the skiff had been for some time tacking towards the distant and deserted Farallone; and presently the figure of Herrick might have been observed to board her, to pass for a while into the house, thence forward to the forecastle, and at last to plunge into the main hatch. In all these quarters, his visit was followed by a coil of smoke; and he had scarce entered his boat again and shoved off, before flames broke forth upon the schooner. They burned gaily; kerosene had not been spared, and the bellows of the Trade incited the conflagration. About half way on the return voyage, when Herrick looked back, he beheld the Farallone wrapped to the topmasts in leaping arms of fire, and the voluminous smoke pursuing him along the face of the lagoon. In one hour's time, he computed, the waters would have closed over the stolen ship.

It so chanced that, as his boat flew before the wind with much vivacity, and his eyes were continually busy in the wake, measuring the progress of the flames, he found himself embayed to the northward of the point of palms, and here became aware at the same time of the figure of Davis immersed in his devotion. An exclamation, part of annoyance, part of amusement, broke from him: and he touched the helm and ran the prow upon the beach not twenty feet from the unconscious devotee. Taking the painter in his hand, he landed, and drew near, and stood over him. And still the voluble and incoherent stream of prayer continued unabated. It was not possible for him to overhear the suppliant's petitions, which he listened to some while in a very mingled mood of humour and pity: and it was only when his own name began to occur and to be conjoined with epithets, that he at last laid his hand on the captain's shoulder.

'Sorry to interrupt the exercise,' said he; 'but I want you to look at the Farallone.'

The captain scrambled to his feet, and stood gasping and staring. 'Mr Herrick, don't startle a man like that!' he said. 'I don't seem someways rightly myself since...' he broke off. 'What did you say anyway? O, the Farallone,' and he looked languidly out.

'Yes,' said Herrick. 'There she burns! and you may guess from that what the news is.'

'The Trinity Hall, I guess,' said the captain.

'The same,' said Herrick; 'sighted half an hour ago, and coming up hand over fist.'

'Well, it don't amount to a hill of beans,' said the captain with a sigh.

'O, come, that's rank ingratitude!' cried Herrick.

'Well,' replied the captain, meditatively, 'you mayn't just see the way that I view it in, but I'd 'most rather stay here upon this island. I found peace here, peace in believing. Yes, I guess this island is about good enough for John

145

Davis.'

'I never heard such nonsense!' cried Herrick. 'What! with all turning out in your favour the way it does, the Farallone wiped out, the crew disposed of, a sure thing for your wife and family, and you, yourself, Attwater's spoiled darling and pet penitent!'

'Now, Mr Herrick, don't say that,' said the captain gently; 'when you know he don't make no difference between us. But, O! why not be one of us? why not come to Jesus right away, and let's meet in yon beautiful land? That's just the one thing wanted; just say, Lord, I believe, help thou mine unbelief! And He'll fold you in His arms. You see, I know! I've been a sinner myself!'

DAVID BALFOUR

DEDICATION.

To

CHARLES BAXTER, *Writer to the Signet.*

My Dear Charles,

It is the fate of sequels to disappoint those who have waited for them; and my David, having been left to kick his heels for more than a lustre in the British Linen Company's office, must expect his late re-appearance to be greeted with hoots, if not with missiles. Yet, when I remember the days of our explorations, I am not without hope. There should be left in our native city some seed of the elect; some long-legged, hot-headed youth must repeat to-day our dreams and wanderings of so many years ago; he will relish the pleasure, which should have been ours, to follow among named streets and numbered houses the country walks of David Balfour, to identify Dean, and Silvermills, and Broughton, and Hope Park, and Pilrig, and poor old Lochend—if it still be standing, and the Figgate Whins—if there be any of them left; or to push (on a long holiday) so far afield as Gillane or the Bass. So, perhaps, his eye shall be opened to behold the series of the generations, and he shall weigh with surprise his momentous and nugatory gift of life.

You are still—as when first I saw, as when I last addressed you—in the venerable city which I must always think of as my home. And I have come so far; and the sights and thoughts of my youth pursue me; and I see like a vision the youth of my father, and of his father, and the whole stream of lives flowing down there far in the north, with the sound of laughter and tears, to cast me out in the end, as by a sudden freshet, on these ultimate islands. And I admire and bow my head before the romance of destiny.

R. L. S.

Vailima, Upolu,

Samoa, 1892.

PART I—THE LORD ADVOCATE

CHAPTER I—A BEGGAR ON HORSEBACK

The 25th day of August, 1751, about two in the afternoon, I, David Balfour, came forth of the British Linen Company, a porter attending me with a bag of money, and some of the chief of these merchants bowing me from their doors. Two days before, and even so late as yestermorning, I was like a beggar-man by the wayside, clad in rags, brought down to my last shillings, my companion a condemned traitor, a price set on my own head for a crime with the news of which the country rang. To-day I was served heir to my position in life, a landed laird, a bank porter by me carrying my gold, recommendations in my pocket, and (in the words of the saying) the ball directly at my foot.

There were two circumstances that served me as ballast to so much sail. The first was the very difficult and deadly business I had still to handle; the second, the place that I was in. The tall, black city, and the numbers and movement and noise of so many folk, made a new world for me, after the moorland braes, the sea-sands and the still country-sides that I had frequented up to then. The throng of the citizens in particular abashed me. Rankeillor's son was short and small in the girth; his clothes scarce held on me; and it was plain I was ill qualified to strut in the front of a bank-porter. It was plain, if I did so, I should but set folk laughing, and (what was worse in my case) set them asking questions. So that I behooved to come by some clothes of my own, and in the meanwhile to walk by the porter's side, and put my hand on his arm as though we were a pair of friends.

At a merchant's in the Luckenbooths I had myself fitted out: none too fine, for I had no idea to appear like a beggar on horseback; but comely and responsible, so that servants should respect me. Thence to an armourer's, where I got a plain sword, to suit with my degree in life. I felt safer with the weapon, though (for one so ignorant of defence) it might be called an added danger. The porter, who was naturally a man of some experience, judged my accoutrement to be well chosen.

"Naething kenspeckle," [1] said he; "plain, dacent claes. As for the rapier, nae doubt it sits wi' your degree; but an I had been you, I would has waired my siller better-gates than that." And he proposed I should buy winter-hosen from a wife in the Cowgate-back, that was a cousin of his own, and made them "extraordinar endurable."

But I had other matters on my hand more pressing. Here I was in this old, black city, which was for all the world like a rabbit-warren, not only by the number of its indwellers, but the complication of its passages and holes. It was, indeed, a place where no stranger had a chance to find a friend, let be another stranger. Suppose him even to hit on the right close, people dwelt so thronged in these tall houses, he might very well seek a day before he chanced on the right door. The ordinary course was to hire a lad they called a caddie, who was like a guide or pilot, led you where you had occasion, and (your errands being done) brought you again where you were lodging. But these caddies, being always employed in the same sort of services, and having it for obligation to be well informed of every house and person in the city, had grown to form a brotherhood of spies; and I knew from tales of Mr. Campbell's how they communicated one with another, what a rage of curiosity they conceived as to their employer's business, and how they were like eyes and fingers to the police. It would be a piece of little wisdom, the way I was now placed, to take such a ferret to my tails. I had three visits to make, all immediately needful: to my kinsman Mr. Balfour of Pilrig, to Stewart the Writer that was Appin's agent, and to William Grant Esquire of Prestongrange, Lord Advocate of Scotland. Mr. Balfour's was a non-committal visit; and besides (Pilrig being in the country) I made bold to find the way to it myself, with the help of my two legs and a Scots tongue. But the rest were in a different case. Not only was the visit to Appin's agent, in the midst of the cry about the Appin murder, dangerous in itself, but it was highly inconsistent with the other. I was like to have a bad enough time of it with my Lord Advocate Grant, the best of ways; but to go to him hot-foot from Appin's agent, was little likely to mend my own affairs, and might prove the mere ruin of friend Alan's. The whole thing, besides, gave me a look of running with the hare and hunting with the hounds that was little to my fancy. I determined, therefore, to be done at once with Mr. Stewart and the whole Jacobitical side of my business, and to profit for that purpose by the guidance of the porter at my side. But it chanced I had scarce given him the address, when there came a sprinkle of rain—nothing to hurt, only for my new clothes—and we took shelter under a pend at the head of a close or alley.

Being strange to what I saw, I stepped a little farther in. The narrow paved way descended swiftly. Prodigious tall houses sprang upon each side and bulged out, one storey beyond another, as they rose. At the top only a ribbon of sky showed in. By what I could spy in the windows, and by the respectable persons that passed out and in, I saw the houses to be very well occupied; and the whole appearance of the place interested me like a tale.

I was still gazing, when there came a sudden brisk tramp of feet in time and clash of steel behind me. Turning quickly, I was aware of a party of armed soldiers, and, in their midst, a tall man in a great coat. He walked with a stoop that was like a piece of courtesy, genteel and insinuating: he waved his hands plausibly as he went, and his face was sly and handsome. I thought his eye took me in, but could not meet it. This procession went by to a door in the close, which a serving-man in a fine livery set open; and two of the soldier-lads carried the prisoner within, the rest lingering with their firelocks by the door.

There can nothing pass in the streets of a city without some following of idle folk and children. It was so now; but the more part melted away incontinent until but three were left. One was a girl; she was dressed like a lady, and had a screen of the Drummond colours on her head; but her comrades or (I should say) followers were ragged gillies, such as I had seen the matches of by the dozen in my Highland journey. They all spoke together earnestly in Gaelic, the sound of which was pleasant in my ears for the sake of Alan; and, though the rain was by again, and my porter plucked at me to be going, I even drew nearer where they were, to listen. The lady scolded sharply, the others making apologies and cringeing before her, so that I made sure she was come of a chief's house. All the while the three of them sought in their pockets, and by what I could make out, they had the matter of half a farthing among the party; which made me smile a little to see all Highland folk alike for fine obeisances and empty sporrans.

It chanced the girl turned suddenly about, so that I saw her face for the first time. There is no greater wonder than the way the face of a young woman fits in a man's mind, and stays there, and he could never tell you why; it just seems it was the thing he wanted. She had wonderful bright eyes like stars, and I daresay the eyes had a part in it; but what I remember the most clearly was the way her lips were a trifle open as she turned. And, whatever was the cause, I stood there staring like a fool. On her side, as she had not known there was anyone so near, she looked at me a little longer, and perhaps with more surprise, than was entirely civil.

It went through my country head she might be wondering at my new clothes; with that, I blushed to my hair, and at the sight of my colouring it is to be supposed she drew her own conclusions, for she moved her gillies farther down the close, and they fell again to this dispute, where I could hear no more of it.

I had often admired a lassie before then, if scarce so sudden and strong; and it was rather my disposition to withdraw than to come forward, for I was much in fear of mockery from the womenkind. You would have thought I had now all the more reason to pursue my common practice, since I had met this young lady in the city street, seemingly following a prisoner, and accompanied with two very ragged indecent-like Highlandmen. But there was here a different ingredient; it was plain the girl thought I had been prying in her secrets; and with my new clothes and sword, and at the top of my new fortunes, this was more than I could swallow. The beggar on horseback could not bear to be thrust down so low, or, at least of it, not by this young lady.

I followed, accordingly, and took off my new hat to her the best that I was able.

"Madam," said I, "I think it only fair to myself to let you understand I have no Gaelic. It is true I was listening, for I have friends of my own across

154

the Highland line, and the sound of that tongue comes friendly; but for your private affairs, if you had spoken Greek, I might have had more guess at them."

She made me a little, distant curtsey. "There is no harm done," said she, with a pretty accent, most like the English (but more agreeable). "A cat may look at a king."

"I do not mean to offend," said I. "I have no skill of city manners; I never before this day set foot inside the doors of Edinburgh. Take me for a country lad—it's what I am; and I would rather I told you than you found it out."

"Indeed, it will be a very unusual thing for strangers to be speaking to each other on the causeway," she replied. "But if you are landward [2] bred it will be different. I am as landward as yourself; I am Highland, as you see, and think myself the farther from my home."

"It is not yet a week since I passed the line," said I. "Less than a week ago I was on the braes of Balwhidder."

"Balwhither?" she cries. "Come ye from Balwhither! The name of it makes all there is of me rejoice. You will not have been long there, and not known some of our friends or family?"

"I lived with a very honest, kind man called Duncan Dhu Maclaren," I replied.

"Well, I know Duncan, and you give him the true name!" she said; "and if he is an honest man, his wife is honest indeed."

"Ay," said I, "they are fine people, and the place is a bonny place."

"Where in the great world is such another!" she cries; "I am loving the smell of that place and the roots that grow there."

I was infinitely taken with the spirit of the maid. "I could be wishing I had brought you a spray of that heather," says I. "And, though I did ill to speak with you at the first, now it seems we have common acquaintance, I make it my petition you will not forget me. David Balfour is the name I am known by. This is my lucky day, when I have just come into a landed estate, and am not very long out of a deadly peril. I wish you would keep my name in mind for the sake of Balwhidder," said I, "and I will yours for the sake of my lucky day."

"My name is not spoken," she replied, with a great deal of haughtiness. "More than a hundred years it has not gone upon men's tongues, save for a blink. I am nameless, like the Folk of Peace. [3] Catriona Drummond is the one I use."

Now indeed I knew where I was standing. In all broad Scotland there was but the one name proscribed, and that was the name of the Macgregors. Yet so far from fleeing this undesirable acquaintancy, I plunged the deeper in.

"I have been sitting with one who was in the same case with yourself," said I, "and I think he will be one of your friends. They called him Robin Oig."

"Did ye so?" cries she. "Ye met Rob?"

"I passed the night with him," said I.

"He is a fowl of the night," said she.

"There was a set of pipes there," I went on, "so you may judge if the time passed."

"You should be no enemy, at all events," said she. "That was his brother there a moment since, with the red soldiers round him. It is him that I call father."

"Is it so?" cried I. "Are you a daughter of James More's?"

"All the daughter that he has," says she: "the daughter of a prisoner; that I should forget it so, even for one hour, to talk with strangers!"

Here one of the gillies addressed her in what he had of English, to know what "she" (meaning by that himself) was to do about "ta sneeshin." I took some note of him for a short, bandy-legged, red-haired, big-headed man, that

156

I was to know more of to my cost.

"There can be none the day, Neil," she replied. "How will you get 'sneeshin,' wanting siller! It will teach you another time to be more careful; and I think James More will not be very well pleased with Neil of the Tom."

"Miss Drummond," I said, "I told you I was in my lucky day. Here I am, and a bank-porter at my tail. And remember I have had the hospitality of your own country of Balwhidder."

"It was not one of my people gave it," said she.

"Ah, well," said I, "but I am owing your uncle at least for some springs upon the pipes. Besides which, I have offered myself to be your friend, and you have been so forgetful that you did not refuse me in the proper time."

"If it had been a great sum, it might have done you honour," said she; "but I will tell you what this is. James More lies shackled in prison; but this time past they will be bringing him down here daily to the Advocate's. . . ."

"The Advocate's!" I cried. "Is that . . . ?"

"It is the house of the Lord Advocate Grant of Prestongrange," said she. "There they bring my father one time and another, for what purpose I have no thought in my mind; but it seems there is some hope dawned for him. All this same time they will not let me be seeing him, nor yet him write; and we wait upon the King's street to catch him; and now we give him his snuff as he goes by, and now something else. And here is this son of trouble, Neil, son of Duncan, has lost my four-penny piece that was to buy that snuff, and James More must go wanting, and will think his daughter has forgotten him."

I took sixpence from my pocket, gave it to Neil, and bade him go about his errand. Then to her, "That sixpence came with me by Balwhidder," said I.

"Ah!" she said, "you are a friend to the Gregara!"

"I would not like to deceive you, either," said I. "I know very little of the Gregara and less of James More and his doings, but since the while I have been standing in this close, I seem to know something of yourself; and if you will just say 'a friend to Miss Catriona' I will see you are the less cheated."

"The one cannot be without the other," said she.

"I will even try," said I.

"And what will you be thinking of myself!" she cried, "to be holding my hand to the first stranger!"

"I am thinking nothing but that you are a good daughter," said I.

"I must not be without repaying it," she said; "where is it you stop!"

"To tell the truth, I am stopping nowhere yet," said I, "being not full three hours in the city; but if you will give me your direction, I will be so bold as come seeking my sixpence for myself."

"Will I can trust you for that?" she asked.

"You need have little fear," said I.

"James More could not bear it else," said she. "I stop beyond the village of Dean, on the north side of the water, with Mrs. Drummond-Ogilvy of Allardyce, who is my near friend and will be glad to thank you."

"You are to see me, then, so soon as what I have to do permits," said I; and, the remembrance of Alan rolling in again upon my mind, I made haste to say farewell.

I could not but think, even as I did so, that we had made extraordinary free upon short acquaintance, and that a really wise young lady would have shown herself more backward. I think it was the bank-porter that put me from this ungallant train of thought.

"I thoucht ye had been a lad of some kind o' sense," he began, shooting out his lips. "Ye're no likely to gang far this gate. A fule and his siller's shune parted. Eh, but ye're a green callant!" he cried, "an' a veecious, tae! Cleikin' up wi' baubeejoes!"

"If you dare to speak of the young lady. . . " I began.

"Leddy!" he cried. "Haud us and safe us, whatten leddy? Ca' thon

158

a leddy? The toun's fu' o' them. Leddies! Man, its weel seen ye're no very acquant in Embro!"

A clap of anger took me.

"Here," said I, "lead me where I told you, and keep your foul mouth shut!"

He did not wholly obey me, for, though he no more addressed me directly, he very impudent sang at me as he went in a manner of innuendo, and with an exceedingly ill voice and ear—

"As Mally Lee cam doun the street, her capuchin did flee,

She cuist a look ahint her to see her negligee.

And we're a' gaun east and wast, we're a' gann ajee,

We're a' gaun east and wast courtin' Mally Lee."

CHAPTER II—THE HIGHLAND WRITER

Mr. Charles Stewart the Writer dwelt at the top of the longest stair ever mason set a hand to; fifteen flights of it, no less; and when I had come to his door, and a clerk had opened it, and told me his master was within, I had scarce breath enough to send my porter packing.

"Awa' east and west wi' ye!" said I, took the money bag out of his hands, and followed the clerk in.

The outer room was an office with the clerk's chair at a table spread with law papers. In the inner chamber, which opened from it, a little brisk man sat poring on a deed, from which he scarce raised his eyes on my entrance; indeed, he still kept his finger in the place, as though prepared to show me out and fall again to his studies. This pleased me little enough; and what pleased me less, I thought the clerk was in a good posture to overhear what should pass between us.

I asked if he was Mr. Charles Stewart the Writer.

"The same," says he; "and, if the question is equally fair, who may you be yourself?"

"You never heard tell of my name nor of me either," said I, "but I bring you a token from a friend that you know well. That you know well," I repeated, lowering my voice, "but maybe are not just so keen to hear from at this present being. And the bits of business that I have to propone to you are rather in the nature of being confidential. In short, I would like to think we were quite private."

He rose without more words, casting down his paper like a man ill-pleased, sent forth his clerk of an errand, and shut to the house-door behind him.

"Now, sir," said he, returning, "speak out your mind and fear nothing; though before you begin," he cries out, "I tell you mine misgives me! I tell you beforehand, ye're either a Stewart or a Stewart sent ye. A good name it is, and one it would ill-become my father's son to lightly. But I begin to grue at the sound of it."

"My name is called Balfour," said I, "David Balfour of Shaws. As for him that sent me, I will let his token speak." And I showed the silver button.

"Put it in your pocket, sir!" cries he. "Ye need name no names. The deevil's buckie, I ken the button of him! And de'il hae't! Where is he now!"

I told him I knew not where Alan was, but he had some sure place (or thought he had) about the north side, where he was to lie until a ship was found for him; and how and where he had appointed to be spoken with.

"It's been always my opinion that I would hang in a tow for this family of mine," he cried, "and, dod! I believe the day's come now! Get a ship for him, quot' he! And who's to pay for it? The man's daft!"

"That is my part of the affair, Mr. Stewart," said I. "Here is a bag of good money, and if more be wanted, more is to be had where it came from."

"I needn't ask your politics," said he.

"Ye need not," said I, smiling, "for I'm as big a Whig as grows."

"Stop a bit, stop a bit," says Mr. Stewart. "What's all this? A Whig? Then why are you here with Alan's button? and what kind of a black-foot traffic is this that I find ye out in, Mr. Whig? Here is a forfeited rebel and an accused murderer, with two hundred pounds on his life, and ye ask me to meddle in his business, and then tell me ye're a Whig! I have no mind of any such Whigs before, though I've kent plenty of them."

"He's a forfeited rebel, the more's the pity," said I, "for the man's my friend. I can only wish he had been better guided. And an accused murderer, that he is too, for his misfortune; but wrongfully accused."

"I hear you say so," said Stewart.

"More than you are to hear me say so, before long," said I. "Alan Breck is innocent, and so is James."

161

"Oh!" says he, "the two cases hang together. If Alan is out, James can never be in."

Hereupon I told him briefly of my acquaintance with Alan, of the accident that brought me present at the Appin murder, and the various passages of our escape among the heather, and my recovery of my estate. "So, sir, you have now the whole train of these events," I went on, "and can see for yourself how I come to be so much mingled up with the affairs of your family and friends, which (for all of our sakes) I wish had been plainer and less bloody. You can see for yourself, too, that I have certain pieces of business depending, which were scarcely fit to lay before a lawyer chosen at random. No more remains, but to ask if you will undertake my service?"

"I have no great mind to it; but coming as you do with Alan's button, the choice is scarcely left me," said he. "What are your instructions?" he added, and took up his pen.

"The first point is to smuggle Alan forth of this country," said I, "but I need not be repeating that."

"I am little likely to forget it," said Stewart.

"The next thing is the bit money I am owing to Cluny," I went on. "It would be ill for me to find a conveyance, but that should be no stick to you. It was two pounds five shillings and three-halfpence farthing sterling."

He noted it.

"Then," said I, "there's a Mr. Henderland, a licensed preacher and missionary in Ardgour, that I would like well to get some snuff into the hands of; and, as I daresay you keep touch with your friends in Appin (so near by), it's a job you could doubtless overtake with the other."

"How much snuff are we to say?" he asked.

"I was thinking of two pounds," said I.

"Two," said he.

"Then there's the lass Alison Hastie, in Lime Kilns," said I. "Her that helped Alan and me across the Forth. I was thinking if I could get her a good Sunday gown, such as she could wear with decency in her degree, it would be an ease to my conscience; for the mere truth is, we owe her our two lives."

"I am glad so see you are thrifty, Mr. Balfour," says he, making his notes.

"I would think shame to be otherwise the first day of my fortune," said I. "And now, if you will compute the outlay and your own proper charges, I would be glad to know if I could get some spending-money back. It's not that I grudge the whole of it to get Alan safe; it's not that I lack more; but having drawn so much the one day, I think it would have a very ill appearance if I was back again seeking, the next. Only be sure you have enough," I added, "for I am very undesirous to meet with you again."

"Well, and I'm pleased to see you're cautious, too," said the Writer. "But I think ye take a risk to lay so considerable a sum at my discretion."

He said this with a plain sneer.

"I'll have to run the hazard," I replied. "O, and there's another service I would ask, and that's to direct me to a lodging, for I have no roof to my head. But it must be a lodging I may seem to have hit upon by accident, for it would never do if the Lord Advocate were to get any jealousy of our acquaintance."

"Ye may set your weary spirit at rest," said he. "I will never name your name, sir; and it's my belief the Advocate is still so much to be sympathised with that he doesnae ken of your existence."

I saw I had got to the wrong side of the man.

"There's a braw day coming for him, then," said I, "for he'll have to learn of it on the deaf side of his head no later than to-morrow, when I call on him."

"When ye call on him!" repeated Mr. Stewart. "Am I daft, or are you! What takes ye near the Advocate!"

"O, just to give myself up," said I.

"Mr. Balfour," he cried, "are ye making a mock of me?"

"No, sir," said I, "though I think you have allowed yourself some such freedom with myself. But I give you to understand once and for all that I am in no jesting spirit."

"Nor yet me," says Stewart. "And I give yon to understand (if that's to be the word) that I like the looks of your behaviour less and less. You come here to me with all sorts of propositions, which will put me in a train of very doubtful acts and bring me among very undesirable persons this many a day to come. And then you tell me you're going straight out of my office to make your peace with the Advocate! Alan's button here or Alan's button there, the four quarters of Alan wouldnae bribe me further in."

"I would take it with a little more temper," said I, "and perhaps we can avoid what you object to. I can see no way for it but to give myself up, but perhaps you can see another; and if you could, I could never deny but what I would be rather relieved. For I think my traffic with his lordship is little likely to agree with my health. There's just the one thing clear, that I have to give my evidence; for I hope it'll save Alan's character (what's left of it), and James's neck, which is the more immediate."

He was silent for a breathing-space, and then, "My man," said he, "you'll never be allowed to give such evidence."

"We'll have to see about that," said I; "I'm stiff-necked when I like."

"Ye muckle ass!" cried Stewart, "it's James they want; James has got to hang—Alan, too, if they could catch him—but James whatever! Go near the Advocate with any such business, and you'll see! he'll find a way to muzzle, ye."

"I think better of the Advocate than that," said I.

"The Advocate be dammed!" cries he. "It's the Campbells, man! You'll have the whole clanjamfry of them on your back; and so will the Advocate too, poor body! It's extraordinar ye cannot see where ye stand! If there's no fair way to stop your gab, there's a foul one gaping. They can put ye in the dock, do ye no see that?" he cried, and stabbed me with one finger in the leg.

"Ay," said I, "I was told that same no further back than this morning by another lawyer."

"And who was he?" asked Stewart, "He spoke sense at least."

I told I must be excused from naming him, for he was a decent stout old Whig, and had little mind to be mixed up in such affairs.

"I think all the world seems to be mixed up in it!" cries Stewart. "But what said you?"

"I told him what had passed between Rankeillor and myself before the house of Shaws.

"Well, and so ye will hang!" said he. "Ye'll hang beside James Stewart. There's your fortune told."

"I hope better of it yet than that," said I; "but I could never deny there was a risk."

"Risk!" says he, and then sat silent again. "I ought to thank you for your staunchness to my friends, to whom you show a very good spirit," he says, "if you have the strength to stand by it. But I warn you that you're wading deep. I wouldn't put myself in your place (me that's a Stewart born!) for all the Stewarts that ever there were since Noah. Risk? ay, I take over-many; but to be tried in court before a Campbell jury and a Campbell judge, and that in a Campbell country and upon a Campbell quarrel—think what you like of me, Balfour, it's beyond me."

"It's a different way of thinking, I suppose," said I; "I was brought up to this one by my father before me."

"Glory to his bones! he has left a decent son to his name," says he. "Yet I would not have you judge me over-sorely. My case is dooms hard. See, sir, ye tell me ye're a Whig: I wonder what I am. No Whig to be sure; I couldnae be just that. But—laigh in your ear, man—I'm maybe no very keen on the other side."

"Is that a fact?" cried I. "It's what I would think of a man of your intelligence."

"Hut! none of your whillywhas!" [4] cries he. "There's intelligence upon both sides. But for my private part I have no particular desire to harm King George; and as for King James, God bless him! he does very well for me across the water. I'm a lawyer, ye see: fond of my books and my bottle, a good plea, a well-drawn deed, a crack in the Parliament House with other lawyer bodies, and perhaps a turn at the golf on a Saturday at e'en. Where do ye come in with your Hieland plaids and claymores?"

"Well," said I, "it's a fact ye have little of the wild Highlandman."

"Little?" quoth he. "Nothing, man! And yet I'm Hieland born, and when the clan pipes, who but me has to dance! The clan and the name, that goes by all. It's just what you said yourself; my father learned it to me, and a bonny trade I have of it. Treason and traitors, and the smuggling of them out and in; and the French recruiting, weary fall it! and the smuggling through of the recruits; and their pleas—a sorrow of their pleas! Here have I been moving one for young Ardsheil, my cousin; claimed the estate under the marriage contract—a forfeited estate! I told them it was nonsense: muckle they cared! And there was I cocking behind a yadvocate that liked the business as little as myself, for it was fair ruin to the pair of us—a black mark, disaffected, branded on our hurdies, like folk's names upon their kye! And what can I do? I'm a Stewart, ye see, and must fend for my clan and family. Then no later by than yesterday there was one of our Stewart lads carried to the Castle. What for? I ken fine: Act of 1736: recruiting for King Lewie. And you'll see, he'll whistle me in to be his lawyer, and there'll be another black mark on my chara'ter! I tell you fair: if I but kent the heid of a Hebrew word from the hurdies of it, be dammed but I would fling the whole thing up and turn minister!"

"It's rather a hard position," said I.

"Dooms hard!" cries he. "And that's what makes me think so much of ye—you that's no Stewart—to stick your head so deep in Stewart business. And for what, I do not know: unless it was the sense of duty."

"I hope it will be that," said I.

"Well," says he, "it's a grand quality. But here is my clerk back; and, by your leave, we'll pick a bit of dinner, all the three of us. When that's done, I'll give you the direction of a very decent man, that'll be very fain to have you for a lodger. And I'll fill your pockets to ye, forbye, out of your ain bag. For this business'll not be near as dear as ye suppose—not even the ship part of it."

I made him a sign that his clerk was within hearing.

"Hoot, ye neednae mind for Robbie," cries he. "A Stewart, too, puir deevil! and has smuggled out more French recruits and trafficking Papists than what he has hairs upon his face. Why, it's Robin that manages that branch of my affairs. Who will we have now, Rob, for across the water!"

"There'll be Andie Scougal, in the Thristle," replied Rob. "I saw Hoseason the other day, but it seems he's wanting the ship. Then there'll be Tam Stobo; but I'm none so sure of Tam. I've seen him colloguing with some gey queer acquaintances; and if was anybody important, I would give Tam the go-by."

"The head's worth two hundred pounds, Robin," said Stewart.

"Gosh, that'll no be Alan Breck!" cried the clerk.

"Just Alan," said his master.

"Weary winds! that's sayrious," cried Robin. "I'll try Andie, then; Andie'll be the best."

"It seems it's quite a big business," I observed.

"Mr. Balfour, there's no end to it," said Stewart.

"There was a name your clerk mentioned," I went on: "Hoseason. That must be my man, I think: Hoseason, of the brig Covenant. Would you set your trust on him?"

"He didnae behave very well to you and Alan," said Mr. Stewart; "but my mind of the man in general is rather otherwise. If he had taken Alan on board his ship on an agreement, it's my notion he would have proved a just dealer. How say ye, Rob?"

"No more honest skipper in the trade than Eli," said the clerk. "I would lippen to [5] Eli's word—ay, if it was the Chevalier, or Appin himsel'," he added.

"And it was him that brought the doctor, wasnae't?" asked the master.

"He was the very man," said the clerk.

"And I think he took the doctor back?" says Stewart.

"Ay, with his sporran full!" cried Robin. "And Eli kent of that!" [6]

"Well, it seems it's hard to ken folk rightly," said I.

"That was just what I forgot when ye came in, Mr. Balfour!" says the Writer.

CHAPTER III—I GO TO PILRIG

The next morning, I was no sooner awake in my new lodging than I was up and into my new clothes; and no sooner the breakfast swallowed, than I was forth on my adventurers. Alan, I could hope, was fended for; James was like to be a more difficult affair, and I could not but think that enterprise might cost me dear, even as everybody said to whom I had opened my opinion. It seemed I was come to the top of the mountain only to cast myself down; that I had clambered up, through so many and hard trials, to be rich, to be recognised, to wear city clothes and a sword to my side, all to commit mere suicide at the last end of it, and the worst kind of suicide, besides, which is to get hanged at the King's charges.

What was I doing it for? I asked, as I went down the high Street and out north by Leith Wynd. First I said it was to save James Stewart; and no doubt the memory of his distress, and his wife's cries, and a word or so I had let drop on that occasion worked upon me strongly. At the same time I reflected that it was (or ought to be) the most indifferent matter to my father's son, whether James died in his bed or from a scaffold. He was Alan's cousin, to be sure; but so far as regarded Alan, the best thing would be to lie low, and let the King, and his Grace of Argyll, and the corbie crows, pick the bones of his kinsman their own way. Nor could I forget that, while we were all in the pot together, James had shown no such particular anxiety whether for Alan or me.

Next it came upon me I was acting for the sake of justice: and I thought that a fine word, and reasoned it out that (since we dwelt in polities, at some discomfort to each one of us) the main thing of all must still be justice, and the death of any innocent man a wound upon the whole community. Next, again, it was the Accuser of the Brethren that gave me a turn of his argument; bade me think shame for pretending myself concerned in these high matters, and told me I was but a prating vain child, who had spoken big words to Rankeillor and to Stewart, and held myself bound upon my vanity to make good that boastfulness. Nay, and he hit me with the other end of the stick;

for he accused me of a kind of artful cowardice, going about at the expense of a little risk to purchase greater safety. No doubt, until I had declared and cleared myself, I might any day encounter Mungo Campbell or the sheriff's officer, and be recognised, and dragged into the Appin murder by the heels; and, no doubt, in case I could manage my declaration with success, I should breathe more free for ever after. But when I looked this argument full in the face I could see nothing to be ashamed of. As for the rest, "Here are the two roads," I thought, "and both go to the same place. It's unjust that James should hang if I can save him; and it would be ridiculous in me to have talked so much and then do nothing. It's lucky for James of the Glens that I have boasted beforehand; and none so unlucky for myself, because now I'm committed to do right. I have the name of a gentleman and the means of one; it would be a poor duty that I was wanting in the essence." And then I thought this was a Pagan spirit, and said a prayer in to myself, asking for what courage I might lack, and that I might go straight to my duty like a soldier to battle, and come off again scatheless, as so many do.

This train of reasoning brought me to a more resolved complexion; though it was far from closing up my sense of the dangers that surrounded me, nor of how very apt I was (if I went on) to stumble on the ladder of the gallows. It was a plain, fair morning, but the wind in the east. The little chill of it sang in my blood, and gave me a feeling of the autumn, and the dead leaves, and dead folks' bodies in their graves. It seemed the devil was in it, if I was to die in that tide of my fortunes and for other folks' affairs. On the top of the Calton Hill, though it was not the customary time of year for that diversion, some children were crying and running with their kites. These toys appeared very plain against the sky; I remarked a great one soar on the wind to a high altitude and then plump among the whins; and I thought to myself at sight of it, "There goes Davie."

My way lay over Mouter's Hill, and through an end of a clachan on the braeside among fields. There was a whirr of looms in it went from house to house; bees bummed in the gardens; the neighbours that I saw at the doorsteps talked in a strange tongue; and I found out later that this was Picardy, a village where the French weavers wrought for the Linen Company.

Here I got a fresh direction for Pilrig, my destination; and a little beyond, on the wayside, came by a gibbet and two men hanged in chains. They were dipped in tar, as the manner is; the wind span them, the chains clattered, and the birds hung about the uncanny jumping-jacks and cried. The sight coming on me suddenly, like an illustration of my fears, I could scarce be done with examining it and drinking in discomfort. And, as I thus turned and turned about the gibbet, what should I strike on, but a weird old wife, that sat behind a leg of it, and nodded, and talked aloud to herself with becks and courtesies.

"Who are these two, mother?" I asked, and pointed to the corpses.

"A blessing on your precious face!" she cried. "Twa joes [7] o' mine: just two o' my old joes, my hinny dear."

"What did they suffer for?" I asked.

"Ou, just for the guid cause," said she. "Aften I spaed to them the way that it would end. Twa shillin' Scots: no pickle mair; and there are twa bonny callants hingin' for 't! They took it frae a wean [8] belanged to Brouchton."

"Ay!" said I to myself, and not to the daft limmer, "and did they come to such a figure for so poor a business? This is to lose all indeed."

"Gie's your loof, [9] hinny," says she, "and let me spae your weird to ye."

"No, mother," said I, "I see far enough the way I am. It's an unco thing to see too far in front."

"I read it in your bree," she said. "There's a bonnie lassie that has bricht een, and there's a wee man in a braw coat, and a big man in a pouthered wig, and there's the shadow of the wuddy, [10] joe, that lies braid across your path. Gie's your loof, hinny, and let Auld Merren spae it to ye bonny."

The two chance shots that seemed to point at Alan and the daughter of James More struck me hard; and I fled from the eldritch creature, casting her a baubee, which she continued to sit and play with under the moving shadows of the hanged.

My way down the causeway of Leith Walk would have been more

171

pleasant to me but for this encounter. The old rampart ran among fields, the like of them I had never seen for artfulness of agriculture; I was pleased, besides, to be so far in the still countryside; but the shackles of the gibbet clattered in my head; and the mope and mows of the old witch, and the thought of the dead men, hag-rode my spirits. To hang on a gallows, that seemed a hard case; and whether a man came to hang there for two shillings Scots, or (as Mr. Stewart had it) from the sense of duty, once he was tarred and shackled and hung up, the difference seemed small. There might David Balfour hang, and other lads pass on their errands and think light of him; and old daft limmers sit at a leg-foot and spae their fortunes; and the clean genty maids go by, and look to the other aide, and hold a nose. I saw them plain, and they had grey eyes, and their screens upon their heads were of the Drummed colours.

I was thus in the poorest of spirits, though still pretty resolved, when I came in view of Pilrig, a pleasant gabled house set by the walkside among some brave young woods. The laird's horse was standing saddled at the door as I came up, but himself was in the study, where he received me in the midst of learned works and musical instruments, for he was not only a deep philosopher but much of a musician. He greeted me at first pretty well, and when he had read Rankeillor's letter, placed himself obligingly at my disposal.

"And what is it, cousin David!" said he—"since it appears that we are cousins—what is this that I can do for you! A word to Prestongrange! Doubtless that is easily given. But what should be the word?"

"Mr. Balfour," said I, "if I were to tell you my whole story the way it fell out, it's my opinion (and it was Rankeillor's before me) that you would be very little made up with it."

"I am sorry to hear this of you, kinsman," says he.

"I must not take that at your hands, Mr. Balfour," said I; "I have nothing to my charge to make me sorry, or you for me, but just the common infirmities of mankind. 'The guilt of Adam's first sin, the want of original righteousness, and the corruption of my whole nature,' so much I must answer for, and I hope I have been taught where to look for help," I said; for I judged from

172

the look of the man he would think the better of me if I knew my questions. [11] "But in the way of worldly honour I have no great stumble to reproach myself with; and my difficulties have befallen me very much against my will and (by all that I can see) without my fault. My trouble is to have become dipped in a political complication, which it is judged you would be blythe to avoid a knowledge of."

"Why, very well, Mr. David," he replied, "I am pleased to see you are all that Rankeillor represented. And for what you say of political complications, you do me no more than justice. It is my study to be beyond suspicion, and indeed outside the field of it. The question is," says he, "how, if I am to know nothing of the matter, I can very well assist you?"

"Why sir," said I, "I propose you should write to his lordship, that I am a young man of reasonable good family and of good means: both of which I believe to be the case."

"I have Rankeillor's word for it," said Mr. Balfour, "and I count that a warran-dice against all deadly."

"To which you might add (if you will take my word for so much) that I am a good churchman, loyal to King George, and so brought up," I went on.

"None of which will do you any harm," said Mr. Balfour.

"Then you might go on to say that I sought his lordship on a matter of great moment, connected with His Majesty's service and the administration of justice," I suggested.

"As I am not to hear the matter," says the laird, "I will not take upon myself to qualify its weight. 'Great moment' therefore falls, and 'moment' along with it. For the rest I might express myself much as you propose."

"And then, sir," said I, and rubbed my neck a little with my thumb, "then I would be very desirous if you could slip in a word that might perhaps tell for my protection."

"Protection?" says he, "for your protection! Here is a phrase that somewhat dampens me. If the matter be so dangerous, I own I would be a little loath to move in it blindfold."

"I believe I could indicate in two words where the thing sticks," said I.

"Perhaps that would be the best," said he.

"Well, it's the Appin murder," said I.

He held up both his hands. "Sirs! sirs!" cried he.

I thought by the expression of his face and voice that I had lost my helper.

"Let me explain. . ." I began.

"I thank you kindly, I will hear no more of it," says he. "I decline in toto to hear more of it. For your name's sake and Rankeillor's, and perhaps a little for your own, I will do what I can to help you; but I will hear no more upon the facts. And it is my first clear duty to warn you. These are deep waters, Mr. David, and you are a young man. Be cautious and think twice."

"It is to be supposed I will have thought oftener than that, Mr. Balfour," said I, "and I will direct your attention again to Rankeillor's letter, where (I hope and believe) he has registered his approval of that which I design."

"Well, well," said he; and then again, "Well, well! I will do what I can for you." There with he took a pen and paper, sat a while in thought, and began to write with much consideration. "I understand that Rankeillor approved of what you have in mind?" he asked presently.

"After some discussion, sir, he bade me to go forward in God's name," said I.

"That is the name to go in," said Mr. Balfour, and resumed his writing. Presently, he signed, re-read what he had written, and addressed me again. "Now here, Mr. David," said he, "is a letter of introduction, which I will seal without closing, and give into your hands open, as the form requires. But, since I am acting in the dark, I will just read it to you, so that you may see if it will secure your end—

"Pilrig, August 26th, 1751.

"My Lord,—This is to bring to your notice my namesake and cousin, David Balfour Esquire of Shaws, a young gentleman of unblemished descent and good estate. He has enjoyed, besides, the more valuable advantages of a godly training, and his political principles are all that your lordship can desire. I am not in Mr. Balfour's confidence, but I understand him to have a matter to declare, touching His Majesty's service and the administration of justice; purposes for which your Lordship's zeal is known. I should add that the young gentleman's intention is known to and approved by some of his friends, who will watch with hopeful anxiety the event of his success or failure.

"Whereupon," continued Mr. Balfour, "I have subscribed myself with the usual compliments. You observe I have said 'some of your friends'; I hope you can justify my plural?"

"Perfectly, sir; my purpose is known and approved by more than one," said I. "And your letter, which I take a pleasure to thank you for, is all I could have hoped."

"It was all I could squeeze out," said he; "and from what I know of the matter you design to meddle in, I can only pray God that it may prove sufficient."

CHAPTER IV—LORD ADVOCATE PRESTONGRANGE

My kinsman kept me to a meal, "for the honour of the roof," he said; and I believe I made the better speed on my return. I had no thought but to be done with the next stage, and have myself fully committed; to a person circumstanced as I was, the appearance of closing a door on hesitation and temptation was itself extremely tempting; and I was the more disappointed, when I came to Prestongrange's house, to be informed he was abroad. I believe it was true at the moment, and for some hours after; and then I have no doubt the Advocate came home again, and enjoyed himself in a neighbouring chamber among friends, while perhaps the very fact of my arrival was forgotten. I would have gone away a dozen times, only for this strong drawing to have done with my declaration out of hand and be able to lay me down to sleep with a free conscience. At first I read, for the little cabinet where I was left contained a variety of books. But I fear I read with little profit; and the weather falling cloudy, the dusk coming up earlier than usual, and my cabinet being lighted with but a loophole of a window, I was at last obliged to desist from this diversion (such as it was), and pass the rest of my time of waiting in a very burthensome vacuity. The sound of people talking in a near chamber, the pleasant note of a harpsichord, and once the voice of a lady singing, bore me a kind of company.

I do not know the hour, but the darkness was long come, when the door of the cabinet opened, and I was aware, by the light behind him, of a tall figure of a man upon the threshold. I rose at once.

"Is anybody there?" he asked. "Who in that?"

"I am bearer of a letter from the laird of Pilrig to the Lord Advocate," said I.

"Have you been here long?" he asked.

"I would not like to hazard an estimate of how many hours," said I.

"It is the first I hear of it," he replied, with a chuckle. "The lads must have forgotten you. But you are in the bit at last, for I am Prestongrange."

So saying, he passed before me into the next room, whither (upon his sign) I followed him, and where he lit a candle and took his place before a business-table. It was a long room, of a good proportion, wholly lined with books. That small spark of light in a corner struck out the man's handsome person and strong face. He was flushed, his eye watered and sparkled, and before he sat down I observed him to sway back and forth. No doubt, he had been supping liberally; but his mind and tongue were under full control.

"Well, sir, sit ye down," said he, "and let us see Pilrig's letter."

He glanced it through in the beginning carelessly, looking up and bowing when he came to my name; but at the last words I thought I observed his attention to redouble, and I made sure he read them twice. All this while you are to suppose my heart was beating, for I had now crossed my Rubicon and was come fairly on the field of battle.

"I am pleased to make your acquaintance, Mr. Balfour," he said, when he had done. "Let me offer you a glass of claret."

"Under your favour, my lord, I think it would scarce be fair on me," said I. "I have come here, as the letter will have mentioned, on a business of some gravity to myself; and, as I am little used with wine, I might be the sooner affected."

"You shall be the judge," said he. "But if you will permit, I believe I will even have the bottle in myself."

He touched a bell, and a footman came, as at a signal, bringing wine and glasses.

"You are sure you will not join me?" asked the Advocate. "Well, here is to our better acquaintance! In what way can I serve you?"

"I should, perhaps, begin by telling you, my lord, that I am here at your own pressing invitation," said I.

"You have the advantage of me somewhere," said he, "for I profess I think I never heard of you before this evening."

"Right, my lord; the name is, indeed, new to you," said I. "And yet you have been for some time extremely wishful to make my acquaintance, and have declared the same in public."

"I wish you would afford me a clue," says he. "I am no Daniel."

"It will perhaps serve for such," said I, "that if I was in a jesting humour—which is far from the case—I believe I might lay a claim on your lordship for two hundred pounds."

"In what sense?" he inquired.

"In the sense of rewards offered for my person," said I.

He thrust away his glass once and for all, and sat straight up in the chair where he had been previously lolling. "What am I to understand?" said he.

"A tall strong lad of about eighteen," I quoted, "speaks like a Lowlander and has no beard."

"I recognise those words," said he, "which, if you have come here with any ill-judged intention of amusing yourself, are like to prove extremely prejudicial to your safety."

"My purpose in this," I replied, "is just entirely as serious as life and death, and you have understood me perfectly. I am the boy who was speaking with Glenure when he was shot."

"I can only suppose (seeing you here) that you claim to be innocent," said he.

"The inference is clear," I said. "I am a very loyal subject to King George, but if I had anything to reproach myself with, I would have had more discretion than to walk into your den."

"I am glad of that," said he. "This horrid crime, Mr. Balfour, is of a dye which cannot permit any clemency. Blood has been barbarously shed. It has been shed in direct opposition to his Majesty and our whole frame of laws, by those who are their known and public oppugnants. I take a very high sense of this. I will not deny that I consider the crime as directly personal to his Majesty."

"And unfortunately, my lord," I added, a little drily, "directly personal to another great personage who may be nameless."

"If you mean anything by those words, I must tell you I consider them unfit for a good subject; and were they spoke publicly I should make it my business to take note of them," said he. "You do not appear to me to recognise the gravity of your situation, or you would be more careful not to pejorate the same by words which glance upon the purity of justice. Justice, in this country, and in my poor hands, is no respecter of persons."

"You give me too great a share in my own speech, my lord," said I. "I did but repeat the common talk of the country, which I have heard everywhere, and from men of all opinions as I came along."

"When you are come to more discretion you will understand such talk in not to be listened to, how much less repeated," says the Advocate. "But I acquit you of an ill intention. That nobleman, whom we all honour, and who has indeed been wounded in a near place by the late barbarity, sits too high to be reached by these aspersions. The Duke of Argyle—you see that I deal plainly with you—takes it to heart as I do, and as we are both bound to do by our judicial functions and the service of his Majesty; and I could wish that all hands, in this ill age, were equally clean of family rancour. But from the accident that this is a Campbell who has fallen martyr to his duty—as who else but the Campbells have ever put themselves foremost on that path?—I may say it, who am no Campbell—and that the chief of that great house happens (for all our advantages) to be the present head of the College of Justice, small minds and disaffected tongues are set agog in every changehouse in the country; and I find a young gentleman like Mr. Balfour so ill-advised as to make himself their echo." So much he spoke with a very oratorical delivery, as if in court, and then declined again upon the manner of a gentleman. "All this apart," said he. "It now remains that I should learn what I am to do with you."

"I had thought it was rather I that should learn the same from your lordship," said I.

"Ay, true," says the Advocate. "But, you see, you come to me well recommended. There is a good honest Whig name to this letter," says he, picking it up a moment from the table. "And—extra-judicially, Mr. Balfour—there is always the possibility of some arrangement, I tell you, and I tell you beforehand that you may be the more upon your guard, your fate lies with me singly. In such a matter (be it said with reverence) I am more powerful than the King's Majesty; and should you please me—and of course satisfy my conscience—in what remains to be held of our interview, I tell you it may remain between ourselves."

"Meaning how?" I asked.

"Why, I mean it thus, Mr. Balfour," said he, "that if you give satisfaction, no soul need know so much as that you visited my house; and you may observe that I do not even call my clerk."

I saw what way he was driving. "I suppose it is needless anyone should be informed upon my visit," said I, "though the precise nature of my gains by that I cannot see. I am not at all ashamed of coming here."

"And have no cause to be," says he, encouragingly. "Nor yet (if you are careful) to fear the consequences."

"My lord," said I, "speaking under your correction, I am not very easy to be frightened."

"And I am sure I do not seek to frighten you," says he. "But to the interrogation; and let me warn you to volunteer nothing beyond the questions I shall ask you. It may consist very immediately with your safety. I have a great discretion, it is true, but there are bounds to it."

"I shall try to follow your lordship's advice," said I.

He spread a sheet of paper on the table and wrote a heading. "It appears you were present, by the way, in the wood of Lettermore at the moment of the fatal shot," he began. "Was this by accident?"

180

"By accident," said I.

"How came you in speech with Colin Campbell?" he asked.

"I was inquiring my way of him to Aucharn," I replied.

I observed he did not write this answer down.

"H'm, true," said he, "I had forgotten that. And do you know, Mr. Balfour, I would dwell, if I were you, as little as might be on your relations with these Stewarts. It might be found to complicate our business. I am not yet inclined to regard these matters as essential."

"I had thought, my lord, that all points of fact were equally material in such a case," said I.

"You forget we are now trying these Stewarts," he replied, with great significance. "If we should ever come to be trying you, it will be very different; and I shall press these very questions that I am now willing to glide upon. But to resume: I have it here in Mr. Mungo Campbell's precognition that you ran immediately up the brae. How came that?"

"Not immediately, my lord, and the cause was my seeing of the murderer."

"You saw him, then?"

"As plain as I see your lordship, though not so near hand."

"You know him?"

"I should know him again."

"In your pursuit you were not so fortunate, then, as to overtake him?"

"I was not."

"Was he alone?"

"He was alone."

"There was no one else in that neighbourhood?"

"Alan Breck Stewart was not far off, in a piece of a wood."

The Advocate laid his pen down. "I think we are playing at cross purposes," said he, "which you will find to prove a very ill amusement for yourself."

"I content myself with following your lordship's advice, and answering what I am asked," said I.

"Be so wise as to bethink yourself in time," said he, "I use you with the most anxious tenderness, which you scarce seem to appreciate, and which (unless you be more careful) may prove to be in vain."

"I do appreciate your tenderness, but conceive it to be mistaken," I replied, with something of a falter, for I saw we were come to grips at last. "I am here to lay before you certain information, by which I shall convince you Alan had no hand whatever in the killing of Glenure."

The Advocate appeared for a moment at a stick, sitting with pursed lips, and blinking his eyes upon me like an angry cat. "Mr. Balfour," he said at last, "I tell you pointedly you go an ill way for your own interests."

"My lord," I said, "I am as free of the charge of considering my own interests in this matter as your lordship. As God judges me, I have but the one design, and that is to see justice executed and the innocent go clear. If in pursuit of that I come to fall under your lordship's displeasure, I must bear it as I may."

At this he rose from his chair, lit a second candle, and for a while gazed upon me steadily. I was surprised to see a great change of gravity fallen upon his face, and I could have almost thought he was a little pale.

"You are either very simple, or extremely the reverse, and I see that I must deal with you more confidentially," says he. "This is a political case—ah, yes, Mr. Balfour! whether we like it or no, the case is political—and I tremble when I think what issues may depend from it. To a political case, I need scarce tell a young man of your education, we approach with very different thoughts from one which is criminal only. Salus populi suprema lex is a maxim susceptible of great abuse, but it has that force which we find elsewhere only in the laws of nature: I mean it has the force of necessity. I will open this out to you, if you will allow me, at more length. You would have me believe—"

"Under your pardon, my lord, I would have you to believe nothing but that which I can prove," said I.

"Tut! tut; young gentleman," says he, "be not so pragmatical, and suffer a man who might be your father (if it was nothing more) to employ his own imperfect language, and express his own poor thoughts, even when they have the misfortune not to coincide with Mr. Balfour's. You would have me to believe Breck innocent. I would think this of little account, the more so as we cannot catch our man. But the matter of Breck's innocence shoots beyond itself. Once admitted, it would destroy the whole presumptions of our case against another and a very different criminal; a man grown old in treason, already twice in arms against his king and already twice forgiven; a fomentor of discontent, and (whoever may have fired the shot) the unmistakable original of the deed in question. I need not tell you that I mean James Stewart."

"And I can just say plainly that the innocence of Alan and of James is what I am here to declare in private to your lordship, and what I am prepared to establish at the trial by my testimony," said I.

"To which I can only answer by an equal plainness, Mr. Balfour," said he, "that (in that case) your testimony will not be called by me, and I desire you to withhold it altogether."

"You are at the head of Justice in this country," I cried, "and you propose to me a crime!"

"I am a man nursing with both hands the interests of this country," he replied, "and I press on you a political necessity. Patriotism is not always moral in the formal sense. You might be glad of it, I think: it is your own protection; the facts are heavy against you; and if I am still trying to except you from a very dangerous place, it is in part of course because I am not insensible to your honesty in coming here; in part because of Pilrig's letter;

but in part, and in chief part, because I regard in this matter my political duty first and my judicial duty only second. For the same reason—I repeat it to you in the same frank words—I do not want your testimony."

"I desire not to be thought to make a repartee, when I express only the plain sense of our position," said I. "But if your lordship has no need of my testimony, I believe the other side would be extremely blythe to get it."

Prestongrange arose and began to pace to and fro in the room. "You are not so young," he said, "but what you must remember very clearly the year '45 and the shock that went about the country. I read in Pilrig's letter that you are sound in Kirk and State. Who saved them in that fatal year? I do not refer to His Royal Highness and his ramrods, which were extremely useful in their day; but the country had been saved and the field won before ever Cumberland came upon Drummossie. Who saved it? I repeat; who saved the Protestant religion and the whole frame of our civil institutions? The late Lord President Culloden, for one; he played a man's part, and small thanks he got for it—even as I, whom you see before you, straining every nerve in the same service, look for no reward beyond the conscience of my duties done. After the President, who else? You know the answer as well as I do; 'tis partly a scandal, and you glanced at it yourself, and I reproved you for it, when you first came in. It was the Duke and the great clan of Campbell. Now here is a Campbell foully murdered, and that in the King's service. The Duke and I are Highlanders. But we are Highlanders civilised, and it is not so with the great mass of our clans and families. They have still savage virtues and defects. They are still barbarians, like these Stewarts; only the Campbells were barbarians on the right side, and the Stewarts were barbarians on the wrong. Now be you the judge. The Campbells expect vengeance. If they do not get it—if this man James escape—there will be trouble with the Campbells. That means disturbance in the Highlands, which are uneasy and very far from being disarmed: the disarming is a farce. . ."

"I can bear you out in that," said I.

"Disturbance in the Highlands makes the hour of our old watchful enemy," pursued his lordship, holding out a finger as he paced; "and I give you

184

my word we may have a '45 again with the Campbells on the other side. To protect the life of this man Stewart—which is forfeit already on half-a-dozen different counts if not on this—do you propose to plunge your country in war, to jeopardise the faith of your fathers, and to expose the lives and fortunes of how many thousand innocent persons? . . . These are considerations that weigh with me, and that I hope will weigh no less with yourself, Mr. Balfour, as a lover of your country, good government, and religious truth."

"You deal with me very frankly, and I thank you for it," said I. "I will try on my side to be no less honest. I believe your policy to be sound. I believe these deep duties may lie upon your lordship; I believe you may have laid them on your conscience when you took the oath of the high office which you hold. But for me, who am just a plain man—or scarce a man yet—the plain duties must suffice. I can think but of two things, of a poor soul in the immediate and unjust danger of a shameful death, and of the cries and tears of his wife that still tingle in my head. I cannot see beyond, my lord. It's the way that I am made. If the country has to fall, it has to fall. And I pray God, if this be wilful blindness, that He may enlighten me before too late."

He had heard me motionless, and stood so a while longer.

"This is an unexpected obstacle," says he, aloud, but to himself.

"And how is your lordship to dispose of me?" I asked.

"If I wished," said he, "you know that you might sleep in gaol?"

"My lord," said I, "I have slept in worse places."

"Well, my boy," said he, "there is one thing appears very plainly from our interview, that I may rely on your pledged word. Give me your honour that you will be wholly secret, not only on what has passed to-night, but in the matter of the Appin case, and I let you go free."

"I will give it till to-morrow or any other near day that you may please to set," said I. "I would not be thought too wily; but if I gave the promise without qualification your lordship would have attained his end."

"I had no thought to entrap you," said he.

"I am sure of that," said I.

"Let me see," he continued. "To-morrow is the Sabbath. Come to me on Monday by eight in the morning, and give me your promise until then."

"Freely given, my lord," said I. "And with regard to what has fallen from yourself, I will give it for an long as it shall please God to spare your days."

"You will observe," he said next, "that I have made no employment of menaces."

"It was like your lordship's nobility," said I. "Yet I am not altogether so dull but what I can perceive the nature of those you have not uttered."

"Well," said he, "good-night to you. May you sleep well, for I think it is more than I am like to do."

With that he sighed, took up a candle, and gave me his conveyance as far as the street door.

CHAPTER V—IN THE ADVOCATE'S HOUSE

The next day, Sabbath, August 27th, I had the occasion I had long looked forward to, to hear some of the famous Edinburgh preachers, all well known to me already by the report of Mr Campbell. Alas! and I might just as well have been at Essendean, and sitting under Mr. Campbell's worthy self! the turmoil of my thoughts, which dwelt continually on the interview with Prestongrange, inhibiting me from all attention. I was indeed much less impressed by the reasoning of the divines than by the spectacle of the thronged congregation in the churches, like what I imagined of a theatre or (in my then disposition) of an assize of trial; above all at the West Kirk, with its three tiers of galleries, where I went in the vain hope that I might see Miss Drummond.

On the Monday I betook me for the first time to a barber's, and was very well pleased with the result. Thence to the Advocate's, where the red coats of the soldiers showed again about his door, making a bright place in the close. I looked about for the young lady and her gillies: there was never a sign of them. But I was no sooner shown into the cabinet or antechamber where I had spent so wearyful a time upon the Saturday, than I was aware of the tall figure of James More in a corner. He seemed a prey to a painful uneasiness, reaching forth his feet and hands, and his eyes speeding here and there without rest about the walls of the small chamber, which recalled to me with a sense of pity the man's wretched situation. I suppose it was partly this, and partly my strong continuing interest in his daughter, that moved me to accost him.

"Give you a good-morning, sir," said I.

"And a good-morning to you, sir," said he.

"You bide tryst with Prestongrange?" I asked.

"I do, sir, and I pray your business with that gentleman be more agreeable than mine," was his reply.

"I hope at least that yours will be brief, for I suppose you pass before me," said I.

"All pass before me," he said, with a shrug and a gesture upward of the open hands. "It was not always so, sir, but times change. It was not so when the sword was in the scale, young gentleman, and the virtues of the soldier might sustain themselves."

There came a kind of Highland snuffle out of the man that raised my dander strangely.

"Well, Mr. Macgregor," said I, "I understand the main thing for a soldier is to be silent, and the first of his virtues never to complain."

"You have my name, I perceive"—he bowed to me with his arms crossed—"though it's one I must not use myself. Well, there is a publicity—I have shown my face and told my name too often in the beards of my enemies. I must not wonder if both should be known to many that I know not."

"That you know not in the least, sir," said I, "nor yet anybody else; but the name I am called, if you care to hear it, is Balfour."

"It is a good name," he replied, civilly; "there are many decent folk that use it. And now that I call to mind, there was a young gentleman, your namesake, that marched surgeon in the year '45 with my battalion."

"I believe that would be a brother to Balfour of Baith," said I, for I was ready for the surgeon now.

"The same, sir," said James More. "And since I have been fellow-soldier with your kinsman, you must suffer me to grasp your hand."

He shook hands with me long and tenderly, beaming on me the while as though he had found a brother.

"Ah!" says he, "these are changed days since your cousin and I heard the balls whistle in our lugs."

"I think he was a very far-away cousin," said I, drily, "and I ought to tell you that I never clapped eyes upon the man."

188

"Well, well," said he, "it makes no change. And you—I do not think you were out yourself, sir—I have no clear mind of your face, which is one not probable to be forgotten."

"In the year you refer to, Mr. Macgregor, I was getting skelped in the parish school," said I.

"So young!" cries he. "Ah, then, you will never be able to think what this meeting is to me. In the hour of my adversity, and here in the house of my enemy, to meet in with the blood of an old brother-in-arms—it heartens me, Mr. Balfour, like the skirling of the highland pipes! Sir, this is a sad look back that many of us have to make: some with falling tears. I have lived in my own country like a king; my sword, my mountains, and the faith of my friends and kinsmen sufficed for me. Now I lie in a stinking dungeon; and do you know, Mr. Balfour," he went on, taking my arm and beginning to lead me about, "do you know, sir, that I lack mere necessaries? The malice of my foes has quite sequestered my resources. I lie, as you know, sir, on a trumped-up charge, of which I am as innocent as yourself. They dare not bring me to my trial, and in the meanwhile I am held naked in my prison. I could have wished it was your cousin I had met, or his brother Baith himself. Either would, I know, have been rejoiced to help me; while a comparative stranger like yourself—"

I would be ashamed to set down all he poured out to me in this beggarly vein, or the very short and grudging answers that I made to him. There were times when I was tempted to stop his mouth with some small change; but whether it was from shame or pride—whether it was for my own sake or Catriona's—whether it was because I thought him no fit father for his daughter, or because I resented that grossness of immediate falsity that clung about the man himself—the thing was clean beyond me. And I was still being wheedled and preached to, and still being marched to and fro, three steps and a turn, in that small chamber, and had already, by some very short replies, highly incensed, although not finally discouraged, my beggar, when Prestongrange appeared in the doorway and bade me eagerly into his big chamber.

"I have a moment's engagements," said he; "and that you may not sit empty-handed I am going to present you to my three braw daughters, of whom perhaps you may have heard, for I think they are more famous than papa. This way."

He led me into another long room above, where a dry old lady sat at a frame of embroidery, and the three handsomest young women (I suppose) in Scotland stood together by a window.

"This is my new friend, Mr Balfour," said he, presenting me by the arm, "David, here is my sister, Miss Grant, who is so good as keep my house for me, and will be very pleased if she can help you. And here," says he, turning to the three younger ladies, "here are my three braw dauchters. A fair question to ye, Mr. Davie: which of the three is the best favoured? And I wager he will never have the impudence to propound honest Alan Ramsay's answer!"

Hereupon all three, and the old Miss Grant as well, cried out against this sally, which (as I was acquainted with the verses he referred to) brought shame into my own check. It seemed to me a citation unpardonable in a father, and I was amazed that these ladies could laugh even while they reproved, or made believe to.

Under cover of this mirth, Prestongrange got forth of the chamber, and I was left, like a fish upon dry land, in that very unsuitable society. I could never deny, in looking back upon what followed, that I was eminently stockish; and I must say the ladies were well drilled to have so long a patience with me. The aunt indeed sat close at her embroidery, only looking now and again and smiling; but the misses, and especially the eldest, who was besides the most handsome, paid me a score of attentions which I was very ill able to repay. It was all in vain to tell myself I was a young follow of some worth as well as a good estate, and had no call to feel abashed before these lasses, the eldest not so much older than myself, and no one of them by any probability half as learned. Reasoning would not change the fact; and there were times when the colour came into my face to think I was shaved that day for the first time.

The talk going, with all their endeavours, very heavily, the eldest took

190

pity on my awkwardness, sat down to her instrument, of which she was a passed mistress, and entertained me for a while with playing and singing, both in the Scots and in the Italian manners; this put me more at my ease, and being reminded of Alan's air that he had taught me in the hole near Carriden, I made so bold as to whistle a bar or two, and ask if she knew that.

She shook her head. "I never heard a note of it," said she. "Whistle it all through. And now once again," she added, after I had done so.

Then she picked it out upon the keyboard, and (to my surprise) instantly enriched the same with well-sounding chords, and sang, as she played, with a very droll expression and broad accent—

"Haenae I got just the lilt of it?

Isnae this the tune that ye whustled?"

"You see," she says, "I can do the poetry too, only it won't rhyme. And then again:

"I am Miss Grant, sib to the Advocate:

You, I believe, are Dauvit Balfour."

I told her how much astonished I was by her genius.

"And what do you call the name of it?" she asked.

"I do not know the real name," said I. "I just call it Alan's air."

She looked at me directly in the face. "I shall call it David's air," said she; "though if it's the least like what your namesake of Israel played to Saul I would never wonder that the king got little good by it, for it's but melancholy music. Your other name I do not like; so if you was ever wishing to hear your tune again you are to ask for it by mine."

This was said with a significance that gave my heart a jog. "Why that, Miss Grant?" I asked.

"Why," says she, "if ever you should come to get hanged, I will set your last dying speech and confession to that tune and sing it."

This put it beyond a doubt that she was partly informed of my story and peril. How, or just how much, it was more difficult to guess. It was plain she knew there was something of danger in the name of Alan, and thus warned me to leave it out of reference; and plain she knew that I stood under some criminal suspicion. I judged besides that the harshness of her last speech (which besides she had followed up immediately with a very noisy piece of music) was to put an end to the present conversation. I stood beside her, affecting to listen and admire, but truly whirled away by my own thoughts. I have always found this young lady to be a lover of the mysterious; and certainly this first interview made a mystery that was beyond my plummet. One thing I learned long after, the hours of the Sunday had been well employed, the bank porter had been found and examined, my visit to Charles Stewart was discovered, and the deduction made that I was pretty deep with James and Alan, and most likely in a continued correspondence with the last. Hence this broad hint that was given me across the harpsichord.

In the midst of the piece of music, one of the younger misses, who was at a window over the close, cried on her sisters to come quick, for there was "Grey eyes again." The whole family trooped there at once, and crowded one another for a look. The window whither they ran was in an odd corner of that room, gave above the entrance door, and flanked up the close.

"Come, Mr. Balfour," they cried, "come and see. She is the most beautiful creature! She hangs round the close-head these last days, always with some wretched-like gillies, and yet seems quite a lady."

I had no need to look; neither did I look twice, or long. I was afraid she might have seen me there, looking down upon her from that chamber of music, and she without, and her father in the same house, perhaps begging for his life with tears, and myself come but newly from rejecting his petitions. But even that glance set me in a better conceit of myself and much less awe of the young ladies. They were beautiful, that was beyond question, but Catriona was beautiful too, and had a kind of brightness in her like a coal of fire. As much as the others cast me down, she lifted me up. I remembered I had talked easily with her. If I could make no hand of it with these fine maids, it was perhaps something their own fault. My embarrassment began to be a little mingled and lightened with a sense of fun; and when the aunt smiled at me from her embroidery, and the three daughters unbent to me like a baby, all with "papa's orders" written on their faces, there were times when I could have found it in my heart to smile myself.

Presently papa returned, the same kind, happy-like, pleasant-spoken man.

"Now, girls," said he, "I must take Mr. Balfour away again; but I hope you have been able to persuade him to return where I shall be always gratified to find him."

So they each made me a little farthing compliment, and I was led away.

If this visit to the family had been meant to soften my resistance, it was the worst of failures. I was no such ass but what I understood how poor a figure I had made, and that the girls would be yawning their jaws off as soon as my stiff back was turned. I felt I had shown how little I had in me of what was soft and graceful; and I longed for a chance to prove that I had something of the other stuff, the stern and dangerous.

Well, I was to be served to my desire, for the scene to which he was conducting me was of a different character.

CHAPTER VI—UMQUILE THE MASTER OF LOVAT

There was a man waiting us in Prestongrange's study, whom I distasted at the first look, as we distaste a ferret or an earwig. He was bitter ugly, but seemed very much of a gentleman; had still manners, but capable of sudden leaps and violences; and a small voice, which could ring out shrill and dangerous when he so desired.

The Advocate presented us in a familiar, friendly way.

"Here, Fraser," said he, "here is Mr. Balfour whom we talked about. Mr. David, this is Mr. Simon Fraser, whom we used to call by another title, but that is an old song. Mr. Fraser has an errand to you."

With that he stepped aside to his book-shelves, and made believe to consult a quarto volume in the far end.

I was thus left (in a sense) alone with perhaps the last person in the world I had expected. There was no doubt upon the terms of introduction; this could be no other than the forfeited Master of Lovat and chief of the great clan Fraser. I knew he had led his men in the Rebellion; I knew his father's head—my old lord's, that grey fox of the mountains—to have fallen on the block for that offence, the lands of the family to have been seized, and their nobility attainted. I could not conceive what he should be doing in Grant's house; I could not conceive that he had been called to the bar, had eaten all his principles, and was now currying favour with the Government even to the extent of acting Advocate-Depute in the Appin murder.

"Well, Mr. Balfour," said he, "what is all this I hear of ye?"

"It would not become me to prejudge," said I, "but if the Advocate was your authority he is fully possessed of my opinions."

"I may tell you I am engaged in the Appin case," he went on; "I am to appear under Prestongrange; and from my study of the precognitions I can assure you your opinions are erroneous. The guilt of Breck is manifest;

and your testimony, in which you admit you saw him on the hill at the very moment, will certify his hanging."

"It will be rather ill to hang him till you catch him," I observed. "And for other matters I very willingly leave you to your own impressions."

"The Duke has been informed," he went on. "I have just come from his Grace, and he expressed himself before me with an honest freedom like the great nobleman he is. He spoke of you by name, Mr. Balfour, and declared his gratitude beforehand in case you would be led by those who understand your own interests and those of the country so much better than yourself. Gratitude is no empty expression in that mouth: experto-crede. I daresay you know something of my name and clan, and the damnable example and lamented end of my late father, to say nothing of my own errata. Well, I have made my peace with that good Duke; he has intervened for me with our friend Prestongrange; and here I am with my foot in the stirrup again and some of the responsibility shared into my hand of prosecuting King George's enemies and avenging the late daring and barefaced insult to his Majesty."

"Doubtless a proud position for your father's son," says I.

He wagged his bald eyebrows at me. "You are pleased to make experiments in the ironical, I think," said he. "But I am here upon duty, I am here to discharge my errand in good faith, it is in vain you think to divert me. And let me tell you, for a young fellow of spirit and ambition like yourself, a good shove in the beginning will do more than ten years' drudgery. The shove is now at your command; choose what you will to be advanced in, the Duke will watch upon you with the affectionate disposition of a father."

"I am thinking that I lack the docility of the son," says I.

"And do you really suppose, sir, that the whole policy of this country is to be suffered to trip up and tumble down for an ill-mannered colt of a boy?" he cried. "This has been made a test case, all who would prosper in the future must put a shoulder to the wheel. Look at me! Do you suppose it is for my pleasure that I put myself in the highly invidious position of persecuting a man that I have drawn the sword alongside of? The choice is not left me."

"But I think, sir, that you forfeited your choice when you mixed in with that unnatural rebellion," I remarked. "My case is happily otherwise; I am a true man, and can look either the Duke or King George in the face without concern."

"Is it so the wind sits?" says he. "I protest you are fallen in the worst sort of error. Prestongrange has been hitherto so civil (he tells me) as not to combat your allegations; but you must not think they are not looked upon with strong suspicion. You say you are innocent. My dear sir, the facts declare you guilty."

"I was waiting for you there," said I.

"The evidence of Mungo Campbell; your flight after the completion of the murder; your long course of secrecy—my good young man!" said Mr. Simon, "here is enough evidence to hang a bullock, let be a David Balfour! I shall be upon that trial; my voice shall be raised; I shall then speak much otherwise from what I do to-day, and far less to your gratification, little as you like it now! Ah, you look white!" cries he. "I have found the key of your impudent heart. You look pale, your eyes waver, Mr. David! You see the grave and the gallows nearer by than you had fancied."

"I own to a natural weakness," said I. "I think no shame for that. Shame. . ." I was going on.

"Shame waits for you on the gibbet," he broke in.

"Where I shall but be even'd with my lord your father," said I.

"Aha, but not so!" he cried, "and you do not yet see to the bottom of this business. My father suffered in a great cause, and for dealing in the affairs of kings. You are to hang for a dirty murder about boddle-pieces. Your personal part in it, the treacherous one of holding the poor wretch in talk, your accomplices a pack of ragged Highland gillies. And it can be shown, my great Mr. Balfour—it can be shown, and it will be shown, trust me that has a finger in the pie—it can be shown, and shall be shown, that you were paid to do it. I think I can see the looks go round the court when I adduce my evidence, and it shall appear that you, a young man of education, let

196

yourself be corrupted to this shocking act for a suit of cast clothes, a bottle of Highland spirits, and three-and-fivepence-halfpenny in copper money."

There was a touch of the truth in these words that knocked me like a blow: clothes, a bottle of usquebaugh, and three-and-fivepence-halfpenny in change made up, indeed, the most of what Alan and I had carried from Auchurn; and I saw that some of James's people had been blabbing in their dungeons.

"You see I know more than you fancied," he resumed in triumph. "And as for giving it this turn, great Mr. David, you must not suppose the Government of Great Britain and Ireland will ever be stuck for want of evidence. We have men here in prison who will swear out their lives as we direct them; as I direct, if you prefer the phrase. So now you are to guess your part of glory if you choose to die. On the one hand, life, wine, women, and a duke to be your handgun: on the other, a rope to your craig, and a gibbet to clatter your bones on, and the lousiest, lowest story to hand down to your namesakes in the future that was ever told about a hired assassin. And see here!" he cried, with a formidable shrill voice, "see this paper that I pull out of my pocket. Look at the name there: it is the name of the great David, I believe, the ink scarce dry yet. Can you guess its nature? It is the warrant for your arrest, which I have but to touch this bell beside me to have executed on the spot. Once in the Tolbooth upon this paper, may God help you, for the die is cast!"

I must never deny that I was greatly horrified by so much baseness, and much unmanned by the immediacy and ugliness of my danger. Mr. Simon had already gloried in the changes of my hue; I make no doubt I was now no ruddier than my shirt; my speech besides trembled.

"There is a gentleman in this room," cried I. "I appeal to him. I put my life and credit in his hands."

Prestongrange shut his book with a snap. "I told you so, Simon," said he; "you have played your hand for all it was worth, and you have lost. Mr. David," he went on, "I wish you to believe it was by no choice of mine you were subjected to this proof. I wish you could understand how glad I am you should come forth from it with so much credit. You may not quite see how, but it is a little of a service to myself. For had our friend here been more successful than I was last night, it might have appeared that he was a better judge of men than I; it might have appeared we were altogether in the wrong situations, Mr. Simon and myself. And I know our friend Simon to be ambitious," says he, striking lightly on Fraser's shoulder. "As for this stage play, it is over; my sentiments are very much engaged in your behalf; and whatever issue we can find to this unfortunate affair, I shall make it my business to see it is adopted with tenderness to you."

These were very good words, and I could see besides that there was little love, and perhaps a spice of genuine ill-will, between these two who were opposed to me. For all that, it was unmistakable this interview had been designed, perhaps rehearsed, with the consent of both; it was plain my adversaries were in earnest to try me by all methods; and now (persuasion, flattery, and menaces having been tried in vain) I could not but wonder what would be their next expedient. My eyes besides were still troubled, and my knees loose under me, with the distress of the late ordeal; and I could do no more than stammer the same form of words: "I put my life and credit in your hands."

"Well, well," said he, "we must try to save them. And in the meanwhile let us return to gentler methods. You must not bear any grudge upon my friend, Mr. Simon, who did but speak by his brief. And even if you did conceive some malice against myself, who stood by and seemed rather to hold a candle, I must not let that extend to innocent members of my family. These are greatly engaged to see more of you, and I cannot consent to have my young womenfolk disappointed. To-morrow they will be going to Hope Park, where I think it very proper you should make your bow. Call for me first, when I may possibly have something for your private hearing; then you shall be turned abroad again under the conduct of my misses; and until that time repeat to me your promise of secrecy."

I had done better to have instantly refused, but in truth I was beside the power of reasoning; did as I was bid; took my leave I know not how; and when I was forth again in the close, and the door had shut behind me, was glad to lean on a house wall and wipe my face. That horrid apparition (as I may call it) of Mr. Simon rang in my memory, as a sudden noise rings after it is over in the ear. Tales of the man's father, of his falseness, of his manifold perpetual treacheries, rose before me from all that I had heard and read, and joined on with what I had just experienced of himself. Each time it occurred to me, the ingenious foulness of that calumny he had proposed to nail upon my character startled me afresh. The case of the man upon the gibbet by Leith Walk appeared scarce distinguishable from that I was now to consider as my own. To rob a child of so little more than nothing was certainly a paltry enterprise for two grown men; but my own tale, as it was to be represented in a court by Simon Fraser, appeared a fair second in every possible point of view of sordidness and cowardice.

The voices of two of Prestongrange's liveried men upon his doorstep recalled me to myself.

"Ha'e," said the one, "this billet as fast as ye can link to the captain."

"Is that for the cateran back again?" asked the other.

"It would seem sae," returned the first. "Him and Simon are seeking him."

"I think Prestongrange is gane gyte," says the second. "He'll have James More in bed with him next."

"Weel, it's neither your affair nor mine's," said the first.

And they parted, the one upon his errand, and the other back into the house.

This looked as ill as possible. I was scarce gone and they were sending already for James More, to whom I thought Mr. Simon must have pointed when he spoke of men in prison and ready to redeem their lives by all extremities. My scalp curdled among my hair, and the next moment the blood leaped in me to remember Catriona. Poor lass! her father stood to be hanged for pretty indefensible misconduct. What was yet more unpalatable, it now seemed he was prepared to save his four quarters by the worst of shame and the most foul of cowardly murders—murder by the false oath; and to complete our misfortunes, it seemed myself was picked out to be the victim.

I began to walk swiftly and at random, conscious only of a desire for movement, air, and the open country.

CHAPTER VII—I MAKE A FAULT IN HONOUR

I came forth, I vow I know not how, on the Lang Dykes [12]. This is a rural road which runs on the north side over against the city. Thence I could see the whole black length of it tail down, from where the castle stands upon its crags above the loch in a long line of spires and gable ends, and smoking chimneys, and at the sight my heart swelled in my bosom. My youth, as I have told, was already inured to dangers; but such danger as I had seen the face of but that morning, in the midst of what they call the safety of a town, shook me beyond experience. Peril of slavery, peril of shipwreck, peril of sword and shot, I had stood all of these without discredit; but the peril there was in the sharp voice and the fat face of Simon, properly Lord Lovat, daunted me wholly.

I sat by the lake side in a place where the rushes went down into the water, and there steeped my wrists and laved my temples. If I could have done so with any remains of self-esteem, I would now have fled from my foolhardy enterprise. But (call it courage or cowardice, and I believe it was both the one and the other) I decided I was ventured out beyond the possibility of a retreat. I had out-faced these men, I would continue to out-face them; come what might, I would stand by the word spoken.

The sense of my own constancy somewhat uplifted my spirits, but not much. At the best of it there was an icy place about my heart, and life seemed a black business to be at all engaged in. For two souls in particular my pity flowed. The one was myself, to be so friendless and lost among dangers. The other was the girl, the daughter of James More. I had seen but little of her; yet my view was taken and my judgment made. I thought her a lass of a clean honour, like a man's; I thought her one to die of a disgrace; and now I believed her father to be at that moment bargaining his vile life for mine. It made a bond in my thoughts betwixt the girl and me. I had seen her before only as a wayside appearance, though one that pleased me strangely; I saw her now in a sudden nearness of relation, as the daughter of my blood foe, and I might say, my murderer. I reflected it was hard I should be so plagued and persecuted all my days for other folks' affairs, and have no manner of pleasure myself. I got meals and a bed to sleep in when my concerns would suffer it; beyond that my wealth was of no help to me. If I was to hang, my days were like to be short; if I was not to hang but to escape out of this trouble, they might yet seem long to me ere I was done with them. Of a sudden her face appeared in my memory, the way I had first seen it, with the parted lips; at that, weakness came in my bosom and strength into my legs; and I set resolutely forward on the way to Dean. If I was to hang to-morrow, and it was sure enough I might very likely sleep that night in a dungeon, I determined I should hear and speak once more with Catriona.

The exercise of walking and the thought of my destination braced me yet more, so that I began to pluck up a kind of spirit. In the village of Dean, where it sits in the bottom of a glen beside the river, I inquired my way of a miller's man, who sent me up the hill upon the farther side by a plain path, and so to a decent-like small house in a garden of lawns and apple-trees. My heart beat high as I stepped inside the garden hedge, but it fell low indeed when I came face to face with a grim and fierce old lady, walking there in a white mutch with a man's hat strapped upon the top of it.

"What do ye come seeking here?" she asked.

I told her I was after Miss Drummond.

"And what may be your business with Miss Drummond?" says she.

I told her I had met her on Saturday last, had been so fortunate as to render her a trifling service, and was come now on the young lady's invitation.

"O, so you're Saxpence!" she cried, with a very sneering manner. "A braw gift, a bonny gentleman. And hae ye ony ither name and designation, or were ye bapteesed Saxpence?" she asked.

I told my name.

"Preserve me!" she cried. "Has Ebenezer gotten a son?"

"No, ma'am," said I. "I am a son of Alexander's. It's I that am the Laird

202

of Shaws."

"Ye'll find your work cut out for ye to establish that," quoth she.

"I perceive you know my uncle," said I; "and I daresay you may be the better pleased to hear that business is arranged."

"And what brings ye here after Miss Drummond?" she pursued.

"I'm come after my saxpence, mem," said I. "It's to be thought, being my uncle's nephew, I would be found a careful lad."

"So ye have a spark of sleeness in ye?" observed the old lady, with some approval. "I thought ye had just been a cuif—you and your saxpence, and your lucky day and your sake of Balwhidder"—from which I was gratified to learn that Catriona had not forgotten some of our talk. "But all this is by the purpose," she resumed. "Am I to understand that ye come here keeping company?"

"This is surely rather an early question," said I. "The maid is young, so am I, worse fortune. I have but seen her the once. I'll not deny," I added, making up my mind to try her with some frankness, "I'll not deny but she has run in my head a good deal since I met in with her. That is one thing; but it would be quite another, and I think I would look very like a fool, to commit myself."

"You can speak out of your mouth, I see," said the old lady. "Praise God, and so can I! I was fool enough to take charge of this rogue's daughter: a fine charge I have gotten; but it's mine, and I'll carry it the way I want to. Do ye mean to tell me, Mr. Balfour of Shaws, that you would marry James More's daughter, and him hanged! Well, then, where there's no possible marriage there shall be no manner of carryings on, and take that for said. Lasses are bruckle things," she added, with a nod; "and though ye would never think it by my wrunkled chafts, I was a lassie mysel', and a bonny one."

"Lady Allardyce," said I, "for that I suppose to be your name, you seem to do the two sides of the talking, which is a very poor manner to come to an agreement. You give me rather a home thrust when you ask if I would marry, at the gallow's foot, a young lady whom I have seen but once. I have told you already I would never be so untenty as to commit myself. And yet I'll go some way with you. If I continue to like the lass as well as I have reason to expect, it will be something more than her father, or the gallows either, that keeps the two of us apart. As for my family, I found it by the wayside like a lost bawbee! I owe less than nothing to my uncle and if ever I marry, it will be to please one person: that's myself."

"I have heard this kind of talk before ye were born," said Mrs. Ogilvy, "which is perhaps the reason that I think of it so little. There's much to be considered. This James More is a kinsman of mine, to my shame be it spoken. But the better the family, the mair men hanged or headed, that's always been poor Scotland's story. And if it was just the hanging! For my part I think I would be best pleased with James upon the gallows, which would be at least an end to him. Catrine's a good lass enough, and a good-hearted, and lets herself be deaved all day with a runt of an auld wife like me. But, ye see, there's the weak bit. She's daft about that long, false, fleeching beggar of a father of hers, and red-mad about the Gregara, and proscribed names, and King James, and a wheen blethers. And you might think ye could guide her, ye would find yourself sore mista'en. Ye say ye've seen her but the once. . ."

"Spoke with her but the once, I should have said," I interrupted. "I saw her again this morning from a window at Prestongrange's."

This I daresay I put in because it sounded well; but I was properly paid for my ostentation on the return.

"What's this of it?" cries the old lady, with a sudden pucker of her face. "I think it was at the Advocate's door-cheek that ye met her first."

I told her that was so.

"H'm," she said; and then suddenly, upon rather a scolding tone, "I have your bare word for it," she cries, "as to who and what you are. By your way of it, you're Balfour of the Shaws; but for what I ken you may be Balfour of the Deevil's oxter. It's possible ye may come here for what ye say, and it's equally possible ye may come here for deil care what! I'm good enough Whig to sit quiet, and to have keepit all my men-folk's heads upon their shoulders. But I'm not just a good enough Whig to be made a fool of neither. And I tell you fairly, there's too much Advocate's door and Advocate's window here for a man that comes taigling after a Macgregor's daughter. Ye can tell that to the Advocate that sent ye, with my fond love. And I kiss my loof to ye, Mr. Balfour," says she, suiting the action to the word; "and a braw journey to ye back to where ye cam frae."

"If you think me a spy," I broke out, and speech stuck in my throat. I stood and looked murder at the old lady for a space, then bowed and turned away.

"Here! Hoots! The callant's in a creel!" she cried. "Think ye a spy? what else would I think ye—me that kens naething by ye? But I see that I was wrong; and as I cannot fight, I'll have to apologise. A bonny figure I would be with a broadsword. Ay! ay!" she went on, "you're none such a bad lad in your way; I think ye'll have some redeeming vices. But, O! Davit Balfour, ye're damned countryfeed. Ye'll have to win over that, lad; ye'll have to soople your back-bone, and think a wee pickle less of your dainty self; and ye'll have to try to find out that women-folk are nae grenadiers. But that can never be. To your last day you'll ken no more of women-folk than what I do of sow-gelding."

I had never been used with such expressions from a lady's tongue, the only two ladies I had known, Mrs. Campbell and my mother, being most devout and most particular women; and I suppose my amazement must have been depicted in my countenance, for Mrs. Ogilvy burst forth suddenly in a fit of laughter.

"Keep me!" she cried, struggling with her mirth, "you have the finest timber face—and you to marry the daughter of a Hieland cateran! Davie, my dear, I think we'll have to make a match of it—if it was just to see the weans. And now," she went on, "there's no manner of service in your daidling here, for the young woman is from home, and it's my fear that the old woman is no suitable companion for your father's son. Forbye that I have nobody but myself to look after my reputation, and have been long enough alone with a sedooctive youth. And come back another day for your saxpence!" she cried after me as I left.

My skirmish with this disconcerting lady gave my thoughts a boldness they had otherwise wanted. For two days the image of Catriona had mixed in all my meditations; she made their background, so that I scarce enjoyed my own company without a glint of her in a corner of my mind. But now she came immediately near; I seemed to touch her, whom I had never touched but the once; I let myself flow out to her in a happy weakness, and looking all about, and before and behind, saw the world like an undesirable desert, where men go as soldiers on a march, following their duty with what constancy they have, and Catriona alone there to offer me some pleasure of my days. I wondered at myself that I could dwell on such considerations in that time of my peril and disgrace; and when I remembered my youth I was ashamed. I had my studies to complete: I had to be called into some useful business; I had yet to take my part of service in a place where all must serve; I had yet to learn, and know, and prove myself a man; and I had so much sense as blush that I should be already tempted with these further-on and holier delights and duties. My education spoke home to me sharply; I was never brought up on sugar biscuits but on the hard food of the truth. I knew that he was quite unfit to be a husband who was not prepared to be a father also; and for a boy like me to play the father was a mere derision.

When I was in the midst of these thoughts and about half-way back to town I saw a figure coming to meet me, and the trouble of my heart was heightened. It seemed I had everything in the world to say to her, but nothing to say first; and remembering how tongue-tied I had been that morning at the Advocate's I made sure that I would find myself struck dumb. But when she came up my fears fled away; not even the consciousness of what I had been privately thinking disconcerted me the least; and I found I could talk with her as easily and rationally as I might with Alan.

"O!" she cried, "you have been seeking your sixpence; did you get it?"

I told her no; but now I had met with her my walk was not in vain. "Though I have seen you to-day already," said I, and told her where and when.

206

"I did not see you," she said. "My eyes are big, but there are better than mine at seeing far. Only I heard singing in the house."

"That was Miss Grant," said I, "the eldest and the bonniest."

"They say they are all beautiful," said she.

"They think the same of you, Miss Drummond," I replied, "and were all crowding to the window to observe you."

"It is a pity about my being so blind," said she, "or I might have seen them too. And you were in the house? You must have been having the fine time with the fine music and the pretty ladies."

"There is just where you are wrong," said I; "for I was as uncouth as a sea-fish upon the brae of a mountain. The truth is that I am better fitted to go about with rudas men than pretty ladies."

"Well, I would think so too, at all events!" said she, at which we both of us laughed.

"It is a strange thing, now," said I. "I am not the least afraid with you, yet I could have run from the Miss Grants. And I was afraid of your cousin too."

"O, I think any man will be afraid of her," she cried. "My father is afraid of her himself."

The name of her father brought me to a stop. I looked at her as she walked by my side; I recalled the man, and the little I knew and the much I guessed of him; and comparing the one with the other, felt like a traitor to be silent.

"Speaking of which," said I, "I met your father no later than this morning."

"Did you?" she cried, with a voice of joy that seemed to mock at me. "You saw James More? You will have spoken with him then?"

"I did even that," said I.

207

Then I think things went the worst way for me that was humanly possible. She gave me a look of mere gratitude. "Ah, thank you for that!" says she.

"You thank me for very little," said I, and then stopped. But it seemed when I was holding back so much, something at least had to come out. "I spoke rather ill to him," said I; "I did no like him very much; I spoke him rather ill, and he was angry."

"I think you had little to do then, and less to tell it to his daughter!" she cried out. "But those that do not love and cherish him I will not know."

"I will take the freedom of a word yet," said I, beginning to tremble. "Perhaps neither your father nor I are in the best of spirits at Prestongrange's. I daresay we both have anxious business there, for it's a dangerous house. I was sorry for him too, and spoke to him the first, if I could but have spoken the wiser. And for one thing, in my opinion, you will soon find that his affairs are mending."

"It will not be through your friendship, I am thinking," said she; "and he is much made up to you for your sorrow."

"Miss Drummond," cried I, "I am alone in this world."

"And I am not wondering at that," said she.

"O, let me speak!" said I. "I will speak but the once, and then leave you, if you will, for ever. I came this day in the hopes of a kind word that I am sore in want of. I know that what I said must hurt you, and I knew it then. It would have been easy to have spoken smooth, easy to lie to you; can you not think how I was tempted to the same? Cannot you see the truth of my heart shine out?"

"I think here is a great deal of work, Mr. Balfour," said she. "I think we will have met but the once, and will can part like gentle folk."

"O, let me have one to believe in me!" I pleaded, "I cannae bear it else. The whole world is clanned against me. How am I to go through with my dreadful fate? If there's to be none to believe in me I cannot do it. The man must just die, for I cannot do it."

She had still looked straight in front of her, head in air; but at my words or the tone of my voice she came to a stop. "What is this you say?" she asked. "What are you talking of?"

"It is my testimony which may save an innocent life," said I, "and they will not suffer me to bear it. What would you do yourself? You know what this is, whose father lies in danger. Would you desert the poor soul? They have tried all ways with me. They have sought to bribe me; they offered me hills and valleys. And to-day that sleuth-hound told me how I stood, and to what a length he would go to butcher and disgrace me. I am to be brought in a party to the murder; I am to have held Glenure in talk for money and old clothes; I am to be killed and shamed. If this is the way I am to fall, and me scarce a man—if this is the story to be told of me in all Scotland—if you are to believe it too, and my name is to be nothing but a by-word—Catriona, how can I go through with it? The thing's not possible; it's more than a man has in his heart."

I poured my words out in a whirl, one upon the other; and when I stopped I found her gazing on me with a startled face.

"Glenure! It is the Appin murder," she said softly, but with a very deep surprise.

I had turned back to bear her company, and we were now come near the head of the brae above Dean village. At this word I stepped in front of her like one suddenly distracted.

"For God's sake!" I cried, "for God's sake, what is this that I have done?" and carried my fists to my temples. "What made me do it? Sure, I am bewitched to say these things!"

"In the name of heaven, what ails you now!" she cried.

"I gave my honour," I groaned, "I gave my honour and now I have broke it. O, Catriona!"

"I am asking you what it is," she said; "was it these things you should not have spoken? And do you think I have no honour, then? or that I am one that would betray a friend? I hold up my right hand to you and swear."

"O, I knew you would be true!" said I. "It's me—it's here. I that stood but this morning and out-faced them, that risked rather to die disgraced upon the gallows than do wrong—and a few hours after I throw my honour away by the roadside in common talk! 'There is one thing clear upon our interview,' says he, 'that I can rely on your pledged word.' Where is my word now? Who could believe me now? You could not believe me. I am clean fallen down; I had best die!" All this I said with a weeping voice, but I had no tears in my body.

"My heart is sore for you," said she, "but be sure you are too nice. I would not believe you, do you say? I would trust you with anything. And these men? I would not be thinking of them! Men who go about to entrap and to destroy you! Fy! this is no time to crouch. Look up! Do you not think I will be admiring you like a great hero of the good—and you a boy not much older than myself? And because you said a word too much in a friend's ear, that would die ere she betrayed you—to make such a matter! It is one thing that we must both forget."

"Catriona," said I, looking at her, hang-dog, "is this true of it? Would ye trust me yet?"

"Will you not believe the tears upon my face?" she cried. "It is the world I am thinking of you, Mr. David Balfour. Let them hang you; I will never forget, I will grow old and still remember you. I think it is great to die so: I will envy you that gallows."

"And maybe all this while I am but a child frighted with bogles," said I. "Maybe they but make a mock of me."

"It is what I must know," she said. "I must hear the whole. The harm is done at all events, and I must hear the whole."

I had sat down on the wayside, where she took a place beside me, and I told her all that matter much as I have written it, my thoughts about her father's dealings being alone omitted.

"Well," she said, when I had finished, "you are a hero, surely, and I never would have thought that same! And I think you are in peril, too. O, Simon Fraser! to think upon that man! For his life and the dirty money, to be dealing in such traffic!" And just then she called out aloud with a queer word that was common with her, and belongs, I believe, to her own language. "My torture!" says she, "look at the sun!"

Indeed, it was already dipping towards the mountains.

She bid me come again soon, gave me her hand, and left me in a turmoil of glad spirits. I delayed to go home to my lodging, for I had a terror of immediate arrest; but got some supper at a change house, and the better part of that night walked by myself in the barley-fields, and had such a sense of Catriona's presence that I seemed to bear her in my arms.

CHAPTER VIII—THE BRAVO

The next day, August 29th, I kept my appointment at the Advocate's in a coat that I had made to my own measure, and was but newly ready.

"Aha," says Prestongrange, "you are very fine to-day; my misses are to have a fine cavalier. Come, I take that kind of you. I take that kind of you, Mr. David. O, we shall do very well yet, and I believe your troubles are nearly at an end."

"You have news for me?" cried I.

"Beyond anticipation," he replied. "Your testimony is after all to be received; and you may go, if you will, in my company to the trial, which in to be held at Inverary, Thursday, 21st proximo."

I was too much amazed to find words.

"In the meanwhile," he continued, "though I will not ask you to renew your pledge, I must caution you strictly to be reticent. To-morrow your precognition must be taken; and outside of that, do you know, I think least said will be soonest mended."

"I shall try to go discreetly," said I. "I believe it is yourself that I must thank for this crowning mercy, and I do thank you gratefully. After yesterday, my lord, this is like the doors of Heaven. I cannot find it in my heart to get the thing believed."

"Ah, but you must try and manage, you must try and manage to believe it," says he, soothing-like, "and I am very glad to hear your acknowledgment of obligation, for I think you may be able to repay me very shortly"—he coughed—"or even now. The matter is much changed. Your testimony, which I shall not trouble you for to-day, will doubtless alter the complexion of the case for all concerned, and this makes it less delicate for me to enter with you on a side issue."

"My Lord," I interrupted, "excuse me for interrupting you, but how has this been brought about? The obstacles you told me of on Saturday appeared even to me to be quite insurmountable; how has it been contrived?"

"My dear Mr. David," said he, "it would never do for me to divulge (even to you, as you say) the councils of the Government; and you must content yourself, if you please, with the gross fact."

He smiled upon me like a father as he spoke, playing the while with a new pen; methought it was impossible there could be any shadow of deception in the man: yet when he drew to him a sheet of paper, dipped his pen among the ink, and began again to address me, I was somehow not so certain, and fell instinctively into an attitude of guard.

"There is a point I wish to touch upon," he began. "I purposely left it before upon one side, which need be now no longer necessary. This is not, of course, a part of your examination, which is to follow by another hand; this is a private interest of my own. You say you encountered Alan Breck upon the hill?"

"I did, my lord," said I.

"This was immediately after the murder?"

"It was."

"Did you speak to him?"

"I did."

"You had known him before, I think?" says my lord, carelessly.

"I cannot guess your reason for so thinking, my lord," I replied, "but such in the fact."

"And when did you part with him again?" said he.

"I reserve my answer," said I. "The question will be put to me at the assize."

"Mr. Balfour," said he, "will you not understand that all this is without prejudice to yourself? I have promised you life and honour; and, believe me,

I can keep my word. You are therefore clear of all anxiety. Alan, it appears, you suppose you can protect; and you talk to me of your gratitude, which I think (if you push me) is not ill-deserved. There are a great many different considerations all pointing the same way; and I will never be persuaded that you could not help us (if you chose) to put salt on Alan's tail."

"My lord," said I, "I give you my word I do not so much as guess where Alan is."

He paused a breath. "Nor how he might be found?" he asked.

I sat before him like a log of wood.

"And so much for your gratitude, Mr. David!" he observed. Again there was a piece of silence. "Well," said he, rising, "I am not fortunate, and we are a couple at cross purposes. Let us speak of it no more; you will receive notice when, where, and by whom, we are to take your precognition. And in the meantime, my misses must be waiting you. They will never forgive me if I detain their cavalier."

Into the hands of these Graces I was accordingly offered up, and found them dressed beyond what I had thought possible, and looking fair as a posy.

As we went forth from the doors a small circumstance occurred which came afterwards to look extremely big. I heard a whistle sound loud and brief like a signal, and looking all about, spied for one moment the red head of Neil of the Tom, the son of Duncan. The next moment he was gone again, nor could I see so much as the skirt-tail of Catriona, upon whom I naturally supposed him to be then attending.

My three keepers led me out by Bristo and the Bruntsfield Links; whence a path carried us to Hope Park, a beautiful pleasance, laid with gravel-walks, furnished with seats and summer-sheds, and warded by a keeper. The way there was a little longsome; the two younger misses affected an air of genteel weariness that damped me cruelly, the eldest considered me with something that at times appeared like mirth; and though I thought I did myself more justice than the day before, it was not without some effort. Upon our reaching the park I was launched on a bevy of eight or ten young gentlemen (some

214

of them cockaded officers, the rest chiefly advocates) who crowded to attend upon these beauties; and though I was presented to all of them in very good words, it seemed I was by all immediately forgotten. Young folk in a company are like to savage animals: they fall upon or scorn a stranger without civility, or I may say, humanity; and I am sure, if I had been among baboons, they would have shown me quite as much of both. Some of the advocates set up to be wits, and some of the soldiers to be rattles; and I could not tell which of these extremes annoyed me most. All had a manner of handling their swords and coat-skirts, for the which (in mere black envy) I could have kicked them from the park. I daresay, upon their side, they grudged me extremely the fine company in which I had arrived; and altogether I had soon fallen behind, and stepped stiffly in the rear of all that merriment with my own thoughts.

From these I was recalled by one of the officers, Lieutenant Hector Duncansby, a gawky, leering Highland boy, asking if my name was not "Palfour."

I told him it was, not very kindly, for his manner was scant civil.

"Ha, Palfour," says he, and then, repeating it, "Palfour, Palfour!"

"I am afraid you do not like my name, sir," says I, annoyed with myself to be annoyed with such a rustical fellow.

"No," says he, "but I wass thinking."

"I would not advise you to make a practice of that, sir," says I. "I feel sure you would not find it to agree with you."

"Tit you effer hear where Alan Grigor fand the tangs?" said he.

I asked him what he could possibly mean, and he answered, with a heckling laugh, that he thought I must have found the poker in the same place and swallowed it.

There could be no mistake about this, and my cheek burned.

"Before I went about to put affronts on gentlemen," said I, "I think I would learn the English language first."

215

He took me by the sleeve with a nod and a wink and led me quietly outside Hope Park. But no sooner were we beyond the view of the promenaders, than the fashion of his countenance changed. "You tam lowland scoon'rel!" cries he, and hit me a buffet on the jaw with his closed fist.

I paid him as good or better on the return; whereupon he stepped a little back and took off his hat to me decorously.

"Enough plows I think," says he. "I will be the offended shentleman, for who effer heard of such suffeeciency as tell a shentlemans that is the king's officer he cannae speak Cot's English? We have swords at our hurdles, and here is the King's Park at hand. Will ye walk first, or let me show ye the way?"

I returned his bow, told him to go first, and followed him. As he went I heard him grumble to himself about Cot's English and the King's coat, so that I might have supposed him to be seriously offended. But his manner at the beginning of our interview was there to belie him. It was manifest he had come prepared to fasten a quarrel on me, right or wrong; manifest that I was taken in a fresh contrivance of my enemies; and to me (conscious as I was of my deficiencies) manifest enough that I should be the one to fall in our encounter.

As we came into that rough rocky desert of the King's Park I was tempted half-a-dozen times to take to my heels and run for it, so loath was I to show my ignorance in fencing, and so much averse to die or even to be wounded. But I considered if their malice went as far as this, it would likely stick at nothing; and that to fall by the sword, however ungracefully, was still an improvement on the gallows. I considered besides that by the unguarded pertness of my words and the quickness of my blow I had put myself quite out of court; and that even if I ran, my adversary would probably pursue and catch me, which would add disgrace to my misfortune. So that, taking all in all, I continued marching behind him, much as a man follows the hangman, and certainly with no more hope.

We went about the end of the long craigs, and came into the Hunter's Bog. Here, on a piece of fair turf, my adversary drew. There was nobody there to see us but some birds; and no resource for me but to follow his

216

example, and stand on guard with the best face I could display. It seems it was not good enough for Mr. Dancansby, who spied some flaw in my manœuvres, paused, looked upon me sharply, and came off and on, and menaced me with his blade in the air. As I had seen no such proceedings from Alan, and was besides a good deal affected with the proximity of death, I grew quite bewildered, stood helpless, and could have longed to run away.

"Fat deil ails her?" cries the lieutenant.

And suddenly engaging, he twitched the sword out of my grasp and sent it flying far among the rushes.

Twice was this manœuvre repeated; and the third time when I brought back my humiliated weapon, I found he had returned his own to the scabbard, and stood awaiting me with a face of some anger, and his hands clasped under his skirt.

"Pe tamned if I touch you!" he cried, and asked me bitterly what right I had to stand up before "shentlemans" when I did not know the back of a sword from the front of it.

I answered that was the fault of my upbringing; and would he do me the justice to say I had given him all the satisfaction it was unfortunately in my power to offer, and had stood up like a man?

"And that is the truth," said he. "I am fery prave myself, and pold as a lions. But to stand up there—and you ken naething of fence!—the way that you did, I declare it was peyond me. And I am sorry for the plow; though I declare I pelief your own was the elder brother, and my heid still sings with it. And I declare if I had kent what way it wass, I would not put a hand to such a piece of pusiness."

"That is handsomely said," I replied, "and I am sure you will not stand up a second time to be the actor for my private enemies."

"Indeed, no, Palfour," said he; "and I think I was used extremely suffeeciently myself to be set up to fecht with an auld wife, or all the same as a bairn whateffer! And I will tell the Master so, and fecht him, by Cot, himself!"

"And if you knew the nature of Mr. Simon's quarrel with me," said I, "you would be yet the more affronted to be mingled up with such affairs."

He swore he could well believe it; that all the Lovats were made of the same meal and the devil was the miller that ground that; then suddenly shaking me by the hand, he vowed I was a pretty enough fellow after all, that it was a thousand pities I had been neglected, and that if he could find the time, he would give an eye himself to have me educated.

"You can do me a better service than even what you propose," said I; and when he had asked its nature—"Come with me to the house of one of my enemies, and testify how I have carried myself this day," I told him. "That will be the true service. For though he has sent me a gallant adversary for the first, the thought in Mr. Simon's mind is merely murder. There will be a second and then a third; and by what you have seen of my cleverness with the cold steel, you can judge for yourself what is like to be the upshot."

"And I would not like it myself, if I was no more of a man than what you wass!" he cried. "But I will do you right, Palfour. Lead on!"

If I had walked slowly on the way into that accursed park my heels were light enough on the way out. They kept time to a very good old air, that is as ancient as the Bible, and the words of it are: "Surely the bitterness of death is passed." I mind that I was extremely thirsty, and had a drink at Saint Margaret's well on the road down, and the sweetness of that water passed belief. We went through the sanctuary, up the Canongate, in by the Netherbow, and straight to Prestongrange's door, talking as we came and arranging the details of our affair. The footman owned his master was at home, but declared him engaged with other gentlemen on very private business, and his door forbidden.

"My business is but for three minutes, and it cannot wait," said I. "You may say it is by no means private, and I shall be even glad to have some witnesses."

As the man departed unwillingly enough upon this errand, we made so bold as to follow him to the ante-chamber, whence I could hear for a while the murmuring of several voices in the room within. The truth is, they were three at the one table—Prestongrange, Simon Fraser, and Mr. Erskine, Sheriff of Perth; and as they were met in consultation on the very business of the Appin murder, they were a little disturbed at my appearance, but decided to receive me.

"Well, well, Mr. Balfour, and what brings you here again? and who is this you bring with you?" says Prestongrange.

As for Fraser, he looked before him on the table.

"He is here to bear a little testimony in my favour, my lord, which I think it very needful you should hear," said I, and turned to Duncansby.

"I have only to say this," said the lieutenant, "that I stood up this day with Palfour in the Hunter's Pog, which I am now fery sorry for, and he behaved himself as pretty as a shentlemans could ask it. And I have creat respects for Palfour," he added.

"I thank you for your honest expressions," said I.

Whereupon Duncansby made his bow to the company, and left the chamber, as we had agreed upon before.

"What have I to do with this?" says Prestongrange.

"I will tell your lordship in two words," said I. "I have brought this gentleman, a King's officer, to do me so much justice. Now I think my character is covered, and until a certain date, which your lordship can very well supply, it will be quite in vain to despatch against me any more officers. I will not consent to fight my way through the garrison of the castle."

The veins swelled on Prestongrange's brow, and he regarded me with fury.

"I think the devil uncoupled this dog of a lad between my legs!" he cried; and then, turning fiercely on his neighbour, "This is some of your work, Simon," he said. "I spy your hand in the business, and, let me tell you, I resent it. It is disloyal, when we are agreed upon one expedient, to follow another in the dark. You are disloyal to me. What! you let me send this lad to the place with my very daughters! And because I let drop a word to you..... Fy, sir, keep your dishonours to yourself!"

Simon was deadly pale. "I will be a kick-ball between you and the Duke no longer," he exclaimed. "Either come to an agreement, or come to a differ, and have it out among yourselves. But I will no longer fetch and carry, and get your contrary instructions, and be blamed by both. For if I were to tell you what I think of all your Hanover business it would make your head sing."

But Sheriff Erskine had preserved his temper, and now intervened smoothly. "And in the meantime," says he, "I think we should tell Mr. Balfour that his character for valour is quite established. He may sleep in peace. Until the date he was so good as to refer to it shall be put to the proof no more."

His coolness brought the others to their prudence; and they made haste, with a somewhat distracted civility, to pack me from the house.

220

CHAPTER IX—THE HEATHER ON FIRE

When I left Prestongrange that afternoon I was for the first time angry. The Advocate had made a mock of me. He had pretended my testimony was to be received and myself respected; and in that very hour, not only was Simon practising against my life by the hands of the Highland soldier, but (as appeared from his own language) Prestongrange himself had some design in operation. I counted my enemies; Prestongrange with all the King's authority behind him; and the Duke with the power of the West Highlands; and the Lovat interest by their side to help them with so great a force in the north, and the whole clan of old Jacobite spies and traffickers. And when I remembered James More, and the red head of Neil the son of Duncan, I thought there was perhaps a fourth in the confederacy, and what remained of Rob Roy's old desperate sept of caterans would be banded against me with the others. One thing was requisite—some strong friend or wise adviser. The country must be full of such, both able and eager to support me, or Lovat and the Duke and Prestongrange had not been nosing for expedients; and it made me rage to think that I might brush against my champions in the street and be no wiser.

And just then (like an answer) a gentleman brushed against me going by, gave me a meaning look, and turned into a close. I knew him with the tail of my eye—it was Stewart the Writer; and, blessing my good fortune, turned in to follow him. As soon as I had entered the close I saw him standing in the mouth of a stair, where he made me a signal and immediately vanished. Seven storeys up, there he was again in a house door, the which he looked behind us after we had entered. The house was quite dismantled, with not a stick of furniture; indeed, it was one of which Stewart had the letting in his hands.

"We'll have to sit upon the floor," said he; "but we're safe here for the time being, and I've been wearying to see ye, Mr. Balfour."

"How's it with Alan?" I asked.

"Brawly," said he. "Andie picks him up at Gillane sands to-morrow,

Wednesday. He was keen to say good-bye to ye, but the way that things were going, I was feared the pair of ye was maybe best apart. And that brings me to the essential: how does your business speed?"

"Why," said I, "I was told only this morning that my testimony was accepted, and I was to travel to Inverary with the Advocate, no less."

"Hout awa!" cried Stewart. "I'll never believe that."

"I have maybe a suspicion of my own," says I, "but I would like fine to hear your reasons."

"Well, I tell ye fairly, I'm horn-mad," cries Stewart. "If my one hand could pull their Government down I would pluck it like a rotten apple. I'm doer for Appin and for James of the Glens; and, of course, it's my duty to defend my kinsman for his life. Hear how it goes with me, and I'll leave the judgment of it to yourself. The first thing they have to do is to get rid of Alan. They cannae bring in James as art and part until they've brought in Alan first as principal; that's sound law: they could never put the cart before the horse."

"And how are they to bring in Alan till they can catch him?" says I.

"Ah, but there is a way to evite that arrestment," said he. "Sound law, too. It would be a bonny thing if, by the escape of one ill-doer another was to go scatheless, and the remeid is to summon the principal and put him to outlawry for the non-compearance. Now there's four places where a person can be summoned: at his dwelling-house; at a place where he has resided forty days; at the head burgh of the shire where he ordinarily resorts; or lastly (if there be ground to think him forth of Scotland) at the cross of Edinburgh, and the pier and shore of Leith, for sixty days. The purpose of which last provision is evident upon its face: being that outgoing ships may have time to carry news of the transaction, and the summonsing be something other than a form. Now take the case of Alan. He has no dwelling-house that ever I could hear of; I would be obliged if anyone would show me where he has lived forty days together since the '45; there is no shire where he resorts whether ordinarily or extraordinarily; if he has a domicile at all, which I misdoubt, it must be with his regiment in France; and if he is not yet forth of Scotland (as we happen to know and they happen to guess) it must be evident to the most dull it's what he's aiming for. Where, then, and what way should he be summoned? I ask it at yourself, a layman."

"You have given the very words," said I. "Here at the cross, and at the pier and shore of Leith, for sixty days."

"Ye're a sounder Scots lawyer than Prestongrange, then!" cries the Writer. "He has had Alan summoned once; that was on the twenty-fifth, the day that we first met. Once, and done with it. And where? Where, but at the cross of Inverary, the head burgh of the Campbells? A word in your ear, Mr. Balfour—they're not seeking Alan."

"What do you mean?" I cried. "Not seeking him?"

"By the best that I can make of it," said he. "Not wanting to find him, in my poor thought. They think perhaps he might set up a fair defence, upon the back of which James, the man they're really after, might climb out. This is not a case, ye see, it's a conspiracy."

"Yet I can tell you Prestongrange asked after Alan keenly," said I; "though, when I come to think of it, he was something of the easiest put by."

"See that!" says he. "But there! I may be right or wrong, that's guesswork at the best, and let me get to my facts again. It comes to my ears that James and the witnesses—the witnesses, Mr. Balfour!—lay in close dungeons, and shackled forbye, in the military prison at Fort William; none allowed in to them, nor they to write. The witnesses, Mr. Balfour; heard ye ever the match of that? I assure ye, no old, crooked Stewart of the gang ever out-faced the law more impudently. It's clean in the two eyes of the Act of Parliament of 1700, anent wrongous imprisonment. No sooner did I get the news than I petitioned the Lord Justice Clerk. I have his word to-day. There's law for ye! here's justice!"

He put a paper in my hand, that same mealy-mouthed, false-faced paper that was printed since in the pamphlet "by a bystander," for behoof (as the title says) of James's "poor widow and five children."

"See," said Stewart, "he couldn't dare to refuse me access to my client,

223

so he recommends the commanding officer to let me in. Recommends!—the Lord Justice Clerk of Scotland recommends. Is not the purpose of such language plain? They hope the officer may be so dull, or so very much the reverse, as to refuse the recommendation. I would have to make the journey back again betwixt here and Fort William. Then would follow a fresh delay till I got fresh authority, and they had disavowed the officer—military man, notoriously ignorant of the law, and that—I ken the cant of it. Then the journey a third time; and there we should be on the immediate heels of the trial before I had received my first instruction. Am I not right to call this a conspiracy?"

"It will bear that colour," said I.

"And I'll go on to prove it you outright," said he. "They have the right to hold James in prison, yet they cannot deny me to visit him. They have no right to hold the witnesses; but am I to get a sight of them, that should be as free as the Lord Justice Clerk himself! See—read: For the rest, refuses to give any orders to keepers of prisons who are not accused as having done anything contrary to the duties of their office. Anything contrary! Sirs! And the Act of seventeen hunner? Mr. Balfour, this makes my heart to burst; the heather is on fire inside my wame."

"And the plain English of that phrase," said I, "is that the witnesses are still to lie in prison and you are not to see them?"

"And I am not to see them until Inverary, when the court is set!" cries he, "and then to hear Prestongrange upon the anxious responsibilities of his office and the great facilities afforded the defence! But I'll begowk them there, Mr. David. I have a plan to waylay the witnesses upon the road, and see if I cannae get I a little harle of justice out of the military man notoriously ignorant of the law that shall command the party."

It was actually so—it was actually on the wayside near Tynedrum, and by the connivance of a soldier officer, that Mr. Stewart first saw the witnesses upon the case.

"There is nothing that would surprise me in this business," I remarked.

224

"I'll surprise you ere I'm done!" cries he. "Do ye see this?"—producing a print still wet from the press. "This is the libel: see, there's Prestongrange's name to the list of witnesses, and I find no word of any Balfour. But here is not the question. Who do ye think paid for the printing of this paper?"

"I suppose it would likely be King George," said I.

"But it happens it was me!" he cried. "Not but it was printed by and for themselves, for the Grants and the Erskines, and yon thief of the black midnight, Simon Fraser. But could I win to get a copy! No! I was to go blindfold to my defence; I was to hear the charges for the first time in court alongst the jury."

"Is not this against the law?" I asked.

"I cannot say so much," he replied. "It was a favour so natural and so constantly rendered (till this nonesuch business) that the law has never looked to it. And now admire the hand of Providence! A stranger is in Fleming's printing house, spies a proof on the floor, picks it up, and carries it to me. Of all things, it was just this libel. Whereupon I had it set again—printed at the expense of the defence: sumptibus moesti rei; heard ever man the like of it?—and here it is for anybody, the muckle secret out—all may see it now. But how do you think I would enjoy this, that has the life of my kinsman on my conscience?"

"Troth, I think you would enjoy it ill," said I.

"And now you see how it is," he concluded, "and why, when you tell me your evidence is to be let in, I laugh aloud in your face."

It was now my turn. I laid before him in brief Mr. Simon's threats and offers, and the whole incident of the bravo, with the subsequent scene at Prestongrange's. Of my first talk, according to promise, I said nothing, nor indeed was it necessary. All the time I was talking Stewart nodded his head like a mechanical figure; and no sooner had my voice ceased, than he opened his mouth and gave me his opinion in two words, dwelling strong on both of them.

"Disappear yourself," said he.

"I do not take you," said I.

"Then I'll carry you there," said he. "By my view of it you're to disappear whatever. O, that's outside debate. The Advocate, who is not without some spunks of a remainder decency, has wrung your life-safe out of Simon and the Duke. He has refused to put you on your trial, and refused to have you killed; and there is the clue to their ill words together, for Simon and the Duke can keep faith with neither friend nor enemy. Ye're not to be tried then, and ye're not to be murdered; but I'm in bitter error if ye're not to be kidnapped and carried away like the Lady Grange. Bet me what ye please—there was their expedient!"

"You make me think," said I, and told him of the whistle and the red-headed retainer, Neil.

"Wherever James More is there's one big rogue, never be deceived on that," said he. "His father was none so ill a man, though a kenning on the wrong side of the law, and no friend to my family, that I should waste my breath to be defending him! But as for James he's a brock and a blagyard. I like the appearance of this red-headed Neil as little as yourself. It looks uncanny: fiegh! it smells bad. It was old Lovat that managed the Lady Grange affair; if young Lovat is to handle yours, it'll be all in the family. What's James More in prison for? The same offence: abduction. His men have had practice in the business. He'll be to lend them to be Simon's instruments; and the next thing we'll be hearing, James will have made his peace, or else he'll have escaped; and you'll be in Benbecula or Applecross."

"Ye make a strong case," I admitted.

"And what I want," he resumed, "is that you should disappear yourself ere they can get their hands upon ye. Lie quiet until just before the trial, and spring upon them at the last of it when they'll be looking for you least. This is always supposing Mr. Balfour, that your evidence is worth so very great a measure of both risk and fash."

"I will tell you one thing," said I. "I saw the murderer and it was not Alan."

226

"Then, by God, my cousin's saved!" cried Stewart. "You have his life upon your tongue; and there's neither time, risk, nor money to be spared to bring you to the trial." He emptied his pockets on the floor. "Here is all that I have by me," he went on, "Take it, ye'll want it ere ye're through. Go straight down this close, there's a way out by there to the Lang Dykes, and by my will of it! see no more of Edinburgh till the clash is over."

"Where am I to go, then?" I inquired.

"And I wish that I could tell ye!" says he, "but all the places that I could send ye to, would be just the places they would seek. No, ye must fend for yourself, and God be your guiding! Five days before the trial, September the sixteen, get word to me at the King's Arms in Stirling; and if ye've managed for yourself as long as that, I'll see that ye reach Inverary."

"One thing more," said I. "Can I no see Alan?"

He seemed boggled. "Hech, I would rather you wouldnae," said he. "But I can never deny that Alan is extremely keen of it, and is to lie this night by Silvermills on purpose. If you're sure that you're not followed, Mr. Balfour—but make sure of that—lie in a good place and watch your road for a clear hour before ye risk it. It would be a dreadful business if both you and him was to miscarry!"

CHAPTER X—THE RED-HEADED MAN

It was about half-past three when I came forth on the Lang Dykes. Dean was where I wanted to go. Since Catriona dwelled there, and her kinsfolk the Glengyle Macgregors appeared almost certainly to be employed against me, it was just one of the few places I should have kept away from; and being a very young man, and beginning to be very much in love, I turned my face in that direction without pause. As a slave to my conscience and common sense, however, I took a measure of precaution. Coming over the crown of a bit of a rise in the road, I clapped down suddenly among the barley and lay waiting. After a while, a man went by that looked to be a Highlandman, but I had never seen him till that hour. Presently after came Neil of the red head. The next to go past was a miller's cart, and after that nothing but manifest country people. Here was enough to have turned the most foolhardy from his purpose, but my inclination ran too strong the other way. I argued it out that if Neil was on that road, it was the right road to find him in, leading direct to his chief's daughter; as for the other Highlandman, if I was to be startled off by every Highlandman I saw, I would scarce reach anywhere. And having quite satisfied myself with this disingenuous debate, I made the better speed of it, and came a little after four to Mrs. Drummond-Ogilvy's.

Both ladies were within the house; and upon my perceiving them together by the open door, I plucked off my hat and said, "Here was a lad come seeking saxpence," which I thought might please the dowager.

Catriona ran out to greet me heartily, and, to my surprise, the old lady seemed scarce less forward than herself. I learned long afterwards that she had despatched a horseman by daylight to Rankeillor at the Queensferry, whom she knew to be the doer for Shaws, and had then in her pocket a letter from that good friend of mine, presenting, in the most favourable view, my character and prospects. But had I read it I could scarce have seen more clear in her designs. Maybe I was countryfeed; at least, I was not so much so as she thought; and it was even to my homespun wits, that she was bent to hammer up a match between her cousin and a beardless boy that was something of a laird in Lothian.

"Saxpence had better take his broth with us, Catrine," says she. "Run and tell the lasses."

And for the little while we were alone was at a good deal of pains to flatter me; always cleverly, always with the appearance of a banter, still calling me Saxpence, but with such a turn that should rather uplift me in my own opinion. When Catriona returned, the design became if possible more obvious; and she showed off the girl's advantages like a horse-couper with a horse. My face flamed that she should think me so obtuse. Now I would fancy the girl was being innocently made a show of, and then I could have beaten the old carline wife with a cudgel; and now, that perhaps these two had set their heads together to entrap me, and at that I sat and gloomed betwixt them like the very image of ill-will. At last the matchmaker had a better device, which was to leave the pair of us alone. When my suspicions are anyway roused it is sometimes a little the wrong side of easy to allay them. But though I knew what breed she was of, and that was a breed of thieves, I could never look in Catriona's face and disbelieve her.

"I must not ask?" says she, eagerly, the same moment we were left alone.

"Ah, but to-day I can talk with a free conscience," I replied. "I am lightened of my pledge, and indeed (after what has come and gone since morning) I would not have renewed it were it asked."

"Tell me," she said. "My cousin will not be so long."

So I told her the tale of the lieutenant from the first step to the last of it, making it as mirthful as I could, and, indeed, there was matter of mirth in that absurdity.

"And I think you will be as little fitted for the rudas men as for the pretty ladies, after all!" says she, when I had done. "But what was your father that he could not learn you to draw the sword! It is most ungentle; I have not heard the match of that in anyone."

"It is most misconvenient at least," said I; "and I think my father (honest man!) must have been wool-gathering to learn me Latin in the place of it. But you see I do the best I can, and just stand up like Lot's wife and let them hammer at me."

"Do you know what makes me smile?" said she. "Well, it is this. I am made this way, that I should have been a man child. In my own thoughts it is so I am always; and I go on telling myself about this thing that is to befall and that. Then it comes to the place of the fighting, and it comes over me that I am only a girl at all events, and cannot hold a sword or give one good blow; and then I have to twist my story round about, so that the fighting is to stop, and yet me have the best of it, just like you and the lieutenant; and I am the boy that makes the fine speeches all through, like Mr. David Balfour."

"You are a bloodthirsty maid," said I.

"Well, I know it is good to sew and spin, and to make samplers," she said, "but if you were to do nothing else in the great world, I think you will say yourself it is a driech business; and it is not that I want to kill, I think. Did ever you kill anyone?"

"That I have, as it chances. Two, no less, and me still a lad that should be at the college," said I. "But yet, in the look-back, I take no shame for it."

"But how did you feel, then—after it?" she asked.

"'Deed, I sat down and grat like a bairn," said I.

"I know that, too," she cried. "I feel where these tears should come from. And at any rate, I would not wish to kill, only to be Catherine Douglas that put her arm through the staples of the bolt, where it was broken. That is my chief hero. Would you not love to die so—for your king?" she asked.

"Troth," said I, "my affection for my king, God bless the puggy face of him, is under more control; and I thought I saw death so near to me this day already, that I am rather taken up with the notion of living."

"Right," she said, "the right mind of a man! Only you must learn arms; I would not like to have a friend that cannot strike. But it will not have been with the sword that you killed these two?"

"Indeed, no," said I, "but with a pair of pistols. And a fortunate thing it was the men were so near-hand to me, for I am about as clever with the pistols as I am with the sword."

So then she drew from me the story of our battle in the brig, which I had omitted in my first account of my affairs.

"Yes," said she, "you are brave. And your friend, I admire and love him."

"Well, and I think anyone would!" said I. "He has his faults like other folk; but he is brave and staunch and kind, God bless him! That will be a strange day when I forget Alan." And the thought of him, and that it was within my choice to speak with him that night, had almost overcome me.

"And where will my head be gone that I have not told my news!" she cried, and spoke of a letter from her father, bearing that she might visit him to-morrow in the castle whither he was now transferred, and that his affairs were mending. "You do not like to hear it," said she. "Will you judge my father and not know him?"

"I am a thousand miles from judging," I replied. "And I give you my word I do rejoice to know your heart is lightened. If my face fell at all, as I suppose it must, you will allow this is rather an ill day for compositions, and the people in power extremely ill persons to be compounding with. I have Simon Fraser extremely heavy on my stomach still."

"Ah!" she cried, "you will not be evening these two; and you should bear in mind that Prestongrange and James More, my father, are of the one blood."

"I never heard tell of that," said I.

"It is rather singular how little you are acquainted with," said she. "One part may call themselves Grant, and one Macgregor, but they are still of the same clan. They are all the sons of Alpin, from whom, I think, our country has its name."

"What country is that?" I asked.

"My country and yours," said she.

"This is my day for discovering I think," said I, "for I always thought the name of it was Scotland."

"Scotland is the name of what you call Ireland," she replied. "But the old ancient true name of this place that we have our foot-soles on, and that our bones are made of, will be Alban. It was Alban they called it when our forefathers will be fighting for it against Rome and Alexander; and it is called so still in your own tongue that you forget."

"Troth," said I, "and that I never learned!" For I lacked heart to take her up about the Macedonian.

"But your fathers and mothers talked it, one generation with another," said she. "And it was sung about the cradles before you or me were ever dreamed of; and your name remembers it still. Ah, if you could talk that language you would find me another girl. The heart speaks in that tongue."

I had a meal with the two ladies, all very good, served in fine old plate, and the wine excellent, for it seems that Mrs. Ogilvy was rich. Our talk, too, was pleasant enough; but as soon as I saw the sun decline sharply and the shadows to run out long, I rose to take my leave. For my mind was now made up to say farewell to Alan; and it was needful I should see the trysting wood, and reconnoitre it, by daylight. Catriona came with me as far as to the garden gate.

"It is long till I see you now?" she asked.

"It is beyond my judging," I replied. "It will be long, it may be never."

"It may be so," said she. "And you are sorry?"

I bowed my head, looking upon her.

"So am I, at all events," said she. "I have seen you but a small time, but I put you very high. You are true, you are brave; in time I think you will be more of a man yet. I will be proud to hear of that. If you should speed worse, if it will come to fall as we are afraid—O well! think you have the one friend. Long after you are dead and me an old wife, I will be telling the bairns about David Balfour, and my tears running. I will be telling how we parted, and

232

what I said to you, and did to you. God go with you and guide you, prays your little friend: so I said—I will be telling them—and here is what I did."

She took up my hand and kissed it. This so surprised my spirits that I cried out like one hurt. The colour came strong in her face, and she looked at me and nodded.

"O yes, Mr. David," said she, "that is what I think of you. The head goes with the lips."

I could read in her face high spirit, and a chivalry like a brave child's; not anything besides. She kissed my hand, as she had kissed Prince Charlie's, with a higher passion than the common kind of clay has any sense of. Nothing before had taught me how deep I was her lover, nor how far I had yet to climb to make her think of me in such a character. Yet I could tell myself I had advanced some way, and that her heart had beat and her blood flowed at thoughts of me.

After that honour she had done me I could offer no more trivial civility. It was even hard for me to speak; a certain lifting in her voice had knocked directly at the door of my own tears.

"I praise God for your kindness, dear," said I. "Farewell, my little friend!" giving her that name which she had given to herself; with which I bowed and left her.

My way was down the glen of the Leith River, towards Stockbridge and Silvermills. A path led in the foot of it, the water bickered and sang in the midst; the sunbeams overhead struck out of the west among long shadows and (as the valley turned) made like a new scene and a new world of it at every corner. With Catriona behind and Alan before me, I was like one lifted up. The place besides, and the hour, and the talking of the water, infinitely pleased me; and I lingered in my steps and looked before and behind me as I went. This was the cause, under Providence, that I spied a little in my rear a red head among some bushes.

Anger sprang in my heart, and I turned straight about and walked at a stiff pace to where I came from. The path lay close by the bushes where I had remarked the head. The cover came to the wayside, and as I passed I was all strung up to meet and to resist an onfall. No such thing befell, I went by unmeddled with; and at that fear increased upon me. It was still day indeed, but the place exceeding solitary. If my haunters had let slip that fair occasion I could but judge they aimed at something more than David Balfour. The lives of Alan and James weighed upon my spirit with the weight of two grown bullocks.

Catriona was yet in the garden walking by herself.

"Catriona," said I, "you see me back again."

"With a changed face," said she.

"I carry two men's lives besides my own," said I. "It would be a sin and shame not to walk carefully. I was doubtful whether I did right to come here. I would like it ill, if it was by that means we were brought to harm."

"I could tell you one that would be liking it less, and will like little enough to hear you talking at this very same time," she cried. "What have I done, at all events?"

"O, you I you are not alone," I replied. "But since I went off I have been dogged again, and I can give you the name of him that follows me. It is Neil, son of Duncan, your man or your father's."

"To be sure you are mistaken there," she said, with a white face. "Neil is in Edinburgh on errands from my father."

"It is what I fear," said I, "the last of it. But for his being in Edinburgh I think I can show you another of that. For sure you have some signal, a signal of need, such as would bring him to your help, if he was anywhere within the reach of ears and legs?"

"Why, how will you know that?" says she.

"By means of a magical talisman God gave to me when I was born, and the name they call it by is Common-sense," said I. "Oblige me so far as make your signal, and I will show you the red head of Neil."

234

No doubt but I spoke bitter and sharp. My heart was bitter. I blamed myself and the girl and hated both of us: her for the vile crew that she was come of, myself for my wanton folly to have stuck my head in such a byke of wasps.

Catriona set her fingers to her lips and whistled once, with an exceeding clear, strong, mounting note, as full as a ploughman's. A while we stood silent; and I was about to ask her to repeat the same, when I heard the sound of some one bursting through the bushes below on the braeside. I pointed in that direction with a smile, and presently Neil leaped into the garden. His eyes burned, and he had a black knife (as they call it on the Highland side) naked in his hand; but, seeing me beside his mistress, stood like a man struck.

"He has come to your call," said I; "judge how near he was to Edinburgh, or what was the nature of your father's errands. Ask himself. If I am to lose my life, or the lives of those that hang by me, through the means of your clan, let me go where I have to go with my eyes open."

She addressed him tremulously in the Gaelic. Remembering Alan's anxious civility in that particular, I could have laughed out loud for bitterness; here, sure, in the midst of these suspicions, was the hour she should have stuck by English.

Twice or thrice they spoke together, and I could make out that Neil (for all his obsequiousness) was an angry man.

Then she turned to me. "He swears it is not," she said.

"Catriona," said I, "do you believe the man yourself?"

She made a gesture like wringing the hands.

"How will I can know?" she cried.

"But I must find some means to know," said I. "I cannot continue to go dovering round in the black night with two men's lives at my girdle! Catriona, try to put yourself in my place, as I vow to God I try hard to put myself in yours. This is no kind of talk that should ever have fallen between me and you; no kind of talk; my heart is sick with it. See, keep him here till

235

two of the morning, and I care not. Try him with that."

They spoke together once more in the Gaelic.

"He says he has James More my father's errand," said she. She was whiter than ever, and her voice faltered as she said it.

"It is pretty plain now," said I, "and may God forgive the wicked!"

She said never anything to that, but continued gazing at me with the same white face.

"This is a fine business," said I again. "Am I to fall, then, and those two along with me?"

"O, what am I to do?" she cried. "Could I go against my father's orders, him in prison, in the danger of his life!"

"But perhaps we go too fast," said I. "This may be a lie too. He may have no right orders; all may be contrived by Simon, and your father knowing nothing."

She burst out weeping between the pair of us; and my heart smote me hard, for I thought this girl was in a dreadful situation.

"Here," said I, "keep him but the one hour; and I'll chance it, and may God bless you."

She put out her hand to me, "I will he needing one good word," she sobbed.

"The full hour, then?" said I, keeping her hand in mine. "Three lives of it, my lass!"

"The full hour!" she said, and cried aloud on her Redeemer to forgive her.

I thought it no fit place for me, and fled.

236

CHAPTER XI—THE WOOD BY SILVERMILLS

I lost no time, but down through the valley and by Stockbridge and Silvermills as hard as I could stave. It was Alan's tryst to be every night between twelve and two "in a bit scrog of wood by east of Silvermills and by south the south mill-lade." This I found easy enough, where it grew on a steep brae, with the mill-lade flowing swift and deep along the foot of it; and here I began to walk slower and to reflect more reasonably on my employment. I saw I had made but a fool's bargain with Catriona. It was not to be supposed that Neil was sent alone upon his errand, but perhaps he was the only man belonging to James More; in which case I should have done all I could to hang Catriona's father, and nothing the least material to help myself. To tell the truth, I fancied neither one of these ideas. Suppose by holding back Neil, the girl should have helped to hang her father, I thought she would never forgive herself this side of time. And suppose there were others pursuing me that moment, what kind of a gift was I come bringing to Alan? and how would I like that?

I was up with the west end of that wood when these two considerations struck me like a cudgel. My feet stopped of themselves and my heart along with them. "What wild game is this that I have been playing?" thought I; and turned instantly upon my heels to go elsewhere.

This brought my face to Silvermills; the path came past the village with a crook, but all plainly visible; and, Highland or Lowland, there was nobody stirring. Here was my advantage, here was just such a conjuncture as Stewart had counselled me to profit by, and I ran by the side of the mill-lade, fetched about beyond the east corner of the wood, threaded through the midst of it, and returned to the west selvage, whence I could again command the path, and yet be myself unseen. Again it was all empty, and my heart began to rise.

For more than an hour I sat close in the border of the trees, and no hare or eagle could have kept a more particular watch. When that hour began the sun was already set, but the sky still all golden and the daylight clear; before the hour was done it had fallen to be half mirk, the images and distances of things were mingled, and observation began to be difficult. All that time not a foot of man had come east from Silvermills, and the few that had gone west were honest countryfolk and their wives upon the road to bed. If I were tracked by the most cunning spies in Europe, I judged it was beyond the course of nature they could have any jealousy of where I was: and going a little further home into the wood I lay down to wait for Alan.

The strain of my attention had been great, for I had watched not the path only, but every bush and field within my vision. That was now at an end. The moon, which was in her first quarter, glinted a little in the wood; all round there was a stillness of the country; and as I lay there on my back, the next three or four hours, I had a fine occasion to review my conduct.

Two things became plain to me first: that I had no right to go that day to Dean, and (having gone there) had now no right to be lying where I was. This (where Alan was to come) was just the one wood in all broad Scotland that was, by every proper feeling, closed against me; I admitted that, and yet stayed on, wondering at myself. I thought of the measure with which I had meted to Catriona that same night; how I had prated of the two lives I carried, and had thus forced her to enjeopardy her father's; and how I was here exposing them again, it seemed in wantonness. A good conscience is eight parts of courage. No sooner had I lost conceit of my behaviour, than I seemed to stand disarmed amidst a throng of terrors. Of a sudden I sat up. How if I went now to Prestongrange, caught him (as I still easily might) before he slept, and made a full submission? Who could blame me? Not Stewart the Writer; I had but to say that I was followed, despaired of getting clear, and so gave in. Not Catriona: here, too, I had my answer ready; that I could not bear she should expose her father. So, in a moment, I could lay all these troubles by, which were after all and truly none of mine; swim clear of the Appin Murder; get forth out of hand-stroke of all the Stewarts and Campbells, all the Whigs and Tories, in the land; and live henceforth to my own mind, and be able to enjoy and to improve my fortunes, and devote some hours of my youth to courting Catriona, which would be surely a more suitable occupation than to hide and run and be followed like a hunted thief,

238

and begin over again the dreadful miseries of my escape with Alan.

At first I thought no shame of this capitulation; I was only amazed I had not thought upon the thing and done it earlier; and began to inquire into the causes of the change. These I traced to my lowness of spirits, that back to my late recklessness, and that again to the common, old, public, disconsidered sin of self-indulgence. Instantly the text came in my head, "How can Satan cast out Satan?" What? (I thought) I had, by self-indulgence; and the following of pleasant paths, and the lure of a young maid, cast myself wholly out of conceit with my own character, and jeopardised the lives of James and Alan? And I was to seek the way out by the same road as I had entered in? No; the hurt that had been caused by self-indulgence must be cured by self-denial; the flesh I had pampered must be crucified. I looked about me for that course which I least liked to follow: this was to leave the wood without waiting to see Alan, and go forth again alone, in the dark and in the midst of my perplexed and dangerous fortunes.

I have been the more careful to narrate this passage of my reflections, because I think it is of some utility, and may serve as an example to young men. But there is reason (they say) in planting kale, and even in ethic and religion, room for common sense. It was already close on Alan's hour, and the moon was down. If I left (as I could not very decently whistle to my spies to follow me) they might miss me in the dark and tack themselves to Alan by mistake. If I stayed, I could at the least of it set my friend upon his guard which might prove his mere salvation. I had adventured other peoples' safety in a course of self-indulgence; to have endangered them again, and now on a mere design of penance, would have been scarce rational. Accordingly, I had scarce risen from my place ere I sat down again, but already in a different frame of spirits, and equally marvelling at my past weakness and rejoicing in my present composure.

Presently after came a crackling in the thicket. Putting my mouth near down to the ground, I whistled a note or two, of Alan's air; an answer came in the like guarded tone, and soon we had knocked together in the dark.

"Is this you at last, Davie?" he whispered.

"Just myself," said I.

"God, man, but I've been wearying to see ye!" says he. "I've had the longest kind of a time. A' day, I've had my dwelling into the inside of a stack of hay, where I couldnae see the nebs of my ten fingers; and then two hours of it waiting here for you, and you never coming! Dod, and ye're none too soon the way it is, with me to sail the morn! The morn? what am I saying?—the day, I mean."

"Ay, Alan, man, the day, sure enough," said I. "It's past twelve now, surely, and ye sail the day. This'll be a long road you have before you."

"We'll have a long crack of it first," said he.

"Well, indeed, and I have a good deal it will be telling you to hear," said I.

And I told him what behooved, making rather a jumble of it, but clear enough when done. He heard me out with very few questions, laughing here and there like a man delighted: and the sound of his laughing (above all there, in the dark, where neither one of us could see the other) was extraordinary friendly to my heart.

"Ay, Davie, ye're a queer character," says he, when I had done: "a queer bitch after a', and I have no mind of meeting with the like of ye. As for your story, Prestongrange is a Whig like yoursel', so I'll say the less of him; and, dod! I believe he was the best friend ye had, if ye could only trust him. But Simon Fraser and James More are my ain kind of cattle, and I'll give them the name that they deserve. The muckle black deil was father to the Frasers, a'body kens that; and as for the Gregara, I never could abye the reek of them since I could stotter on two feet. I bloodied the nose of one, I mind, when I was still so wambly on my legs that I cowped upon the top of him. A proud man was my father that day, God rest him! and I think he had the cause. I'll never can deny but what Robin was something of a piper," he added; "but as for James More, the deil guide him for me!"

"One thing we have to consider," said I. "Was Charles Stewart right or wrong? Is it only me they're after, or the pair of us?"

240

"And what's your ain opinion, you that's a man of so much experience?" said he.

"It passes me," said I.

"And me too," says Alan. "Do ye think this lass would keep her word to ye?" he asked.

"I do that," said I.

"Well, there's nae telling," said he. "And anyway, that's over and done: he'll be joined to the rest of them lang syne."

"How many would ye think there would be of them?" I asked.

"That depends," said Alan. "If it was only you, they would likely send two-three lively, brisk young birkies, and if they thought that I was to appear in the employ, I daresay ten or twelve," said he.

It was no use, I gave a little crack of laughter.

"And I think your own two eyes will have seen me drive that number, or the double of it, nearer hand!" cries he.

"It matters the less," said I, "because I am well rid of them for this time."

"Nae doubt that's your opinion," said he; "but I wouldnae be the least surprised if they were hunkering this wood. Ye see, David man; they'll be Hieland folk. There'll be some Frasers, I'm thinking, and some of the Gregara; and I would never deny but what the both of them, and the Gregara in especial, were clever experienced persons. A man kens little till he's driven a spreagh of neat cattle (say) ten miles through a throng lowland country and the black soldiers maybe at his tail. It's there that I learned a great part of my penetration. And ye need nae tell me: it's better than war; which is the next best, however, though generally rather a bauchle of a business. Now the Gregara have had grand practice."

"No doubt that's a branch of education that was left out with me," said I.

"And I can see the marks of it upon ye constantly," said Alan. "But that's

241

the strange thing about you folk of the college learning: ye're ignorat, and ye cannae see 't. Wae's me for my Greek and Hebrew; but, man, I ken that I dinnae ken them—there's the differ of it. Now, here's you. Ye lie on your wame a bittie in the bield of this wood, and ye tell me that ye've cuist off these Frasers and Macgregors. Why? Because I couldnae see them, says you. Ye blockhead, that's their livelihood."

"Take the worst of it," said I, "and what are we to do?"

"I am thinking of that same," said he. "We might twine. It wouldnae be greatly to my taste; and forbye that, I see reasons against it. First, it's now unco dark, and it's just humanly possible we might give them the clean slip. If we keep together, we make but the ae line of it; if we gang separate, we make twae of them: the more likelihood to stave in upon some of these gentry of yours. And then, second, if they keep the track of us, it may come to a fecht for it yet, Davie; and then, I'll confess I would be blythe to have you at my oxter, and I think you would be none the worse of having me at yours. So, by my way of it, we should creep out of this wood no further gone than just the inside of next minute, and hold away east for Gillane, where I'm to find my ship. It'll be like old days while it lasts, Davie; and (come the time) we'll have to think what you should be doing. I'm wae to leave ye here, wanting me."

"Have with ye, then!" says I. "Do ye gang back where you were stopping?"

"Deil a fear!" said Alan. "They were good folks to me, but I think they would be a good deal disappointed if they saw my bonny face again. For (the way times go) I am nae just what ye could call a Walcome Guest. Which makes me the keener for your company, Mr. David Balfour of the Shaws, and set ye up! For, leave aside twa cracks here in the wood with Charlie Stewart, I have scarce said black or white since the day we parted at Corstorphine."

With which he rose from his place, and we began to move quietly eastward through the wood.

CHAPTER XII—ON THE MARCH AGAIN WITH ALAN

It was likely between one and two; the moon (as I have said) was down; a strongish wind, carrying a heavy wrack of cloud, had set in suddenly from the west; and we began our movement in as black a night as ever a fugitive or a murderer wanted. The whiteness of the path guided us into the sleeping town of Broughton, thence through Picardy, and beside my old acquaintance the gibbet of the two thieves. A little beyond we made a useful beacon, which was a light in an upper window of Lochend. Steering by this, but a good deal at random, and with some trampling of the harvest, and stumbling and falling down upon the banks, we made our way across country, and won forth at last upon the linky, boggy muirland that they call the Figgate Whins. Here, under a bush of whin, we lay down the remainder of that night and slumbered.

The day called us about five. A beautiful morning it was, the high westerly wind still blowing strong, but the clouds all blown away to Europe. Alan was already sitting up and smiling to himself. It was my first sight of my friend since we were parted, and I looked upon him with enjoyment. He had still the same big great-coat on his back; but (what was new) he had now a pair of knitted boot-hose drawn above the knee. Doubtless these were intended for disguise; but, as the day promised to be warm, he made a most unseasonable figure.

"Well, Davie," said he, "is this no a bonny morning? Here is a day that looks the way that a day ought to. This is a great change of it from the belly of my haystack; and while you were there sottering and sleeping I have done a thing that maybe I do very seldom."

"And what was that?" said I.

"O, just said my prayers," said he.

"And where are my gentry, as ye call them?" I asked.

"Gude kens," says he; "and the short and the long of it is that we must take our chance of them. Up with your foot-soles, Davie! Forth, Fortune, once again of it! And a bonny walk we are like to have."

So we went east by the beach of the sea, towards where the salt-pans were smoking in by the Esk mouth. No doubt there was a by-ordinary bonny blink of morning sun on Arthur's Seat and the green Pentlands; and the pleasantness of the day appeared to set Alan among nettles.

"I feel like a gomeral," says he, "to be leaving Scotland on a day like this. It sticks in my head; I would maybe like it better to stay here and hing."

"Ay, but ye wouldnae, Alan," said I.

"No, but what France is a good place too," he explained; "but it's some way no the same. It's brawer I believe, but it's no Scotland. I like it fine when I'm there, man; yet I kind of weary for Scots divots and the Scots peat-reek."

"If that's all you have to complain of, Alan, it's no such great affair," said I.

"And it sets me ill to be complaining, whatever," said he, "and me but new out of yon deil's haystack."

"And so you were unco weary of your haystack?" I asked.

"Weary's nae word for it," said he. "I'm not just precisely a man that's easily cast down; but I do better with caller air and the lift above my head. I'm like the auld Black Douglas (wasnae't?) that likit better to hear the laverock sing than the mouse cheep. And yon place, ye see, Davie—whilk was a very suitable place to hide in, as I'm free to own—was pit mirk from dawn to gloaming. There were days (or nights, for how would I tell one from other?) that seemed to me as long as a long winter."

"How did you know the hour to bide your tryst?" I asked.

"The goodman brought me my meat and a drop brandy, and a candle-dowp to eat it by, about eleeven," said he. "So, when I had swallowed a bit, it would be time to be getting to the wood. There I lay and wearied for ye sore, Davie," says he, laying his hand on my shoulder "and guessed when the two hours would be about by—unless Charlie Stewart would come and tell me on his watch—and then back to the dooms haystack. Na, it was a driech employ, and praise the Lord that I have warstled through with it!"

"What did you do with yourself?" I asked.

"Faith," said he, "the best I could! Whiles I played at the knucklebones. I'm an extraordinar good hand at the knucklebones, but it's a poor piece of business playing with naebody to admire ye. And whiles I would make songs."

"What were they about?" says I.

"O, about the deer and the heather," says he, "and about the ancient old chiefs that are all by with it lang syne, and just about what songs are about in general. And then whiles I would make believe I had a set of pipes and I was playing. I played some grand springs, and I thought I played them awful bonny; I vow whiles that I could hear the squeal of them! But the great affair is that it's done with."

With that he carried me again to my adventures, which he heard all over again with more particularity, and extraordinary approval, swearing at intervals that I was "a queer character of a callant."

"So ye were frich'ened of Sim Fraser?" he asked once.

"In troth was I!" cried I.

"So would I have been, Davie," said he. "And that is indeed a driedful man. But it is only proper to give the deil his due: and I can tell you he is a most respectable person on the field of war."

"Is he so brave?" I asked.

"Brave!" said he. "He is as brave as my steel sword."

The story of my duel set him beside himself.

"To think of that!" he cried. "I showed ye the trick in Corrynakiegh too. And three times—three times disarmed! It's a disgrace upon my character that learned ye! Here, stand up, out with your airn; ye shall walk no step beyond this place upon the road till ye can do yoursel' and me mair credit."

"Alan," said I, "this is midsummer madness. Here is no time for fencing lessons."

"I cannae well say no to that," he admitted. "But three times, man! And you standing there like a straw bogle and rinning to fetch your ain sword like a doggie with a pocket-napkin! David, this man Duncansby must be something altogether by-ordinar! He maun be extraordinar skilly. If I had the time, I would gang straight back and try a turn at him mysel'. The man must be a provost."

"You silly fellow," said I, "you forget it was just me."

"Na," said he, "but three times!"

"When ye ken yourself that I am fair incompetent," I cried.

"Well, I never heard tell the equal of it," said he.

"I promise you the one thing, Alan," said I. "The next time that we forgather, I'll be better learned. You shall not continue to bear the disgrace of a friend that cannot strike."

"Ay, the next time!" says he. "And when will that be, I would like to ken?"

"Well, Alan, I have had some thoughts of that, too," said I; "and my plan is this. It's my opinion to be called an advocate."

"That's but a weary trade, Davie," says Alan, "and rather a blagyard one forby. Ye would be better in a king's coat than that."

"And no doubt that would be the way to have us meet," cried I. "But as you'll be in King Lewie's coat, and I'll be in King Geordie's, we'll have a dainty meeting of it."

"There's some sense in that," he admitted.

"An advocate, then, it'll have to be," I continued, "and I think it a more suitable trade for a gentleman that was three times disarmed. But the beauty of the thing is this: that one of the best colleges for that kind of learning—and the one where my kinsman, Pilrig, made his studies—is the college of Leyden in Holland. Now, what say you, Alan? Could not a cadet of Royal Ecossais get a furlough, slip over the marches, and call in upon a Leyden student?"

"Well, and I would think he could!" cried he. "Ye see, I stand well in with my colonel, Count Drummond-Melfort; and, what's mair to the purpose I have a cousin of mine lieutenant-colonel in a regiment of the Scots-Dutch. Naething could be mair proper than what I would get a leave to see Lieutenant-Colonel Stewart of Halkett's. And Lord Melfort, who is a very scienteefic kind of a man, and writes books like Cæsar, would be doubtless very pleased to have the advantage of my observes."

"Is Lord Meloort an author, then?" I asked, for much as Alan thought of soldiers, I thought more of the gentry that write books.

"The very same, Davie," said he. "One would think a colonel would have something better to attend to. But what can I say that make songs?"

"Well, then," said I, "it only remains you should give me an address to write you at in France; and as soon as I am got to Leyden I will send you mine."

"The best will be to write me in the care of my chieftain," said he, "Charles Stewart, of Ardsheil, Esquire, at the town of Melons, in the Isle of France. It might take long, or it might take short, but it would aye get to my hands at the last of it."

We had a haddock to our breakfast in Musselburgh, where it amused me vastly to hear Alan. His great-coat and boot-hose were extremely remarkable this warm morning, and perhaps some hint of an explanation had been wise; but Alan went into that matter like a business, or I should rather say, like a diversion. He engaged the goodwife of the house with some compliments upon the rizzoring of our haddocks; and the whole of the rest of our stay held her in talk about a cold he had taken on his stomach, gravely relating all manner of symptoms and sufferings, and hearing with a vast show of interest all the old wives' remedies she could supply him with in return.

We left Musselburgh before the first ninepenny coach was due from Edinburgh for (as Alan said) that was a rencounter we might very well avoid. The wind although still high, was very mild, the sun shone strong, and Alan began to suffer in proportion. From Prestonpans he had me aside to the field of Gladsmuir, where he exerted himself a great deal more than needful to describe the stages of the battle. Thence, at his old round pace, we travelled to Cockenzie. Though they were building herring-busses there at Mrs. Cadell's, it seemed a desert-like, back-going town, about half full of ruined houses; but the ale-house was clean, and Alan, who was now in a glowing heat, must indulge himself with a bottle of ale, and carry on to the new luckie with the old story of the cold upon his stomach, only now the symptoms were all different.

I sat listening; and it came in my mind that I had scarce ever heard him address three serious words to any woman, but he was always drolling and fleering and making a private mock of them, and yet brought to that business a remarkable degree of energy and interest. Something to this effect I remarked to him, when the good-wife (as chanced) was called away.

"What do ye want?" says he. "A man should aye put his best foot forrit with the womankind; he should aye give them a bit of a story to divert them, the poor lambs! It's what ye should learn to attend to, David; ye should get the principles, it's like a trade. Now, if this had been a young lassie, or onyways bonnie, she would never have heard tell of my stomach, Davie. But aince they're too old to be seeking joes, they a' set up to be apotecaries. Why? What do I ken? They'll be just the way God made them, I suppose. But I think a man would be a gomeral that didnae give his attention to the same."

And here, the luckie coming back, he turned from me as if with impatience to renew their former conversation. The lady had branched some while before from Alan's stomach to the case of a goodbrother of her own in Aberlady, whose last sickness and demise she was describing at extraordinary length. Sometimes it was merely dull, sometimes both dull and awful, for she talked with unction. The upshot was that I fell in a deep muse, looking forth

248

of the window on the road, and scarce marking what I saw. Presently had any been looking they might have seen me to start.

"We pit a fomentation to his feet," the good-wife was saying, "and a het stane to his wame, and we gied him hyssop and water of pennyroyal, and fine, clean balsam of sulphur for the hoast. . . "

"Sir," says I, cutting very quietly in, "there's a friend of mine gone by the house."

"Is that e'en sae?" replies Alan, as though it were a thing of small account. And then, "Ye were saying, mem?" says he; and the wearyful wife went on.

Presently, however, he paid her with a half-crown piece, and she must go forth after the change.

"Was it him with the red head?" asked Alan.

"Ye have it," said I.

"What did I tell you in the wood?" he cried. "And yet it's strange he should be here too! Was he his lane?"

"His lee-lane for what I could see," said I.

"Did he gang by?" he asked.

"Straight by," said I, "and looked neither to the right nor left."

"And that's queerer yet," said Alan. "It sticks in my mind, Davie, that we should be stirring. But where to?—deil hae't! This is like old days fairly," cries he.

"There is one big differ, though," said I, "that now we have money in our pockets."

"And another big differ, Mr. Balfour," says he, "that now we have dogs at our tail. They're on the scent; they're in full cry, David. It's a bad business and be damned to it." And he sat thinking hard with a look of his that I knew well.

"I'm saying, Luckie," says he, when the goodwife returned, "have ye a back road out of this change house?"

She told him there was and where it led to.

"Then, sir," says he to me, "I think that will be the shortest road for us. And here's good-bye to ye, my braw woman; and I'll no forget thon of the cinnamon water."

We went out by way of the woman's kale yard, and up a lane among fields. Alan looked sharply to all sides, and seeing we were in a little hollow place of the country, out of view of men, sat down.

"Now for a council of war, Davie," said he. "But first of all, a bit lesson to ye. Suppose that I had been like you, what would yon old wife have minded of the pair of us! Just that we had gone out by the back gate. And what does she mind now? A fine, canty, friendly, cracky man, that suffered with the stomach, poor body! and was real ta'en up about the goodbrother. O man, David, try and learn to have some kind of intelligence!"

"I'll try, Alan," said I.

"And now for him of the red head," says he; "was he gaun fast or slow?"

"Betwixt and between," said I.

"No kind of a hurry about the man?" he asked.

"Never a sign of it," said I.

"Nhm!" said Alan, "it looks queer. We saw nothing of them this morning on the Whins; he's passed us by, he doesnae seem to be looking, and yet here he is on our road! Dod, Davie, I begin to take a notion. I think it's no you they're seeking, I think it's me; and I think they ken fine where they're gaun."

"They ken?" I asked.

"I think Andie Scougal's sold me—him or his mate wha kent some part of the affair—or else Charlie's clerk callant, which would be a pity too," says Alan; "and if you askit me for just my inward private conviction, I think there'll be heads cracked on Gillane sands."

250

"Alan," I cried, "if you're at all right there'll be folk there and to spare. It'll be small service to crack heads."

"It would aye be a satisfaction though," says Alan. "But bide a bit; bide a bit; I'm thinking—and thanks to this bonny westland wind, I believe I've still a chance of it. It's this way, Davie. I'm no trysted with this man Scougal till the gloaming comes. But," says he, "if I can get a bit of a wind out of the west I'll be there long or that," he says, "and lie-to for ye behind the Isle of Fidra. Now if your gentry kens the place, they ken the time forbye. Do ye see me coming, Davie? Thanks to Johnnie Cope and other red-coat gomerals, I should ken this country like the back of my hand; and if ye're ready for another bit run with Alan Breck, we'll can cast back inshore, and come to the seaside again by Dirleton. If the ship's there, we'll try and get on board of her. If she's no there, I'll just have to get back to my weary haystack. But either way of it, I think we will leave your gentry whistling on their thumbs."

"I believe there's some chance in it," said I. "Have on with ye, Alan!"

CHAPTER XIII—GILLANE SANDS

I did not profit by Alan's pilotage as he had done by his marchings under General Cope; for I can scarce tell what way we went. It is my excuse that we travelled exceeding fast. Some part we ran, some trotted, and the rest walked at a vengeance of a pace. Twice, while we were at top speed, we ran against country-folk; but though we plumped into the first from round a corner, Alan was as ready as a loaded musket.

"Has ye seen my horse?" he gasped.

"Na, man, I haenae seen nae horse the day," replied the countryman.

And Alan spared the time to explain to him that we were travelling "ride and tie"; that our charger had escaped, and it was feared he had gone home to Linton. Not only that, but he expended some breath (of which he had not very much left) to curse his own misfortune and my stupidity which was said to be its cause.

"Them that cannae tell the truth," he observed to myself as we went on again, "should be aye mindful to leave an honest, handy lee behind them. If folk dinnae ken what ye're doing, Davie, they're terrible taken up with it; but if they think they ken, they care nae mair for it than what I do for pease porridge."

As we had first made inland, so our road came in the end to lie very near due north; the old Kirk of Aberlady for a landmark on the left; on the right, the top of the Berwick Law; and it was thus we struck the shore again, not far from Dirleton. From north Berwick west to Gillane Ness there runs a string of four small islets, Craiglieth, the Lamb, Fidra, and Eyebrough, notable by their diversity of size and shape. Fidra is the most particular, being a strange grey islet of two humps, made the more conspicuous by a piece of ruin; and I mind that (as we drew closer to it) by some door or window of these ruins the sea peeped through like a man's eye. Under the lee of Fidra there is a good anchorage in westerly winds, and there, from a far way off, we could see the

Thistle riding.

The shore in face of these islets is altogether waste. Here is no dwelling of man, and scarce any passage, or at most of vagabond children running at their play. Gillane is a small place on the far side of the Ness, the folk of Dirleton go to their business in the inland fields, and those of North Berwick straight to the sea-fishing from their haven; so that few parts of the coast are lonelier. But I mind, as we crawled upon our bellies into that multiplicity of heights and hollows, keeping a bright eye upon all sides, and our hearts hammering at our ribs, there was such a shining of the sun and the sea, such a stir of the wind in the bent grass, and such a bustle of down-popping rabbits and up-flying gulls, that the desert seemed to me, like a place alive. No doubt it was in all ways well chosen for a secret embarcation, if the secret had been kept; and even now that it was out, and the place watched, we were able to creep unperceived to the front of the sandhills, where they look down immediately on the beach and sea.

But here Alan came to a full stop.

"Davie," said he, "this is a kittle passage! As long as we lie here we're safe; but I'm nane sae muckle nearer to my ship or the coast of France. And as soon as we stand up and signal the brig, it's another matter. For where will your gentry be, think ye?"

"Maybe they're no come yet," said I. "And even if they are, there's one clear matter in our favour. They'll be all arranged to take us, that's true. But they'll have arranged for our coming from the east and here we are upon their west."

"Ay," says Alan, "I wish we were in some force, and this was a battle, we would have bonnily out-manœuvred them! But it isnae, Davit; and the way it is, is a wee thing less inspiring to Alan Breck. I swither, Davie."

"Time flies, Alan," said I.

"I ken that," said Alan. "I ken naething else, as the French folk say. But this is a dreidful case of heids or tails. O! if I could but ken where your gentry were!"

"Alan," said I, "this is no like you. It's got to be now or never."

"This is no me, quo' he,"

sang Alan, with a queer face betwixt shame and drollery.

"Neither you nor me, quo' he, neither you nor me.

Wow, na, Johnnie man! neither you nor me."

And then of a sudden he stood straight up where he was, and with a handkerchief flying in his right hand, marched down upon the beach. I stood up myself, but lingered behind him, scanning the sand-hills to the east. His appearance was at first unremarked: Scougal not expecting him so early, and my gentry watching on the other side. Then they awoke on board the Thistle, and it seemed they had all in readiness, for there was scarce a second's bustle on the deck before we saw a skiff put round her stern and begin to pull lively for the coast. Almost at the same moment of time, and perhaps half a mile away towards Gillane Ness, the figure of a man appeared for a blink upon a sandhill, waving with his arms; and though he was gone again in the same flash, the gulls in that part continued a little longer to fly wild.

Alan had not seen this, looking straight to seaward at the ship and skiff.

"It maun be as it will!" said he, when I had told him, "Weel may yon boatie row, or my craig'll have to thole a raxing."

That part of the beach was long and flat, and excellent walking when the tide was down; a little cressy burn flowed over it in one place to the sea; and the sandhills ran along the head of it like the rampart of a town. No eye of ours could spy what was passing behind there in the bents, no hurry of ours could mend the speed of the boat's coming: time stood still with us through that uncanny period of waiting.

"There is one thing I would like to ken," say Alan. "I would like to ken these gentry's orders. We're worth four hunner pound the pair of us: how if they took the guns to us, Davie! They would get a bonny shot from the top of that lang sandy bank."

"Morally impossible," said I. "The point is that they can have no guns.

This thing has been gone about too secret; pistols they may have, but never guns."

"I believe ye'll be in the right," says Alan. "For all which I am wearing a good deal for yon boat."

And he snapped his fingers and whistled to it like a dog.

It was now perhaps a third of the way in, and we ourselves already hard on the margin of the sea, so that the soft sand rose over my shoes. There was no more to do whatever but to wait, to look as much as we were able at the creeping nearer of the boat, and as little as we could manage at the long impenetrable front of the sandhills, over which the gulls twinkled and behind which our enemies were doubtless marshalling.

"This is a fine, bright, caller place to get shot in," says Alan suddenly; "and, man, I wish that I had your courage!"

"Alan!" I cried, "what kind of talk is this of it! You're just made of courage; it's the character of the man, as I could prove myself if there was nobody else."

"And you would be the more mistaken," said he. "What makes the differ with me is just my great penetration and knowledge of affairs. But for auld, cauld, dour, deadly courage, I am not fit to hold a candle to yourself. Look at us two here upon the sands. Here am I, fair hotching to be off; here's you (for all that I ken) in two minds of it whether you'll no stop. Do you think that I could do that, or would? No me! Firstly, because I havenae got the courage and wouldnae daur; and secondly, because I am a man of so much penetration and would see ye damned first."

"It's there ye're coming, is it?" I cried. "Ah, man Alan, you can wile your old wives, but you never can wile me."

Remembrance of my temptation in the wood made me strong as iron.

"I have a tryst to keep," I continued. "I am trysted with your cousin Charlie; I have passed my word."

"Braw trysts that you'll can keep," said Alan. "Ye'll just mistryst aince and for a' with the gentry in the bents. And what for?" he went on with an extreme threatening gravity. "Just tell me that, my mannie! Are ye to be speerited away like Lady Grange? Are they to drive a dirk in your inside and bury ye in the bents? Or is it to be the other way, and are they to bring ye in with James? Are they folk to be trustit? Would ye stick your head in the mouth of Sim Fraser and the ither Whigs?" he added with extraordinary bitterness.

"Alan," cried I, "they're all rogues and liars, and I'm with ye there. The more reason there should be one decent man in such a land of thieves! My word is passed, and I'll stick to it. I said long syne to your kinswoman that I would stumble at no risk. Do ye mind of that?—the night Red Colin fell, it was. No more I will, then. Here I stop. Prestongrange promised me my life: if he's to be mansworn, here I'll have to die."

"Aweel aweel," said Alan.

All this time we had seen or heard no more of our pursuers. In truth we had caught them unawares; their whole party (as I was to learn afterwards) had not yet reached the scene; what there was of them was spread among the bents towards Gillane. It was quite an affair to call them in and bring them over, and the boat was making speed. They were besides but cowardly fellows: a mere leash of Highland cattle-thieves, of several clans, no gentleman there to be the captain and the more they looked at Alan and me upon the beach, the less (I must suppose) they liked the look of us.

Whoever had betrayed Alan it was not the captain: he was in the skiff himself, steering and stirring up his oarsmen, like a man with his heart in his employ. Already he was near in, and the boat securing—already Alan's face had flamed crimson with the excitement of his deliverance, when our friends in the bents, either in their despair to see their prey escape them or with some hope of scaring Andie, raised suddenly a shrill cry of several voices.

This sound, arising from what appeared to be a quite deserted coast, was really very daunting, and the men in the boat held water instantly.

"What's this of it?" sings out the captain, for he was come within an easy hail.

"Freens o'mine," says Alan, and began immediately to wade forth in the shallow water towards the boat. "Davie," he said, pausing, "Davie, are ye no coming? I am swier to leave ye."

"Not a hair of me," said I.

"He stood part of a second where he was to his knees in the salt water, hesitating.

"He that will to Cupar, maun to Cupar," said he, and swashing in deeper than his waist, was hauled into the skiff, which was immediately directed for the ship.

I stood where he had left me, with my hands behind my back; Alan sat with his head turned watching me; and the boat drew smoothly away. Of a sudden I came the nearest hand to shedding tears, and seemed to myself the most deserted solitary lad in Scotland. With that I turned my back upon the sea and faced the sandhills. There was no sight or sound of man; the sun shone on the wet sand and the dry, the wind blew in the bents, the gulls made a dreary piping. As I passed higher up the beach, the sand-lice were hopping nimbly about the stranded tangles. The devil any other sight or sound in that unchancy place. And yet I knew there were folk there, observing me, upon some secret purpose. They were no soldiers, or they would have fallen on and taken us ere now; doubtless they were some common rogues hired for my undoing, perhaps to kidnap, perhaps to murder me outright. From the position of those engaged, the first was the more likely; from what I knew of their character and ardency in this business, I thought the second very possible; and the blood ran cold about my heart.

I had a mad idea to loosen my sword in the scabbard; for though I was very unfit to stand up like a gentleman blade to blade, I thought I could do some scathe in a random combat. But I perceived in time the folly of resistance. This was no doubt the joint "expedient" on which Prestongrange and Fraser were agreed. The first, I was very sure, had done something to secure my life; the second was pretty likely to have slipped in some contrary hints into the ears of Neil and his companions; and if I were to show bare steel I might play straight into the hands of my worst enemy and seal my own doom.

These thoughts brought me to the head of the beach. I cast a look behind, the boat was nearing the brig, and Alan flew his handkerchief for a farewell, which I replied to with the waving of my hand. But Alan himself was shrunk to a small thing in my view, alongside of this pass that lay in front of me. I set my hat hard on my head, clenched my teeth, and went right before me up the face of the sand-wreath. It made a hard climb, being steep, and the sand like water underfoot. But I caught hold at last by the long bent-grass on the brae-top, and pulled myself to a good footing. The same moment men stirred and stood up here and there, six or seven of them, ragged-like knaves, each with a dagger in his hand. The fair truth is, I shut my eyes and prayed. When I opened them again, the rogues were crept the least thing nearer without speech or hurry. Every eye was upon mine, which struck me with a strange sensation of their brightness, and of the fear with which they continued to approach me. I held out my hands empty; whereupon one asked, with a strong Highland brogue, if I surrendered.

"Under protest," said I, "if ye ken what that means, which I misdoubt."

At that word, they came all in upon me like a flight of birds upon a carrion, seized me, took my sword, and all the money from my pockets, bound me hand and foot with some strong line, and cast me on a tussock of bent. There they sat about their captive in a part of a circle and gazed upon him silently like something dangerous, perhaps a lion or a tiger on the spring. Presently this attention was relaxed. They drew nearer together, fell to speech in the Gaelic, and very cynically divided my property before my eyes. It was my diversion in this time that I could watch from my place the progress of my friend's escape. I saw the boat come to the brig and be hoisted in, the sails fill, and the ship pass out seaward behind the isles and by North Berwick.

In the course of two hours or so, more and more ragged Highlandmen kept collecting. Neil among the first, until the party must have numbered near a score. With each new arrival there was a fresh bout of talk, that sounded like complaints and explanations; but I observed one thing, none of those who came late had any share in the division of my spoils. The last discussion was very violent and eager, so that once I thought they would have quarrelled; on the heels of which their company parted, the bulk of them returning westward in a troop, and only three, Neil and two others, remaining sentries on the prisoner.

"I could name one who would be very ill pleased with your day's work, Neil Duncanson," said I, when the rest had moved away.

He assured me in answer I should be tenderly used, for he knew he was "acquent wi' the leddy."

This was all our talk, nor did any other son of man appear upon that portion of the coast until the sun had gone down among the Highland mountains, and the gloaming was beginning to grow dark. At which hour I was aware of a long, lean, bony-like Lothian man of a very swarthy countenance, that came towards us among the bents on a farm horse.

"Lads," cried he, "has ye a paper like this?" and held up one in his hand. Neil produced a second, which the newcomer studied through a pair of horn spectacles, and saying all was right and we were the folk he was seeking, immediately dismounted. I was then set in his place, my feet tied under the horse's belly, and we set forth under the guidance of the Lowlander. His path must have been very well chosen, for we met but one pair—a pair of lovers—the whole way, and these, perhaps taking us to be free-traders, fled on our approach. We were at one time close at the foot of Berwick Law on the south side; at another, as we passed over some open hills, I spied the lights of a clachan and the old tower of a church among some trees not far off, but too far to cry for help, if I had dreamed of it. At last we came again within sound of the sea. There was moonlight, though not much; and by this I could see the three huge towers and broken battlements of Tantallon, that old chief place of the Red Douglases. The horse was picketed in the bottom of the ditch to graze, and I was led within, and forth into the court, and thence into the tumble-down stone hall. Here my conductors built a brisk fire in the midst of the pavement, for there was a chill in the night. My hands were loosed,

I was set by the wall in the inner end, and (the Lowlander having produced provisions) I was given oatmeal bread and a pitcher of French brandy. This done, I was left once more alone with my three Highlandmen. They sat close by the fire drinking and talking; the wind blew in by the breaches, cast about the smoke and flames, and sang in the tops of the towers; I could hear the sea under the cliffs, and, my mind being reassured as to my life, and my body and spirits wearied with the day's employment, I turned upon one side and slumbered.

I had no means of guessing at what hour I was wakened, only the moon was down and the fire was low. My feet were now loosed, and I was carried through the ruins and down the cliff-side by a precipitous path to where I found a fisher's boat in a haven of the rocks. This I was had on board of, and we began to put forth from the shore in a fine starlight.

CHAPTER XIV—THE BASS

I had no thought where they were taking me; only looked here and there for the appearance of a ship; and there ran the while in my head a word of Ransome's—the twenty-pounders. If I were to be exposed a second time to that same former danger of the plantations, I judged it must turn ill with me; there was no second Alan; and no second shipwreck and spare yard to be expected now; and I saw myself hoe tobacco under the whip's lash. The thought chilled me; the air was sharp upon the water, the stretchers of the boat drenched with a cold dew: and I shivered in my place beside the steersman. This was the dark man whom I have called hitherto the Lowlander; his name was Dale, ordinarily called Black Andie. Feeling the thrill of my shiver, he very kindly handed me a rough jacket full of fish-scales, with which I was glad to cover myself.

"I thank you for this kindness," said I, "and will make so free as to repay it with a warning. You take a high responsibility in this affair. You are not like these ignorant, barbarous Highlanders, but know what the law is and the risks of those that break it."

"I am no just exactly what ye would ca' an extremist for the law," says he, "at the best of times; but in this business I act with a good warranty."

"What are you going to do with me?" I asked.

"Nae harm," said he, "nae harm ava'. Ye'll have strong freens, I'm thinking. Ye'll be richt eneuch yet."

There began to fall a greyness on the face of the sea; little dabs of pink and red, like coals of slow fire, came in the east; and at the same time the geese awakened, and began crying about the top of the Bass. It is just the one crag of rock, as everybody knows, but great enough to carve a city from. The sea was extremely little, but there went a hollow plowter round the base of it. With the growing of the dawn I could see it clearer and clearer; the straight crags painted with sea-birds' droppings like a morning frost, the sloping top of it green with grass, the clan of white geese that cried about the sides, and the black, broken buildings of the prison sitting close on the sea's edge.

At the sight the truth came in upon me in a clap.

"It's there you're taking me!" I cried.

"Just to the Bass, mannie," said he: "Whaur the auld saints were afore ye, and I misdoubt if ye have come so fairly by your preeson."

"But none dwells there now," I cried; "the place is long a ruin."

"It'll be the mair pleisand a change for the solan geese, then," quoth Andie dryly.

The day coming slowly brighter I observed on the bilge, among the big stones with which fisherfolk ballast their boats, several kegs and baskets, and a provision of fuel. All these were discharged upon the crag. Andie, myself, and my three Highlanders (I call them mine, although it was the other way about), landed along with them. The sun was not yet up when the boat moved away again, the noise of the oars on the thole-pins echoing from the cliffs, and left us in our singular reclusion:

Andie Dale was the Prefect (as I would jocularly call him) of the Bass, being at once the shepherd and the gamekeeper of that small and rich estate. He had to mind the dozen or so of sheep that fed and fattened on the grass of the sloping part of it, like beasts grazing the roof of a cathedral. He had charge besides of the solan geese that roosted in the crags; and from these an extraordinary income is derived. The young are dainty eating, as much as two shillings a-piece being a common price, and paid willingly by epicures; even the grown birds are valuable for their oil and feathers; and a part of the minister's stipend of North Berwick is paid to this day in solan geese, which makes it (in some folks' eyes) a parish to be coveted. To perform these several businesses, as well as to protect the geese from poachers, Andie had frequent occasion to sleep and pass days together on the crag; and we found the man at home there like a farmer in his steading. Bidding us all shoulder some of the packages, a matter in which I made haste to bear a hand, he led us in by a locked gate, which was the only admission to the island, and through the ruins of the fortress, to the governor's house. There we saw by the ashes in the chimney and a standing bed-place in one corner, that he made his usual occupation.

This bed he now offered me to use, saying he supposed I would set up to be gentry.

"My gentrice has nothing to do with where I lie," said I. "I bless God I have lain hard ere now, and can do the same again with thankfulness. While I am here, Mr. Andie, if that be your name, I will do my part and take my place beside the rest of you; and I ask you on the other hand to spare me your mockery, which I own I like ill."

He grumbled a little at this speech, but seemed upon reflection to approve it. Indeed, he was a long-headed, sensible man, and a good Whig and Presbyterian; read daily in a pocket Bible, and was both able and eager to converse seriously on religion, leaning more than a little towards the Cameronian extremes. His morals were of a more doubtful colour. I found he was deep in the free trade, and used the ruins of Tantallon for a magazine of smuggled merchandise. As for a gauger, I do not believe he valued the life of one at half-a-farthing. But that part of the coast of Lothian is to this day as wild a place, and the commons there as rough a crew, as any in Scotland.

One incident of my imprisonment is made memorable by a consequence it had long after. There was a warship at this time stationed in the Firth, the Seahorse, Captain Palliser. It chanced she was cruising in the month of September, plying between Fife and Lothian, and sounding for sunk dangers. Early one fine morning she was seen about two miles to east of us, where she lowered a boat, and seemed to examine the Wildfire Rocks and Satan's Bush, famous dangers of that coast. And presently after having got her boat again, she came before the wind and was headed directly for the Bass. This was very troublesome to Andie and the Highlanders; the whole business of my sequestration was designed for privacy, and here, with a navy captain perhaps blundering ashore, it looked to become public enough, if it were nothing worse. I was in a minority of one, I am no Alan to fall upon so many, and I was far from sure that a warship was the least likely to improve my condition. All which considered, I gave Andie my parole of good behaviour and obedience, and was had briskly to the summit of the rock, where we all lay down, at the cliff's edge, in different places of observation and concealment. The Seahorse came straight on till I thought she would have struck, and we (looking giddily down) could see the ship's company at their quarters and hear the leadsman singing at the lead. Then she suddenly wore and let fly a volley of I know not how many great guns. The rock was shaken with the thunder of the sound, the smoke flowed over our heads, and the geese rose in number beyond computation or belief. To hear their screaming and to see the twinkling of their wings, made a most inimitable curiosity; and I suppose it was after this somewhat childish pleasure that Captain Palliser had come so near the Bass. He was to pay dear for it in time. During his approach I had the opportunity to make a remark upon the rigging of that ship by which I ever after knew it miles away; and this was a means (under Providence) of my averting from a friend a great calamity, and inflicting on Captain Palliser himself a sensible disappointment.

All the time of my stay on the rock we lived well. We had small ale and brandy, and oatmeal, of which we made our porridge night and morning. At times a boat came from the Castleton and brought us a quarter of mutton, for the sheep upon the rock we must not touch, these being specially fed to market. The geese were unfortunately out of season, and we let them be. We fished ourselves, and yet more often made the geese to fish for us: observing one when he had made a capture and scaring him from his prey ere he had swallowed it.

The strange nature of this place, and the curiosities with which it abounded, held me busy and amused. Escape being impossible, I was allowed my entire liberty, and continually explored the surface of the isle wherever it might support the foot of man. The old garden of the prison was still to be observed, with flowers and pot-herbs running wild, and some ripe cherries on a bush. A little lower stood a chapel or a hermit's cell; who built or dwelt in it, none may know, and the thought of its age made a ground of many meditations. The prison, too, where I now bivouacked with Highland cattle-thieves, was a place full of history, both human and divine. I thought it strange so many saints and martyrs should have gone by there so recently, and left not so much as a leaf out of their Bibles, or a name carved upon the wall, while the rough soldier lads that mounted guard upon the battlements had filled the neighbourhood with their mementoes—broken tobacco-pipes for the most part, and that in a surprising plenty, but also metal buttons from their coats. There were times when I thought I could have heard the pious sound of psalms out of the martyr's dungeons, and seen the soldiers tramp the ramparts with their glinting pipes, and the dawn rising behind them out of the North Sea.

No doubt it was a good deal Andie and his tales that put these fancies in my head. He was extraordinarily well acquainted with the story of the rock in all particulars, down to the names of private soldiers, his father having served there in that same capacity. He was gifted besides with a natural genius for narration, so that the people seemed to speak and the things to be done before your face. This gift of his and my assiduity to listen brought us the more close together. I could not honestly deny but what I liked him; I soon saw that he liked me; and indeed, from the first I had set myself out to capture his good-will. An odd circumstance (to be told presently) effected this beyond my expectation; but even in early days we made a friendly pair to be a prisoner and his gaoler.

I should trifle with my conscience if I pretended my stay upon the Bass was wholly disagreeable. It seemed to me a safe place, as though I was escaped there out of my troubles. No harm was to be offered me; a material impossibility, rock and the deep sea, prevented me from fresh attempts; I felt I had my life safe and my honour safe, and there were times when I allowed myself to gloat on them like stolen waters. At other times my thoughts were very different, I recalled how strong I had expressed myself both to Rankeillor and to Stewart; I reflected that my captivity upon the Bass, in view of a great part of the coasts of Fife and Lothian, was a thing I should be thought more likely to have invented than endured; and in the eyes of these two gentlemen, at least, I must pass for a boaster and a coward. Now I would take this lightly enough; tell myself that so long as I stood well with Catriona Drummond, the opinion of the rest of man was but moonshine and spilled water; and thence pass off into those meditations of a lover which are so delightful to himself and must always appear so surprisingly idle to a reader. But anon the fear would take me otherwise; I would be shaken with a perfect panic of self-esteem, and these supposed hard judgments appear an injustice impossible to be supported. With that another train of thought would be presented, and I had scarce begun to be concerned about men's judgments of myself, than I was haunted with the remembrance of James Stewart in his dungeon and the lamentations of his wife. Then, indeed, passion began to work in me; I could not forgive myself to sit there idle: it seemed (if I were a man at all) that I could fly or swim out of my place of safety; and it was in such humours and to amuse my self-reproaches that I would set the more particularly to win the good side of Andie Dale.

At last, when we two were alone on the summit of the rock on a bright morning, I put in some hint about a bribe. He looked at me, cast back his head, and laughed out loud.

"Ay, you're funny, Mr. Dale," said I, "but perhaps if you'll glance an eye upon that paper you may change your note."

The stupid Highlanders had taken from me at the time of my seizure nothing but hard money, and the paper I now showed Andie was an acknowledgment from the British Linen Company for a considerable sum.

He read it. "Troth, and ye're nane sae ill aff," said he.

"I thought that would maybe vary your opinions," said I.

"Hout!" said he. "It shows me ye can bribe; but I'm no to be bribit."

"We'll see about that yet a while," says I. "And first, I'll show you that I know what I am talking. You have orders to detain me here till after Thursday, 21st September."

"Ye're no a'thegether wrong either," says Andie. "I'm to let you gang, bar orders contrair, on Saturday, the 23rd."

I could not but feel there was something extremely insidious in this arrangement. That I was to re-appear precisely in time to be too late would

266

cast the more discredit on my tale, if I were minded to tell one; and this screwed me to fighting point.

"Now then, Andie, you that kens the world, listen to me, and think while ye listen," said I. "I know there are great folks in the business, and I make no doubt you have their names to go upon. I have seen some of them myself since this affair began, and said my say into their faces too. But what kind of a crime would this be that I had committed? or what kind of a process is this that I am fallen under? To be apprehended by some ragged John-Hielandman on August 30th, carried to a rickle of old stones that is now neither fort nor gaol (whatever it once was) but just the gamekeeper's lodge of the Bass Rock, and set free again, September 23rd, as secretly as I was first arrested—does that sound like law to you? or does it sound like justice? or does it not sound honestly like a piece of some low dirty intrigue, of which the very folk that meddle with it are ashamed?"

"I canna gainsay ye, Shaws. It looks unco underhand," says Andie. "And werenae the folk guid sound Whigs and true-blue Presbyterians I would has seen them ayont Jordan and Jeroozlem or I would have set hand to it."

"The Master of Lovat'll be a braw Whig," says I, "and a grand Presbyterian."

"I ken naething by him," said he. "I hae nae trokings wi' Lovats."

"No, it'll be Prestongrange that you'll be dealing with," said I.

"Ah, but I'll no tell ye that," said Andie.

"Little need when I ken," was my retort.

"There's just the ae thing ye can be fairly sure of, Shaws," says Andie. "And that is that (try as ye please) I'm no dealing wi' yoursel'; nor yet I amnae goin' to," he added.

"Well, Andie, I see I'll have to be speak out plain with you," I replied. And told him so much as I thought needful of the facts.

He heard me out with some serious interest, and when I had done, seemed to consider a little with himself.

"Shaws," said he at last, "I'll deal with the naked hand. It's a queer tale, and no very creditable, the way you tell it; and I'm far frae minting that is other than the way that ye believe it. As for yoursel', ye seem to me rather a dacent-like young man. But me, that's aulder and mair judeecious, see perhaps a wee bit further forrit in the job than what ye can dae. And here the maitter clear and plain to ye. There'll be nae skaith to yoursel' if I keep ye here; far free that, I think ye'll be a hantle better by it. There'll be nae skaith to the kintry—just ae mair Hielantman hangit—Gude kens, a guid riddance! On the ither hand, it would be considerable skaith to me if I would let you free. Sae, speakin' as a guid Whig, an honest freen' to you, and an anxious freen' to my ainsel', the plain fact is that I think ye'll just have to bide here wi' Andie an' the solans."

"Andie," said I, laying my hand upon his knee, "this Hielantman's innocent."

"Ay, it's a peety about that," said he. "But ye see, in this warld, the way God made it, we cannae just get a'thing that we want."

CHAPTER XV—BLACK ANDIE'S TALE OF TOD LAPRAIK

I have yet said little of the Highlanders. They were all three of the followers of James More, which bound the accusation very tight about their master's neck. All understood a word or two of English, but Neil was the only one who judged he had enough of it for general converse, in which (when once he got embarked) his company was often tempted to the contrary opinion. They were tractable, simple creatures; showed much more courtesy than might have been expected from their raggedness and their uncouth appearance, and fell spontaneously to be like three servants for Andie and myself.

Dwelling in that isolated place, in the old falling ruins of a prison, and among endless strange sounds of the sea and the sea-birds, I thought I perceived in them early the effects of superstitious fear. When there was nothing doing they would either lie and sleep, for which their appetite appeared insatiable, or Neil would entertain the others with stories which seemed always of a terrifying strain. If neither of these delights were within reach—if perhaps two were sleeping and the third could find no means to follow their example—I would see him sit and listen and look about him in a progression of uneasiness, starting, his face blenching, his hands clutched, a man strung like a bow. The nature of these fears I had never an occasion to find out, but the sight of them was catching, and the nature of the place that we were in favourable to alarms. I can find no word for it in the English, but Andie had an expression for it in the Scots from which he never varied.

"Ay," he would say, "it's an unco place, the Bass."

It is so I always think of it. It was an unco place by night, unco by day; and these were unco sounds, of the calling of the solans, and the plash of the sea and the rock echoes, that hung continually in our ears. It was chiefly so in moderate weather. When the waves were anyway great they roared about the rock like thunder and the drums of armies, dreadful but merry to hear; and it was in the calm days that a man could daunt himself with listening—not a

Highlandman only, as I several times experimented on myself, so many still, hollow noises haunted and reverberated in the porches of the rock.

This brings me to a story I heard, and a scene I took part in, which quite changed our terms of living, and had a great effect on my departure. It chanced one night I fell in a muse beside the fire and (that little air of Alan's coming back to my memory) began to whistle. A hand was laid upon my arm, and the voice of Neil bade me to stop, for it was not "canny musics."

"Not canny?" I asked. "How can that be?"

"Na," said he; "it will be made by a bogle and her wanting ta heid upon his body." [13]

"Well," said I, "there can be no bogles here, Neil; for it's not likely they would fash themselves to frighten geese."

"Ay?" says Andie, "is that what ye think of it! But I'll can tell ye there's been waur nor bogles here."

"What's waur than bogles, Andie?" said I.

"Warlocks," said he. "Or a warlock at the least of it. And that's a queer tale, too," he added. "And if ye would like, I'll tell it ye."

To be sure we were all of the one mind, and even the Highlander that had the least English of the three set himself to listen with all his might.

The Tale of Tod Lapraik

My faither, Tam Dale, peace to his banes, was a wild, sploring lad in his young days, wi' little wisdom and little grace. He was fond of a lass and fond of a glass, and fond of a ran-dan; but I could never hear tell that he was muckle use for honest employment. Frae ae thing to anither, he listed at last for a sodger and was in the garrison of this fort, which was the first way that ony of the Dales cam to set foot upon the Bass. Sorrow upon that service! The governor brewed his ain ale; it seems it was the warst conceivable. The rock was proveesioned free the shore with vivers, the thing was ill-guided, and there were whiles when they but to fish and shoot solans for their diet. To

270

crown a', thir was the Days of the Persecution. The perishin' cauld chalmers were all occupeed wi' sants and martyrs, the saut of the yearth, of which it wasnae worthy. And though Tam Dale carried a firelock there, a single sodger, and liked a lass and a glass, as I was sayin', the mind of the man was mair just than set with his position. He had glints of the glory of the kirk; there were whiles when his dander rase to see the Lord's sants misguided, and shame covered him that he should be haulding a can'le (or carrying a firelock) in so black a business. There were nights of it when he was here on sentry, the place a' wheesht, the frosts o' winter maybe riving in the wa's, and he would hear ane o' the prisoners strike up a psalm, and the rest join in, and the blessed sounds rising from the different chalmers—or dungeons, I would raither say—so that this auld craig in the sea was like a pairt of Heev'n. Black shame was on his saul; his sins hove up before him muckle as the Bass, and above a', that chief sin, that he should have a hand in hagging and hashing at Christ's Kirk. But the truth is that he resisted the spirit. Day cam, there were the rousing compainions, and his guid resolves depairtit.

In thir days, dwalled upon the Bass a man of God, Peden the Prophet was his name. Ye'll have heard tell of Prophet Peden. There was never the wale of him sinsyne, and it's a question wi' mony if there ever was his like afore. He was wild's a peat-hag, fearsome to look at, fearsome to hear, his face like the day of judgment. The voice of him was like a solan's and dinnle'd in folks' lugs, and the words of him like coals of fire.

Now there was a lass on the rock, and I think she had little to do, for it was nae place far decent weemen; but it seems she was bonny, and her and Tam Dale were very well agreed. It befell that Peden was in the gairden his lane at the praying when Tam and the lass cam by; and what should the lassie do but mock with laughter at the sant's devotions? He rose and lookit at the twa o' them, and Tam's knees knoitered thegether at the look of him. But whan he spak, it was mair in sorrow than in anger. "Poor thing, poor thing!" says he, and it was the lass he lookit at, "I hear you skirl and laugh," he says, "but the Lord has a deid shot prepared for you, and at that surprising judgment ye shall skirl but the ae time!" Shortly thereafter she was daundering on the craigs wi' twa-three sodgers, and it was a blawy day.

There cam a gowst of wind, claught her by the coats, and awa' wi' her bag and baggage. And it was remarked by the sodgers that she gied but the ae skirl.

Nae doubt this judgment had some weicht upon Tam Dale; but it passed again and him none the better. Ae day he was flyting wi' anither sodger-lad. "Deil hae me!" quo' Tam, for he was a profane swearer. And there was Peden glowering at him, gash an' waefu'; Peden wi' his lang chafts an' luntin' een, the maud happed about his kist, and the hand of him held out wi' the black nails upon the finger-nebs—for he had nae care of the body. "Fy, fy, poor man!" cries he, "the poor fool man! Deil hae me, quo' he; an' I see the deil at his oxter." The conviction of guilt and grace cam in on Tam like the deep sea; he flang doun the pike that was in his hands—"I will nae mair lift arms against the cause o' Christ!" says he, and was as gude's word. There was a sair fyke in the beginning, but the governor, seeing him resolved, gied him his discharge, and he went and dwallt and married in North Berwick, and had aye a gude name with honest folk free that day on.

It was in the year seeventeen hunner and sax that the Bass cam in the hands o' the Da'rymples, and there was twa men soucht the chairge of it. Baith were weel qualified, for they had baith been sodgers in the garrison, and kent the gate to handle solans, and the seasons and values of them. Forby that they were baith—or they baith seemed—earnest professors and men of comely conversation. The first of them was just Tam Dale, my faither. The second was ane Lapraik, whom the folk ca'd Tod Lapraik maistly, but whether for his name or his nature I could never hear tell. Weel, Tam gaed to see Lapraik upon this business, and took me, that was a toddlin' laddie, by the hand. Tod had his dwallin' in the lang loan benorth the kirkyaird. It's a dark uncanny loan, forby that the kirk has aye had an ill name since the days o' James the Saxt and the deevil's cantrips played therein when the Queen was on the seas; and as for Tod's house, it was in the mirkest end, and was little liked by some that kenned the best. The door was on the sneck that day, and me and my faither gaed straucht in. Tod was a wabster to his trade; his loom stood in the but. There he sat, a muckle fat, white hash of a man like creish, wi' a kind of a holy smile that gart me scunner. The hand of him aye cawed the shuttle, but his een was steeked. We cried to him by his name, we skirled in the deid lug of him, we shook him by the shou'ther. Nae mainner o' service! There he sat on his dowp, an' cawed the shuttle and smiled like creish.

"God be guid to us," says Tam Dale, "this is no canny?"

He had jimp said the word, when Tod Lapraik cam to himsel'.

"Is this you, Tam?" says he. "Haith, man! I'm blythe to see ye. I whiles fa' into a bit dwam like this," he says; "its frae the stamach."

Weel, they began to crack about the Bass and which of them twa was to get the warding o't, and little by little cam to very ill words, and twined in anger. I mind weel that as my faither and me gaed hame again, he cam ower and ower the same expression, how little he likit Tod Lapraik and his dwams.

"Dwam!" says he. "I think folk hae brunt for dwams like yon."

Aweel, my faither got the Bass and Tod had to go wantin'. It was remembered sinsyne what way he had ta'en the thing. "Tam," says he, "ye hae gotten the better o' me aince mair, and I hope," says he, "ye'll find at least a' that ye expeckit at the Bass." Which have since been thought remarkable expressions. At last the time came for Tam Dale to take young solans. This was a business he was weel used wi', he had been a craigsman frae a laddie, and trustit nane but himsel'. So there was he hingin' by a line an' speldering on the craig face, whaur its hieest and steighest. Fower tenty lads were on the tap, hauldin' the line and mindin' for his signals. But whaur Tam hung there was naething but the craig, and the sea belaw, and the solans skirlin and flying. It was a braw spring morn, and Tam whustled as he claught in the young geese. Mony's the time I've heard him tell of this experience, and aye the swat ran upon the man.

It chanced, ye see, that Tam keeked up, and he was awaur of a muckle solan, and the solan pyking at the line. He thocht this by-ordinar and outside the creature's habits. He minded that ropes was unco saft things, and the solan's neb and the Bass Rock unco hard, and that twa hunner feet were raither mair than he would care to fa'.

"Shoo!" says Tam. "Awa', bird! Shoo, awa' wi' ye!" says he.

The solan keekit doon into Tam's face, and there was something unco in the creature's ee. Just the ae keek it gied, and back to the rope. But now it wroucht and warstl't like a thing dementit. There never was the solan made that wroucht as that solan wroucht; and it seemed to understand its employ brawly, birzing the saft rope between the neb of it and a crunkled jag o' stane.

There gaed a cauld stend o' fear into Tam's heart. "This thing is nae bird," thinks he. His een turnt backward in his heid and the day gaed black aboot him. "If I get a dwam here," he toucht, "it's by wi' Tam Dale." And he signalled for the lads to pu' him up.

And it seemed the solan understood about signals. For nae sooner was the signal made than he let be the rope, spried his wings, squawked out loud, took a turn flying, and dashed straucht at Tam Dale's een. Tam had a knife, he gart the cauld steel glitter. And it seemed the solan understood about knives, for nae suner did the steel glint in the sun than he gied the ae squawk, but laighter, like a body disappointit, and flegged aff about the roundness of the craig, and Tam saw him nae mair. And as sune as that thing was gane, Tam's heid drapt upon his shouther, and they pu'd him up like a deid corp, dadding on the craig.

A dram of brandy (which he went never without) broucht him to his mind, or what was left of it. Up he sat.

"Rin, Geordie, rin to the boat, mak' sure of the boat, man—rin!" he cries, "or yon solan'll have it awa'," says he.

The fower lads stared at ither, an' tried to whilly-wha him to be quiet. But naething would satisfy Tam Dale, till ane o' them had startit on aheid to stand sentry on the boat. The ithers askit if he was for down again.

"Na," says he, "and niether you nor me," says he, "and as sune as I can win to stand on my twa feet we'll be aff frae this craig o' Sawtan."

Sure eneuch, nae time was lost, and that was ower muckle; for before they won to North Berwick Tam was in a crying fever. He lay a' the simmer; and wha was sae kind as come speiring for him, but Tod Lapraik! Folk thocht afterwards that ilka time Tod cam near the house the fever had worsened. I

274

kenna for that; but what I ken the best, that was the end of it.

It was about this time o' the year; my grandfaither was out at the white fishing; and like a bairn, I but to gang wi' him. We had a grand take, I mind, and the way that the fish lay broucht us near in by the Bass, whaur we foregaithered wi' anither boat that belanged to a man Sandie Fletcher in Castleton. He's no lang deid neither, or ye could speir at himsel'. Weel, Sandie hailed.

"What's yon on the Bass?" says he.

"On the Bass?" says grandfaither.

"Ay," says Sandie, "on the green side o't."

"Whatten kind of a thing?" says grandfaither. "There cannae be naething on the Bass but just the sheep."

"It looks unco like a body," quo' Sandie, who was nearer in.

"A body!" says we, and we none of us likit that. For there was nae boat that could have brought a man, and the key o' the prison yett hung ower my faither's at hame in the press bed.

We keepit the twa boats close for company, and crap in nearer hand. Grandfaither had a gless, for he had been a sailor, and the captain of a smack, and had lost her on the sands of Tay. And when we took the glass to it, sure eneuch there was a man. He was in a crunkle o' green brae, a wee below the chaipel, a' by his lee lane, and lowped and flang and danced like a daft quean at a waddin'.

"It's Tod," says grandfather, and passed the gless to Sandie.

"Ay, it's him," says Sandie.

"Or ane in the likeness o' him," says grandfaither.

"Sma' is the differ," quo' Sandie. "De'il or warlock, I'll try the gun at him," quo' he, and broucht up a fowling-piece that he aye carried, for Sandie was a notable famous shot in all that country.

"Haud your hand, Sandie," says grandfaither; "we maun see clearer first," says he, "or this may be a dear day's wark to the baith of us."

"Hout!" says Sandie, "this is the Lord's judgment surely, and be damned to it," says he.

"Maybe ay, and maybe no," says my grandfaither, worthy man! "But have you a mind of the Procurator Fiscal, that I think ye'll have foregaithered wi' before," says he.

This was ower true, and Sandie was a wee thing set ajee. "Aweel, Edie," says he, "and what would be your way of it?"

"Ou, just this," says grandfaither. "Let me that has the fastest boat gang back to North Berwick, and let you bide here and keep an eye on Thon. If I cannae find Lapraik, I'll join ye and the twa of us'll have a crack wi' him. But if Lapraik's at hame, I'll rin up the flag at the harbour, and ye can try Thon Thing wi' the gun."

Aweel, so it was agreed between them twa. I was just a bairn, an' clum in Sandie's boat, whaur I thocht I would see the best of the employ. My grandsire gied Sandie a siller tester to pit in his gun wi' the leid draps, bein mair deidly again bogles. And then the as boat set aff for North Berwick, an' the tither lay whaur it was and watched the wanchancy thing on the brae-side.

A' the time we lay there it lowped and flang and capered and span like a teetotum, and whiles we could hear it skelloch as it span. I hae seen lassies, the daft queans, that would lowp and dance a winter's nicht, and still be lowping and dancing when the winter's day cam in. But there would be fowk there to hauld them company, and the lads to egg them on; and this thing was its lee-lane. And there would be a fiddler diddling his elbock in the chimney-side; and this thing had nae music but the skirling of the solans. And the lassies were bits o' young things wi' the reid life dinnling and stending in their members; and this was a muckle, fat, creishy man, and him fa'n in the vale o' years. Say what ye like, I maun say what I believe. It was joy was in the creature's heart, the joy o' hell, I daursay: joy whatever. Mony a time I have askit mysel' why witches and warlocks should sell their sauls (whilk are their maist dear possessions) and be auld, duddy, wrunkl't wives or auld, feckless, doddered men; and then I mind upon Tod Lapraik dancing a' the hours by his lane in the black glory of his heart. Nae doubt they burn for it muckle in hell, but they have a grand time here of it, whatever!—and the Lord forgie us!

Weel, at the hinder end, we saw the wee flag yirk up to the mast-heid upon the harbour rocks. That was a' Sandie waited for. He up wi' the gun, took a deleeberate aim, an' pu'd the trigger. There cam' a bang and then ae waefu' skirl frae the Bass. And there were we rubbin' our een and lookin' at ither like daft folk. For wi' the bang and the skirl the thing had clean disappeared. The sun glintit, the wund blew, and there was the bare yaird whaur the Wonder had been lowping and flinging but ae second syne.

The hale way hame I roared and grat wi' the terror o' that dispensation. The grawn folk were nane sae muckle better; there was little said in Sandie's boat but just the name of God; and when we won in by the pier, the harbour rocks were fair black wi' the folk waitin' us. It seems they had fund Lapraik in ane of his dwams, cawing the shuttle and smiling. Ae lad they sent to hoist the flag, and the rest abode there in the wabster's house. You may be sure they liked it little; but it was a means of grace to severals that stood there praying in to themsel's (for nane cared to pray out loud) and looking on thon awesome thing as it cawed the shuttle. Syne, upon a suddenty, and wi' the ae dreidfu' skelloch, Tod sprang up frae his hinderlands and fell forrit on the wab, a bluidy corp.

When the corp was examined the leid draps hadnae played buff upon the warlock's body; sorrow a leid drap was to be fund! but there was grandfaither's siller tester in the puddock's heart of him.

Andie had scarce done when there befell a mighty silly affair that had its consequence. Neil, as I have said, was himself a great narrator. I have heard since that he knew all the stories in the Highlands; and thought much of himself, and was thought much of by others on the strength of it. Now Andie's tale reminded him of one he had already heard.

"She would ken that story afore," he said. "She was the story of Uistean

277

More M'Gillie Phadrig and the Gavar Vore."

"It is no sic a thing," cried Andie. "It is the story of my faither (now wi' God) and Tod Lapraik. And the same in your beard," says he; "and keep the tongue of ye inside your Hielant chafts!"

In dealing with Highlanders it will be found, and has been shown in history, how well it goes with Lowland gentlefolk; but the thing appears scarce feasible for Lowland commons. I had already remarked that Andie was continually on the point of quarrelling with our three MacGregors, and now, sure enough, it was to come.

"Thir will be no words to use to shentlemans," says Neil.

"Shentlemans!" cries Andie. "Shentlemans, ye hielant stot! If God would give ye the grace to see yoursel' the way that ithers see ye, ye would throw your denner up."

There came some kind of a Gaelic oath from Neil, and the black knife was in his hand that moment.

There was no time to think; and I caught the Highlander by the leg, and had him down, and his armed hand pinned out, before I knew what I was doing. His comrades sprang to rescue him, Andie and I were without weapons, the Gregara three to two. It seemed we were beyond salvation, when Neil screamed in his own tongue, ordering the others back, and made his submission to myself in a manner the most abject, even giving me up his knife which (upon a repetition of his promises) I returned to him on the morrow.

Two things I saw plain: the first, that I must not build too high on Andie, who had shrunk against the wall and stood there, as pale as death, till the affair was over; the second, the strength of my own position with the Highlanders, who must have received extraordinary charges to be tender of my safety. But if I thought Andie came not very well out in courage, I had no fault to find with him upon the account of gratitude. It was not so much that he troubled me with thanks, as that his whole mind and manner appeared changed; and as he preserved ever after a great timidity of our companions, he and I were yet more constantly together.

278

CHAPTER XVI—THE MISSING WITNESS

On the seventeenth, the day I was trysted with the Writer, I had much rebellion against fate. The thought of him waiting in the King's Arms, and of what he would think, and what he would say when next we met, tormented and oppressed me. The truth was unbelievable, so much I had to grant, and it seemed cruel hard I should be posted as a liar and a coward, and have never consciously omitted what it was possible that I should do. I repeated this form of words with a kind of bitter relish, and re-examined in that light the steps of my behaviour. It seemed I had behaved to James Stewart as a brother might; all the past was a picture that I could be proud of, and there was only the present to consider. I could not swim the sea, nor yet fly in the air, but there was always Andie. I had done him a service, he liked me; I had a lever there to work on; if it were just for decency, I must try once more with Andie.

It was late afternoon; there was no sound in all the Bass but the lap and bubble of a very quiet sea; and my four companions were all crept apart, the three Macgregors higher on the rock, and Andie with his Bible to a sunny place among the ruins; there I found him in deep sleep, and, as soon as he was awake, appealed to him with some fervour of manner and a good show of argument.

"If I thoucht it was to do guid to ye, Shaws!" said he, staring at me over his spectacles.

"It's to save another," said I, "and to redeem my word. What would be more good than that? Do ye no mind the scripture, Andie? And you with the Book upon your lap! What shall it profit a man if he gain the whole world?"

"Ay," said he, "that's grand for you. But where do I come in! I have my word to redeem the same's yoursel'. And what are ye asking me to do, but just to sell it ye for siller?"

"Andie! have I named the name of siller?" cried I.

"Ou, the name's naething", said he; "the thing is there, whatever. It just comes to this; if I am to service ye the way that you propose, I'll lose my lifelihood. Then it's clear ye'll have to make it up to me, and a pickle mair, for your ain credit like. And what's that but just a bribe? And if even I was certain of the bribe! But by a' that I can learn, it's far frae that; and if you were to hang, where would I be? Na: the thing's no possible. And just awa' wi' ye like a bonny lad! and let Andie read his chapter."

I remember I was at bottom a good deal gratified with this result; and the next humour I fell into was one (I had near said) of gratitude to Prestongrange, who had saved me, in this violent, illegal manner, out of the midst of my dangers, temptations, and perplexities. But this was both too flimsy and too cowardly to last me long, and the remembrance of James began to succeed to the possession of my spirits. The 21st, the day set for the trial, I passed in such misery of mind as I can scarce recall to have endured, save perhaps upon Isle Earraid only. Much of the time I lay on a brae-side betwixt sleep and waking, my body motionless, my mind full of violent thoughts. Sometimes I slept indeed; but the court-house of Inverary and the prisoner glancing on all sides to find his missing witness, followed me in slumber; and I would wake again with a start to darkness of spirit and distress of body. I thought Andie seemed to observe me, but I paid him little heed. Verily, my bread was bitter to me, and my days a burthen.

Early the next morning (Friday, 22nd) a boat came with provisions, and Andie placed a packet in my hand. The cover was without address but sealed with a Government seal. It enclosed two notes. "Mr. Balfour can now see for himself it is too late to meddle. His conduct will be observed and his discretion rewarded." So ran the first, which seemed to be laboriously writ with the left hand. There was certainly nothing in these expressions to compromise the writer, even if that person could be found; the seal, which formidably served instead of signature, was affixed to a separate sheet on which there was no scratch of writing; and I had to confess that (so far) my adversaries knew what they were doing, and to digest as well as I was able the threat that peeped under the promise.

But the second enclosure was by far the more surprising. It was in a lady's hand of writ. "Maister Dauvit Balfour is informed a friend was speiring for him and her eyes were of the grey," it ran—and seemed so extraordinary a piece to come to my hands at such a moment and under cover of a Government seal, that I stood stupid. Catriona's grey eyes shone in my remembrance. I thought, with a bound of pleasure, she must be the friend. But who should the writer be, to have her billet thus enclosed with Prestongrange's? And of all wonders, why was it thought needful to give me this pleasing but most inconsequent intelligence upon the Bass? For the writer, I could hit upon none possible except Miss Grant. Her family, I remembered, had remarked on Catriona's eyes and even named her for their colour; and she herself had been much in the habit to address me with a broad pronunciation, by way of a sniff, I supposed, at my rusticity. No doubt, besides, but she lived in the same house as this letter came from. So there remained but one step to be accounted for; and that was how Prestongrange should have permitted her at all in an affair so secret, or let her daft-like billet go in the same cover with his own. But even here I had a glimmering. For, first of all, there was something rather alarming about the young lady, and papa might be more under her domination than I knew. And, second, there was the man's continual policy to be remembered, how his conduct had been continually mingled with caresses, and he had scarce ever, in the midst of so much contention, laid aside a mask of friendship. He must conceive that my imprisonment had incensed me. Perhaps this little jesting, friendly message was intended to disarm my rancour?

I will be honest—and I think it did. I felt a sudden warmth towards that beautiful Miss Grant, that she should stoop to so much interest in my affairs. The summoning up of Catriona moved me of itself to milder and more cowardly counsels. If the Advocate knew of her and our acquaintance—if I should please him by some of that "discretion" at which his letter pointed— to what might not this lead! In vain is the net prepared in the sight of any fowl, the Scripture says. Well, fowls must be wiser than folk! For I thought I perceived the policy, and yet fell in with it.

I was in this frame, my heart beating, the grey eyes plain before me like two stars, when Andie broke in upon my musing.

"I see ye has gotten guid news," said he.

I found him looking curiously in my face; with that there came before me like a vision of James Stewart and the court of Inverary; and my mind turned at once like a door upon its hinges. Trials, I reflected, sometimes draw out longer than is looked for. Even if I came to Inverary just too late, something might yet be attempted in the interests of James—and in those of my own character, the best would be accomplished. In a moment, it seemed without thought, I had a plan devised.

"Andie," said I, "is it still to be to-morrow?"

He told me nothing was changed.

"Was anything said about the hour?" I asked.

He told me it was to be two o'clock afternoon.

"And about the place?" I pursued.

"Whatten place?" says Andie.

"The place I am to be landed at?" said I.

He owned there was nothing as to that.

"Very well, then," I said, "this shall be mine to arrange. The wind is in the east, my road lies westward: keep your boat, I hire it; let us work up the Forth all day; and land me at two o'clock to-morrow at the westmost we'll can have reached."

"Ye daft callant!" he cried; "ye would try for Inverary after a'!"

"Just that, Andie," says I.

"Weel, ye're ill to beat!" says he. "And I was a kind o' sorry for ye a' day yesterday," he added. "Ye see, I was never entirely sure till then, which way of it ye really wantit."

Here was a spur to a lame horse!

"A word in your ear, Andie," said I. "This plan of mine has another advantage yet. We can leave these Hielandman behind us on the rock, and

282

one of your boats from the Castleton can bring them off to-morrow. Yon Neil has a queer eye when he regards you; maybe, if I was once out of the gate there might be knives again; these red-shanks are unco grudgeful. And if there should come to be any question, here is your excuse. Our lives were in danger by these savages; being answerable for my safety, you chose the part to bring me from their neighbourhood and detain me the rest of the time on board your boat: and do you know, Andie?" says I, with a smile, "I think it was very wisely chosen."

"The truth is I have nae goo for Neil," says Andie, "nor he for me, I'm thinking; and I would like ill to come to my hands wi' the man. Tam Anster will make a better hand of it with the cattle onyway." (For this man, Anster, came from Fife, where the Gaelic is still spoken.) "Ay, ay!" says Andie, "Tam'll can deal with them the best. And troth! the mair I think of it, the less I see we would be required. The place—ay, feggs! they had forgot the place. Eh, Shaws, ye're a lang-heided chield when ye like! Forby that I'm awing ye my life," he added, with more solemnity, and offered me his hand upon the bargain.

Whereupon, with scarce more words, we stepped suddenly on board the boat, cast off, and set the lug. The Gregara were then busy upon breakfast, for the cookery was their usual part; but, one of them stepping to the battlements, our flight was observed before we were twenty fathoms from the rock; and the three of them ran about the ruins and the landing-shelf, for all the world like ants about a broken nest, hailing and crying on us to return. We were still in both the lee and the shadow of the rock, which last lay broad upon the waters, but presently came forth in almost the same moment into the wind and sunshine; the sail filled, the boat heeled to the gunwale, and we swept immediately beyond sound of the men's voices. To what terrors they endured upon the rock, where they were now deserted without the countenance of any civilised person or so much as the protection of a Bible, no limit can be set; nor had they any brandy left to be their consolation, for even in the haste and secrecy of our departure Andie had managed to remove it.

It was our first care to set Anster ashore in a cove by the Glenteithy Rocks, so that the deliverance of our maroons might be duly seen to the next day. Thence we kept away up Firth. The breeze, which was then so spirited, swiftly declined, but never wholly failed us. All day we kept moving, though often not much more; and it was after dark ere we were up with the Queensferry. To keep the letter of Andie's engagement (or what was left of it) I must remain on board, but I thought no harm to communicate with the shore in writing. On Prestongrange's cover, where the Government seal must have a good deal surprised my correspondent, I writ, by the boat's lantern, a few necessary words, aboard and Andie carried them to Rankeillor. In about an hour he came again, with a purse of money and the assurance that a good horse should be standing saddled for me by two to-morrow at Clackmannan Pool. This done, and the boat riding by her stone anchor, we lay down to sleep under the sail.

We were in the Pool the next day long ere two; and there was nothing left for me but to sit and wait. I felt little alacrity upon my errand. I would have been glad of any passable excuse to lay it down; but none being to be found, my uneasiness was no less great than if I had been running to some desired pleasure. By shortly after one the horse was at the waterside, and I could see a man walking it to and fro till I should land, which vastly swelled my impatience. Andie ran the moment of my liberation very fine, showing himself a man of his bare word, but scarce serving his employers with a heaped measure; and by about fifty seconds after two I was in the saddle and on the full stretch for Stirling. In a little more than an hour I had passed that town, and was already mounting Alan Water side, when the weather broke in a small tempest. The rain blinded me, the wind had nearly beat me from the saddle, and the first darkness of the night surprised me in a wilderness still some way east of Balwhidder, not very sure of my direction and mounted on a horse that began already to be weary.

In the press of my hurry, and to be spared the delay and annoyance of a guide, I had followed (so far as it was possible for any horseman) the line of my journey with Alan. This I did with open eyes, foreseeing a great risk in it, which the tempest had now brought to a reality. The last that I knew of where I was, I think it must have been about Uam Var; the hour perhaps six at night. I must still think it great good fortune that I got about eleven to my destination, the house of Duncan Dhu. Where I had wandered in the interval perhaps the horse could tell. I know we were twice down, and once over the saddle and for a moment carried away in a roaring burn. Steed and rider were bemired up to the eyes.

From Duncan I had news of the trial. It was followed in all these Highland regions with religious interest; news of it spread from Inverary as swift as men could travel; and I was rejoiced to learn that, up to a late hour that Saturday it was not yet concluded; and all men began to suppose it must spread over the Monday. Under the spur of this intelligence I would not sit to eat; but, Duncan having agreed to be my guide, took the road again on foot, with the piece in my hand and munching as I went. Duncan brought with him a flask of usquebaugh and a hand-lantern; which last enlightened us just so long as we could find houses where to rekindle it, for the thing leaked outrageously and blew out with every gust. The more part of the night we walked blindfold among sheets of rain, and day found us aimless on the mountains. Hard by we struck a hut on a burn-side, where we got bite and a direction; and, a little before the end of the sermon, came to the kirk doors of Inverary.

The rain had somewhat washed the upper parts of me, but I was still bogged as high as to the knees; I streamed water; I was so weary I could hardly limp, and my face was like a ghost's. I stood certainly more in need of a change of raiment and a bed to lie on, than of all the benefits in Christianity. For all which (being persuaded the chief point for me was to make myself immediately public) I set the door of the church with the dirty Duncan at my tails, and finding a vacant place sat down.

"Thirteently, my brethren, and in parenthesis, the law itself must be regarded as a means of grace," the minister was saying, in the voice of one delighting to pursue an argument.

The sermon was in English on account of the assize. The judges were present with their armed attendants, the halberts glittered in a corner by the door, and the seats were thronged beyond custom with the array of lawyers. The text was in Romans 5th and 13th—the minister a skilled hand; and the whole of that able churchful—from Argyle, and my Lords Elchies and

285

Kilkerran, down to the halbertmen that came in their attendance—was sunk with gathered brows in a profound critical attention. The minister himself and a sprinkling of those about the door observed our entrance at the moment and immediately forgot the same; the rest either did not hear or would not hear or would not be heard; and I sat amongst my friends and enemies unremarked.

The first that I singled out was Prestongrange. He sat well forward, like an eager horseman in the saddle, his lips moving with relish, his eyes glued on the minister; the doctrine was clearly to his mind. Charles Stewart, on the other hand, was half asleep, and looked harassed and pale. As for Simon Fraser, he appeared like a blot, and almost a scandal, in the midst of that attentive congregation, digging his hands in his pockets, shifting his legs, clearing his throat, and rolling up his bald eyebrows and shooting out his eyes to right and left, now with a yawn, now with a secret smile. At times, too, he would take the Bible in front of him, run it through, seem to read a bit, run it through again, and stop and yawn prodigiously: the whole as if for exercise.

In the course of this restlessness his eye alighted on myself. He sat a second stupefied, then tore a half-leaf out of the Bible, scrawled upon it with a pencil, and passed it with a whispered word to his next neighbour. The note came to Prestongrange, who gave me but the one look; thence it voyaged to the hands of Mr. Erskine; thence again to Argyle, where he sat between the other two lords of session, and his Grace turned and fixed me with an arrogant eye. The last of those interested in my presence was Charlie Stewart, and he too began to pencil and hand about dispatches, none of which I was able to trace to their destination in the crowd.

But the passage of these notes had aroused notice; all who were in the secret (or supposed themselves to be so) were whispering information—the rest questions; and the minister himself seemed quite discountenanced by the flutter in the church and sudden stir and whispering. His voice changed, he plainly faltered, nor did he again recover the easy conviction and full tones of his delivery. It would be a puzzle to him till his dying day, why a sermon that had gone with triumph through four parts, should thus miscarry in the fifth.

As for me, I continued to sit there, very wet and weary, and a good deal anxious as to what should happen next, but greatly exulting in my success.

286

CHAPTER XVII—THE MEMORIAL

The last word of the blessing was scarce out of the minister's mouth before Stewart had me by the arm. We were the first to be forth of the church, and he made such extraordinary expedition that we were safe within the four walls of a house before the street had begun to be thronged with the home-going congregation.

"Am I yet in time?" I asked.

"Ay and no," said he. "The case is over; the jury is enclosed, and will so kind as let us ken their view of it to-morrow in the morning, the same as I could have told it my own self three days ago before the play began. The thing has been public from the start. The panel kent it, 'Ye may do what ye will for me,' whispers he two days ago. 'Ye ken my fate by what the Duke of Argyle has just said to Mr. Macintosh.' O, it's been a scandal!

"The great Agyle he gaed before,

He gart the cannons and guns to roar,"

and the very macer cried 'Cruachan!' But now that I have got you again I'll never despair. The oak shall go over the myrtle yet; we'll ding the Campbells yet in their own town. Praise God that I should see the day!"

He was leaping with excitement, emptied out his mails upon the floor that I might have a change of clothes, and incommoded me with his assistance as I changed. What remained to be done, or how I was to do it, was what he never told me nor, I believe, so much as thought of. "We'll ding the Campbells yet!" that was still his overcome. And it was forced home upon my mind how this, that had the externals of a sober process of law, was in its essence a clan battle between savage clans. I thought my friend the Writer none of the least savage. Who that had only seen him at a counsel's back before the Lord Ordinary or following a golf ball and laying down his clubs on Bruntsfield links, could have recognised for the same person this voluble and violent clansman?

James Stewart's counsel were four in number—Sheriffs Brown of Colstoun and Miller, Mr. Robert Macintosh, and Mr. Stewart younger of Stewart Hall. These were covenanted to dine with the Writer after sermon, and I was very obligingly included of the party. No sooner the cloth lifted, and the first bowl very artfully compounded by Sheriff Miller, than we fell to the subject in hand. I made a short narration of my seizure and captivity, and was then examined and re-examined upon the circumstances of the murder. It will be remembered this was the first time I had had my say out, or the matter at all handled, among lawyers; and the consequence was very dispiriting to the others and (I must own) disappointing to myself.

"To sum up," said Colstoun, "you prove that Alan was on the spot; you have heard him proffer menaces against Glenure; and though you assure us he was not the man who fired, you leave a strong impression that he was in league with him, and consenting, perhaps immediately assisting, in the act. You show him besides, at the risk of his own liberty, actively furthering the criminal's escape. And the rest of your testimony (so far as the least material) depends on the bare word of Alan or of James, the two accused. In short, you do not at all break, but only lengthen by one personage, the chain that binds our client to the murderer; and I need scarcely say that the introduction of a third accomplice rather aggravates that appearance of a conspiracy which has been our stumbling block from the beginning."

"I am of the same opinion," said Sheriff Miller. "I think we may all be very much obliged to Prestongrange for taking a most uncomfortable witness out of our way. And chiefly, I think, Mr. Balfour himself might be obliged. For you talk of a third accomplice, but Mr. Balfour (in my view) has very much the appearance of a fourth."

"Allow me, sirs!" interposed Stewart the Writer. "There is another view. Here we have a witness—never fash whether material or not—a witness in this cause, kidnapped by that old, lawless, bandit crew of the Glengyle Macgregors, and sequestered for near upon a month in a bourock of old ruins on the Bass. Move that and see what dirt you fling on the proceedings! Sirs, this is a tale to make the world ring with! It would be strange, with such a grip as this, if we couldnae squeeze out a pardon for my client."

288

"And suppose we took up Mr. Balfour's cause to-morrow?" said Stewart Hall. "I am much deceived or we should find so many impediments thrown in our path, as that James should have been hanged before we had found a court to hear us. This is a great scandal, but I suppose we have none of us forgot a greater still, I mean the matter of the Lady Grange. The woman was still in durance; my friend Mr. Hope of Rankeillor did what was humanly possible; and how did he speed? He never got a warrant! Well, it'll be the same now; the same weapons will be used. This is a scene, gentleman, of clan animosity. The hatred of the name which I have the honour to bear, rages in high quarters. There is nothing here to be viewed but naked Campbell spite and scurvy Campbell intrigue."

You may be sure this was to touch a welcome topic, and I sat for some time in the midst of my learned counsel, almost deaved with their talk but extremely little the wiser for its purport. The Writer was led into some hot expressions; Colstoun must take him up and set him right; the rest joined in on different sides, but all pretty noisy; the Duke of Argyle was beaten like a blanket; King George came in for a few digs in the by-going and a great deal of rather elaborate defence; and there was only one person that seemed to be forgotten, and that was James of the Glens.

Through all this Mr. Miller sat quiet. He was a slip of an oldish gentleman, ruddy and twinkling; he spoke in a smooth rich voice, with an infinite effect of pawkiness, dealing out each word the way an actor does, to give the most expression possible; and even now, when he was silent, and sat there with his wig laid aside, his glass in both hands, his mouth funnily pursed, and his chin out, he seemed the mere picture of a merry slyness. It was plain he had a word to say, and waited for the fit occasion.

It came presently. Colstoun had wound up one of his speeches with some expression of their duty to their client. His brother sheriff was pleased, I suppose, with the transition. He took the table in his confidence with a gesture and a look.

"That suggests to me a consideration which seems overlooked," said he. "The interest of our client goes certainly before all, but the world does not

289

come to an end with James Stewart." Whereat he cocked his eye. "I might condescend, exempli gratia, upon a Mr. George Brown, a Mr. Thomas Miller, and a Mr. David Balfour. Mr. David Balfour has a very good ground of complaint, and I think, gentlemen—if his story was properly redd out—I think there would be a number of wigs on the green."

The whole table turned to him with a common movement.

"Properly handled and carefully redd out, his is a story that could scarcely fail to have some consequence," he continued. "The whole administration of justice, from its highest officer downward, would be totally discredited; and it looks to me as if they would need to be replaced." He seemed to shine with cunning as he said it. "And I need not point out to ye that this of Mr. Balfour's would be a remarkable bonny cause to appear in," he added.

Well, there they all were started on another hare; Mr. Balfour's cause, and what kind of speeches could be there delivered, and what officials could be thus turned out, and who would succeed to their positions. I shall give but the two specimens. It was proposed to approach Simon Fraser, whose testimony, if it could be obtained, would prove certainly fatal to Argyle and to Prestongrange. Miller highly approved of the attempt. "We have here before us a dreeping roast," said he, "here is cut-and-come-again for all." And methought all licked their lips. The other was already near the end. Stewart the Writer was out of the body with delight, smelling vengeance on his chief enemy, the Duke.

"Gentlemen," cried he, charging his glass, "here is to Sheriff Miller. His legal abilities are known to all. His culinary, this bowl in front of us is here to speak for. But when it comes to the poleetical!"—cries he, and drains the glass.

"Ay, but it will hardly prove politics in your meaning, my friend," said the gratified Miller. "A revolution, if you like, and I think I can promise you that historical writers shall date from Mr. Balfour's cause. But properly guided, Mr. Stewart, tenderly guided, it shall prove a peaceful revolution."

"And if the damned Campbells get their ears rubbed, what care I?" cries

Stewart, smiting down his fist.

It will be thought I was not very well pleased with all this, though I could scarce forbear smiling at a kind of innocency in these old intriguers. But it was not my view to have undergone so many sorrows for the advancement of Sheriff Miller or to make a revolution in the Parliament House: and I interposed accordingly with as much simplicity of manner as I could assume.

"I have to thank you, gentlemen, for your advice," said I. "And now I would like, by your leave, to set you two or three questions. There is one thing that has fallen rather on one aide, for instance: Will this cause do any good to our friend James of the Glens?"

They seemed all a hair set back, and gave various answers, but concurring practically in one point, that James had now no hope but in the King's mercy.

"To proceed, then," said I, "will it do any good to Scotland? We have a saying that it is an ill bird that fouls his own nest. I remember hearing we had a riot in Edinburgh when I was an infant child, which gave occasion to the late Queen to call this country barbarous; and I always understood that we had rather lost than gained by that. Then came the year 'Forty-five, which made Scotland to be talked of everywhere; but I never heard it said we had anyway gained by the 'Forty-five. And now we come to this cause of Mr. Balfour's, as you call it. Sheriff Miller tells us historical writers are to date from it, and I would not wonder. It is only my fear they would date from it as a period of calamity and public reproach."

The nimble-witted Miller had already smelt where I was travelling to, and made haste to get on the same road. "Forcibly put, Mr. Balfour," says he. "A weighty observe, sir."

"We have next to ask ourselves if it will be good for King George," I pursued. "Sheriff Miller appears pretty easy upon this; but I doubt you will scarce be able to pull down the house from under him, without his Majesty coming by a knock or two, one of which might easily prove fatal."

I gave them a chance to answer, but none volunteered.

"Of those for whom the case was to be profitable," I went on, "Sheriff

Miller gave us the names of several, among the which he was good enough to mention mine. I hope he will pardon me if I think otherwise. I believe I hung not the least back in this affair while there was life to be saved; but I own I thought myself extremely hazarded, and I own I think it would be a pity for a young man, with some idea of coming to the Bar, to ingrain upon himself the character of a turbulent, factious fellow before he was yet twenty. As for James, it seems—at this date of the proceedings, with the sentence as good as pronounced—he has no hope but in the King's mercy. May not his Majesty, then, be more pointedly addressed, the characters of these high officers sheltered from the public, and myself kept out of a position which I think spells ruin for me?"

They all sat and gazed into their glasses, and I could see they found my attitude on the affair unpalatable. But Miller was ready at all events.

"If I may be allowed to put my young friend's notion in more formal shape," says he, "I understand him to propose that we should embody the fact of his sequestration, and perhaps some heads of the testimony he was prepared to offer, in a memorial to the Crown. This plan has elements of success. It is as likely as any other (and perhaps likelier) to help our client. Perhaps his Majesty would have the goodness to feel a certain gratitude to all concerned in such a memorial, which might be construed into an expression of a very delicate loyalty; and I think, in the drafting of the same, this view might be brought forward."

They all nodded to each other, not without sighs, for the former alternative was doubtless more after their inclination.

"Paper, then, Mr. Stewart, if you please," pursued Miller; "and I think it might very fittingly be signed by the five of us here present, as procurators for the condemned man.'"

"It can do none of us any harm, at least," says Colstoun, heaving another sigh, for he had seen himself Lord Advocate the last ten minutes.

Thereupon they set themselves, not very enthusiastically, to draft the memorial—a process in the course of which they soon caught fire; and I had no more ado but to sit looking on and answer an occasional question. The paper was very well expressed; beginning with a recitation of the facts about myself, the reward offered for my apprehension, my surrender, the pressure brought to bear upon me; my sequestration; and my arrival at Inverary in time to be too late; going on to explain the reasons of loyalty and public interest for which it was agreed to waive any right of action; and winding up with a forcible appeal to the King's mercy on behalf of James.

Methought I was a good deal sacrificed, and rather represented in the light of a firebrand of a fellow whom my cloud of lawyers had restrained with difficulty from extremes. But I let it pass, and made but the one suggestion, that I should be described as ready to deliver my own evidence and adduce that of others before any commission of inquiry—and the one demand, that I should be immediately furnished with a copy.

Colstoun hummed and hawed. "This is a very confidential document," said he.

"And my position towards Prestongrange is highly peculiar," I replied. "No question but I must have touched his heart at our first interview, so that he has since stood my friend consistently. But for him, gentlemen, I must now be lying dead or awaiting my sentence alongside poor James. For which reason I choose to communicate to him the fact of this memorial as soon as it is copied. You are to consider also that this step will make for my protection. I have enemies here accustomed to drive hard; his Grace is in his own country, Lovat by his side; and if there should hang any ambiguity over our proceedings I think I might very well awake in gaol."

Not finding any very ready answer to these considerations, my company of advisers were at the last persuaded to consent, and made only this condition that I was to lay the paper before Prestongrange with the express compliments of all concerned.

The Advocate was at the castle dining with his Grace. By the hand of one of Colstoun's servants I sent him a billet asking for an interview, and received a summons to meet him at once in a private house of the town. Here I found him alone in a chamber; from his face there was nothing to be

293

gleaned; yet I was not so unobservant but what I spied some halberts in the hall, and not so stupid but what I could gather he was prepared to arrest me there and then, should it appear advisable.

"So, Mr. David, this is you?" said he.

"Where I fear I am not overly welcome, my lord," said I. "And I would like before I go further to express my sense of your lordship's good offices, even should they now cease."

"I have heard of your gratitude before," he replied drily, "and I think this can scarce be the matter you called me from my wine to listen to. I would remember also, if I were you, that you still stand on a very boggy foundation."

"Not now, my lord, I think," said I; "and if your lordship will but glance an eye along this, you will perhaps think as I do."

He read it sedulously through, frowning heavily; then turned back to one part and another which he seemed to weigh and compare the effect of. His face a little lightened.

"This is not so bad but what it might be worse," said he; "though I am still likely to pay dear for my acquaintance with Mr. David Balfour."

"Rather for your indulgence to that unlucky young man, my lord," said I.

He still skimmed the paper, and all the while his spirits seemed to mend.

"And to whom am I indebted for this?" he asked presently. "Other counsels must have been discussed, I think. Who was it proposed this private method? Was it Miller?"

"My lord, it was myself," said I. "These gentlemen have shown me no such consideration, as that I should deny myself any credit I can fairly claim, or spare them any responsibility they should properly bear. And the mere truth is, that they were all in favour of a process which should have remarkable consequences in the Parliament House, and prove for them (in one of their own expressions) a dripping roast. Before I intervened, I think they were on the point of sharing out the different law appointments. Our friend Mr. Simon was to be taken in upon some composition."

Prestongrange smiled. "These are our friends," said he. "And what were your reasons for dissenting, Mr. David?"

I told them without concealment, expressing, however, with more force and volume those which regarded Prestongrange himself.

"You do me no more than justice," said he. "I have fought as hard in your interest as you have fought against mine. And how came you here to-day?" he asked. "As the case drew out, I began to grow uneasy that I had clipped the period so fine, and I was even expecting you to-morrow. But to-day—I never dreamed of it."

I was not of course, going to betray Andie.

"I suspect there is some very weary cattle by the road," said I.

"If I had known you were such a mosstrooper you should have tasted longer of the Bass," says he.

"Speaking of which, my lord, I return your letter." And I gave him the enclosure in the counterfeit hand.

"There was the cover also with the seal," said he.

"I have it not," said I. "It bore not even an address, and could not compromise a cat. The second enclosure I have, and with your permission, I desire to keep it."

I thought he winced a little, but he said nothing to the point. "To-morrow," he resumed, "our business here is to be finished, and I proceed by Glasgow. I would be very glad to have you of my party, Mr David."

"My lord . . ." I began.

"I do not deny it will be of service to me," he interrupted. "I desire even that, when we shall come to Edinburgh, you should alight at my house. You have very warm friends in the Miss Grants, who will be overjoyed to have you to themselves. If you think I have been of use to you, you can thus easily repay me, and so far from losing, may reap some advantage by the way. It is not every strange young man who is presented in society by the King's Advocate."

Often enough already (in our brief relations) this gentleman had caused my head to spin; no doubt but what for a moment he did so again now. Here was the old fiction still maintained of my particular favour with his daughters, one of whom had been so good as to laugh at me, while the other two had scarce deigned to remark the fact of my existence. And now I was to ride with my lord to Glasgow; I was to dwell with him in Edinburgh; I was to be brought into society under his protection! That he should have so much good-nature as to forgive me was surprising enough; that he could wish to take me up and serve me seemed impossible; and I began to seek some ulterior meaning. One was plain. If I became his guest, repentance was excluded; I could never think better of my present design and bring any action. And besides, would not my presence in his house draw out the whole pungency of the memorial? For that complaint could not be very seriously regarded, if the person chiefly injured was the guest of the official most incriminated. As I thought upon this I could not quite refrain from smiling.

"This is in the nature of a countercheck to the memorial?" said I.

"You are cunning, Mr. David," said he, "and you do not wholly guess wrong the fact will be of use to me in my defence. Perhaps, however, you underrate friendly sentiments, which are perfectly genuine. I have a respect for you, David, mingled with awe," says he, smiling.

"I am more than willing, I am earnestly desirous to meet your wishes," said I. "It is my design to be called to the Bar, where your lordship's countenance would be invaluable; and I am besides sincerely grateful to yourself and family for different marks of interest and of indulgence. The difficulty is here. There is one point in which we pull two ways. You are trying to hang James Stewart, I am trying to save him. In so far as my riding with you would better your lordship's defence, I am at your lordships orders; but in so far as it would help to hang James Stewart, you see me at a stick."

I thought he swore to himself. "You should certainly be called; the Bar is the true scene for your talents," says he, bitterly, and then fell a while silent. "I will tell you," he presently resumed, "there is no question of James Stewart, for or against, James is a dead man; his life is given and taken—bought (if you like it better) and sold; no memorial can help—no defalcation of a faithful Mr. David hurt him. Blow high, blow low, there will be no pardon for James Stewart: and take that for said! The question is now of myself: am I to stand or fall? and I do not deny to you that I am in some danger. But will Mr. David Balfour consider why? It is not because I pushed the case unduly against James; for that, I am sure of condonation. And it is not because I have sequestered Mr. David on a rock, though it will pass under that colour; but because I did not take the ready and plain path, to which I was pressed repeatedly, and send Mr. David to his grave or to the gallows. Hence the scandal—hence this damned memorial," striking the paper on his leg. "My tenderness for you has brought me in this difficulty. I wish to know if your tenderness to your own conscience is too great to let you help me out of it."

No doubt but there was much of the truth in what he said; if James was past helping, whom was it more natural that I should turn to help than just the man before me, who had helped myself so often, and was even now setting me a pattern of patience? I was besides not only weary, but beginning to be ashamed, of my perpetual attitude of suspicion and refusal.

"If you will name the time and place, I will be punctually ready to attend your lordship," said I.

He shook hands with me. "And I think my misses have some news for you," says he, dismissing me.

I came away, vastly pleased to have my peace made, yet a little concerned in conscience; nor could I help wondering, as I went back, whether, perhaps, I had not been a scruple too good-natured. But there was the fact, that this was a man that might have been my father, an able man, a great dignitary, and one that, in the hour of my need, had reached a hand to my assistance. I was in the better humour to enjoy the remainder of that evening, which I passed with the advocates, in excellent company no doubt, but perhaps with rather more than a sufficiency of punch: for though I went early to bed I have no clear mind of how I got there.

CHAPTER XVIII—THE TEE'D BALL

On the morrow, from the justices' private room, where none could see me, I heard the verdict given in and judgment rendered upon James. The Duke's words I am quite sure I have correctly; and since that famous passage has been made a subject of dispute, I may as well commemorate my version. Having referred to the year '45, the chief of the Campbells, sitting as Justice-General upon the bench, thus addressed the unfortunate Stewart before him: "If you had been successful in that rebellion, you might have been giving the law where you have now received the judgment of it; we, who are this day your judges, might have been tried before one of your mock courts of judicature; and then you might have been satiated with the blood of any name or clan to which you had an aversion."

"This is to let the cat out of the bag, indeed," thought I. And that was the general impression. It was extraordinary how the young advocate lads took hold and made a mock of this speech, and how scarce a meal passed but what someone would get in the words: "And then you might have been satiated." Many songs were made in time for the hour's diversion, and are near all forgot. I remember one began:

> "What do ye want the bluid of, bluid of?
>
> Is it a name, or is it a clan,
>
> Or is it an aefauld Hielandman,
>
> That ye want the bluid of, bluid of?"

Another went to my old favourite air, The House of Airlie, and began thus:

> "It fell on a day when Argyle was on the bench,
>
> That they served him a Stewart for his denner."

And one of the verses ran:

"Then up and spak' the Duke, and flyted on his cook,

I regard it as a sensible aspersion,

That I would sup ava', an' satiate my maw,

With the bluid of ony clan of my aversion."

James was as fairly murdered as though the Duke had got a fowling-piece and stalked him. So much of course I knew: but others knew not so much, and were more affected by the items of scandal that came to light in the progress of the cause. One of the chief was certainly this sally of the justice's. It was run hard by another of a juryman, who had struck into the midst of Coulston's speech for the defence with a "Pray, sir, cut it short, we are quite weary," which seemed the very excess of impudence and simplicity. But some of my new lawyer friends were still more staggered with an innovation that had disgraced and even vitiated the proceedings. One witness was never called. His name, indeed, was printed, where it may still be seen on the fourth page of the list: "James Drummond, alias Macgregor, alias James More, late tenant in Inveronachile"; and his precognition had been taken, as the manner is, in writing. He had remembered or invented (God help him) matter which was lead in James Stewart's shoes, and I saw was like to prove wings to his own. This testimony it was highly desirable to bring to the notice of the jury, without exposing the man himself to the perils of cross-examination; and the way it was brought about was a matter of surprise to all. For the paper was handed round (like a curiosity) in court; passed through the jury-box, where it did its work; and disappeared again (as though by accident) before it reached the counsel for the prisoner. This was counted a most insidious device; and that the name of James More should be mingled up with it filled me with shame for Catriona and concern for myself.

The following day, Prestongrange and I, with a considerable company, set out for Glasgow, where (to my impatience) we continued to linger some time in a mixture of pleasure and affairs. I lodged with my lord, with whom I was encouraged to familiarity; had my place at entertainments; was presented to the chief guests; and altogether made more of than I thought accorded either with my parts or station; so that, on strangers being present, I would often blush for Prestongrange. It must be owned the view I had taken of the world in these last months was fit to cast a gloom upon my character. I had met many men, some of them leaders in Israel whether by their birth or talents; and who among them all had shown clean hands? As for the Browns and Millers, I had seen their self-seeking, I could never again respect them. Prestongrange was the best yet; he had saved me, spared me rather, when others had it in their minds to murder me outright; but the blood of James lay at his door; and I thought his present dissimulation with myself a thing below pardon. That he should affect to find pleasure in my discourse almost surprised me out of my patience. I would sit and watch him with a kind of a slow fire of anger in my bowels. "Ah, friend, friend," I would think to myself, "if you were but through with this affair of the memorial, would you not kick me in the streets?" Here I did him, as events have proved, the most grave injustice; and I think he was at once far more sincere, and a far more artful performer, than I supposed.

But I had some warrant for my incredulity in the behaviour of that court of young advocates that hung about in the hope of patronage. The sudden favour of a lad not previously heard of troubled them at first out of measure; but two days were not gone by before I found myself surrounded with flattery and attention. I was the same young man, and neither better nor bonnier, that they had rejected a month before; and now there was no civility too fine for me! The same, do I say? It was not so; and the by-name by which I went behind my back confirmed it. Seeing me so firm with the Advocate, and persuaded that I was to fly high and far, they had taken a word from the golfing green, and called me the Tee'd Ball. [14] I was told I was now "one of themselves"; I was to taste of their soft lining, who had already made my own experience of the roughness of the outer husk; and one, to whom I had been presented in Hope Park, was so aspired as even to remind me of that meeting. I told him I had not the pleasure of remembering it.

"Why" says he, "it was Miss Grant herself presented me! My name is so-and-so."

"It may very well be, sir," said I; "but I have kept no mind of it."

At which he desisted; and in the midst of the disgust that commonly overflowed my spirits I had a glisk of pleasure.

But I have not patience to dwell upon that time at length. When I was in company with these young politics I was borne down with shame for myself and my own plain ways, and scorn for them and their duplicity. Of the two evils, I thought Prestongrange to be the least; and while I was always as stiff as buckram to the young bloods, I made rather a dissimulation of my hard feelings towards the Advocate, and was (in old Mr. Campbell's word) "soople to the laird." Himself commented on the difference, and bid me be more of my age, and make friends with my young comrades.

I told him I was slow of making friends.

"I will take the word back," said he. "But there is such a thing as Fair gude s'en and fair gude day, Mr. David. These are the same young men with whom you are to pass your days and get through life: your backwardness has a look of arrogance; and unless you can assume a little more lightness of manner, I fear you will meet difficulties in the path."

"It will be an ill job to make a silk purse of a sow's ear," said I.

On the morning of October 1st I was awakened by the clattering in of an express; and getting to my window almost before he had dismounted, I saw the messenger had ridden hard. Somewhile after I was called to Prestongrange, where he was sitting in his bedgown and nightcap, with his letters round him.

"Mr. David," add he, "I have a piece of news for you. It concerns some friends of yours, of whom I sometimes think you are a little ashamed, for you have never referred to their existence."

I suppose I blushed.

"See you understand, since you make the answering signal," said he. "And I must compliment you on your excellent taste in beauty. But do you know, Mr. David? this seems to me a very enterprising lass. She crops up from every side. The Government of Scotland appears unable to proceed for Mistress Katrine Drummond, which was somewhat the case (no great while back) with a certain Mr. David Balfour. Should not these make a good match? Her first intromission in politics—but I must not tell you that story, the authorities have decided you are to hear it otherwise and from a livelier narrator. This new example is more serious, however; and I am afraid I must alarm you with the intelligence that she is now in prison."

I cried out.

"Yes," said he, "the little lady is in prison. But I would not have you to despair. Unless you (with your friends and memorials) shall procure my downfall, she is to suffer nothing."

"But what has she done? What is her offence?" I cried.

"It might be almost construed a high treason," he returned, "for she has broke the king's Castle of Edinburgh."

"The lady is much my friend," I said. "I know you would not mock me if the thing were serious."

"And yet it is serious in a sense," said he; "for this rogue of a Katrine—or Cateran, as we may call her—has set adrift again upon the world that very doubtful character, her papa."

Here was one of my previsions justified: James More was once again at liberty. He had lent his men to keep me a prisoner; he had volunteered his testimony in the Appin case, and the same (no matter by what subterfuge) had been employed to influence the jury. Now came his reward, and he was free. It might please the authorities to give to it the colour of an escape; but I knew better—I knew it must be the fulfilment of a bargain. The same course of thought relieved me of the least alarm for Catriona. She might be thought to have broke prison for her father; she might have believed so herself. But the chief hand in the whole business was that of Prestongrange; and I was sure, so far from letting her come to punishment, he would not suffer her to be even tried. Whereupon thus came out of me the not very politic ejaculation:

"Ah! I was expecting that!"

302

"You have at times a great deal of discretion, too!" says Prestongrange.

"And what is my lord pleased to mean by that?" I asked.

"I was just marvelling", he replied, "that being so clever as to draw these inferences, you should not be clever enough to keep them to yourself. But I think you would like to hear the details of the affair. I have received two versions: and the least official is the more full and far the more entertaining, being from the lively pen of my eldest daughter. 'Here is all the town bizzing with a fine piece of work,' she writes, 'and what would make the thing more noted (if it were only known) the malefactor is a protégée of his lordship my papa. I am sure your heart is too much in your duty (if it were nothing else) to have forgotten Grey Eyes. What does she do, but get a broad hat with the flaps open, a long hairy-like man's greatcoat, and a big gravatt; kilt her coats up to Gude kens whaur, clap two pair of boot-hose upon her legs, take a pair of clouted brogues [15] in her hand, and off to the Castle! Here she gives herself out to be a soutar [16] in the employ of James More, and gets admitted to his cell, the lieutenant (who seems to have been full of pleasantry) making sport among his soldiers of the soutar's greatcoat. Presently they hear disputation and the sound of blows inside. Out flies the cobbler, his coat flying, the flaps of his hat beat about his face, and the lieutenant and his soldiers mock at him as he runs off. They laughed no so hearty the next time they had occasion to visit the cell and found nobody but a tall, pretty, grey-eyed lass in the female habit! As for the cobbler, he was 'over the hills ayout Dumblane,' and it's thought that poor Scotland will have to console herself without him. I drank Catriona's health this night in public. Indeed, the whole town admires her; and I think the beaux would wear bits of her garters in their button-holes if they could only get them. I would have gone to visit her in prison too, only I remembered in time I was papa's daughter; so I wrote her a billet instead, which I entrusted to the faithful Doig, and I hope you will admit I can be political when I please. The same faithful gomeral is to despatch this letter by the express along with those of the wiseacres, so that you may hear Tom Fool in company with Solomon. Talking of gomerals, do tell Dauvit Balfour. I would I could see the face of him at the thought of a long-legged lass in such a predicament; to say nothing of the levities of your affectionate daughter, and his respectful friend.' So my rascal signs herself!" continued Prestongrange. "And you see, Mr. David, it is quite true what I tell you, that my daughters regard you with the most affectionate playfulness."

"The gomeral is much obliged," said I.

"And was not this prettily done!" he went on. "Is not this Highland maid a piece of a heroine?"

"I was always sure she had a great heart," said I. "And I wager she guessed nothing . . . But I beg your pardon, this is to tread upon forbidden subjects."

"I will go bail she did not," he returned, quite openly. "I will go bail she thought she was flying straight into King George's face."

Remembrance of Catriona and the thought of her lying in captivity, moved me strangely. I could see that even Prestongrange admired, and could not withhold his lips from smiling when he considered her behaviour. As for Miss Grant, for all her ill habit of mockery, her admiration shone out plain. A kind of a heat came on me.

"I am not your lordship's daughter. . . " I began.

"That I know of!" he put in, smiling.

"I speak like a fool," said I; "or rather I began wrong. It would doubtless be unwise in Mistress Grant to go to her in prison; but for me, I think I would look like a half-hearted friend if I did not fly there instantly."

"So-ho, Mr. David," says he; "I thought that you and I were in a bargain?"

"My lord," I said, "when I made that bargain I was a good deal affected by your goodness, but I'll never can deny that I was moved besides by my own interest. There was self-seeking in my heart, and I think shame of it now. It may be for your lordship's safety to say this fashious Davie Balfour is your friend and housemate. Say it then; I'll never contradict you. But as for your patronage, I give it all back. I ask but the one thing—let me go, and give me a pass to see her in her prison."

He looked at me with a hard eye. "You put the cart before the horse, I think," says he. "That which I had given was a portion of my liking, which your thankless nature does not seem to have remarked. But for my patronage, it is not given, nor (to be exact) is it yet offered." He paused a bit. "And I warn you, you do not know yourself," he added. "Youth is a hasty season; you will think better of all this before a year."

"Well, and I would like to be that kind of youth!" I cried. "I have seen too much of the other party in these young advocates that fawn upon your lordship and are even at the pains to fawn on me. And I have seen it in the old ones also. They are all for by-ends, the whole clan of them! It's this that makes me seem to misdoubt your lordship's liking. Why would I think that you would like me? But ye told me yourself ye had an interest!"

I stopped at this, confounded that I had run so far; he was observing me with an unfathomable face.

"My lord, I ask your pardon," I resumed. "I have nothing in my chafts but a rough country tongue. I think it would be only decent-like if I would go to see my friend in her captivity; but I'm owing you my life—I'll never forget that; and if it's for your lordship's good, here I'll stay. That's barely gratitude."

"This might have been reached in fewer words," says Prestongrange grimly. "It is easy, and it is at times gracious, to say a plain Scots 'ay'."

"Ah, but, my lord, I think ye take me not yet entirely!" cried I. "For your sake, for my life-safe, and the kindness that ye say ye bear to me—for these, I'll consent; but not for any good that might be coming to myself. If I stand aside when this young maid is in her trial, it's a thing I will be noways advantaged by; I will lose by it, I will never gain. I would rather make a shipwreck wholly than to build on that foundation."

He was a minute serious, then smiled. "You mind me of the man with the long nose," said he; "was you to see the moon by a telescope you would see David Balfour there! But you shall have your way of it. I will ask at you one service, and then set you free: My clerks are overdriven; be so good as copy me these few pages, and when that is done, I shall bid you God speed! I would never charge myself with Mr. David's conscience; and if you could cast some part of it (as you went by) in a moss hag, you would find yourself to ride much easier without it."

"Perhaps not just entirely in the same direction though, my lord!" says I.

"And you shall have the last word, too!" cries he gaily.

Indeed, he had some cause for gaiety, having now found the means to gain his purpose. To lessen the weight of the memorial, or to have a readier answer at his hand, he desired I should appear publicly in the character of his intimate. But if I were to appear with the same publicity as a visitor to Catriona in her prison the world would scarce stint to draw conclusions, and the true nature of James More's escape must become evident to all. This was the little problem I had to set him of a sudden, and to which he had so briskly found an answer. I was to be tethered in Glasgow by that job of copying, which in mere outward decency I could not well refuse; and during these hours of employment Catriona was privately got rid of. I think shame to write of this man that loaded me with so many goodnesses. He was kind to me as any father, yet I ever thought him as false as a cracked bell.

CHAPTER XIX—I AM MUCH IN THE HANDS OF THE LADIES

The copying was a weary business, the more so as I perceived very early there was no sort of urgency in the matters treated, and began very early to consider my employment a pretext. I had no sooner finished than I got to horse, used what remained of daylight to the best purpose, and being at last fairly benighted, slept in a house by Almond-Water side. I was in the saddle again before the day, and the Edinburgh booths were just opening when I clattered in by the West Bow and drew up a smoking horse at my lord Advocate's door. I had a written word for Doig, my lord's private hand that was thought to be in all his secrets—a worthy little plain man, all fat and snuff and self-sufficiency. Him I found already at his desk and already bedabbled with maccabaw, in the same anteroom where I rencountered with James More. He read the note scrupulously through like a chapter in his Bible.

"H'm," says he; "ye come a wee thing ahint-hand, Mr. Balfour. The bird's flaen—we hae letten her out."

"Miss Drummond is set free?" I cried.

"Achy!" said he. "What would we keep her for, ye ken? To hae made a steer about the bairn would has pleased naebody."

"And where'll she be now?" says I.

"Gude kens!" says Doig, with a shrug.

"She'll have gone home to Lady Allardyce, I'm thinking," said I.

"That'll be it," said he.

"Then I'll gang there straight," says I.

"But ye'll be for a bite or ye go?" said he.

"Neither bite nor sup," said I. "I had a good wauch of milk in by Ratho."

"Aweel, aweel," says Doig. "But ye'll can leave your horse here and your bags, for it seems we're to have your up-put."

"Na, na", said I. "Tamson's mear [17] would never be the thing for me this day of all days."

Doig speaking somewhat broad, I had been led by imitation into an accent much more countrified than I was usually careful to affect a good deal broader, indeed, than I have written it down; and I was the more ashamed when another voice joined in behind me with a scrap of a ballad:

"Gae saddle me the bonny black,

Gae saddle sune and mak' him ready

For I will down the Gatehope-slack,

And a' to see my bonny leddy."

The young lady, when I turned to her, stood in a morning gown, and her hands muffled in the same, as if to hold me at a distance. Yet I could not but think there was kindness in the eye with which she saw me.

"My best respects to you, Mistress Grant," said I, bowing.

"The like to yourself, Mr. David," she replied with a deep courtesy. "And I beg to remind you of an old musty saw, that meat and mass never hindered man. The mass I cannot afford you, for we are all good Protestants. But the meat I press on your attention. And I would not wonder but I could find something for your private ear that would be worth the stopping for."

"Mistress Grant," said I, "I believe I am already your debtor for some merry words—and I think they were kind too—on a piece of unsigned paper."

"Unsigned paper?" says she, and made a droll face, which was likewise wondrous beautiful, as of one trying to remember.

"Or else I am the more deceived," I went on. "But to be sure, we shall have the time to speak of these, since your father is so good as to make me for a while your inmate; and the gomeral begs you at this time only for the favour of his liberty."

"You give yourself hard names," said she.

"Mr. Doig and I would be blythe to take harder at your clever pen," says I.

"Once more I have to admire the discretion of all men-folk," she replied. "But if you will not eat, off with you at once; you will be back the sooner, for you go on a fool's errand. Off with you, Mr. David," she continued, opening the door.

> "He has lowpen on his bonny grey,
>
> He rade the richt gate and the ready
>
> I trow he would neither stint nor stay,
>
> For he was seeking his bonny leddy."

I did not wait to be twice bidden, and did justice to Miss Grant's citation on the way to Dean.

Old Lady Allardyce walked there alone in the garden, in her hat and mutch, and having a silver-mounted staff of some black wood to lean upon. As I alighted from my horse, and drew near to her with congees, I could see the blood come in her face, and her head fling into the air like what I had conceived of empresses.

"What brings you to my poor door?" she cried, speaking high through her nose. "I cannot bar it. The males of my house are dead and buried; I have neither son nor husband to stand in the gate for me; any beggar can pluck me by the baird [18]—and a baird there is, and that's the worst of it yet!" she added partly to herself.

I was extremely put out at this reception, and the last remark, which seemed like a daft wife's, left me near hand speechless.

"I see I have fallen under your displeasure, ma'am," said I. "Yet I will still be so bold as ask after Mistress Drummond."

She considered me with a burning eye, her lips pressed close together into twenty creases, her hand shaking on her staff. "This cows all!" she cried. "Ye come to me to speir for her? Would God I knew!"

"She is not here?" I cried.

She threw up her chin and made a step and a cry at me, so that I fell back incontinent.

"Out upon your leeing throat!" she cried. "What! ye come and speir at me! She's in jyle, whaur ye took her to—that's all there is to it. And of a' the beings ever I beheld in breeks, to think it should be to you! Ye timmer scoun'rel, if I had a male left to my name I would have your jaicket dustit till ye raired."

I thought it not good to delay longer in that place, because I remarked her passion to be rising. As I turned to the horse-post she even followed me; and I make no shame to confess that I rode away with the one stirrup on and scrambling for the other.

As I knew no other quarter where I could push my inquiries, there was nothing left me but to return to the Advocate's. I was well received by the four ladies, who were now in company together, and must give the news of Prestongrange and what word went in the west country, at the most inordinate length and with great weariness to myself; while all the time that young lady, with whom I so much desired to be alone again, observed me quizzically and seemed to find pleasure in the sight of my impatience. At last, after I had endured a meal with them, and was come very near the point of appealing for an interview before her aunt, she went and stood by the music-case, and picking out a tune, sang to it on a high key—"He that will not when he may, When he will he shall have nay." But this was the end of her rigours, and presently, after making some excuse of which I have no mind, she carried me away in private to her father's library. I should not fail to say she was dressed to the nines, and appeared extraordinary handsome.

"Now, Mr. David, sit ye down here and let us have a two-handed crack," said she. "For I have much to tell you, and it appears besides that I have been

310

grossly unjust to your good taste."

"In what manner, Mistress Grant?" I asked. "I trust I have never seemed to fail in due respect."

"I will be your surety, Mr. David," said she. "Your respect, whether to yourself or your poor neighbours, has been always and most fortunately beyond imitation. But that is by the question. You got a note from me?" she asked.

"I was so bold as to suppose so upon inference," said I, "and it was kindly thought upon."

"It must have prodigiously surprised you," said she. "But let us begin with the beginning. You have not perhaps forgot a day when you were so kind as to escort three very tedious misses to Hope Park? I have the less cause to forget it myself, because you was so particular obliging as to introduce me to some of the principles of the Latin grammar, a thing which wrote itself profoundly on my gratitude."

"I fear I was sadly pedantical," said I, overcome with confusion at the memory. "You are only to consider I am quite unused with the society of ladies."

"I will say the less about the grammar then," she replied. "But how came you to desert your charge? 'He has thrown her out, overboard, his ain dear Annie!'" she hummed; "and his ain dear Annie and her two sisters had to taigle home by theirselves like a string of green geese! It seems you returned to my papa's, where you showed yourself excessively martial, and then on to realms unknown, with an eye (it appears) to the Bass Rock; solan geese being perhaps more to your mind than bonny lasses."

Through all this raillery there was something indulgent in the lady's eye which made me suppose there might be better coming.

"You take a pleasure to torment me," said I, "and I make a very feckless plaything; but let me ask you to be more merciful. At this time there is but the one thing that I care to hear of, and that will be news of Catriona."

"Do you call her by that name to her face, Mr. Balfour?" she asked.

"In troth, and I am not very sure," I stammered.

"I would not do so in any case to strangers," said Miss Grant. "And why are you so much immersed in the affairs of this young lady?"

"I heard she was in prison," said I.

"Well, and now you hear that she is out of it," she replied, "and what more would you have? She has no need of any further champion."

"I may have the greater need of her, ma'am," said I.

"Come, this is better!" says Miss Grant. "But look me fairly in the face; am I not bonnier than she?"

"I would be the last to be denying it," said I. "There is not your marrow in all Scotland."

"Well, here you have the pick of the two at your hand, and must needs speak of the other," said she. "This is never the way to please the ladies, Mr. Balfour."

"But, mistress," said I, "there are surely other things besides mere beauty."

"By which I am to understand that I am no better than I should be, perhaps?" she asked.

"By which you will please understand that I am like the cock in the midden in the fable book," said I. "I see the braw jewel—and I like fine to see it too—but I have more need of the pickle corn."

"Bravissimo!" she cried. "There is a word well said at last, and I will reward you for it with my story. That same night of your desertion I came late from a friend's house—where I was excessively admired, whatever you may think of it—and what should I hear but that a lass in a tartan screen desired to speak with me? She had been there an hour or better, said the servant-lass, and she grat in to herself as she sat waiting. I went to her direct; she rose as I came in, and I knew her at a look. 'Grey Eyes!' says I to myself, but was more wise than to let on. You will be Miss Grant at last? she says, rising and looking at me hard and pitiful. Ay, it was true he said, you are bonny at all events.—The way God made me, my dear, I said, but I would be gey and obliged if you could tell me what brought you here at such a time of the night.—Lady, she said, we are kinsfolk, we are both come of the blood of the sons of Alpin.—My dear, I replied, I think no more of Alpin or his sons than what I do of a kalestock. You have a better argument in these tears upon your bonny face. And at that I was so weak-minded as to kiss her, which is what you would like to do dearly, and I wager will never find the courage of. I say it was weak-minded of me, for I knew no more of her than the outside; but it was the wisest stroke I could have hit upon. She is a very staunch, brave nature, but I think she has been little used with tenderness; and at that caress (though to say the truth, it was but lightly given) her heart went out to me. I will never betray the secrets of my sex, Mr. Davie; I will never tell you the way she turned me round her thumb, because it is the same she will use to twist yourself. Ay, it is a fine lass! She is as clean as hill well water."

"She is e'en't!" I cried.

"Well, then, she told me her concerns," pursued Miss Grant, "and in what a swither she was in about her papa, and what a taking about yourself, with very little cause, and in what a perplexity she had found herself after you was gone away. And then I minded at long last, says she, that we were kinswomen, and that Mr. David should have given you the name of the bonniest of the bonny, and I was thinking to myself 'If she is so bonny she will be good at all events'; and I took up my foot soles out of that. That was when I forgave yourself, Mr. Davie. When you was in my society, you seemed upon hot iron: by all marks, if ever I saw a young man that wanted to be gone, it was yourself, and I and my two sisters were the ladies you were so desirous to be gone from; and now it appeared you had given me some notice in the by-going, and was so kind as to comment on my attractions! From that hour you may date our friendship, and I began to think with tenderness upon the Latin grammar."

"You will have many hours to rally me in," said I; "and I think besides you do yourself injustice. I think it was Catriona turned your heart in my

313

The Ebb-Tide. A Trio and a Quartette & David Balfour

direction. She is too simple to perceive as you do the stiffness of her friend."

"I would not like to wager upon that, Mr. David," said she. "The lasses have clear eyes. But at least she is your friend entirely, as I was to see. I carried her in to his lordship my papa; and his Advocacy being in a favourable stage of claret, was so good as to receive the pair of us. Here is Grey Eyes that you have been deaved with these days past, said I, she is come to prove that we spoke true, and I lay the prettiest lass in the three Lothians at your feet—making a papistical reservation of myself. She suited her action to my words: down she went upon her knees to him—I would not like to swear but he saw two of her, which doubtless made her appeal the more irresistible, for you are all a pack of Mahomedans—told him what had passed that night, and how she had withheld her father's man from following of you, and what a case she was in about her father, and what a flutter for yourself; and begged with weeping for the lives of both of you (neither of which was in the slightest danger), till I vow I was proud of my sex because it was done so pretty, and ashamed for it because of the smallness of the occasion. She had not gone far, I assure you, before the Advocate was wholly sober, to see his inmost politics ravelled out by a young lass and discovered to the most unruly of his daughters. But we took him in hand, the pair of us, and brought that matter straight. Properly managed—and that means managed by me—there is no one to compare with my papa."

"He has been a good man to me," said I.

"Well, he was a good man to Katrine, and I was there to see to it," said she.

"And she pled for me?" say I.

"She did that, and very movingly," said Miss Grant. "I would not like to tell you what she said—I find you vain enough already."

"God reward her for it!" cried I.

"With Mr. David Balfour, I suppose?" says she.

"You do me too much injustice at the last!" I cried. "I would tremble to think of her in such hard hands. Do you think I would presume, because she begged my life? She would do that for a new whelped puppy! I have had more than that to set me up, if you but ken'd. She kissed that hand of mine. Ay, but she did. And why? because she thought I was playing a brave part and might be going to my death. It was not for my sake—but I need not be telling that to you, that cannot look at me without laughter. It was for the love of what she thought was bravery. I believe there is none but me and poor Prince Charlie had that honour done them. Was this not to make a god of me? and do you not think my heart would quake when I remember it?"

"I do laugh at you a good deal, and a good deal more than is quite civil," said she; "but I will tell you one thing: if you speak to her like that, you have some glimmerings of a chance."

"Me?" I cried, "I would never dare. I can speak to you, Miss Grant, because it's a matter of indifference what ye think of me. But her? no fear!" said I.

"I think you have the largest feet in all broad Scotland," says she.

"Troth they are no very small," said I, looking down.

"Ah, poor Catriona!" cries Miss Grant.

And I could but stare upon her; for though I now see very well what she was driving at (and perhaps some justification for the same), I was never swift at the uptake in such flimsy talk.

"Ah well, Mr. David," she said, "it goes sore against my conscience, but I see I shall have to be your speaking board. She shall know you came to her straight upon the news of her imprisonment; she shall know you would not pause to eat; and of our conversation she shall hear just so much as I think convenient for a maid of her age and inexperience. Believe me, you will be in that way much better served than you could serve yourself, for I will keep the big feet out of the platter."

"You know where she is, then?" I exclaimed.

"That I do, Mr. David, and will never tell," said she.

"Why that?" I asked.

"Well," she said, "I am a good friend, as you will soon discover; and the chief of those that I am friend to is my papa. I assure you, you will never heat nor melt me out of that, so you may spare me your sheep's eyes; and adieu to your David-Balfourship for the now."

"But there is yet one thing more," I cried. "There is one thing that must be stopped, being mere ruin to herself, and to me too."

"Well," she said, "be brief; I have spent half the day on you already."

"My Lady Allardyce believes," I began—"she supposes—she thinks that I abducted her."

The colour came into Miss Grant's face, so that at first I was quite abashed to find her ear so delicate, till I bethought me she was struggling rather with mirth, a notion in which I was altogether confirmed by the shaking of her voice as she replied—

"I will take up the defence of your reputation," she said. "You may leave it in my hands."

And with that she withdrew out of the library.

CHAPTER XX—I CONTINUE TO MOVE IN GOOD SOCIETY

For about exactly two months I remained a guest in Prestongrange's family, where I bettered my acquaintance with the bench, the bar, and the flower of Edinburgh company. You are not to suppose my education was neglected; on the contrary, I was kept extremely busy. I studied the French, so as to be more prepared to go to Leyden; I set myself to the fencing, and wrought hard, sometimes three hours in the day, with notable advancement; at the suggestion of my cousin, Pilrig, who was an apt musician, I was put to a singing class; and by the orders of my Miss Grant, to one for the dancing, at which I must say I proved far from ornamental. However, all were good enough to say it gave me an address a little more genteel; and there is no question but I learned to manage my coat skirts and sword with more dexterity, and to stand in a room as though the same belonged to me. My clothes themselves were all earnestly re-ordered; and the most trifling circumstance, such as where I should tie my hair, or the colour of my ribbon, debated among the three misses like a thing of weight. One way with another, no doubt I was a good deal improved to look at, and acquired a bit of modest air that would have surprised the good folks at Essendean.

The two younger misses were very willing to discuss a point of my habiliment, because that was in the line of their chief thoughts. I cannot say that they appeared any other way conscious of my presence; and though always more than civil, with a kind of heartless cordiality, could not hide how much I wearied them. As for the aunt, she was a wonderful still woman; and I think she gave me much the same attention as she gave the rest of the family, which was little enough. The eldest daughter and the Advocate himself were thus my principal friends, and our familiarity was much increased by a pleasure that we took in common. Before the court met we spent a day or two at the house of Grange, living very nobly with an open table, and here it was that we three began to ride out together in the fields, a practice afterwards maintained in Edinburgh, so far as the Advocate's continual affairs permitted. When we were put in a good frame by the briskness of the exercise, the difficulties of the way, or the accidents of bad weather, my shyness wore entirely off; we forgot that we were strangers, and speech not being required, it flowed the more naturally on. Then it was that they had my story from me, bit by bit, from the time that I left Essendean, with my voyage and battle in the Covenant, wanderings in the heather, etc.; and from the interest they found in my adventures sprung the circumstance of a jaunt we made a little later on, on a day when the courts were not sitting, and of which I will tell a trifle more at length.

We took horse early, and passed first by the house of Shaws, where it stood smokeless in a great field of white frost, for it was yet early in the day. Here Prestongrange alighted down, gave me his horse, an proceeded alone to visit my uncle. My heart, I remember, swelled up bitter within me at the sight of that bare house and the thought of the old miser sitting chittering within in the cold kitchen!

"There is my home," said I; "and my family."

"Poor David Balfour!" said Miss Grant.

What passed during the visit I have never heard; but it would doubtless not be very agreeable to Ebenezer, for when the Advocate came forth again his face was dark.

"I think you will soon be the laird indeed, Mr. Davie," says he, turning half about with the one foot in the stirrup.

"I will never pretend sorrow," said I; and, to say the truth, during his absence Miss Grant and I had been embellishing the place in fancy with plantations, parterres, and a terrace—much as I have since carried out in fact.

Thence we pushed to the Queensferry, where Rankeillor gave us a good welcome, being indeed out of the body to receive so great a visitor. Here the Advocate was so unaffectedly good as to go quite fully over my affairs, sitting perhaps two hours with the Writer in his study, and expressing (I was told) a great esteem for myself and concern for my fortunes. To while this time, Miss Grant and I and young Rankeillor took boat and passed the Hope to Limekilns. Rankeillor made himself very ridiculous (and, I thought, offensive) with his admiration for the young lady, and to my wonder (only it is so common a weakness of her sex) she seemed, if anything, to be a little gratified. One use it had: for when we were come to the other side, she laid her commands on him to mind the boat, while she and I passed a little further to the alehouse. This was her own thought, for she had been taken with my account of Alison Hastie, and desired to see the lass herself. We found her once more alone—indeed, I believe her father wrought all day in the fields—and she curtsied dutifully to the gentry-folk and the beautiful young lady in the riding-coat.

"Is this all the welcome I am to get?" said I, holding out my hand. "And have you no more memory of old friends?"

"Keep me! wha's this of it?" she cried, and then, "God's truth, it's the tautit [19] laddie!"

"The very same," says I.

"Mony's the time I've thocht upon you and your freen, and blythe am I to see in your braws," [20] she cried. "Though I kent ye were come to your ain folk by the grand present that ye sent me and that I thank ye for with a' my heart."

"There," said Miss Grant to me, "run out by with ye, like a guid bairn. I didnae come here to stand and haud a candle; it's her and me that are to crack."

I suppose she stayed ten minutes in the house, but when she came forth I observed two things—that her eyes were reddened, and a silver brooch was gone out of her bosom. This very much affected me.

"I never saw you so well adorned," said I.

"O Davie man, dinna be a pompous gowk!" said she, and was more than usually sharp to me the remainder of the day.

About candlelight we came home from this excursion.

For a good while I heard nothing further of Catriona—my Miss Grant remaining quite impenetrable, and stopping my mouth with pleasantries. At last, one day that she returned from walking and found me alone in the parlour over my French, I thought there was something unusual in her looks; the colour heightened, the eyes sparkling high, and a bit of a smile continually bitten in as she regarded me. She seemed indeed like the very spirit of mischief, and, walking briskly in the room, had soon involved me in a kind of quarrel over nothing and (at the least) with nothing intended on my side. I was like Christian in the slough—the more I tried to clamber out upon the side, the deeper I became involved; until at last I heard her declare, with a great deal of passion, that she would take that answer from the hands of none, and I must down upon my knees for pardon.

The causelessness of all this fuff stirred my own bile. "I have said nothing you can properly object to," said I, "and as for my knees, that is an attitude I keep for God."

"And as a goddess I am to be served!" she cried, shaking her brown locks at me and with a bright colour. "Every man that comes within waft of my petticoats shall use me so!"

"I will go so far as ask your pardon for the fashion's sake, although I vow I know not why," I replied. "But for these play-acting postures, you can go to others."

"O Davie!" she said. "Not if I was to beg you?"

I bethought me I was fighting with a woman, which is the same as to say a child, and that upon a point entirely formal.

"I think it a bairnly thing," I said, "not worthy in you to ask, or me to render. Yet I will not refuse you, neither," said I; "and the stain, if there be any, rests with yourself." And at that I kneeled fairly down.

"There!" she cried. "There is the proper station, there is where I have been manoeuvring to bring you." And then, suddenly, "Kep," [21] said she, flung me a folded billet, and ran from the apartment laughing.

The billet had neither place nor date. "Dear Mr. David," it began, "I get your news continually by my cousin, Miss Grant, and it is a pleisand hearing. I am very well, in a good place, among good folk, but necessitated to be quite private, though I am hoping that at long last we may meet again. All your friendships have been told me by my loving cousin, who loves us both. She bids me to send you this writing, and oversees the same. I will be asking you to do all her commands, and rest your affectionate friend, Catriona Macgregor-Drummond. P.S.—Will you not see my cousin, Allardyce?"

I think it not the least brave of my campaigns (as the soldiers say) that I should have done as I was here bidden and gone forthright to the house by Dean. But the old lady was now entirely changed and supple as a glove. By what means Miss Grant had brought this round I could never guess; I am sure, at least, she dared not to appear openly in the affair, for her papa was compromised in it pretty deep. It was he, indeed, who had persuaded Catriona to leave, or rather, not to return, to her cousin's, placing her instead with a family of Gregorys—decent people, quite at the Advocate's disposition, and in whom she might have the more confidence because they were of his own clan and family. These kept her private till all was ripe, heated and helped her to attempt her father's rescue, and after she was discharged from prison received her again into the same secrecy. Thus Prestongrange obtained and used his instrument; nor did there leak out the smallest word of his acquaintance with the daughter of James More. There was some whispering, of course, upon the escape of that discredited person; but the Government replied by a show of rigour, one of the cell porters was flogged, the lieutenant of the guard (my poor friend, Duncansby) was broken of his rank, and as for Catriona, all men were well enough pleased that her fault should be passed by in silence.

I could never induce Miss Grant to carry back an answer. "No," she would say, when I persisted, "I am going to keep the big feet out of the platter." This was the more hard to bear, as I was aware she saw my little friend many times in the week, and carried her my news whenever (as she said) I "had behaved myself." At last she treated me to what she called an indulgence, and I thought rather more of a banter. She was certainly a strong, almost a violent, friend to all she liked, chief among whom was a certain frail old gentlewoman, very blind and very witty, who dwelt on the top of a tall land on a strait close, with a nest of linnets in a cage, and thronged all day with visitors. Miss Grant was very fond to carry me there and put me to entertain her friend with the narrative of my misfortunes: and Miss Tibbie Ramsay (that was her name) was particular kind, and told me a great deal that was worth knowledge of old folks and past affairs in Scotland. I should say that from her chamber window, and not three feet away, such is the straitness of that close, it was possible to look into a barred loophole lighting the stairway of the opposite house.

Here, upon some pretext, Miss Grant left me one day alone with Miss Ramsay. I mind I thought that lady inattentive and like one preoccupied. I was besides very uncomfortable, for the window, contrary to custom, was left open and the day was cold. All at once the voice of Miss Grant sounded in my ears as from a distance.

"Here, Shaws!" she cried, "keek out of the window and see what I have broughten you."

I think it was the prettiest sight that ever I beheld. The well of the close was all in clear shadow where a man could see distinctly, the walls very black and dingy; and there from the barred loophole I saw two faces smiling across at me—Miss Grant's and Catriona's.

"There!" says Miss Grant, "I wanted her to see you in your braws like the lass of Limekilns. I wanted her to see what I could make of you, when I buckled to the job in earnest!"

It came in my mind that she had been more than common particular that day upon my dress; and I think that some of the same care had been bestowed upon Catriona. For so merry and sensible a lady, Miss Grant was certainly wonderful taken up with duds.

"Catriona!" was all I could get out.

As for her, she said nothing in the world, but only waved her hand and smiled to me, and was suddenly carried away again from before the loophole.

That vision was no sooner lost than I ran to the house door, where I found I was locked in; thence back to Miss Ramsay, crying for the key, but might as well have cried upon the castle rock. She had passed her word, she said, and I must be a good lad. It was impossible to burst the door, even if it had been mannerly; it was impossible I should leap from the window, being seven storeys above ground. All I could do was to crane over the close and watch for their reappearance from the stair. It was little to see, being no more than the tops of their two heads each on a ridiculous bobbin of skirts, like to a pair of pincushions. Nor did Catriona so much as look up for a farewell; being prevented (as I heard afterwards) by Miss Grant, who told her folk were never seen to less advantage than from above downward.

On the way home, as soon as I was set free, I upbraided Miss Grant with her cruelty.

"I am sorry you was disappointed," says she demurely. "For my part I was very pleased. You looked better than I dreaded; you looked—if it will not make you vain—a mighty pretty young man when you appeared in the window. You are to remember that she could not see your feet," says she, with the manner of one reassuring me.

"O!" cried I, "leave my feet be—they are no bigger than my neighbours'."

"They are even smaller than some," said she, "but I speak in parables like a Hebrew prophet."

"I marvel little they were sometimes stoned!" says I. "But, you miserable girl, how could you do it? Why should you care to tantalise me with a moment?"

"Love is like folk," says she; "it needs some kind of vivers." [22]

"Oh, Barbara, let me see her properly!" I pleaded. "You can—you see her when you please; let me have half an hour."

"Who is it that is managing this love affair! You! Or me?" she asked, and as I continued to press her with my instances, fell back upon a deadly expedient: that of imitating the tones of my voice when I called on Catriona by name; with which, indeed, she held me in subjection for some days to follow.

There was never the least word heard of the memorial, or none by me. Prestongrange and his grace the Lord President may have heard of it (for what I know) on the deafest sides of their heads; they kept it to themselves, at least—the public was none the wiser; and in course of time, on November 8th, and in the midst of a prodigious storm of wind and rain, poor James of the Glens was duly hanged at Lettermore by Ballachulish.

So there was the final upshot of my politics! Innocent men have perished before James, and are like to keep on perishing (in spite of all our wisdom) till the end of time. And till the end of time young folk (who are not yet used with the duplicity of life and men) will struggle as I did, and make heroical resolves, and take long risks; and the course of events will push them upon the one side and go on like a marching army. James was hanged; and here was I dwelling in the house of Prestongrange, and grateful to him for his fatherly attention. He was hanged; and behold! when I met Mr. Simon in the causeway, I was fain to pull off my beaver to him like a good little boy before his dominie. He had been hanged by fraud and violence, and the world wagged along, and there was not a pennyweight of difference; and the villains of that horrid plot were decent, kind, respectable fathers of families, who went to kirk and took the sacrament!

But I had had my view of that detestable business they call politics—I had seen it from behind, when it is all bones and blackness; and I was cured for life of any temptations to take part in it again. A plain, quiet, private path was that which I was ambitious to walk in, when I might keep my head out of the way of dangers and my conscience out of the road of temptation. For, upon a retrospect, it appeared I had not done so grandly, after all; but with the greatest possible amount of big speech and preparation, had accomplished nothing.

The 25th of the same month a ship was advertised to sail from Leith; and I was suddenly recommended to make up my mails for Leyden. To Prestongrange I could, of course, say nothing; for I had already been a long while sorning on his house and table. But with his daughter I was more open, bewailing my fate that I should be sent out of the country, and assuring her, unless she should bring me to farewell with Catriona, I would refuse at the last hour.

"Have I not given you my advice?" she asked.

"I know you have," said I, "and I know how much I am beholden to you already, and that I am bidden to obey your orders. But you must confess you are something too merry a lass at times to lippen [23] to entirely."

"I will tell you, then," said she. "Be you on board by nine o'clock forenoon; the ship does not sail before one; keep your boat alongside; and if you are not pleased with my farewells when I shall send them, you can come ashore again and seek Katrine for yourself."

Since I could make no more of her, I was fain to be content with this.

The day came round at last when she and I were to separate. We had been extremely intimate and familiar; I was much in her debt; and what way we were to part was a thing that put me from my sleep, like the vails I was to give to the domestic servants. I knew she considered me too backward, and rather desired to rise in her opinion on that head. Besides which, after so much affection shown and (I believe) felt upon both sides, it would have looked cold-like to be anyways stiff. Accordingly, I got my courage up and my words ready, and the last chance we were like to be alone, asked pretty boldly to be allowed to salute her in farewell.

"You forget yourself strangely, Mr. Balfour," said she. "I cannot call to mind that I have given you any right to presume on our acquaintancy."

I stood before her like a stopped clock, and knew not what to think, far less to say, when of a sudden she cast her arms about my neck and kissed me with the best will in the world.

"You inimitable bairn!" she cried. "Did you think that I would let us part like strangers? Because I can never keep my gravity at you five minutes on end, you must not dream I do not love you very well: I am all love and laughter, every time I cast an eye on you! And now I will give you an advice to conclude your education, which you will have need of before it's very long. Never ask womenfolk. They're bound to answer 'No'; God never made the lass that could resist the temptation. It's supposed by divines to be the curse of Eve: because she did not say it when the devil offered her the apple, her daughters can say nothing else."

"Since I am so soon to lose my bonny professor," I began.

"This is gallant, indeed," says she curtseying.

"I would put the one question," I went on. "May I ask a lass to marry to me?"

"You think you could not marry her without!" she asked. "Or else get her to offer?"

"You see you cannot be serious," said I.

"I shall be very serious in one thing, David," said she: "I shall always be your friend."

As I got to my horse the next morning, the four ladies were all at that same window whence we had once looked down on Catriona, and all cried farewell and waved their pocket napkins as I rode away. One out of the four I knew was truly sorry; and at the thought of that, and how I had come to the door three months ago for the first time, sorrow and gratitude made a confusion in my mind.

PART II—FATHER AND DAUGHTER

CHAPTER XXI—THE VOYAGE INTO HOLLAND

The ship lay at a single anchor, well outside the pier of Leith, so that all we passengers must come to it by the means of skiffs. This was very little troublesome, for the reason that the day was a flat calm, very frosty and cloudy, and with a low shifting fog upon the water. The body of the vessel was thus quite hid as I drew near, but the tall spars of her stood high and bright in a sunshine like the flickering of a fire. She proved to be a very roomy, commodious merchant, but somewhat blunt in the bows, and loaden extraordinary deep with salt, salted salmon, and fine white linen stockings for the Dutch. Upon my coming on board, the captain welcomed me—one Sang (out of Lesmahago, I believe), a very hearty, friendly tarpaulin of a man, but at the moment in rather of a bustle. There had no other of the passengers yet appeared, so that I was left to walk about upon the deck, viewing the prospect and wondering a good deal what these farewells should be which I was promised.

All Edinburgh and the Pentland Hills glinted above me in a kind of smuisty brightness, now and again overcome with blots of cloud; of Leith there was no more than the tops of chimneys visible, and on the face of the water, where the haar [24] lay, nothing at all. Out of this I was presently aware of a sound of oars pulling, and a little after (as if out of the smoke of a fire) a boat issued. There sat a grave man in the stern sheets, well muffled from the cold, and by his side a tall, pretty, tender figure of a maid that brought my heart to a stand. I had scarce the time to catch my breath in, and be ready to meet her, as she stepped upon the deck, smiling, and making my best bow, which was now vastly finer than some months before, when first I made it to her ladyship. No doubt we were both a good deal changed: she seemed to have shot up like a young, comely tree. She had now a kind of pretty backwardness that became her well as of one that regarded herself more highly and was fairly woman; and for another thing, the hand of the same magician had been at work upon the pair of us, and Miss Grant had made us both braw, if she could make but the one bonny.

The same cry, in words not very different, came from both of us, that the other was come in compliment to say farewell, and then we perceived in a flash we were to ship together.

"O, why will not Baby have been telling me!" she cried; and then remembered a letter she had been given, on the condition of not opening it till she was well on board. Within was an enclosure for myself, and ran thus:

"Dear Davie,—What do you think of my farewell? and what do you say to your fellow passenger? Did you kiss, or did you ask? I was about to have signed here, but that would leave the purport of my question doubtful, and in my own case I ken the answer. So fill up here with good advice. Do not be too blate, [25] and for God's sake do not try to be too forward; nothing acts you worse. I am

"Your affectionate friend and governess,

"Barbara Grant."

I wrote a word of answer and compliment on a leaf out of my pocketbook, put it in with another scratch from Catriona, sealed the whole with my new signet of the Balfour arms, and despatched it by the hand of Prestongrange's servant that still waited in my boat.

Then we had time to look upon each other more at leisure, which we had not done for a piece of a minute before (upon a common impulse) we shook hands again.

"Catriona?" said I. It seemed that was the first and last word of my eloquence.

"You will be glad to see me again?" says she.

"And I think that is an idle word," said I. "We are too deep friends to make speech upon such trifles."

"Is she not the girl of all the world?" she cried again. "I was never knowing such a girl so honest and so beautiful."

"And yet she cared no more for Alpin than what she did for a kale-stock," said I.

"Ah, she will say so indeed!" cries Catriona. "Yet it was for the name and the gentle kind blood that she took me up and was so good to me."

"Well, I will tell you why it was," said I. "There are all sorts of people's faces in this world. There is Barbara's face, that everyone must look at and admire, and think her a fine, brave, merry girl. And then there is your face, which is quite different—I never knew how different till to-day. You cannot see yourself, and that is why you do not understand; but it was for the love of your face that she took you up and was so good to you. And everybody in the world would do the same."

"Everybody?" says she.

"Every living soul!" said I.

"Ah, then, that will be why the soldiers at the castle took me up!" she cried.

"Barbara has been teaching you to catch me," said I.

"She will have taught me more than that at all events. She will have taught me a great deal about Mr. David—all the ill of him, and a little that was not so ill either, now and then," she said, smiling. "She will have told me all there was of Mr. David, only just that he would sail upon this very same ship. And why it is you go?"

I told her.

"Ah, well," said she, "we will be some days in company and then (I suppose) good-bye for altogether! I go to meet my father at a place of the name of Helvoetsluys, and from there to France, to be exiles by the side of our chieftain."

I could say no more than just "O!" the name of James More always drying up my very voice.

She was quick to perceive it, and to guess some portion of my thought.

"There is one thing I must be saying first of all, Mr. David," said she. "I think two of my kinsfolk have not behaved to you altogether very well. And the one of them two is James More, my father, and the other is the Laird of Prestongrange. Prestongrange will have spoken by himself, or his daughter in the place of him. But for James More, my father, I have this much to say: he lay shackled in a prison; he is a plain honest soldier and a plain Highland gentleman; what they would be after he would never be guessing; but if he had understood it was to be some prejudice to a young gentleman like yourself, he would have died first. And for the sake of all your friendships, I will be asking you to pardon my father and family for that same mistake."

"Catriona," said I, "what that mistake was I do not care to know. I know but the one thing—that you went to Prestongrange and begged my life upon your knees. O, I ken well enough it was for your father that you went, but when you were there you pleaded for me also. It is a thing I cannot speak of. There are two things I cannot think of into myself: and the one is your good words when you called yourself my little friend, and the other that you pleaded for my life. Let us never speak more, we two, of pardon or offence."

We stood after that silent, Catriona looking on the deck and I on her; and before there was more speech, a little wind having sprung up in the nor'-west, they began to shake out the sails and heave in upon the anchor.

There were six passengers besides our two selves, which made of it a full cabin. Three were solid merchants out of Leith, Kirkcaldy, and Dundee, all engaged in the same adventure into High Germany. One was a Hollander returning; the rest worthy merchants' wives, to the charge of one of whom Catriona was recommended. Mrs. Gebbie (for that was her name) was by great good fortune heavily incommoded by the sea, and lay day and night on the broad of her back. We were besides the only creatures at all young on board the Rose, except a white-faced boy that did my old duty to attend upon the table; and it came about that Catriona and I were left almost entirely to ourselves. We had the next seats together at the table, where I waited on her with extraordinary pleasure. On deck, I made her a soft place with my cloak; and the weather being singularly fine for that season, with bright frosty days and nights, a steady, gentle wind, and scarce a sheet started all the way through the North Sea, we sat there (only now and again walking to and fro for warmth) from the first blink of the sun till eight or nine at night under the clear stars. The merchants or Captain Sang would sometimes glance and smile upon us, or pass a merry word or two and give us the go-by again; but the most part of the time they were deep in herring and chintzes and linen, or in computations of the slowness of the passage, and left us to our own concerns, which were very little important to any but ourselves.

At the first, we had a great deal to say, and thought ourselves pretty witty; and I was at a little pains to be the beau, and she (I believe) to play the young lady of experience. But soon we grew plainer with each other. I laid aside my high, clipped English (what little there was left of it) and forgot to make my Edinburgh bows and scrapes; she, upon her side, fell into a sort of kind familiarity; and we dwelt together like those of the same household, only (upon my side) with a more deep emotion. About the same time the bottom seemed to fall out of our conversation, and neither one of us the less pleased. Whiles she would tell me old wives' tales, of which she had a wonderful variety, many of them from my friend red-headed Niel. She told them very pretty, and they were pretty enough childish tales; but the pleasure to myself was in the sound of her voice, and the thought that she was telling and I listening. Whiles, again, we would sit entirely silent, not communicating even with a look, and tasting pleasure enough in the sweetness of that neighbourhood. I speak here only for myself. Of what was in the maid's mind, I am not very sure that ever I asked myself; and what was in my own, I was afraid to consider. I need make no secret of it now, either to myself or to the reader; I was fallen totally in love. She came between me and the sun. She had grown suddenly taller, as I say, but with a wholesome growth; she seemed all health, and lightness, and brave spirits; and I thought she walked like a young deer, and stood like a birch upon the mountains. It was enough for me to sit near by her on the deck; and I declare I scarce spent two thoughts upon the future, and was so well content with what I then enjoyed that I was never at the pains to imagine any further step; unless perhaps that I would be sometimes tempted to take her hand in mine and hold it there. But I was too like a miser of what joys I had, and would venture nothing on a hazard.

What we spoke was usually of ourselves or of each other, so that if anyone had been at so much pains as overhear us, he must have supposed us the most egotistical persons in the world. It befell one day when we were at this practice, that we came on a discourse of friends and friendship, and I think now that we were sailing near the wind. We said what a fine thing friendship was, and how little we had guessed of it, and how it made life a new thing, and a thousand covered things of the same kind that will have been said, since the foundation of the world, by young folk in the same predicament. Then we remarked upon the strangeness of that circumstance, that friends came together in the beginning as if they were there for the first time, and yet each had been alive a good while, losing time with other people.

"It is not much that I have done," said she, "and I could be telling you the five-fifths of it in two-three words. It is only a girl I am, and what can befall a girl, at all events? But I went with the clan in the year '45. The men marched with swords and fire-locks, and some of them in brigades in the same set of tartan; they were not backward at the marching, I can tell you. And there were gentlemen from the Low Country, with their tenants mounted and trumpets to sound, and there was a grand skirling of war-pipes. I rode on a little Highland horse on the right hand of my father, James More, and of Glengyle himself. And here is one fine thing that I remember, that Glengyle kissed me in the face, because (says he) 'my kinswoman, you are the only lady of the clan that has come out,' and me a little maid of maybe twelve years old! I saw Prince Charlie too, and the blue eyes of him; he was pretty indeed! I had his hand to kiss in front of the army. O, well, these were the good days, but it is all like a dream that I have seen and then awakened. It went what way you very well know; and these were the worst days of all, when the red-coat soldiers were out, and my father and uncles lay in the hill, and I was to be carrying them their meat in the middle night, or at the short sight of day when the cocks crow. Yes, I have walked in the night, many's the time, and my heart great in me for terror of the darkness. It is a strange thing I will never have been meddled with by a bogle; but they say a maid goes safe.

Next there was my uncle's marriage, and that was a dreadful affair beyond all. Jean Kay was that woman's name; and she had me in the room with her that night at Inversnaid, the night we took her from her friends in the old, ancient manner. She would and she wouldn't; she was for marrying Rob the one minute, and the next she would be for none of him. I will never have seen such a feckless creature of a woman; surely all there was of her would tell her ay or no. Well, she was a widow; and I can never be thinking a widow a good woman."

"Catriona!" says I, "how do you make out that?"

"I do not know," said she; "I am only telling you the seeming in my heart. And then to marry a new man! Fy! But that was her; and she was married again upon my Uncle Robin, and went with him awhile to kirk and market; and then wearied, or else her friends got claught of her and talked her round, or maybe she turned ashamed; at the least of it, she ran away, and went back to her own folk, and said we had held her in the lake, and I will never tell you all what. I have never thought much of any females since that day. And so in the end my father, James More, came to be cast in prison, and you know the rest of it an well as me."

"And through all you had no friends?" said I.

"No," said she; "I have been pretty chief with two-three lasses on the braes, but not to call it friends."

"Well, mine is a plain tale," said I. "I never had a friend to my name till I met in with you."

"And that brave Mr. Stewart?" she asked.

"O, yes, I was forgetting him," I said. "But he is a man, and that in very different."

"I would think so," said she. "O, yes, it is quite different."

"And then there was one other," said I. "I once thought I had a friend, but it proved a disappointment."

She asked me who she was?

"It was a he, then," said I. "We were the two best lads at my father's school, and we thought we loved each other dearly. Well, the time came when he went to Glasgow to a merchant's house, that was his second cousin once removed; and wrote me two-three times by the carrier; and then he found new friends, and I might write till I was tired, he took no notice. Eh, Catriona, it took me a long while to forgive the world. There is not anything more bitter than to lose a fancied friend."

Then she began to question me close upon his looks and character, for we were each a great deal concerned in all that touched the other; till at last, in a very evil hour, I minded of his letters and went and fetched the bundle from the cabin.

"Here are his letters," said I, "and all the letters that ever I got. That will be the last I'll can tell of myself; ye know the lave [26] as well as I do."

"Will you let me read them, then?" says she.

I told her, if she would be at the pains; and she bade me go away and she would read them from the one end to the other. Now, in this bundle that I gave her, there were packed together not only all the letters of my false friend, but one or two of Mr. Campbell's when he was in town at the Assembly, and to make a complete roll of all that ever was written to me, Catriona's little word, and the two I had received from Miss Grant, one when I was on the Bass and one on board that ship. But of these last I had no particular mind at the moment.

I was in that state of subjection to the thought of my friend that it mattered not what I did, nor scarce whether I was in her presence or out of it; I had caught her like some kind of a noble fever that lived continually in my bosom, by night and by day, and whether I was waking or asleep. So it befell that after I was come into the fore-part of the ship where the broad bows splashed into the billows, I was in no such hurry to return as you might fancy; rather prolonged my absence like a variety in pleasure. I do not think I am by nature much of an Epicurean: and there had come till then so small a share of pleasure in my way that I might be excused perhaps to dwell on it unduly.

When I returned to her again, I had a faint, painful impression as of a buckle slipped, so coldly she returned the packet.

"You have read them?" said I; and I thought my voice sounded not wholly natural, for I was turning in my mind for what could ail her.

"Did you mean me to read all?" she asked.

I told her "Yes," with a drooping voice.

"The last of them as well?" said she.

I knew where we were now; yet I would not lie to her either. "I gave them all without afterthought," I said, "as I supposed that you would read them. I see no harm in any."

"I will be differently made," said she. "I thank God I am differently made. It was not a fit letter to be shown me. It was not fit to be written."

"I think you are speaking of your own friend, Barbara Grant?" said I.

"There will not be anything as bitter as to lose a fancied friend," said she, quoting my own expression.

"I think it is sometimes the friendship that was fancied!" I cried. "What kind of justice do you call this, to blame me for some words that a tomfool of a madcap lass has written down upon a piece of paper? You know yourself with what respect I have behaved—and would do always."

"Yet you would show me that same letter!" says she. "I want no such friends. I can be doing very well, Mr. Balfour, without her—or you."

"This is your fine gratitude!" says I.

"I am very much obliged to you," said she. "I will be asking you to take away your—letters." She seemed to choke upon the word, so that it sounded like an oath.

"You shall never ask twice," said I; picked up that bundle, walked a little way forward and cast them as far as possible into the sea. For a very little more I could have cast myself after them.

The rest of the day I walked up and down raging. There were few names so ill but what I gave her them in my own mind before the sun went down. All that I had ever heard of Highland pride seemed quite outdone; that a girl (scarce grown) should resent so trifling an allusion, and that from her next friend, that she had near wearied me with praising of! I had bitter, sharp, hard thoughts of her, like an angry boy's. If I had kissed her indeed (I thought), perhaps she would have taken it pretty well; and only because it had been written down, and with a spice of jocularity, up she must fuff in this ridiculous passion. It seemed to me there was a want of penetration in the female sex, to make angels weep over the case of the poor men.

We were side by side again at supper, and what a change was there! She was like curdled milk to me; her face was like a wooden doll's; I could have indifferently smitten her or grovelled at her feet, but she gave me not the least occasion to do either. No sooner the meal done than she betook herself to attend on Mrs. Gebbie, which I think she had a little neglected heretofore. But she was to make up for lost time, and in what remained of the passage was extraordinary assiduous with the old lady, and on deck began to make a great deal more than I thought wise of Captain Sang. Not but what the Captain seemed a worthy, fatherly man; but I hated to behold her in the least familiarity with anyone except myself.

Altogether, she was so quick to avoid me, and so constant to keep herself surrounded with others, that I must watch a long while before I could find my opportunity; and after it was found, I made not much of it, as you are now to hear.

"I have no guess how I have offended," said I; "it should scarce be beyond pardon, then. O, try if you can pardon me."

"I have no pardon to give," said she; and the words seemed to come out of her throat like marbles. "I will be very much obliged for all your friendships." And she made me an eighth part of a curtsey.

But I had schooled myself beforehand to say more, and I was going to say it too.

"There is one thing," said I. "If I have shocked your particularity by the showing of that letter, it cannot touch Miss Grant. She wrote not to you, but to a poor, common, ordinary lad, who might have had more sense than show it. If you are to blame me—"

"I will advise you to say no more about that girl, at all events!" said Catriona. "It is her I will never look the road of, not if she lay dying." She turned away from me, and suddenly back. "Will you swear you will have no more to deal with her?" she cried.

"Indeed, and I will never be so unjust then," said I; "nor yet so ungrateful."

And now it was I that turned away.

CHAPTER XXII—HELVOETSLUYS

The weather in the end considerably worsened; the wind sang in the shrouds, the sea swelled higher, and the ship began to labour and cry out among the billows. The song of the leadsman in the chains was now scarce ceasing, for we thrid all the way among shoals. About nine in the morning, in a burst of wintry sun between two squalls of hail, I had my first look of Holland—a line of windmills birling in the breeze. It was besides my first knowledge of these daft-like contrivances, which gave me a near sense of foreign travel and a new world and life. We came to an anchor about half-past eleven, outside the harbour of Helvoetsluys, in a place where the sea sometimes broke and the ship pitched outrageously. You may be sure we were all on deck save Mrs. Gebbie, some of us in cloaks, others mantled in the ship's tarpaulins, all clinging on by ropes, and jesting the most like old sailor-folk that we could imitate.

Presently a boat, that was backed like a partancrab, came gingerly alongside, and the skipper of it hailed our master in the Dutch. Thence Captain Sang turned, very troubled-like, to Catriona; and the rest of us crowding about, the nature of the difficulty was made plain to all. The Rose was bound to the port of Rotterdam, whither the other passengers were in a great impatience to arrive, in view of a conveyance due to leave that very evening in the direction of the Upper Germany. This, with the present half-gale of wind, the captain (if no time were lost) declared himself still capable to save. Now James More had trysted in Helvoet with his daughter, and the captain had engaged to call before the port and place her (according to the custom) in a shore boat. There was the boat, to be sure, and here was Catriona ready: but both our master and the patroon of the boat scrupled at the risk, and the first was in no humour to delay.

"Your father," said he, "would be gey an little pleased if we was to break a leg to ye, Miss Drummond, let-a-be drowning of you. Take my way of it," says he, "and come on-by with the rest of us here to Rotterdam. Ye can get a passage down the Maes in a sailing scoot as far as to the Brill, and thence on again, by a place in a rattel-waggon, back to Helvoet."

But Catriona would hear of no change. She looked white-like as she beheld the bursting of the sprays, the green seas that sometimes poured upon the fore-castle, and the perpetual bounding and swooping of the boat among the billows; but she stood firmly by her father's orders. "My father, James More, will have arranged it so," was her first word and her last. I thought it very idle and indeed wanton in the girl to be so literal and stand opposite to so much kind advice; but the fact is she had a very good reason, if she would have told us. Sailing scoots and rattel-waggons are excellent things; only the use of them must first be paid for, and all she was possessed of in the world was just two shillings and a penny halfpenny sterling. So it fell out that captain and passengers, not knowing of her destitution—and she being too proud to tell them—spoke in vain.

"But you ken nae French and nae Dutch neither," said one.

"It is very true," says she, "but since the year '46 there are so many of the honest Scotch abroad that I will be doing very well. I thank you."

There was a pretty country simplicity in this that made some laugh, others looked the more sorry, and Mr. Gebbie fall outright in a passion. I believe he knew it was his duty (his wife having accepted charge of the girl) to have gone ashore with her and seen her safe: nothing would have induced him to have done so, since it must have involved the lose of his conveyance; and I think he made it up to his conscience by the loudness of his voice. At least he broke out upon Captain Sang, raging and saying the thing was a disgrace; that it was mere death to try to leave the ship, and at any event we could not cast down an innocent maid in a boatful of nasty Holland fishers, and leave her to her fate. I was thinking something of the same; took the mate upon one side, arranged with him to send on my chests by track-scoot to an address I had in Leyden, and stood up and signalled to the fishers.

"I will go ashore with the young lady, Captain Sang," said I. "It is all one what way I go to Leyden;" and leaped at the same time into the boat, which I managed not so elegantly but what I fell with two of the fishers in the bilge.

From the boat the business appeared yet more precarious than from the ship, she stood so high over us, swung down so swift, and menaced us so perpetually with her plunging and passaging upon the anchor cable. I began to think I had made a fool's bargain, that it was merely impossible Catriona should be got on board to me, and that I stood to be set ashore at Helvoet all by myself and with no hope of any reward but the pleasure of embracing James More, if I should want to. But this was to reckon without the lass's courage. She had seen me leap with very little appearance (however much reality) of hesitation; to be sure, she was not to be beat by her discarded friend. Up she stood on the bulwarks and held by a stay, the wind blowing in her petticoats, which made the enterprise more dangerous, and gave us rather more of a view of her stockings than would be thought genteel in cities. There was no minute lost, and scarce time given for any to interfere if they had wished the same. I stood up on the other side and spread my arms; the ship swung down on us, the patroon humoured his boat nearer in than was perhaps wholly safe, and Catriona leaped into the air. I was so happy as to catch her, and the fishers readily supporting us, escaped a fall. She held to me a moment very tight, breathing quick and deep; thence (she still clinging to me with both hands) we were passed aft to our places by the steersman; and Captain Sang and all the crew and passengers cheering and crying farewell, the boat was put about for shore.

As soon as Catriona came a little to herself she unhanded me suddenly, but said no word. No more did I; and indeed the whistling of the wind and the breaching of the sprays made it no time for speech; and our crew not only toiled excessively but made extremely little way, so that the Rose had got her anchor and was off again before we had approached the harbour mouth.

We were no sooner in smooth water than the patroon, according to their beastly Hollands custom, stopped his boat and required of us our fares. Two guilders was the man's demand—between three and four shillings English money—for each passenger. But at this Catriona began to cry out with a vast deal of agitation. She had asked of Captain Sang, she said, and the fare was but an English shilling. "Do you think I will have come on board and not ask first?" cries she. The patroon scolded back upon her in a lingo where the oaths were English and the rest right Hollands; till at last (seeing her near tears) I privately slipped in the rogue's hand six shillings, whereupon he was obliging enough to receive from her the other shilling without more complaint. No doubt I was a good deal nettled and ashamed. I like to see folk thrifty, but not with so much passion; and I daresay it would be rather coldly that I asked her, as the boat moved on again for shore, where it was that she was trysted with her father.

"He is to be inquired of at the house of one Sprott, an honest Scotch merchant," says she; and then with the same breath, "I am wishing to thank you very much—you are a brave friend to me."

"It will be time enough when I get you to your father," said I, little thinking that I spoke so true. "I can tell him a fine tale of a loyal daughter."

"O, I do not think I will be a loyal girl, at all events," she cried, with a great deal of painfulness in the expression. "I do not think my heart is true."

"Yet there are very few that would have made that leap, and all to obey a father's orders," I observed.

"I cannot have you to be thinking of me so," she cried again. "When you had done that same, how would I stop behind? And at all events that was not all the reasons." Whereupon, with a burning face, she told me the plain truth upon her poverty.

"Good guide us!" cried I, "what kind of daft-like proceeding is this, to let yourself be launched on the continent of Europe with an empty purse—I count it hardly decent—scant decent!" I cried.

"You forget James More, my father, is a poor gentleman," said she. "He is a hunted exile."

"But I think not all your friends are hunted exiles," I exclaimed. "And was this fair to them that care for you? Was it fair to me? was it fair to Miss Grant that counselled you to go, and would be driven fair horn-mad if she could hear of it? Was it even fair to these Gregory folk that you were living with, and used you lovingly? It's a blessing you have fallen in my hands!

341

Suppose your father hindered by an accident, what would become of you here, and you your lee-lone in a strange place? The thought of the thing frightens me," I said.

"I will have lied to all of them," she replied. "I will have told them all that I had plenty. I told her too. I could not be lowering James More to them."

I found out later on that she must have lowered him in the very dust, for the lie was originally the father's, not the daughter's, and she thus obliged to persevere in it for the man's reputation. But at the time I was ignorant of this, and the mere thought of her destitution and the perils in which see must have fallen, had ruffled me almost beyond reason.

"Well, well, well," said I, "you will have to learn more sense."

I left her mails for the moment in an inn upon the shore, where I got a direction for Sprott's house in my new French, and we walked there—it was some little way—beholding the place with wonder as we went. Indeed, there was much for Scots folk to admire: canals and trees being intermingled with the houses; the houses, each within itself, of a brave red brick, the colour of a rose, with steps and benches of blue marble at the cheek of every door, and the whole town so clean you might have dined upon the causeway. Sprott was within, upon his ledgers, in a low parlour, very neat and clean, and set out with china and pictures, and a globe of the earth in a brass frame. He was a big-chafted, ruddy, lusty man, with a crooked hard look to him; and he made us not that much civility as offer us a seat.

"Is James More Macgregor now in Helvoet, sir?" says I.

"I ken nobody by such a name," says he, impatient-like.

"Since you are so particular," says I, "I will amend my question, and ask you where we are to find in Helvoet one James Drummond, alias Macgregor, alias James More, late tenant in Inveronachile?"

"Sir," says he, "he may be in Hell for what I ken, and for my part I wish he was."

"The young lady is that gentleman's daughter, sir," said I, "before whom, I think you will agree with me, it is not very becoming to discuss his character."

"I have nothing to make either with him, or her, or you!" cries he in his gross voice.

"Under your favour, Mr. Sprott," said I, "this young lady is come from Scotland seeking him, and by whatever mistake, was given the name of your house for a direction. An error it seems to have been, but I think this places both you and me—who am but her fellow-traveller by accident—under a strong obligation to help our countrywoman."

"Will you ding me daft?" he cries. "I tell ye I ken naething and care less either for him or his breed. I tell ye the man owes me money."

"That may very well be, sir," said I, who was now rather more angry than himself. "At least, I owe you nothing; the young lady is under my protection; and I am neither at all used with these manners, nor in the least content with them."

As I said this, and without particularly thinking what I did, I drew a step or two nearer to his table; thus striking, by mere good fortune, on the only argument that could at all affect the man. The blood left his lusty countenance.

"For the Lord's sake dinna be hasty, sir!" he cried. "I am truly wishfu' no to be offensive. But ye ken, sir, I'm like a wheen guid-natured, honest, canty auld fellows—my bark is waur nor my bite. To hear me, ye micht whiles fancy I was a wee thing dour; but na, na! it's a kind auld fallow at heart, Sandie Sprott! And ye could never imagine the fyke and fash this man has been to me."

"Very good, sir," said I. "Then I will make that much freedom with your kindness as trouble you for your last news of Mr. Drummond."

"You're welcome, sir!" said he. "As for the young leddy (my respects to her!), he'll just have clean forgotten her. I ken the man, ye see; I have lost siller by him ere now. He thinks of naebody but just himsel'; clan, king, or dauchter, if he can get his wameful, he would give them a' the go-by! ay, or his correspondent either. For there is a sense in whilk I may be nearly almost said to be his correspondent. The fact is, we are employed thegether in a business affair, and I think it's like to turn out a dear affair for Sandie Sprott. The man's as guid's my pairtner, and I give ye my mere word I ken naething by where he is. He micht be coming here to Helvoet; he micht come here the morn, he michtnae come for a twalmouth; I would wonder at naething—or just at the ae thing, and that's if he was to pay me my siller. Ye see what way I stand with it; and it's clear I'm no very likely to meddle up with the young leddy, as ye ca' her. She cannae stop here, that's ae thing certain sure. Dod, sir, I'm a lone man! If I was to tak her in, its highly possible the hellicat would try and gar me marry her when he turned up."

"Enough of this talk," said I. "I will take the young leddy among better friends. Give me, pen, ink, and paper, and I will leave here for James More the address of my correspondent in Leyden. He can inquire from me where he is to seek his daughter."

This word I wrote and sealed; which while I was doing, Sprott of his own motion made a welcome offer, to charge himself with Miss Drummond's mails, and even send a porter for them to the inn. I advanced him to that effect a dollar or two to be a cover, and he gave me an acknowledgment in writing of the sum.

Whereupon (I giving my arm to Catriona) we left the house of this unpalatable rascal. She had said no word throughout, leaving me to judge and speak in her place; I, upon my side, had been careful not to embarrass her by a glance; and even now, although my heart still glowed inside of me with shame and anger, I made it my affair to seem quite easy.

"Now," said I, "let us get back to yon same inn where they can speak the French, have a piece of dinner, and inquire for conveyances to Rotterdam. I will never be easy till I have you safe again in the hands of Mrs. Gebbie."

"I suppose it will have to be," said Catriona, "though whoever will be pleased, I do not think it will be her. And I will remind you this once again that I have but one shilling, and three baubees."

344

"And just this once again," said I, "I will remind you it was a blessing that I came alongst with you."

"What else would I be thinking all this time?" says she, and I thought weighed a little on my arm. "It is you that are the good friend to me."

CHAPTER XXIII—TRAVELS IN HOLLAND

The rattel-waggon, which is a kind of a long waggon set with benches, carried us in four hours of travel to the great city of Rotterdam. It was long past dark by then, but the streets were pretty brightly lighted and thronged with wild-like, outlandish characters—bearded Hebrews, black men, and the hordes of courtesans, most indecently adorned with finery and stopping seamen by their very sleeves; the clash of talk about us made our heads to whirl; and what was the most unexpected of all, we appeared to be no more struck with all these foreigners than they with us. I made the best face I could, for the lass's sake and my own credit; but the truth is I felt like a lost sheep, and my heart beat in my bosom with anxiety. Once or twice I inquired after the harbour or the berth of the ship Rose: but either fell on some who spoke only Hollands, or my own French failed me. Trying a street at a venture, I came upon a lane of lighted houses, the doors and windows thronged with wauf-like painted women; these jostled and mocked upon us as we passed, and I was thankful we had nothing of their language. A little after we issued forth upon an open place along the harbour.

"We shall be doing now," cries I, as soon as I spied masts. "Let us walk here by the harbour. We are sure to meet some that has the English, and at the best of it we may light upon that very ship."

We did the next best, as happened; for, about nine of the evening, whom should we walk into the arms of but Captain Sang? He told us they had made their run in the most incredible brief time, the wind holding strong till they reached port; by which means his passengers were all gone already on their further travels. It was impossible to chase after the Gebbies into the High Germany, and we had no other acquaintance to fall back upon but Captain Sang himself. It was the more gratifying to find the man friendly and wishful to assist. He made it a small affair to find some good plain family of merchants, where Catriona might harbour till the Rose was loaden; declared he would then blithely carry her back to Leith for nothing and see her safe in the hands of Mr. Gregory; and in the meanwhile carried us to a late ordinary for the meal we stood in need of. He seemed extremely friendly, as I say, but what surprised me a good deal, rather boisterous in the bargain; and the cause of this was soon to appear. For at the ordinary, calling for Rhenish wine and drinking of it deep, he soon became unutterably tipsy. In this case, as too common with all men, but especially with those of his rough trade, what little sense or manners he possessed deserted him; and he behaved himself so scandalous to the young lady, jesting most ill-favouredly at the figure she had made on the ship's rail, that I had no resource but carry her suddenly away.

She came out of the ordinary clinging to me close. "Take me away, David," she said. "You keep me. I am not afraid with you."

"And have no cause, my little friend!" cried I, and could have found it in my heart to weep.

"Where will you be taking me?" she said again. "Don't leave me at all events—never leave me."

"Where am I taking you to?" says I stopping, for I had been staving on ahead in mere blindness. "I must stop and think. But I'll not leave you, Catriona; the Lord do so to me, and more also, if I should fail or fash you."

She crept close into me by way of a reply.

"Here," I said, "is the stillest place we have hit on yet in this busy byke of a city. Let us sit down here under yon tree and consider of our course."

That tree (which I am little like to forget) stood hard by the harbour side. It was like a black night, but lights were in the houses, and nearer hand in the quiet ships; there was a shining of the city on the one hand, and a buzz hung over it of many thousands walking and talking; on the other, it was dark and the water bubbled on the sides. I spread my cloak upon a builder's stone, and made her sit there; she would have kept her hold upon me, for she still shook with the late affronts; but I wanted to think clear, disengaged myself, and paced to and fro before her, in the manner of what we call a smuggler's walk, belabouring my brains for any remedy. By the course of these scattering thoughts I was brought suddenly face to face with a remembrance that, in the

347

heat and haste of our departure, I had left Captain Sang to pay the ordinary. At this I began to laugh out loud, for I thought the man well served; and at the same time, by an instinctive movement, carried my hand to the pocket where my money was. I suppose it was in the lane where the women jostled us; but there is only the one thing certain, that my purse was gone.

"You will have thought of something good," said she, observing me to pause.

At the pinch we were in, my mind became suddenly clear as a perspective glass, and I saw there was no choice of methods. I had not one doit of coin, but in my pocket-book I had still my letter on the Leyden merchant; and there was now but the one way to get to Leyden, and that was to walk on our two feet.

"Catriona," said I, "I know you're brave and I believe you're strong—do you think you could walk thirty miles on a plain road?" We found it, I believe, scarce the two-thirds of that, but such was my notion of the distance.

"David," she said, "if you will just keep near, I will go anywhere and do anything. The courage of my heart, it is all broken. Do not be leaving me in this horrible country by myself, and I will do all else."

"Can you start now and march all night?" said I.

"I will do all that you can ask of me," she said, "and never ask you why. I have been a bad ungrateful girl to you; and do what you please with me now! And I think Miss Barbara Grant is the best lady in the world," she added, "and I do not see what she would deny you for at all events."

This was Greek and Hebrew to me; but I had other matters to consider, and the first of these was to get clear of that city on the Leyden road. It proved a cruel problem; and it may have been one or two at night ere we had solved it. Once beyond the houses, there was neither moon nor stars to guide us; only the whiteness of the way in the midst and a blackness of an alley on both hands. The walking was besides made most extraordinary difficult by a plain black frost that fell suddenly in the small hours and turned that highway into one long slide.

348

"Well, Catriona," said I, "here we are like the king's sons and the old wives' daughters in your daft-like Highland tales. Soon we'll be going over the 'seven Bens, the seven glens and the seven mountain moors'." Which was a common byword or overcome in those tales of hers that had stuck in my memory.

"Ah," says she, "but here are no glens or mountains! Though I will never be denying but what the trees and some of the plain places hereabouts are very pretty. But our country is the best yet."

"I wish we could say as much for our own folk," says I, recalling Sprott and Sang, and perhaps James More himself.

"I will never complain of the country of my friend," said she, and spoke it out with an accent so particular that I seemed to see the look upon her face.

I caught in my breath sharp and came near falling (for my pains) on the black ice.

"I do not know what you think, Catriona," said I, when I was a little recovered, "but this has been the best day yet! I think shame to say it, when you have met in with such misfortunes and disfavours; but for me, it has been the best day yet."

"It was a good day when you showed me so much love," said she.

"And yet I think shame to be happy too," I went on, "and you here on the road in the black night."

"Where in the great world would I be else?" she cried. "I am thinking I am safest where I am with you."

"I am quite forgiven, then?" I asked.

"Will you not forgive me that time so much as not to take it in your mouth again?" she cried. "There is nothing in this heart to you but thanks. But I will be honest too," she added, with a kind of suddenness, "and I'll never can forgive that girl."

"Is this Miss Grant again?" said I. "You said yourself she was the best lady in the world."

"So she will be, indeed!" says Catriona. "But I will never forgive her for all that. I will never, never forgive her, and let me hear tell of her no more."

"Well," said I, "this beats all that ever came to my knowledge; and I wonder that you can indulge yourself in such bairnly whims. Here is a young lady that was the best friend in the world to the both of us, that learned us how to dress ourselves, and in a great manner how to behave, as anyone can see that knew us both before and after."

But Catriona stopped square in the midst of the highway.

"It is this way of it," said she. "Either you will go on to speak of her, and I will go back to yon town, and let come of it what God pleases! Or else you will do me that politeness to talk of other things."

I was the most nonplussed person in this world; but I bethought me that she depended altogether on my help, that she was of the frail sex and not so much beyond a child, and it was for me to be wise for the pair of us.

"My dear girl," said I, "I can make neither head nor tails of this; but God forbid that I should do anything to set you on the jee. As for talking of Miss Grant, I have no such a mind to it, and I believe it was yourself began it. My only design (if I took you up at all) was for your own improvement, for I hate the very look of injustice. Not that I do not wish you to have a good pride and a nice female delicacy; they become you well; but here you show them to excess."

"Well, then, have you done?" said she.

"I have done," said I.

"A very good thing," said she, and we went on again, but now in silence.

It was an eerie employment to walk in the gross night, beholding only shadows and hearing nought but our own steps. At first, I believe our hearts burned against each other with a deal of enmity; but the darkness and the cold, and the silence, which only the cocks sometimes interrupted, or sometimes the farmyard dogs, had pretty soon brought down our pride to the dust; and for my own particular, I would have jumped at any decent opening for speech.

Before the day peeped, came on a warmish rain, and the frost was all wiped away from among our feet. I took my cloak to her and sought to hap her in the same; she bade me, rather impatiently, to keep it.

"Indeed and I will do no such thing," said I. "Here am I, a great, ugly lad that has seen all kinds of weather, and here are you a tender, pretty maid! My dear, you would not put me to a shame?"

Without more words she let me cover her; which as I was doing in the darkness, I let my hand rest a moment on her shoulder, almost like an embrace.

"You must try to be more patient of your friend," said I.

I thought she seemed to lean the least thing in the world against my bosom, or perhaps it was but fancy.

"There will be no end to your goodness," said she.

And we went on again in silence; but now all was changed; and the happiness that was in my heart was like a fire in a great chimney.

The rain passed ere day; it was but a sloppy morning as we came into the town of Delft. The red gabled houses made a handsome show on either hand of a canal; the servant lassies were out slestering and scrubbing at the very stones upon the public highway; smoke rose from a hundred kitchens; and it came in upon me strongly it was time to break our fasts.

"Catriona," said I, "I believe you have yet a shilling and three baubees?"

"Are you wanting it?" said she, and passed me her purse. "I am wishing it was five pounds! What will you want it for?"

"And what have we been walking for all night, like a pair of waif Egyptians!" says I. "Just because I was robbed of my purse and all I possessed in that unchancy town of Rotterdam. I will tell you of it now, because I think the worst is over, but we have still a good tramp before us till we get to where my money is, and if you would not buy me a piece of bread, I were like to go fasting."

She looked at me with open eyes. By the light of the new day she was all black and pale for weariness, so that my heart smote me for her. But as for her, she broke out laughing.

"My torture! are we beggars then!" she cried. "You too? O, I could have wished for this same thing! And I am glad to buy your breakfast to you. But it would be pleisand if I would have had to dance to get a meal to you! For I believe they are not very well acquainted with our manner of dancing over here, and might be paying for the curiosity of that sight."

I could have kissed her for that word, not with a lover's mind, but in a heat of admiration. For it always warms a man to see a woman brave.

We got a drink of milk from a country wife but new come to the town, and in a baker's, a piece of excellent, hot, sweet-smelling bread, which we ate upon the road as we went on. That road from Delft to the Hague is just five miles of a fine avenue shaded with trees, a canal on the one hand, on the other excellent pastures of cattle. It was pleasant here indeed.

"And now, Davie," said she, "what will you do with me at all events?"

"It is what we have to speak of," said I, "and the sooner yet the better. I can come by money in Leyden; that will be all well. But the trouble is how to dispose of you until your father come. I thought last night you seemed a little sweir to part from me?"

"It will be more than seeming then," said she.

"You are a very young maid," said I, "and I am but a very young callant. This is a great piece of difficulty. What way are we to manage? Unless indeed, you could pass to be my sister?"

"And what for no?" said she, "if you would let me!"

"I wish you were so, indeed," I cried. "I would be a fine man if I had such a sister. But the rub is that you are Catriona Drummond."

"And now I will be Catriona Balfour," she said. "And who is to ken? They are all strange folk here."

"If you think that it would do," says I. "I own it troubles me. I would like it very ill, if I advised you at all wrong."

"David, I have no friend here but you," she said.

"The mere truth is, I am too young to be your friend," said I. "I am too young to advise you, or you to be advised. I see not what else we are to do, and yet I ought to warn you."

"I will have no choice left," said she. "My father James More has not used me very well, and it is not the first time, I am cast upon your hands like a sack of barley meal, and have nothing else to think of but your pleasure. If you will have me, good and well. If you will not"—she turned and touched her hand upon my arm—"David, I am afraid," said she.

"No, but I ought to warn you," I began; and then bethought me I was the bearer of the purse, and it would never do to seem too churlish. "Catriona," said I, "don't misunderstand me: I am just trying to do my duty by you, girl! Here am I going alone to this strange city, to be a solitary student there; and here is this chance arisen that you might dwell with me a bit, and be like my sister; you can surely understand this much, my dear, that I would just love to have you?"

"Well, and here I am," said she. "So that's soon settled."

I know I was in duty bounden to have spoke more plain. I know this was a great blot on my character, for which I was lucky that I did not pay more dear. But I minded how easy her delicacy had been startled with a word of kissing her in Barbara's letter; now that she depended on me, how was I to be more bold? Besides, the truth is, I could see no other feasible method to dispose of her. And I daresay inclination pulled me very strong.

A little beyond the Hague she fell very lame and made the rest of the distance heavily enough. Twice she must rest by the wayside, which she did with pretty apologies, calling herself a shame to the Highlands and the race she came of, and nothing but a hindrance to myself. It was her excuse, she said, that she was not much used with walking shod. I would have had her strip off her shoes and stockings and go barefoot. But she pointed out to me that the women of that country, even in the landward roads, appeared to be all shod.

"I must not be disgracing my brother," said she, and was very merry with it all, although her face told tales of her.

There is a garden in that city we were bound to, sanded below with clean sand, the trees meeting overhead, some of them trimmed, some preached, and the whole place beautified with alleys and arbours. Here I left Catriona, and went forward by myself to find my correspondent. There I drew on my credit, and asked to be recommended to some decent, retired lodging. My baggage being not yet arrived, I told him I supposed I should require his caution with the people of the house; and explained that, my sister being come for a while to keep house with me, I should be wanting two chambers. This was all very well; but the trouble was that Mr. Balfour in his letter of recommendation had condescended on a great deal of particulars, and never a word of any sister in the case. I could see my Dutchman was extremely suspicious; and viewing me over the rims of a great pair of spectacles—he was a poor, frail body, and reminded me of an infirm rabbit—he began to question me close.

Here I fell in a panic. Suppose he accept my tale (thinks I), suppose he invite my sister to his house, and that I bring her. I shall have a fine ravelled pirn to unwind, and may end by disgracing both the lassie and myself. Thereupon I began hastily to expound to him my sister's character. She was of a bashful disposition, it appeared, and be extremely fearful of meeting strangers that I had left her at that moment sitting in a public place alone. And then, being launched upon the stream of falsehood, I must do like all the rest of the world in the same circumstance, and plunge in deeper than was any service; adding some altogether needless particulars of Miss Balfour's ill-health and retirement during childhood. In the midst of which I awoke to a sense of my behaviour, and was turned to one blush.

The old gentleman was not so much deceived but what he discovered a willingness to be quit of me. But he was first of all a man of business; and knowing that my money was good enough, however it might be with my conduct, he was so far obliging as to send his son to be my guide and caution in the matter of a lodging. This implied my presenting of the young man to Catriona. The poor, pretty child was much recovered with resting, looked and behaved to perfection, and took my arm and gave me the name of brother more easily than I could answer her. But there was one misfortune: thinking to help, she was rather towardly than otherwise to my Dutchman. And I could not but reflect that Miss Balfour had rather suddenly outgrown her bashfulness. And there was another thing, the difference of our speech. I had the Low Country tongue and dwelled upon my words; she had a hill voice, spoke with something of an English accent, only far more delightful, and was scarce quite fit to be called a deacon in the craft of talking English grammar; so that, for a brother and sister, we made a most uneven pair. But the young Hollander was a heavy dog, without so much spirit in his belly as to remark her prettiness, for which I scorned him. And as soon as he had found a cover to our heads, he left us alone, which was the greater service of the two.

CHAPTER XXIV—FULL STORY OF A COPY OF HEINECCIUS

The place found was in the upper part of a house backed on a canal. We had two rooms, the second entering from the first; each had a chimney built out into the floor in the Dutch manner; and being alongside, each had the same prospect from the window of the top of a tree below us in a little court, of a piece of the canal, and of houses in the Hollands architecture and a church spire upon the further side. A full set of bells hung in that spire and made delightful music; and when there was any sun at all, it shone direct in our two chambers. From a tavern hard by we had good meals sent in.

The first night we were both pretty weary, and she extremely so. There was little talk between us, and I packed her off to her bed as soon as she had eaten. The first thing in the morning I wrote word to Sprott to have her mails sent on, together with a line to Alan at his chief's; and had the same despatched, and her breakfast ready, ere I waked her. I was a little abashed when she came forth in her one habit, and the mud of the way upon her stockings. By what inquiries I had made, it seemed a good few days must pass before her mails could come to hand in Leyden, and it was plainly needful she must have a shift of things. She was unwilling at first that I should go to that expense; but I reminded her she was now a rich man's sister and must appear suitably in the part, and we had not got to the second merchant's before she was entirely charmed into the spirit of the thing, and her eyes shining. It pleased me to see her so innocent and thorough in this pleasure. What was more extraordinary was the passion into which I fell on it myself; being never satisfied that I had bought her enough or fine enough, and never weary of beholding her in different attires. Indeed, I began to understand some little of Miss Grant's immersion in the interest of clothes; for the truth is, when you have the ground of a beautiful person to adorn, the whole business becomes beautiful. The Dutch chintzes I should say were extraordinary cheap and fine; but I would be ashamed to set down what I paid for stockings to her. Altogether I spent so great a sum upon this pleasuring (as I may call it) that I was ashamed for a great while to spend more; and by way of a set-off, I left our chambers pretty bare. If we had beds, if Catriona was a little braw, and I had light to see her by, we were richly enough lodged for me.

By the end of this merchandising I was glad to leave her at the door with all our purchases, and go for a long walk alone in which to read myself a lecture. Here had I taken under my roof, and as good as to my bosom, a young lass extremely beautiful, and whose innocence was her peril. My talk with the old Dutchman, and the lies to which I was constrained, had already given me a sense of how my conduct must appear to others; and now, after the strong admiration I had just experienced and the immoderacy with which I had continued my vain purchases, I began to think of it myself as very hazarded. I bethought me, if I had a sister indeed, whether I would so expose her; then, judging the case too problematical, I varied my question into this, whether I would so trust Catriona in the hands of any other Christian being; the answer to which made my face to burn. The more cause, since I had been entrapped and had entrapped the girl into an undue situation, that I should behave in it with scrupulous nicety. She depended on me wholly for her bread and shelter; in case I should alarm her delicacy, she had no retreat. Besides I was her host and her protector; and the more irregularly I had fallen in these positions, the less excuse for me if I should profit by the same to forward even the most honest suit; for with the opportunities that I enjoyed, and which no wise parent would have suffered for a moment, even the most honest suit would be unfair. I saw I must be extremely hold-off in my relations; and yet not too much so neither; for if I had no right to appear at all in the character of a suitor, I must yet appear continually, and if possible agreeably, in that of host. It was plain I should require a great deal of tact and conduct, perhaps more than my years afforded. But I had rushed in where angels might have feared to tread, and there was no way out of that position save by behaving right while I was in it. I made a set of rules for my guidance; prayed for strength to be enabled to observe them, and as a more human aid to the same end purchased a study-book in law. This being all that I could think of, I relaxed from these grave considerations; whereupon my mind bubbled at once into an effervescency of pleasing spirits, and it was like one treading on air that I turned homeward. As I thought that name of home, and recalled the image of that figure awaiting me between four walls, my heart beat upon my bosom.

My troubles began with my return. She ran to greet me with an obvious and affecting pleasure. She was clad, besides, entirely in the new clothes that I had bought for her; looked in them beyond expression well; and must walk about and drop me curtseys to display them and to be admired. I am sure I did it with an ill grace, for I thought to have choked upon the words.

"Well," she said, "if you will not be caring for my pretty clothes, see what I have done with our two chambers." And she showed me the place all very finely swept, and the fires glowing in the two chimneys.

I was glad of a chance to seem a little more severe than I quite felt. "Catriona," said I, "I am very much displeased with you, and you must never again lay a hand upon my room. One of us two must have the rule while we are here together; it is most fit it should be I who am both the man and the elder; and I give you that for my command."

She dropped me one of her curtseys; which were extraordinary taking. "If you will be cross," said she, "I must be making pretty manners at you, Davie. I will be very obedient, as I should be when every stitch upon all there is of me belongs to you. But you will not be very cross either, because now I have not anyone else."

This struck me hard, and I made haste, in a kind of penitence, to blot out all the good effect of my last speech. In this direction progress was more easy, being down hill; she led me forward, smiling; at the sight of her, in the brightness of the fire and with her pretty becks and looks, my heart was altogether melted. We made our meal with infinite mirth and tenderness; and the two seemed to be commingled into one, so that our very laughter sounded like a kindness.

In the midst of which I awoke to better recollections, made a lame word of excuse, and set myself boorishly to my studies. It was a substantial, instructive book that I had bought, by the late Dr. Heineccius, in which I was to do a great deal reading these next few days, and often very glad that I had no one to question me of what I read. Methought she bit her lip at me a little, and that cut me. Indeed it left her wholly solitary, the more as she was very little of a reader, and had never a book. But what was I to do?

So the rest of the evening flowed by almost without speech.

I could have beat myself. I could not lie in my bed that night for rage and repentance, but walked to and fro on my bare feet till I was nearly perished, for the chimney was gone out and the frost keen. The thought of her in the next room, the thought that she might even hear me as I walked, the remembrance of my churlishness and that I must continue to practise the same ungrateful course or be dishonoured, put me beside my reason. I stood like a man between Scylla and Charybdis: What must she think of me? was my one thought that softened me continually into weakness. What is to become of us? the other which steeled me again to resolution. This was my first night of wakefulness and divided counsels, of which I was now to pass many, pacing like a madman, sometimes weeping like a childish boy, sometimes praying (I fain would hope) like a Christian.

But prayer is not very difficult, and the hitch comes in practice. In her presence, and above all if I allowed any beginning of familiarity, I found I had very little command of what should follow. But to sit all day in the same room with her, and feign to be engaged upon Heineccius, surpassed my strength. So that I fell instead upon the expedient of absenting myself so much as I was able; taking out classes and sitting there regularly, often with small attention, the test of which I found the other day in a note-book of that period, where I had left off to follow an edifying lecture and actually scribbled in my book some very ill verses, though the Latinity is rather better than I thought that I could ever have compassed. The evil of this course was unhappily near as great as its advantage. I had the less time of trial, but I believe, while the time lasted, I was tried the more extremely. For she being so much left to solitude, she came to greet my return with an increasing fervour that came nigh to overmaster me. These friendly offers I must barbarously cast back; and my rejection sometimes wounded her so cruelly that I must unbend and seek to make it up to her in kindness. So that our time passed in ups and downs, tiffs and disappointments, upon the which I could almost say (if it may be said with reverence) that I was crucified.

The base of my trouble was Catriona's extraordinary innocence, at which I was not so much surprised as filled with pity and admiration. She seemed to have no thought of our position, no sense of my struggles; welcomed any mark of my weakness with responsive joy; and when I was drove again to my retrenchments, did not always dissemble her chagrin. There were times when I have thought to myself, "If she were over head in love, and set her cap to catch me, she would scarce behave much otherwise;" and then I would fall again into wonder at the simplicity of woman, from whom I felt (in these moments) that I was not worthy to be descended.

There was one point in particular on which our warfare turned, and of all things, this was the question of her clothes. My baggage had soon followed me from Rotterdam, and hers from Helvoet. She had now, as it were, two wardrobes; and it grew to be understood between us (I could never tell how) that when she was friendly she would wear my clothes, and when otherwise her own. It was meant for a buffet, and (as it were) the renunciation of her gratitude; and I felt it so in my bosom, but was generally more wise than to appear to have observed the circumstance.

Once, indeed, I was betrayed into a childishness greater than her own; it fell in this way. On my return from classes, thinking upon her devoutly with a great deal of love and a good deal of annoyance in the bargain, the annoyance began to fade away out of my mind; and spying in a window one of those forced flowers, of which the Hollanders are so skilled in the artifice, I gave way to an impulse and bought it for Catriona. I do not know the name of that flower, but it was of the pink colour, and I thought she would admire the same, and carried it home to her with a wonderful soft heart. I had left her in my clothes, and when I returned to find her all changed and a face to match, I cast but the one look at her from head to foot, ground my teeth together, flung the window open, and my flower into the court, and then (between rage and prudence) myself out of that room again, of which I slammed she door as I went out.

On the steep stair I came near falling, and this brought me to myself, so that I began at once to see the folly of my conduct. I went, not into the street as I had purposed, but to the house court, which was always a solitary place, and where I saw my flower (that had cost me vastly more than it was worth) hanging in the leafless tree. I stood by the side of the canal, and looked upon the ice. Country people went by on their skates, and I envied them. I could see no way out of the pickle I was in no way so much as to return to the room I had just left. No doubt was in my mind but I had now betrayed the secret of my feelings; and to make things worse, I had shown at the same time (and that with wretched boyishness) incivility to my helpless guest.

I suppose she must have seen me from the open window. It did not seem to me that I had stood there very long before I heard the crunching of footsteps on the frozen snow, and turning somewhat angrily (for I was in no spirit to be interrupted) saw Catriona drawing near. She was all changed again, to the clocked stockings.

"Are we not to have our walk to-day?" said she.

I was looking at her in a maze. "Where is your brooch?" says I.

She carried her hand to her bosom and coloured high. "I will have forgotten it," said she. "I will run upstairs for it quick, and then surely we'll can have our walk?"

There was a note of pleading in that last that staggered me; I had neither words nor voice to utter them; I could do no more than nod by way of answer; and the moment she had left me, climbed into the tree and recovered my flower, which on her return I offered her.

"I bought it for you, Catriona," said I.

She fixed it in the midst of her bosom with the brooch, I could have thought tenderly.

"It is none the better of my handling," said I again, and blushed.

"I will be liking it none the worse, you may be sure of that," said she.

We did not speak so much that day; she seemed a thought on the reserve, though not unkindly. As for me, all the time of our walking, and after we came home, and I had seen her put my flower into a pot of water, I

361

was thinking to myself what puzzles women were. I was thinking, the one moment, it was the most stupid thing on earth she should not have perceived my love; and the next, that she had certainly perceived it long ago, and (being a wise girl with the fine female instinct of propriety) concealed her knowledge.

We had our walk daily. Out in the streets I felt more safe; I relaxed a little in my guardedness; and for one thing, there was no Heineccius. This made these periods not only a relief to myself, but a particular pleasure to my poor child. When I came back about the hour appointed, I would generally find her ready dressed, and glowing with anticipation. She would prolong their duration to the extreme, seeming to dread (as I did myself) the hour of the return; and there is scarce a field or waterside near Leyden, scarce a street or lane there, where we have not lingered. Outside of these, I bade her confine herself entirely to our lodgings; this in the fear of her encountering any acquaintance, which would have rendered our position very difficult. From the same apprehension I would never suffer her to attend church, nor even go myself; but made some kind of shift to hold worship privately in our own chamber—I hope with an honest, but I am quite sure with a very much divided mind. Indeed, there was scarce anything that more affected me, than thus to kneel down alone with her before God like man and wife.

One day it was snowing downright hard. I had thought it not possible that we should venture forth, and was surprised to find her waiting for me ready dressed.

"I will not be doing without my walk," she cried. "You are never a good boy, Davie, in the house; I will never be caring for you only in the open air. I think we two will better turn Egyptian and dwell by the roadside."

That was the best walk yet of all of them; she clung near to me in the falling snow; it beat about and melted on us, and the drops stood upon her bright cheeks like tears and ran into her smiling mouth. Strength seemed to come upon me with the sight like a giant's; I thought I could have caught her up and run with her into the uttermost places in the earth; and we spoke together all that time beyond belief for freedom and sweetness.

It was the dark night when we came to the house door. She pressed my arm upon her bosom. "Thank you kindly for these same good hours," said she, on a deep note of her voice.

The concern in which I fell instantly on this address, put me with the same swiftness on my guard; and we were no sooner in the chamber, and the light made, than she beheld the old, dour, stubborn countenance of the student of Heineccius. Doubtless she was more than usually hurt; and I know for myself, I found it more than usually difficult to maintain any strangeness. Even at the meal, I durst scarce unbuckle and scarce lift my eyes to her; and it was no sooner over than I fell again to my civilian, with more seeming abstraction and less understanding than before. Methought, as I read, I could hear my heart strike like an eight-day clock. Hard as I feigned to study, there was still some of my eyesight that spilled beyond the book upon Catriona. She sat on the floor by the side of my great mail, and the chimney lighted her up, and shone and blinked upon her, and made her glow and darken through a wonder of fine hues. Now she would be gazing in the fire, and then again at me; and at that I would be plunged in a terror of myself, and turn the pages of Heineccius like a man looking for the text in church.

Suddenly she called out aloud. "O, why does not my father come?" she cried, and fell at once into a storm of tears.

I leaped up, flung Heineccius fairly in the fire, ran to her side, and cast an arm around her sobbing body.

She put me from her sharply, "You do not love your friend," says she. "I could be so happy too, if you would let me!" And then, "O, what will I have done that you should hate me so?"

"Hate you!" cries I, and held her firm. "You blind less, can you not see a little in my wretched heart? Do you not think when I sit there, reading in that fool-book that I have just burned and be damned to it, I take ever the least thought of any stricken thing but just yourself? Night after night I could have grat to see you sitting there your lone. And what was I to do? You are here under my honour; would you punish me for that? Is it for that that you would spurn a loving servant?"

At the word, with a small, sudden motion, she clung near to me. I raised her face to mine, I kissed it, and she bowed her brow upon my bosom, clasping me tight. I saw in a mere whirl like a man drunken. Then I heard her voice sound very small and muffled in my clothes.

"Did you kiss her truly?" she asked.

There went through me so great a heave of surprise that I was all shook with it.

"Miss Grant?" I cried, all in a disorder. "Yes, I asked her to kiss me good-bye, the which she did."

"Ah, well!" said she, "you have kissed me too, at all events."

At the strangeness and sweetness of that word, I saw where we had fallen; rose, and set her on her feet.

"This will never do," said I. "This will never, never do. O Catrine, Catrine!" Then there came a pause in which I was debarred from any speaking. And then, "Go away to your bed," said I. "Go away to your bed and leave me."

She turned to obey me like a child, and the next I knew of it, had stopped in the very doorway.

"Good night, Davie!" said she.

"And O, good night, my love!" I cried, with a great outbreak of my soul, and caught her to me again, so that it seemed I must have broken her. The next moment I had thrust her from the room, shut to the door even with violence, and stood alone.

The milk was spilt now, the word was out and the truth told. I had crept like an untrusty man into the poor maid's affections; she was in my hand like any frail, innocent thing to make or mar; and what weapon of defence was left me? It seemed like a symbol that Heineccius, my old protection, was now burned. I repented, yet could not find it in my heart to blame myself for that great failure. It seemed not possible to have resisted the boldness of her innocence or that last temptation of her weeping. And all that I had to excuse me did but make my sin appear the greater—it was upon a nature so defenceless, and with such advantages of the position, that I seemed to have practised.

What was to become of us now? It seemed we could no longer dwell in the one place. But where was I to go? or where she? Without either choice or fault of ours, life had conspired to wall us together in that narrow place. I had a wild thought of marrying out of hand; and the next moment put it from me with revolt. She was a child, she could not tell her own heart; I had surprised her weakness, I must never go on to build on that surprisal; I must keep her not only clear of reproach, but free as she had come to me.

Down I sat before the fire, and reflected, and repented, and beat my brains in vain for any means of escape. About two of the morning, there were three red embers left and the house and all the city was asleep, when I was aware of a small sound of weeping in the next room. She thought that I slept, the poor soul; she regretted her weakness—and what perhaps (God help her!) she called her forwardness—and in the dead of the night solaced herself with tears. Tender and bitter feelings, love and penitence and pity, struggled in my soul; it seemed I was under bond to heal that weeping.

"O, try to forgive me!" I cried out, "try, try to forgive me. Let us forget it all, let us try if we'll no can forget it!"

There came no answer, but the sobbing ceased. I stood a long while with my hands still clasped as I had spoken; then the cold of the night laid hold upon me with a shudder, and I think my reason reawakened.

"You can make no hand of this, Davie," thinks I. "To bed with you like a wise lad, and try if you can sleep. To-morrow you may see your way."

CHAPTER XXV—THE RETURN OF JAMES MORE

I was called on the morrow out of a late and troubled slumber by a knocking on my door, ran to open it, and had almost swooned with the contrariety of my feelings, mostly painful; for on the threshold, in a rough wraprascal and an extraordinary big laced hat, there stood James More.

I ought to have been glad perhaps without admixture, for there was a sense in which the man came like an answer to prayer. I had been saying till my head was weary that Catriona and I must separate, and looking till my head ached for any possible means of separation. Here were the means come to me upon two legs, and joy was the hindmost of my thoughts. It is to be considered, however, that even if the weight of the future were lifted off me by the man's arrival, the present heaved up the more black and menacing; so that, as I first stood before him in my shirt and breeches, I believe I took a leaping step backward like a person shot.

"Ah," said he, "I have found you, Mr. Balfour." And offered me his large, fine hand, the which (recovering at the same time my post in the doorway, as if with some thought of resistance) I took him by doubtfully. "It is a remarkable circumstance how our affairs appear to intermingle," he continued. "I am owing you an apology for an unfortunate intrusion upon yours, which I suffered myself to be entrapped into by my confidence in that false-face, Prestongrange; I think shame to own to you that I was ever trusting to a lawyer." He shrugged his shoulders with a very French air. "But indeed the man is very plausible," says he. "And now it seems that you have busied yourself handsomely in the matter of my daughter, for whose direction I was remitted to yourself."

"I think, sir," said I, with a very painful air, "that it will be necessary we two should have an explanation."

"There is nothing amiss?" he asked. "My agent, Mr. Sprott—"

"For God's sake moderate your voice!" I cried. "She must not hear till we have had an explanation."

"She is in this place?" cries he.

"That is her chamber door," said I.

"You are here with her alone?" he asked.

"And who else would I have got to stay with us?" cries I.

I will do him the justice to admit that he turned pale.

"This is very unusual," said he. "This is a very unusual circumstance. You are right, we must hold an explanation."

So saying he passed me by, and I must own the tall old rogue appeared at that moment extraordinary dignified. He had now, for the first time, the view of my chamber, which I scanned (I may say) with his eyes. A bit of morning sun glinted in by the window pane, and showed it off; my bed, my mails, and washing dish, with some disorder of my clothes, and the unlighted chimney, made the only plenishing; no mistake but it looked bare and cold, and the most unsuitable, beggarly place conceivable to harbour a young lady. At the same time came in on my mind the recollection of the clothes that I had bought for her; and I thought this contrast of poverty and prodigality bore an ill appearance.

He looked all about the chamber for a seat, and finding nothing else to his purpose except my bed, took a place upon the side of it; where, after I had closed the door, I could not very well avoid joining him. For however this extraordinary interview might end, it must pass if possible without waking Catriona; and the one thing needful was that we should sit close and talk low. But I can scarce picture what a pair we made; he in his great coat which the coldness of my chamber made extremely suitable; I shivering in my shirt and breeks; he with very much the air of a judge; and I (whatever I looked) with very much the feelings of a man who has heard the last trumpet.

"Well?" says he.

And "Well," I began, but found myself unable to go further.

"You tell me she is here?" said he again, but now with a spice of impatience that seemed to brace me up.

"She is in this house," said I, "and I knew the circumstance would be called unusual. But you are to consider how very unusual the whole business was from the beginning. Here is a young lady landed on the coast of Europe with two shillings and a penny halfpenny. She is directed to yon man Sprott in Helvoet. I hear you call him your agent. All I can say is he could do nothing but damn and swear at the mere mention of your name, and I must fee him out of my own pocket even to receive the custody of her effects. You speak of unusual circumstances, Mr. Drummond, if that be the name you prefer. Here was a circumstance, if you like, to which it was barbarity to have exposed her."

"But this is what I cannot understand the least," said James. "My daughter was placed into the charge of some responsible persons, whose names I have forgot."

"Gebbie was the name," said I; "and there is no doubt that Mr. Gebbie should have gone ashore with her at Helvoet. But he did not, Mr. Drummond; and I think you might praise God that I was there to offer in his place."

"I shall have a word to say to Mr. Gebbie before long," said he. "As for yourself, I think it might have occurred that you were somewhat young for such a post."

"But the choice was not between me and somebody else, it was between me and nobody," cried I. "Nobody offered in my place, and I must say I think you show a very small degree of gratitude to me that did."

"I shall wait until I understand my obligation a little more in the particular," says he.

"Indeed, and I think it stares you in the face, then," said I. "Your child was deserted, she was clean flung away in the midst of Europe, with scarce two shillings, and not two words of any language spoken there: I must say, a bonny business! I brought her to this place. I gave her the name and the tenderness due to a sister. All this has not gone without expense, but that I scarce need to hint at. They were services due to the young lady's character which I respect; and I think it would be a bonny business too, if I was to be singing her praises to her father."

"You are a young man," he began.

"So I hear you tell me," said I, with a good deal of heat.

"You are a very young man," he repeated, "or you would have understood the significancy of the step."

"I think you speak very much at your ease," cried I. "What else was I to do? It is a fact I might have hired some decent, poor woman to be a third to us, and I declare I never thought of it until this moment! But where was I to find her, that am a foreigner myself? And let me point out to your observation, Mr. Drummond, that it would have cost me money out of my pocket. For here is just what it comes to, that I had to pay through the nose for your neglect; and there is only the one story to it, just that you were so unloving and so careless as to have lost your daughter."

"He that lives in a glass house should not be casting stones," says he; "and we will finish inquiring into the behaviour of Miss Drummond before we go on to sit in judgment on her father."

"But I will be entrapped into no such attitude," said I. "The character of Miss Drummond is far above inquiry, as her father ought to know. So is mine, and I am telling you that. There are but the two ways of it open. The one is to express your thanks to me as one gentleman to another, and to say no more. The other (if you are so difficult as to be still dissatisfied) is to pay me, that which I have expended and be done."

He seemed to soothe me with a hand in the air. "There, there," said he. "You go too fast, you go too fast, Mr. Balfour. It is a good thing that I have learned to be more patient. And I believe you forget that I have yet to see my daughter."

I began to be a little relieved upon this speech and a change in the man's manner that I spied in him as soon as the name of money fell between us.

"I was thinking it would be more fit—if you will excuse the plainness of my dressing in your presence—that I should go forth and leave you to encounter her alone?" said I.

"What I would have looked for at your hands!" says he; and there was no mistake but what he said it civilly.

I thought this better and better still, and as I began to pull on my hose, recalling the man's impudent mendicancy at Prestongrange's, I determined to pursue what seemed to be my victory.

"If you have any mind to stay some while in Leyden," said I, "this room is very much at your disposal, and I can easy find another for myself: in which way we shall have the least amount of flitting possible, there being only one to change."

"Why, sir," said he, making his bosom big, "I think no shame of a poverty I have come by in the service of my king; I make no secret that my affairs are quite involved; and for the moment, it would be even impossible for me to undertake a journey."

"Until you have occasion to communicate with your friends," said I, "perhaps it might be convenient for you (as of course it would be honourable to myself) if you were to regard yourself in the light of my guest?"

"Sir," said he, "when an offer is frankly made, I think I honour myself most to imitate that frankness. Your hand, Mr. David; you have the character that I respect the most; you are one of those from whom a gentleman can take a favour and no more words about it. I am an old soldier," he went on, looking rather disgusted-like around my chamber, "and you need not fear I shall prove burthensome. I have ate too often at a dyke-side, drank of the ditch, and had no roof but the rain."

"I should be telling you," said I, "that our breakfasts are sent customarily in about this time of morning. I propose I should go now to the tavern, and bid them add a cover for yourself and delay the meal the matter of an hour, which will give you an interval to meet your daughter in."

Methought his nostrils wagged at this. "O, an hour?" says he. "That is

370

perhaps superfluous. Half an hour, Mr. David, or say twenty minutes; I shall do very well in that. And by the way," he adds, detaining me by the coat, "what is it you drink in the morning, whether ale or wine?"

"To be frank with you, sir," says I, "I drink nothing else but spare, cold water."

"Tut-tut," says he, "that is fair destruction to the stomach, take an old campaigner's word for it. Our country spirit at home is perhaps the most entirely wholesome; but as that is not come-at-able, Rhenish or a white wine of Burgundy will be next best."

"I shall make it my business to see you are supplied," said I.

"Why, very good," said he, "and we shall make a man of you yet, Mr. David."

By this time, I can hardly say that I was minding him at all, beyond an odd thought of the kind of father-in-law that he was like to prove; and all my cares centred about the lass his daughter, to whom I determined to convey some warning of her visitor. I stepped to the door accordingly, and cried through the panels, knocking thereon at the same time: "Miss Drummond, here is your father come at last."

With that I went forth upon my errand, having (by two words) extraordinarily damaged my affairs.

CHAPTER XXVI—THE THREESOME

Whether or not I was to be so much blamed, or rather perhaps pitied, I must leave others to judge. My shrewdness (of which I have a good deal, too) seems not so great with the ladies. No doubt, at the moment when I awaked her, I was thinking a good deal of the effect upon James More; and similarly when I returned and we were all sat down to breakfast, I continued to behave to the young lady with deference and distance; as I still think to have been most wise. Her father had cast doubts upon the innocence of my friendship; and these, it was my first business to allay. But there is a kind of an excuse for Catriona also. We had shared in a scene of some tenderness and passion, and given and received caresses: I had thrust her from me with violence; I had called aloud upon her in the night from the one room to the other; she had passed hours of wakefulness and weeping; and it is not to be supposed I had been absent from her pillow thoughts. Upon the back of this, to be awaked, with unaccustomed formality, under the name of Miss Drummond, and to be thenceforth used with a great deal of distance and respect, led her entirely in error on my private sentiments; and she was indeed so incredibly abused as to imagine me repentant and trying to draw off!

The trouble betwixt us seems to have been this: that whereas I (since I had first set eyes on his great hat) thought singly of James More, his return and suspicions, she made so little of these that I may say she scarce remarked them, and all her troubles and doings regarded what had passed between us in the night before. This is partly to be explained by the innocence and boldness of her character; and partly because James More, having sped so ill in his interview with me, or had his mouth closed by my invitation, said no word to her upon the subject. At the breakfast, accordingly, it soon appeared we were at cross purposes. I had looked to find her in clothes of her own: I found her (as if her father were forgotten) wearing some of the best that I had bought for her, and which she knew (or thought) that I admired her in. I had looked to find her imitate my affectation of distance, and be most precise and formal; instead I found her flushed and wild-like, with eyes extraordinary bright, and a painful and varying expression, calling me by name with a sort of appeal of tenderness, and referring and deferring to my thoughts and wishes like an anxious or a suspected wife.

But this was not for long. As I behold her so regardless of her own interests, which I had jeopardised and was now endeavouring to recover, I redoubled my own coldness in the manner of a lesson to the girl. The more she came forward, the farther I drew back; the more she betrayed the closeness of our intimacy, the more pointedly civil I became, until even her father (if he had not been so engrossed with eating) might have observed the opposition. In the midst of which, of a sudden, she became wholly changed, and I told myself, with a good deal of relief, that she had took the hint at last.

All day I was at my classes or in quest of my new lodging; and though the hour of our customary walk hung miserably on my hands, I cannot say but I was happy on the whole to find my way cleared, the girl again in proper keeping, the father satisfied or at least acquiescent, and myself free to prosecute my love with honour. At supper, as at all our meals, it was James More that did the talking. No doubt but he talked well if anyone could have believed him. But I will speak of him presently more at large. The meal at an end, he rose, got his great coat, and looking (as I thought) at me, observed he had affairs abroad. I took this for a hint that I was to be going also, and got up; whereupon the girl, who had scarce given me greeting at my entrance, turned her eyes upon me wide open with a look that bade me stay. I stood between them like a fish out of water, turning from one to the other; neither seemed to observe me, she gazing on the floor, he buttoning his coat: which vastly swelled my embarrassment. This appearance of indifference argued, upon her side, a good deal of anger very near to burst out. Upon his, I thought it horribly alarming; I made sure there was a tempest brewing there; and considering that to be the chief peril, turned towards him and put myself (so to speak) in the man's hands.

"Can I do anything for you, Mr. Drummond?" says I.

He stifled a yawn, which again I thought to be duplicity. "Why, Mr. David," said he, "since you are so obliging as to propose it, you might show me the way to a certain tavern" (of which he gave the name) "where I hope to fall in with some old companions in arms."

There was no more to say, and I got my hat and cloak to bear him company.

"And as for you," say he to his daughter, "you had best go to your bed. I shall be late home, and Early to bed and early to rise, gars bonny lasses have bright eyes."

Whereupon he kissed her with a good deal of tenderness, and ushered me before him from the door. This was so done (I thought on purpose) that it was scarce possible there should be any parting salutation; but I observed she did not look at me, and set it down to terror of James More.

It was some distance to that tavern. He talked all the way of matters which did not interest me the smallest, and at the door dismissed me with empty manners. Thence I walked to my new lodging, where I had not so much as a chimney to hold me warm, and no society but my own thoughts. These were still bright enough; I did not so much as dream that Catriona was turned against me; I thought we were like folk pledged; I thought we had been too near and spoke too warmly to be severed, least of all by what were only steps in a most needful policy. And the chief of my concern was only the kind of father-in-law that I was getting, which was not at all the kind I would have chosen: and the matter of how soon I ought to speak to him, which was a delicate point on several sides. In the first place, when I thought how young I was I blushed all over, and could almost have found it in my heart to have desisted; only that if once I let them go from Leyden without explanation, I might lose her altogether. And in the second place, there was our very irregular situation to be kept in view, and the rather scant measure of satisfaction I had given James More that morning. I concluded, on the whole, that delay would not hurt anything, yet I would not delay too long neither; and got to my cold bed with a full heart.

The next day, as James More seemed a little on the complaining hand in the matter of my chamber, I offered to have in more furniture; and coming in the afternoon, with porters bringing chairs and tables, found the girl once more left to herself. She greeted me on my admission civilly, but withdrew at once to her own room, of which she shut the door. I made my disposition, and paid and dismissed the men so that she might hear them go, when I supposed she would at once come forth again to speak to me. I waited yet awhile, then knocked upon her door.

"Catriona!" said I.

The door was opened so quickly, even before I had the word out, that I thought she must have stood behind it listening. She remained there in the interval quite still; but she had a look that I cannot put a name on, as of one in a bitter trouble.

"Are we not to have our walk to-day either?" so I faltered.

"I am thanking you," said she. "I will not be caring much to walk, now that my father is come home."

"But I think he has gone out himself and left you here alone," said I.

"And do you think that was very kindly said?" she asked.

"It was not unkindly meant," I replied. "What ails you, Catriona? What have I done to you that you should turn from me like this?"

"I do not turn from you at all," she said, speaking very carefully. "I will ever be grateful to my friend that was good to me; I will ever be his friend in all that I am able. But now that my father James More is come again, there is a difference to be made, and I think there are some things said and done that would be better to be forgotten. But I will ever be your friend in all that I am able, and if that is not all that . . . . if it is not so much . . . . Not that you will be caring! But I would not have you think of me too hard. It was true what you said to me, that I was too young to be advised, and I am hoping you will remember I was just a child. I would not like to lose your friendship, at all events."

She began this very pale; but before she was done, the blood was in her face like scarlet, so that not her words only, but her face and the trembling of her very hands, besought me to be gentle. I saw, for the first time, how very wrong I had done to place the child in that position, where she had been entrapped into a moment's weakness, and now stood before me like a person shamed.

"Miss Drummond," I said, and stuck, and made the same beginning once again, "I wish you could see into my heart," I cried. "You would read there that my respect is undiminished. If that were possible, I should say it was increased. This is but the result of the mistake we made; and had to come; and the less said of it now the better. Of all of our life here, I promise you it shall never pass my lips; I would like to promise you too that I would never think of it, but it's a memory that will be always dear to me. And as for a friend, you have one here that would die for you."

"I am thanking you," said she.

We stood awhile silent, and my sorrow for myself began to get the upper hand; for here were all my dreams come to a sad tumble, and my love lost, and myself alone again in the world as at the beginning.

"Well," said I, "we shall be friends always, that's a certain thing. But this is a kind of farewell, too: it's a kind of a farewell after all; I shall always ken Miss Drummond, but this is a farewell to my Catriona."

I looked at her; I could hardly say I saw her, but she seemed to grow great and brighten in my eyes; and with that I suppose I must have lost my head, for I called out her name again and made a step at her with my hands reached forth.

She shrank back like a person struck, her face flamed; but the blood sprang no faster up into her cheeks, than what it flowed back upon my own heart, at sight of it, with penitence and concern. I found no words to excuse myself, but bowed before her very deep, and went my ways out of the house with death in my bosom.

I think it was about five days that followed without any change. I saw her scarce ever but at meals, and then of course in the company of James More. If we were alone even for a moment, I made it my devoir to behave the more distantly and to multiply respectful attentions, having always in my mind's eye that picture of the girl shrinking and flaming in a blush, and in my heart more pity for her than I could depict in words. I was sorry enough for myself, I need not dwell on that, having fallen all my length and more than all my height in a few seconds; but, indeed, I was near as sorry for the girl, and sorry enough to be scarce angry with her save by fits and starts. Her plea was good; she had been placed in an unfair position; if she had deceived herself and me, it was no more than was to have been looked for.

And for another thing she was now very much alone. Her father, when he was by, was rather a caressing parent; but he was very easy led away by his affairs and pleasures, neglected her without compunction or remark, spent his nights in taverns when he had the money, which was more often than I could at all account for; and even in the course of these few days, failed once to come to a meal, which Catriona and I were at last compelled to partake of without him. It was the evening meal, and I left immediately that I had eaten, observing I supposed she would prefer to be alone; to which she agreed and (strange as it may seem) I quite believed her. Indeed, I thought myself but an eyesore to the girl, and a reminder of a moment's weakness that she now abhorred to think of. So she must sit alone in that room where she and I had been so merry, and in the blink of that chimney whose light had shone upon our many difficult and tender moments. There she must sit alone, and think of herself as of a maid who had most unmaidenly proffered her affections and had the same rejected. And in the meanwhile I would be alone some other place, and reading myself (whenever I was tempted to be angry) lessons upon human frailty and female delicacy. And altogether I suppose there were never two poor fools made themselves more unhappy in a greater misconception.

As for James, he paid not so much heed to us, or to anything in nature but his pocket, and his belly, and his own prating talk. Before twelve hours were gone he had raised a small loan of me; before thirty, he had asked for a second and been refused. Money and refusal he took with the same kind of high good nature. Indeed, he had an outside air of magnanimity that was very well fitted to impose upon a daughter; and the light in which he was constantly presented in his talk, and the man's fine presence and great ways went together pretty harmoniously. So that a man that had no business with him, and either very little penetration or a furious deal of prejudice, might almost have been taken in. To me, after my first two interviews, he was as plain as print; I saw him to be perfectly selfish, with a perfect innocency in the same; and I would hearken to his swaggering talk (of arms, and "an old soldier," and "a poor Highland gentleman," and "the strength of my country and my friends") as I might to the babbling of a parrot.

The odd thing was that I fancy he believed some part of it himself, or did at times; I think he was so false all through that he scarce knew when he was lying; and for one thing, his moments of dejection must have been wholly genuine. There were times when he would be the most silent, affectionate, clinging creature possible, holding Catriona's hand like a big baby, and begging of me not to leave if I had any love to him; of which, indeed, I had none, but all the more to his daughter. He would press and indeed beseech us to entertain him with our talk, a thing very difficult in the state of our relations; and again break forth in pitiable regrets for his own land and friends, or into Gaelic singing.

"This is one of the melancholy airs of my native land," he would say. "You may think it strange to see a soldier weep, and indeed it is to make a near friend of you," says he. "But the notes of this singing are in my blood, and the words come out of my heart. And when I mind upon my red mountains and the wild birds calling there, and the brave streams of water running down, I would scarce think shame to weep before my enemies." Then he would sing again, and translate to me pieces of the song, with a great deal of boggling and much expressed contempt against the English language. "It says here," he would say, "that the sun is gone down, and the battle is at an end, and the brave chiefs are defeated. And it tells here how the stars see them fleeing into strange countries or lying dead on the red mountain; and they will never more shout the call of battle or wash their feet in the streams of the valley. But if you had only some of this language, you would weep also because the words of it are beyond all expression, and it is mere mockery to tell you it in English."

Well, I thought there was a good deal of mockery in the business, one way and another; and yet, there was some feeling too, for which I hated him, I think, the worst of all. And it used to cut me to the quick to see Catriona so much concerned for the old rogue, and weeping herself to see him weep, when I was sure one half of his distress flowed from his last night's drinking in some tavern. There were times when I was tempted to lend him a round sum, and see the last of him for good; but this would have been to see the last of Catriona as well, for which I was scarcely so prepared; and besides, it went against my conscience to squander my good money on one who was so little of a husband.

CHAPTER XXVII—A TWOSOME

I believe it was about the fifth day, and I know at least that James was in one of his fits of gloom, when I received three letters. The first was from Alan, offering to visit me in Leyden; the other two were out of Scotland and prompted by the same affair, which was the death of my uncle and my own complete accession to my rights. Rankeillor's was, of course, wholly in the business view; Miss Grant's was like herself, a little more witty than wise, full of blame to me for not having written (though how was I to write with such intelligence?) and of rallying talk about Catriona, which it cut me to the quick to read in her very presence.

For it was of course in my own rooms that I found them, when I came to dinner, so that I was surprised out of my news in the very first moment of reading it. This made a welcome diversion for all three of us, nor could any have foreseen the ill consequences that ensued. It was accident that brought the three letters the same day, and that gave them into my hand in the same room with James More; and of all the events that flowed from that accident, and which I might have prevented if I had held my tongue, the truth is that they were preordained before Agricola came into Scotland or Abraham set out upon his travels.

The first that I opened was naturally Alan's; and what more natural than that I should comment on his design to visit me? but I observed James to sit up with an air of immediate attention.

"Is that not Alan Breck that was suspected of the Appin accident?" he inquired.

I told him, "Ay," it was the same; and he withheld me some time from my other letters, asking of our acquaintance, of Alan's manner of life in France, of which I knew very little, and further of his visit as now proposed.

"All we forfeited folk hang a little together," he explained, "and besides I know the gentleman: and though his descent is not the thing, and indeed he has no true right to use the name of Stewart, he was very much admired in the day of Drummossie. He did there like a soldier; if some that need not be named had done as well, the upshot need not have been so melancholy to remember. There were two that did their best that day, and it makes a bond between the pair of us," says he.

I could scarce refrain from shooting out my tongue at him, and could almost have wished that Alan had been there to have inquired a little further into that mention of his birth. Though, they tell me, the same was indeed not wholly regular.

Meanwhile, I had opened Miss Grant's, and could not withhold an exclamation.

"Catriona," I cried, forgetting, the first time since her father was arrived, to address her by a handle, "I am come into my kingdom fairly, I am the laird of Shaws indeed—my uncle is dead at last."

She clapped her hands together leaping from her seat. The next moment it must have come over both of us at once what little cause of joy was left to either, and we stood opposite, staring on each other sadly.

But James showed himself a ready hypocrite. "My daughter," says he, "is this how my cousin learned you to behave? Mr. David has lost a new friend, and we should first condole with him on his bereavement."

"Troth, sir," said I, turning to him in a kind of anger, "I can make no such great faces. His death is as blithe news as ever I got."

"It's a good soldier's philosophy," says James. "'Tis the way of flesh, we must all go, all go. And if the gentleman was so far from your favour, why, very well! But we may at least congratulate you on your accession to your estates."

"Nor can I say that either," I replied, with the same heat. "It is a good estate; what matters that to a lone man that has enough already? I had a good revenue before in my frugality; and but for the man's death—which gratifies me, shame to me that must confess it!—I see not how anyone is to be bettered by this change."

"Come, come," said he, "you are more affected than you let on, or you would never make yourself out so lonely. Here are three letters; that means three that wish you well; and I could name two more, here in this very chamber. I have known you not so very long, but Catriona, when we are alone, is never done with the singing of your praises."

She looked up at him, a little wild at that; and he slid off at once into another matter, the extent of my estate, which (during the most of the dinner time) he continued to dwell upon with interest. But it was to no purpose he dissembled; he had touched the matter with too gross a hand: and I knew what to expect. Dinner was scarce ate when he plainly discovered his designs. He reminded Catriona of an errand, and bid her attend to it. "I do not see you should be one beyond the hour," he added, "and friend David will be good enough to bear me company till you return." She made haste to obey him without words. I do not know if she understood, I believe not; but I was completely satisfied, and sat strengthening my mind for what should follow.

The door had scarce closed behind her departure, when the man leaned back in his chair and addressed me with a good affectation of easiness. Only the one thing betrayed him, and that was his face; which suddenly shone all over with fine points of sweat.

"I am rather glad to have a word alone with you," says he, "because in our first interview there were some expressions you misapprehended and I have long meant to set you right upon. My daughter stands beyond doubt. So do you, and I would make that good with my sword against all gainsayers. But, my dear David, this world is a censorious place—as who should know it better than myself, who have lived ever since the days of my late departed father, God sain him! in a perfect spate of calumnies? We have to face to that; you and me have to consider of that; we have to consider of that." And he wagged his head like a minister in a pulpit.

"To what effect, Mr. Drummond?" said I. "I would be obliged to you if you would approach your point."

"Ay, ay," said he, laughing, "like your character, indeed! and what I most admire in it. But the point, my worthy fellow, is sometimes in a kittle bit." He filled a glass of wine. "Though between you and me, that are such fast friends, it need not bother us long. The point, I need scarcely tell you, is my daughter. And the first thing is that I have no thought in my mind of blaming you. In the unfortunate circumstances, what could you do else? 'Deed, and I cannot tell."

"I thank you for that," said I, pretty close upon my guard.

"I have besides studied your character," he went on; "your talents are fair; you seem to have a moderate competence, which does no harm; and one thing with another, I am very happy to have to announce to you that I have decided on the latter of the two ways open."

"I am afraid I am dull," said I. "What ways are these?"

He bent his brows upon me formidably and uncrossed his legs. "Why, sir," says he, "I think I need scarce describe them to a gentleman of your condition; either that I should cut your throat or that you should marry my daughter."

"You are pleased to be quite plain at last," said I.

"And I believe I have been plain from the beginning!" cries he robustiously. "I am a careful parent, Mr. Balfour; but I thank God, a patient and deleeborate man. There is many a father, sir, that would have hirsled you at once either to the altar or the field. My esteem for your character—"

"Mr. Drummond," I interrupted, "if you have any esteem for me at all, I will beg of you to moderate your voice. It is quite needless to rowt at a gentleman in the same chamber with yourself and lending you his best attention."

"Why, very true," says he, with an immediate change. "And you must excuse the agitations of a parent."

"I understand you then," I continued—"for I will take no note of your other alternative, which perhaps it was a pity you let fall—I understand you rather to offer me encouragement in case I should desire to apply for your daughter's hand?"

"It is not possible to express my meaning better," said he, "and I see we shall do well together."

"That remains to be yet seen," said I. "But so much I need make no secret of, that I bear the lady you refer to the most tender affection, and I could not fancy, even in a dream, a better fortune than to get her."

"I was sure of it, I felt certain of you, David," he cried, and reached out his hand to me.

I put it by. "You go too fast, Mr. Drummond," said I. "There are conditions to be made; and there is a difficulty in the path, which I see not entirely how we shall come over. I have told you that, upon my side, there is no objection to the marriage, but I have good reason to believe there will be much on the young lady's."

"This is all beside the mark," says he. "I will engage for her acceptance."

"I think you forget, Mr. Drummond," said I, "that, even in dealing with myself, you have been betrayed into two-three unpalatable expressions. I will have none such employed to the young lady. I am here to speak and think for the two of us; and I give you to understand that I would no more let a wife be forced upon myself, than what I would let a husband be forced on the young lady."

He sat and glowered at me like one in doubt and a good deal of temper.

"So that is to be the way of it," I concluded. "I will marry Miss Drummond, and that blithely, if she is entirely willing. But if there be the least unwillingness, as I have reason to fear—marry her will I never."

"Well well," said he, "this is a small affair. As soon as she returns I will sound her a bit, and hope to reassure you—"

But I cut in again. "Not a finger of you, Mr. Drummond, or I cry off, and you can seek a husband to your daughter somewhere else," said I. "It is I that am to be the only dealer and the only judge. I shall satisfy myself exactly;

384

and none else shall anyways meddle—you the least of all."

"Upon my word, sir!" he exclaimed, "and who are you to be the judge?"

"The bridegroom, I believe," said I.

"This is to quibble," he cried. "You turn your back upon the fact. The girl, my daughter, has no choice left to exercise. Her character is gone."

"And I ask your pardon," said I, "but while this matter lies between her and you and me, that is not so."

"What security have I!" he cried. "Am I to let my daughter's reputation depend upon a chance?"

"You should have thought of all this long ago," said I, "before you were so misguided as to lose her; and not afterwards when it is quite too late. I refuse to regard myself as any way accountable for your neglect, and I will be browbeat by no man living. My mind is quite made up, and come what may, I will not depart from it a hair's breadth. You and me are to sit here in company till her return: upon which, without either word or look from you, she and I are to go forth again to hold our talk. If she can satisfy me that she is willing to this step, I will then make it; and if she cannot, I will not."

He leaped out of his chair like a man stung. "I can spy your manœuvre," he cried; "you would work upon her to refuse!"

"Maybe ay, and maybe no," said I. "That is the way it is to be, whatever."

"And if I refuse?" cries he.

"Then, Mr. Drummond, it will have to come to the throat-cutting," said I.

What with the size of the man, his great length of arm in which he came near rivalling his father, and his reputed skill at weapons, I did not use this word without trepidation, to say nothing at all of the circumstance that he was Catriona's father. But I might have spared myself alarms. From the poorness of my lodging—he does not seem to have remarked his daughter's dresses, which were indeed all equally new to him—and from the fact that

I had shown myself averse to lend, he had embraced a strong idea of my poverty. The sudden news of my estate convinced him of his error, and he had made but the one bound of it on this fresh venture, to which he was now so wedded, that I believe he would have suffered anything rather than fall to the alternative of fighting.

A little while longer he continued to dispute with me, until I hit upon a word that silenced him.

"If I find you so averse to let me see the lady by herself," said I, "I must suppose you have very good grounds to think me in the right about her unwillingness."

He gabbled some kind of an excuse.

"But all this is very exhausting to both of our tempers," I added, "and I think we would do better to preserve a judicious silence."

The which we did until the girl returned, and I must suppose would have cut a very ridiculous figure had there been any there to view us.

CHAPTER XXVIII—IN WHICH I AM LEFT ALONE

I opened the door to Catriona and stopped her on the threshold.

"Your father wishes us to take our walk," said I.

She looked to James More, who nodded, and at that, like a trained soldier, she turned to go with me.

We took one of our old ways, where we had gone often together, and been more happy than I can tell of in the past. I came a half a step behind, so that I could watch her unobserved. The knocking of her little shoes upon the way sounded extraordinary pretty and sad; and I thought it a strange moment that I should be so near both ends of it at once, and walk in the midst between two destinies, and could not tell whether I was hearing these steps for the last time, or whether the sound of them was to go in and out with me till death should part us.

She avoided even to look at me, only walked before her, like one who had a guess of what was coming. I saw I must speak soon before my courage was run out, but where to begin I knew not. In this painful situation, when the girl was as good as forced into my arms and had already besought my forbearance, any excess of pressure must have seemed indecent; yet to avoid it wholly would have a very cold-like appearance. Between these extremes I stood helpless, and could have bit my fingers; so that, when at last I managed to speak at all, it may be said I spoke at random.

"Catriona," said I, "I am in a very painful situation; or rather, so we are both; and I would be a good deal obliged to you if you would promise to let me speak through first of all, and not to interrupt me till I have done."

She promised me that simply.

"Well," said I, "this that I have got to say is very difficult, and I know very well I have no right to be saying it. After what passed between the two of us last Friday, I have no manner of right. We have got so ravelled up (and all by my fault) that I know very well the least I could do is just to hold my tongue, which was what I intended fully, and there was nothing further from my thoughts than to have troubled you again. But, my dear, it has become merely necessary, and no way by it. You see, this estate of mine has fallen in, which makes of me rather a better match; and the—the business would not have quite the same ridiculous-like appearance that it would before. Besides which, it's supposed that our affairs have got so much ravelled up (as I was saying) that it would be better to let them be the way they are. In my view, this part of the thing is vastly exagerate, and if I were you I would not wear two thoughts on it. Only it's right I should mention the same, because there's no doubt it has some influence on James More. Then I think we were none so unhappy when we dwelt together in this town before. I think we did pretty well together. If you would look back, my dear—"

"I will look neither back nor forward," she interrupted. "Tell me the one thing: this is my father's doing?"

"He approves of it," said I. "He approved I that I should ask your hand in marriage," and was going on again with somewhat more of an appeal upon her feelings; but she marked me not, and struck into the midst.

"He told you to!" she cried. "It is no sense denying it, you said yourself that there was nothing farther from your thoughts. He told you to."

"He spoke of it the first, if that is what you mean," I began.

She was walking ever the faster, and looking fain in front of her; but at this she made a little noise in her head, and I thought she would have run.

"Without which," I went on, "after what you said last Friday, I would never have been so troublesome as make the offer. But when he as good as asked me, what was I to do?"

She stopped and turned round upon me.

"Well, it is refused at all events," she cried, "and there will be an end of that."

And she began again to walk forward.

388

"I suppose I could expect no better," said I, "but I think you might try to be a little kind to me for the last end of it. I see not why you should be harsh. I have loved you very well, Catriona—no harm that I should call you so for the last time. I have done the best that I could manage, I am trying the same still, and only vexed that I can do no better. It is a strange thing to me that you can take any pleasure to be hard to me."

"I am not thinking of you," she said, "I am thinking of that man, my father."

"Well, and that way, too!" said I. "I can be of use to you that way, too; I will have to be. It is very needful, my dear, that we should consult about your father; for the way this talk has gone, an angry man will be James More."

She stopped again. "It is because I am disgraced?" she asked.

"That is what he is thinking," I replied, "but I have told you already to make nought of it."

"It will be all one to me," she cried. "I prefer to be disgraced!"

I did not know very well what to answer, and stood silent.

There seemed to be something working in her bosom after that last cry; presently she broke out, "And what is the meaning of all this? Why is all this shame loundered on my head? How could you dare it, David Balfour?"

"My dear," said I, "what else was I to do?"

"I am not your dear," she said, "and I defy you to be calling me these words."

"I am not thinking of my words," said I. "My heart bleeds for you, Miss Drummond. Whatever I may say, be sure you have my pity in your difficult position. But there is just the one thing that I wish you would bear in view, if it was only long enough to discuss it quietly; for there is going to be a collieshangie when we two get home. Take my word for it, it will need the two of us to make this matter end in peace."

"Ay," said she. There sprang a patch of red in either of her cheeks. "Was he for fighting you?" said she.

"Well, he was that," said I.

She gave a dreadful kind of laugh. "At all events, it is complete!" she cried. And then turning on me. "My father and I are a fine pair," said she, "but I am thanking the good God there will be somebody worse than what we are. I am thanking the good God that he has let me see you so. There will never be the girl made that will not scorn you."

I had borne a good deal pretty patiently, but this was over the mark.

"You have no right to speak to me like that," said I. "What have I done but to be good to you, or try to be? And here is my repayment! O, it is too much."

She kept looking at me with a hateful smile. "Coward!" said she.

"The word in your throat and in your father's!" I cried. "I have dared him this day already in your interest. I will dare him again, the nasty pole-cat; little I care which of us should fall! Come," said I, "back to the house with us; let us be done with it, let me be done with the whole Hieland crew of you! You will see what you think when I am dead."

She shook her head at me with that same smile I could have struck her for.

"O, smile away!" I cried. "I have seen your bonny father smile on the wrong side this day. Not that I mean he was afraid, of course," I added hastily, "but he preferred the other way of it."

"What is this?" she asked.

"When I offered to draw with him," said I.

"You offered to draw upon James More!" she cried.

"And I did so," said I, "and found him backward enough, or how would we be here?"

"There is a meaning upon this," said she. "What is it you are meaning?"

"He was to make you take me," I replied, "and I would not have it. I said you should be free, and I must speak with you alone; little I supposed it would be such a speaking! 'And what if I refuse?' said he.—'Then it must come to the throat-cutting,' says I, 'for I will no more have a husband forced on that young lady, than what I would have a wife forced upon myself.' These were my words, they were a friend's words; bonnily have I paid for them! Now you have refused me of your own clear free will, and there lives no father in the Highlands, or out of them, that can force on this marriage. I will see that your wishes are respected; I will make the same my business, as I have all through. But I think you might have that decency as to affect some gratitude. 'Deed, and I thought you knew me better! I have not behaved quite well to you, but that was weakness. And to think me a coward, and such a coward as that—O, my lass, there was a stab for the last of it!"

"Davie, how would I guess?" she cried. "O, this is a dreadful business! Me and mine,"—she gave a kind of a wretched cry at the word—"me and mine are not fit to speak to you. O, I could be kneeling down to you in the street, I could be kissing your hands for forgiveness!"

"I will keep the kisses I have got from you already," cried I. "I will keep the ones I wanted and that were something worth; I will not be kissed in penitence."

"What can you be thinking of this miserable girl?" says she.

"What I am trying to tell you all this while!" said I, "that you had best leave me alone, whom you can make no more unhappy if you tried, and turn your attention to James More, your father, with whom you are like to have a queer pirn to wind."

"O, that I must be going out into the world alone with such a man!" she cried, and seemed to catch herself in with a great effort. "But trouble yourself no more for that," said she. "He does not know what kind of nature is in my heart. He will pay me dear for this day of it; dear, dear, will he pay."

She turned, and began to go home and I to accompany her. At which she stopped.

"I will be going alone," she said. "It is alone I must be seeing him."

Some little time I raged about the streets, and told myself I was the worst used lad in Christendom. Anger choked me; it was all very well for me to breathe deep; it seemed there was not air enough about Leyden to supply me, and I thought I would have burst like a man at the bottom of the sea. I stopped and laughed at myself at a street corner a minute together, laughing out loud, so that a passenger looked at me, which brought me to myself.

"Well," I thought, "I have been a gull and a ninny and a soft Tommy long enough. Time it was done. Here is a good lesson to have nothing to do with that accursed sex, that was the ruin of the man in the beginning and will be so to the end. God knows I was happy enough before ever I saw her; God knows I can be happy enough again when I have seen the last of her."

That seemed to me the chief affair: to see them go. I dwelled upon the idea fiercely; and presently slipped on, in a kind of malevolence, to consider how very poorly they were likely to fare when Davie Balfour was no longer by to be their milk-cow; at which, to my very own great surprise, the disposition of my mind turned bottom up. I was still angry; I still hated her; and yet I thought I owed it to myself that she should suffer nothing.

This carried me home again at once, where I found the mails drawn out and ready fastened by the door, and the father and daughter with every mark upon them of a recent disagreement. Catriona was like a wooden doll; James More breathed hard, his face was dotted with white spots, and his nose upon one side. As soon as I came in, the girl looked at him with a steady, clear, dark look that might have been followed by a blow. It was a hint that was more contemptuous than a command, and I was surprised to see James More accept it. It was plain he had had a master talking-to; and I could see there must be more of the devil in the girl than I had guessed, and more good humour about the man than I had given him the credit of.

He began, at least, calling me Mr. Balfour, and plainly speaking from a lesson; but he got not very far, for at the first pompous swell of his voice, Catriona cut in.

"I will tell you what James More is meaning," said she. "He means we

392

have come to you, beggar-folk, and have not behaved to you very well, and we are ashamed of our ingratitude and ill-behaviour. Now we are wanting to go away and be forgotten; and my father will have guided his gear so ill, that we cannot even do that unless you will give us some more alms. For that is what we are, at an events, beggar-folk and sorners."

"By your leave, Miss Drummond," said I, "I must speak to your father by myself."

She went into her own room and shut the door, without a word or a look.

"You must excuse her, Mr. Balfour," says James More. "She has no delicacy."

"I am not here to discuss that with you," said I, "but to be quit of you. And to that end I must talk of your position. Now, Mr. Drummond, I have kept the run of your affairs more closely than you bargained for. I know you had money of your own when you were borrowing mine. I know you have had more since you were here in Leyden, though you concealed it even from your daughter."

"I bid you beware. I will stand no more baiting," he broke out. "I am sick of her and you. What kind of a damned trade is this to be a parent! I have had expressions used to me—" There he broke off. "Sir, this is the heart of a soldier and a parent," he went on again, laying his hand on his bosom, "outraged in both characters—and I bid you beware."

"If you would have let me finish," says I, "you would have found I spoke for your advantage."

"My dear friend," he cried, "I know I might have relied upon the generosity of your character."

"Man! will you let me speak?" said I. "The fact is that I cannot win to find out if you are rich or poor. But it is my idea that your means, as they are mysterious in their source, so they are something insufficient in amount; and I do not choose your daughter to be lacking. If I durst speak to herself, you may be certain I would never dream of trusting it to you; because I know you like the back of my hand, and all your blustering talk is that much wind to me. However, I believe in your way you do still care something for your daughter after all; and I must just be doing with that ground of confidence, such as it is."

Whereupon, I arranged with him that he was to communicate with me, as to his whereabouts and Catriona's welfare, in consideration of which I was to serve him a small stipend.

He heard the business out with a great deal of eagerness; and when it was done, "My dear fellow, my dear son," he cried out, "this is more like yourself than any of it yet! I will serve you with a soldier's faithfulness—"

"Let me hear no more of it!" says I. "You have got me to that pitch that the bare name of soldier rises on my stomach. Our traffic is settled; I am now going forth and will return in one half-hour, when I expect to find my chambers purged of you."

I gave them good measure of time; it was my one fear that I might see Catriona again, because tears and weakness were ready in my heart, and I cherished my anger like a piece of dignity. Perhaps an hour went by; the sun had gone down, a little wisp of a new moon was following it across a scarlet sunset; already there were stars in the east, and in my chambers, when at last I entered them, the night lay blue. I lit a taper and reviewed the rooms; in the first there remained nothing so much as to awake a memory of those who were gone; but in the second, in a corner of the floor, I spied a little heap that brought my heart into my mouth. She had left behind at her departure all that she had ever had of me. It was the blow that I felt sorest, perhaps because it was the last; and I fell upon that pile of clothing and behaved myself more foolish than I care to tell of.

Late in the night, in a strict frost, and my teeth chattering, I came again by some portion of my manhood and considered with myself. The sight of these poor frocks and ribbons, and her shifts, and the clocked stockings, was not to be endured; and if I were to recover any constancy of mind, I saw I must be rid of them ere the morning. It was my first thought to have

394

made a fire and burned them; but my disposition has always been opposed to wastery, for one thing; and for another, to have burned these things that she had worn so close upon her body seemed in the nature of a cruelty. There was a corner cupboard in that chamber; there I determined to bestow them. The which I did and made it a long business, folding them with very little skill indeed but the more care; and sometimes dropping them with my tears. All the heart was gone out of me, I was weary as though I had run miles, and sore like one beaten; when, as I was folding a kerchief that she wore often at her neck, I observed there was a corner neatly cut from it. It was a kerchief of a very pretty hue, on which I had frequently remarked; and once that she had it on, I remembered telling her (by way of a banter) that she wore my colours. There came a glow of hope and like a tide of sweetness in my bosom; and the next moment I was plunged back in a fresh despair. For there was the corner crumpled in a knot and cast down by itself in another part of the floor.

But when I argued with myself, I grew more hopeful. She had cut that corner off in some childish freak that was manifestly tender; that she had cast it away again was little to be wondered at; and I was inclined to dwell more upon the first than upon the second, and to be more pleased that she had ever conceived the idea of that keepsake, than concerned because she had flung it from her in an hour of natural resentment.

CHAPTER XXIX—WE MEET IN DUNKIRK

Altogether, then, I was scarce so miserable the next days but what I had many hopeful and happy snatches; threw myself with a good deal of constancy upon my studies; and made out to endure the time till Alan should arrive, or I might hear word of Catriona by the means of James More. I had altogether three letters in the time of our separation. One was to announce their arrival in the town of Dunkirk in France, from which place James shortly after started alone upon a private mission. This was to England and to see Lord Holderness; and it has always been a bitter thought that my good money helped to pay the charges of the same. But he has need of a long spoon who soups with the de'il, or James More either. During this absence, the time was to fall due for another letter; and as the letter was the condition of his stipend, he had been so careful as to prepare it beforehand and leave it with Catriona to be despatched. The fact of our correspondence aroused her suspicions, and he was no sooner gone than she had burst the seal. What I received began accordingly in the writing of James More:

"My dear Sir,—Your esteemed favour came to hand duly, and I have to acknowledge the inclosure according to agreement. It shall be all faithfully expended on my daughter, who is well, and desires to be remembered to her dear friend. I find her in rather a melancholy disposition, but trust in the mercy of God to see her re-established. Our manner of life is very much alone, but we solace ourselves with the melancholy tunes of our native mountains, and by walking up the margin of the sea that lies next to Scotland. It was better days with me when I lay with five wounds upon my body on the field of Gladsmuir. I have found employment here in the haras of a French nobleman, where my experience is valued. But, my dear Sir, the wages are so exceedingly unsuitable that I would be ashamed to mention them, which makes your remittances the more necessary to my daughter's comfort, though I daresay the sight of old friends would be still better.

"My dear Sir,

"Your affectionate, obedient servant,

"James Macgregor Drummond."

Below it began again in the hand of Catriona:—

"Do not be believing him, it is all lies together,—C. M. D."

Not only did she add this postscript, but I think she must have come near suppressing the letter; for it came long after date, and was closely followed by the third. In the time betwixt them, Alan had arrived, and made another life to me with his merry conversation; I had been presented to his cousin of the Scots-Dutch, a man that drank more than I could have thought possible and was not otherwise of interest; I had been entertained to many jovial dinners and given some myself, all with no great change upon my sorrow; and we two (by which I mean Alan and myself, and not at all the cousin) had discussed a good deal the nature of my relations with James More and his daughter. I was naturally diffident to give particulars; and this disposition was not anyway lessened by the nature of Alan's commentary upon those I gave.

"I cannae make heed nor tail of it," he would say, "but it sticks in my mind ye've made a gowk of yourself. There's few people that has had more experience than Alan Breck: and I can never call to mind to have heard tell of a lassie like this one of yours. The way that you tell it, the thing's fair impossible. Ye must have made a terrible hash of the business, David."

"There are whiles that I am of the same mind," said I.

"The strange thing is that ye seem to have a kind of fancy for her too!" said Alan.

"The biggest kind, Alan," said I, "and I think I'll take it to my grave with me."

"Well, ye beat me, whatever!" he would conclude.

I showed him the letter with Catriona's postscript. "And here again!" he cried. "Impossible to deny a kind of decency to this Catriona, and sense forby! As for James More, the man's as boss as a drum; he's just a wame and a wheen words; though I'll can never deny that he fought reasonably well at Gladsmuir, and it's true what he says here about the five wounds. But the loss of him is that the man's boss."

"Ye see, Alan," said I, "it goes against the grain with me to leave the maid in such poor hands."

"Ye couldnae weel find poorer," he admitted. "But what are ye to do with it? It's this way about a man and a woman, ye see, Davie: The weemenfolk have got no kind of reason to them. Either they like the man, and then a' goes fine; or else they just detest him, and ye may spare your breath—ye can do naething. There's just the two sets of them—them that would sell their coats for ye, and them that never look the road ye're on. That's a' that there is to women; and you seem to be such a gomeral that ye cannae tell the tane frae the tither."

"Well, and I'm afraid that's true for me," said I.

"And yet there's naething easier!" cried Alan. "I could easy learn ye the science of the thing; but ye seem to me to be born blind, and there's where the deefficulty comes in."

"And can you no help me?" I asked, "you that are so clever at the trade?"

"Ye see, David, I wasnae here," said he. "I'm like a field officer that has naebody but blind men for scouts and éclaireurs; and what would he ken? But it sticks in my mind that ye'll have made some kind of bauchle; and if I was you I would have a try at her again."

"Would ye so, man Alan?" said I.

"I would e'en't," says he.

The third letter came to my hand while we were deep in some such talk: and it will be seen how pat it fell to the occasion. James professed to be in some concern upon his daughter's health, which I believe was never better; abounded in kind expressions to myself; and finally proposed that I should visit them at Dunkirk.

"You will now be enjoying the society of my old comrade Mr. Stewart,"

398

he wrote. "Why not accompany him so far in his return to France? I have something very particular for Mr. Stewart's ear; and, at any rate, I would be pleased to meet in with an old fellow-soldier and one so mettle as himself. As for you, my dear sir, my daughter and I would be proud to receive our benefactor, whom we regard as a brother and a son. The French nobleman has proved a person of the most filthy avarice of character, and I have been necessitate to leave the haras. You will find us in consequence a little poorly lodged in the auberge of a man Bazin on the dunes; but the situation is caller, and I make no doubt but we might spend some very pleasant days, when Mr. Stewart and I could recall our services, and you and my daughter divert yourselves in a manner more befitting your age. I beg at least that Mr. Stewart would come here; my business with him opens a very wide door."

"What does the man want with me?" cried Alan, when he had read. "What he wants with you is clear enough—it's siller. But what can he want with Alan Breck?"

"O, it'll be just an excuse," said I. "He is still after this marriage, which I wish from my heart that we could bring about. And he asks you because he thinks I would be less likely to come wanting you."

"Well, I wish that I kent," says Alan. "Him and me were never onyways pack; we used to girn at ither like a pair of pipers. 'Something for my ear,' quo' he! I'll maybe have something for his hinder-end, before we're through with it. Dod, I'm thinking it would be a kind of divertisement to gang and see what he'll be after! Forby that I could see your lassie then. What say ye, Davie? Will ye ride with Alan?"

You may be sure I was not backward, and Alan's furlough running towards an end, we set forth presently upon this joint adventure.

It was near dark of a January day when we rode at last into the town of Dunkirk. We left our horses at the post, and found a guide to Bazin's Inn, which lay beyond the walls. Night was quite fallen, so that we were the last to leave that fortress, and heard the doors of it close behind us as we passed the bridge. On the other side there lay a lighted suburb, which we thridded for a while, then turned into a dark lane, and presently found ourselves wading in the night among deep sand where we could hear a bullering of the sea. We travelled in this fashion for some while, following our conductor mostly by the sound of his voice; and I had begun to think he was perhaps misleading us, when we came to the top of a small brae, and there appeared out of the darkness a dim light in a window.

"Voilà l'auberge à Bazin," says the guide.

Alan smacked his lips. "An unco lonely bit," said he, and I thought by his tone he was not wholly pleased.

A little after, and we stood in the lower storey of that house, which was all in the one apartment, with a stairs leading to the chambers at the side, benches and tables by the wall, the cooking fire at the one end of it, and shelves of bottles and the cellar-trap at the other. Here Bazin, who was an ill-looking, big man, told us the Scottish gentleman was gone abroad he knew not where, but the young lady was above, and he would call her down to us.

I took from my breast that kerchief wanting the corner, and knotted it about my throat. I could hear my heart go; and Alan patting me on the shoulder with some of his laughable expressions, I could scarce refrain from a sharp word. But the time was not long to wait. I heard her step pass overhead, and saw her on the stair. This she descended very quietly, and greeted me with a pale face and a certain seeming of earnestness, or uneasiness, in her manner that extremely dashed me.

"My father, James More, will be here soon. He will be very pleased to see you," she said. And then of a sudden her face flamed, her eyes lightened, the speech stopped upon her lips; and I made sure she had observed the kerchief. It was only for a breath that she was discomposed; but methought it was with a new animation that she turned to welcome Alan. "And you will be his friend, Alan Breck?" she cried. "Many is the dozen times I will have heard him tell of you; and I love you already for all your bravery and goodness."

"Well, well," says Alan, holding her hand in his and viewing her, "and so this is the young lady at the last of it! David, ye're an awful poor hand of a description."

400

I do not know that ever I heard him speak so straight to people's hearts; the sound of his voice was like song.

"What? will he have been describing me?" she cried.

"Little else of it since I ever came out of France!" says he, "forby a bit of a speciment one night in Scotland in a shaw of wood by Silvermills. But cheer up, my dear! ye're bonnier than what he said. And now there's one thing sure; you and me are to be a pair of friends. I'm a kind of a henchman to Davie here; I'm like a tyke at his heels; and whatever he cares for, I've got to care for too—and by the holy airn! they've got to care for me! So now you can see what way you stand with Alan Breck, and ye'll find ye'll hardly lose on the transaction. He's no very bonnie, my dear, but he's leal to them he loves."

"I thank you from my heart for your good words," said she. "I have that honour for a brave, honest man that I cannot find any to be answering with."

Using travellers' freedom, we spared to wait for James More, and sat down to meat, we threesome. Alan had Catriona sit by him and wait upon his wants: he made her drink first out of his glass, he surrounded her with continual kind gallantries, and yet never gave me the most small occasion to be jealous; and he kept the talk so much in his own hand, and that in so merry a note, that neither she nor I remembered to be embarrassed. If any had seen us there, it must have been supposed that Alan was the old friend and I the stranger. Indeed, I had often cause to love and to admire the man, but I never loved or admired him better than that night; and I could not help remarking to myself (what I was sometimes rather in danger of forgetting) that he had not only much experience of life, but in his own way a great deal of natural ability besides. As for Catriona, she seemed quite carried away; her laugh was like a peal of bells, her face gay as a May morning; and I own, although I was well pleased, yet I was a little sad also, and thought myself a dull, stockish character in comparison of my friend, and very unfit to come into a young maid's life, and perhaps ding down her gaiety.

But if that was like to be my part, I found that at least I was not alone in it; for, James More returning suddenly, the girl was changed into a piece of stone. Through the rest of that evening, until she made an excuse and slipped to bed, I kept an eye upon her without cease; and I can bear testimony that she never smiled, scarce spoke, and looked mostly on the board in front of her. So that I really marvelled to see so much devotion (as it used to be) changed into the very sickness of hate.

Of James More it is unnecessary to say much; you know the man already, what there was to know of him; and I am weary of writing out his lies. Enough that he drank a great deal, and told us very little that was to any possible purpose. As for the business with Alan, that was to be reserved for the morrow and his private hearing.

It was the more easy to be put off, because Alan and I were pretty weary with four day's ride, and sat not very late after Catriona.

We were soon alone in a chamber where we were to make-shift with a single bed. Alan looked on me with a queer smile.

"Ye muckle ass!" said he.

"What do ye mean by that?" I cried.

"Mean? What do I mean! It's extraordinar, David man," say he, "that you should be so mortal stupit."

Again I begged him to speak out.

"Well, it's this of it," said he. "I told ye there were the two kinds of women—them that would sell their shifts for ye, and the others. Just you try for yoursel, my bonny man! But what's that neepkin at your craig?"

I told him.

"I thocht it was something thereabout," said he.

Nor would he say another word though I besieged him long with importunities.

CHAPTER XXX—THE LETTER FROM THE SHIP

Daylight showed us how solitary the inn stood. It was plainly hard upon the sea, yet out of all view of it, and beset on every side with scabbit hills of sand. There was, indeed, only one thing in the nature of a prospect, where there stood out over a brae the two sails of a windmill, like an ass's ears, but with the ass quite hidden. It was strange (after the wind rose, for at first it was dead calm) to see the turning and following of each other of these great sails behind the hillock. Scarce any road came by there; but a number of footways travelled among the bents in all directions up to Mr. Bazin's door. The truth is, he was a man of many trades, not any one of them honest, and the position of his inn was the best of his livelihood. Smugglers frequented it; political agents and forfeited persons bound across the water came there to await their passages; and I daresay there was worse behind, for a whole family might have been butchered in that house and nobody the wiser.

I slept little and ill. Long ere it was day, I had slipped from beside my bedfellow, and was warming myself at the fire or walking to and fro before the door. Dawn broke mighty sullen; but a little after, sprang up a wind out of the west, which burst the clouds, let through the sun, and set the mill to the turning. There was something of spring in the sunshine, or else it was in my heart; and the appearing of the great sails one after another from behind the hill, diverted me extremely. At times I could hear a creak of the machinery; and by half-past eight of the day, and I thought this dreary, desert place was like a paradise.

For all which, as the day drew on and nobody came near, I began to be aware of an uneasiness that I could scarce explain. It seemed there was trouble afoot; the sails of the windmill, as they came up and went down over the hill, were like persons spying; and outside of all fancy, it was surely a strange neighbourhood and house for a young lady to be brought to dwell in.

At breakfast, which we took late, it was manifest that James More was in some danger or perplexity; manifest that Alan was alive to the same, and watched him close; and this appearance of duplicity upon the one side, and vigilance upon the other, held me on live coals. The meal was no sooner over than James seemed to come began to make apologies. He had an appointment of a private nature in the town (it was with the French nobleman, he told me), and we would please excuse him till about noon. Meanwhile he carried his daughter aside to the far end of the room, where he seemed to speak rather earnestly and she to listen with much inclination.

"I am caring less and less about this man James," said Alan. "There's something no right with the man James, and I shouldnae wonder but what Alan Breck would give an eye to him this day. I would like fine to see yon French nobleman, Davie; and I daresay you could find an employ to yoursel, and that would be to speir at the lassie for some news o' your affair. Just tell it to her plainly—tell her ye're a muckle ass at the off-set; and then, if I were you, and ye could do it naitural, I would just mint to her I was in some kind of a danger; a' weemenfolk likes that."

"I cannae lee, Alan, I cannae do it naitural," says I, mocking him.

"The more fool you!" says he. "Then ye'll can tell her that I recommended it; that'll set her to the laughing; and I wouldnae wonder but what that was the next best. But see to the pair of them! If I didnae feel just sure of the lassie, and that she was awful pleased and chief with Alan, I would think there was some kind of hocus-pocus about you."

"And is she so pleased with ye, then, Alan?" I asked.

"She thinks a heap of me," says he. "And I'm no like you: I'm one that can tell. That she does—she thinks a heap of Alan. And troth! I'm thinking a good deal of him mysel; and with your permission, Shaws, I'll be getting a wee yont amang the bents, so that I can see what way James goes."

One after another went, till I was left alone beside the breakfast table; James to Dunkirk, Alan dogging him, Catriona up the stairs to her own chamber. I could very well understand how she should avoid to be alone with me; yet was none the better pleased with it for that, and bent my mind to entrap her to an interview before the men returned. Upon the whole, the best appeared to me to do like Alan. If I was out of view among the sandhills, the fine morning would decoy her forth; and once I had her in the open, I could please myself.

No sooner said than done; nor was I long under the bield of a hillock before she appeared at the inn door, looked here and there, and (seeing nobody) set out by a path that led directly seaward, and by which I followed her. I was in no haste to make my presence known; the further she went I made sure of the longer hearing to my suit; and the ground being all sandy it was easy to follow her unheard. The path rose and came at last to the head of a knowe. Thence I had a picture for the first time of what a desolate wilderness that inn stood hidden in; where was no man to be seen, nor any house of man, except just Bazin's and the windmill. Only a little further on, the sea appeared and two or three ships upon it, pretty as a drawing. One of these was extremely close in to be so great a vessel; and I was aware of a shock of new suspicion, when I recognised the trim of the Seahorse. What should an English ship be doing so near in to France? Why was Alan brought into her neighbourhood, and that in a place so far from any hope of rescue? and was it by accident, or by design, that the daughter of James More should walk that day to the seaside?

Presently I came forth behind her in the front of the sandhills and above the beach. It was here long and solitary; with a man-o'-war's boat drawn up about the middle of the prospect, and an officer in charge and pacing the sands like one who waited. I sat down where the rough grass a good deal covered me, and looked for what should follow. Catriona went straight to the boat; the officer met her with civilities; they had ten words together; I saw a letter changing hands; and there was Catriona returning. At the same time, as if this were all her business on the Continent, the boat shoved off and was headed for the Seahorse. But I observed the officer to remain behind and disappear among the bents.

I liked the business little; and the more I considered of it, liked it less. Was it Alan the officer was seeking? or Catriona? She drew near with her head down, looking constantly on the sand, and made so tender a picture that I could not bear to doubt her innocence. The next, she raised her face and recognised me; seemed to hesitate, and then came on again, but more slowly, and I thought with a changed colour. And at that thought, all else that was upon my bosom—fears, suspicions, the care of my friend's life—was clean swallowed up; and I rose to my feet and stood waiting her in a drunkenness of hope.

I gave her "good morning" as she came up, which she returned with a good deal of composure.

"Will you forgive my having followed you?" said I.

"I know you are always meaning kindly," she replied; and then, with a little outburst, "but why will you be sending money to that man! It must not be."

"I never sent it for him," said I, "but for you, as you know well."

"And you have no right to be sending it to either one of us," she said. "David, it is not right."

"It is not, it is all wrong," said I, "and I pray God he will help this dull fellow (if it be at all possible) to make it better. Catriona, this is no kind of life for you to lead; and I ask your pardon for the word, but yon man is no fit father to take care of you."

"Do not be speaking of him, even!" was her cry.

"And I need speak of him no more; it is not of him that I am thinking, O, be sure of that!" says I. "I think of the one thing. I have been alone now this long time in Leyden; and when I was by way of at my studies, still I was thinking of that. Next Alan came, and I went among soldier-men to their big dinners; and still I had the same thought. And it was the same before, when I had her there beside me. Catriona, do you see this napkin at my throat! You cut a corner from it once and then cast it from you. They're your colours now; I wear them in my heart. My dear, I cannot be wanting you. O, try to put up with me!"

I stepped before her so as to intercept her walking on.

"Try to put up with me," I was saying, "try and bear me with a little."

Still she had never the word, and a fear began to rise in me like a fear of death.

"Catriona," I cried, gazing on her hard, "is it a mistake again? Am I quite lost?"

She raised her face to me, breathless.

"Do you want me, Davie, truly?" said she, and I scarce could hear her say it.

"I do that," said I. "O, sure you know it—I do that."

"I have nothing left to give or to keep back," said she. "I was all yours from the first day, if you would have had a gift of me!" she said.

This was on the summit of a brae; the place was windy and conspicuous, we were to be seen there even from the English ship; but I kneeled down before her in the sand, and embraced her knees, and burst into that storm of weeping that I thought it must have broken me. All thought was wholly beaten from my mind by the vehemency of my discompose. I knew not where I was. I had forgot why I was happy; only I knew she stooped, and I felt her cherish me to her face and bosom, and heard her words out of a whirl.

"Davie," she was saying, "O, Davie, is this what you think of me! Is it so that you were caring for poor me! O, Davie, Davie!"

With that she wept also, and our tears were commingled in a perfect gladness.

It might have been ten in the day before I came to a clear sense of what a mercy had befallen me; and sitting over against her, with her hands in mine, gazed in her face, and laughed out loud for pleasure like a child, and called her foolish and kind names. I have never seen the place that looked so pretty as those bents by Dunkirk; and the windmill sails, as they bobbed over the knowe, were like a tune of music.

I know not how much longer we might have continued to forget all else besides ourselves, had I not chanced upon a reference to her father, which

407

brought us to reality.

"My little friend," I was calling her again and again, rejoicing to summon up the past by the sound of it, and to gaze across on her, and to be a little distant—"My little friend, now you are mine altogether; mine for good, my little friend and that man's no longer at all."

There came a sudden whiteness in her face, she plucked her hands from mine.

"Davie, take me away from him!" she cried. "There's something wrong; he's not true. There will be something wrong; I have a dreadful terror here at my heart. What will he be wanting at all events with that King's ship? What will this word be saying?" And she held the letter forth. "My mind misgives me, it will be some ill to Alan. Open it, Davie—open it and see."

I took it, and looked at it, and shook my head.

"No," said I, "it goes against me, I cannot open a man's letter."

"Not to save your friend?" she cried.

"I cannae tell," said I. "I think not. If I was only sure!"

"And you have but to break the seal!" said she.

"I know it," said I, "but the thing goes against me."

"Give it here," said she, "and I will open it myself."

"Nor you neither," said I. "You least of all. It concerns your father, and his honour, dear, which we are both misdoubting. No question but the place is dangerous-like, and the English ship being here, and your father having word from it, and yon officer that stayed ashore. He would not be alone either; there must be more along with him; I daresay we are spied upon this minute. Ay, no doubt, the letter should be opened; but somehow, not by you nor me."

I was about thus far with it, and my spirit very much overcome with a sense of danger and hidden enemies, when I spied Alan, come back again from following James and walking by himself among the sand-hills. He was in his soldier's coat, of course, and mighty fine; but I could not avoid to shudder when I thought how little that jacket would avail him, if he were once caught and flung in a skiff, and carried on board of the Seahorse, a deserter, a rebel, and now a condemned murderer.

"There," said I, "there is the man that has the best right to open it: or not, as he thinks fit."

With which I called upon his name, and we both stood up to be a mark for him.

"If it is so—if it be more disgrace—will you can bear it?" she asked, looking upon me with a burning eye.

"I was asked something of the same question when I had seen you but the once," said I. "What do you think I answered? That if I liked you as I thought I did—and O, but I like you better!—I would marry you at his gallows' foot."

The blood rose in her face; she came close up and pressed upon me, holding my hand: and it was so that we awaited Alan.

He came with one of his queer smiles. "What was I telling ye, David?" says he.

"There is a time for all things, Alan," said I, "and this time is serious. How have you sped? You can speak out plain before this friend of ours."

"I have been upon a fool's errand," said he.

"I doubt we have done better than you, then," said I; "and, at least, here is a great deal of matter that you must judge of. Do you see that?" I went on, pointing to the ship. "That is the Seahorse, Captain Palliser."

"I should ken her, too," says Alan. "I had fyke enough with her when she was stationed in the Forth. But what ails the man to come so close?"

"I will tell you why he came there first," said I. "It was to bring this letter to James More. Why he stops here now that it's delivered, what it's likely to be about, why there's an officer hiding in the bents, and whether or not it's probable that he's alone—I would rather you considered for yourself."

"A letter to James More?" said he.

"The same," said I.

"Well, and I can tell ye more than that," said Alan. "For the last night, when you were fast asleep, I heard the man colloguing with some one in the French, and then the door of that inn to be opened and shut."

"Alan!" cried I, "you slept all night, and I am here to prove it."

"Ay, but I would never trust Alan whether he was asleep or waking!" says he. "But the business looks bad. Let's see the letter."

I gave it him.

"Catriona," said he, "you have to excuse me, my dear; but there's nothing less than my fine bones upon the cast of it, and I'll have to break this seal."

"It is my wish," said Catriona.

He opened it, glanced it through, and flung his hand in the air.

"The stinking brock!" says he, and crammed the paper in his pocket. "Here, let's get our things together. This place is fair death to me." And he began to walk towards the inn.

It was Catriona that spoke the first. "He has sold you?" she asked.

"Sold me, my dear," said Alan. "But thanks to you and Davie, I'll can jink him yet. Just let me win upon my horse," he added.

"Catriona must come with us," said I. "She can have no more traffic with that man. She and I are to be married." At which she pressed my hand to her side.

"Are ye there with it?" says Alan, looking back. "The best day's work that ever either of you did yet! And I'm bound to say, my dawtie, ye make a real, bonny couple."

410

The way that he was following brought us close in by the windmill, where I was aware of a man in seaman's trousers, who seemed to be spying from behind it. Only, of course, we took him in the rear.

"See, Alan!"

"Wheesht!" said, he, "this is my affairs."

The man was, no doubt, a little deafened by the clattering of the mill, and we got up close before he noticed. Then he turned, and we saw he was a big fellow with a mahogany face.

"I think, sir," says Alan, "that you speak the English?"

"Non, monsieur," says he, with an incredible bad accent.

"Non, monsieur," cries Alan, mocking him. "Is that how they learn you French on the Seahorse? Ye muckle, gutsey hash, here's a Scots boot to your English hurdies!"

And bounding on him before he could escape, he dealt the man a kick that laid him on his nose. Then he stood, with a savage smile, and watched him scramble to his feet and scamper off into the sand-hills.

"But it's high time I was clear of these empty bents!" said Alan; and continued his way at top speed, and we still following, to the backdoor of Bazin's inn.

It chanced that as we entered by the one door we came face to face with James More entering by the other.

"Here!" said I to Catriona, "quick! upstairs with you and make your packets; this is no fit scene for you."

In the meanwhile James and Alan had met in the midst of the long room. She passed them close by to reach the stairs; and after she was some way up I saw her turn and glance at them again, though without pausing. Indeed, they were worth looking at. Alan wore as they met one of his best appearances of courtesy and friendliness, yet with something eminently warlike, so that James smelled danger off the man, as folk smell fire in a house, and stood prepared for accidents.

Time pressed. Alan's situation in that solitary place, and his enemies about him, might have daunted Cæsar. It made no change in him; and it was in his old spirit of mockery and daffing that he began the interview.

"A braw good day to ye again, Mr. Drummond," said he. "What'll yon business of yours be just about?"

"Why, the thing being private, and rather of a long story," says James, "I think it will keep very well till we have eaten."

"I'm none so sure of that," said Alan. "It sticks in my mind it's either now or never; for the fact is me and Mr. Balfour here have gotten a line, and we're thinking of the road."

I saw a little surprise in James's eye; but he held himself stoutly.

"I have but the one word to say to cure you of that," said he, "and that is the name of my business."

"Say it then," says Alan. "Hout! wha minds for Davie?"

"It is a matter that would make us both rich men," said James.

"Do you tell me that?" cries Alan.

"I do, sir," said James. "The plain fact is that it is Cluny's Treasure."

"No!" cried Alan. "Have ye got word of it?"

"I ken the place, Mr. Stewart, and can take you there," said James.

"This crowns all!" says Alan. "Well, and I'm glad I came to Dunkirk. And so this was your business, was it? Halvers, I'm thinking?"

"That is the business, sir," said James.

"Well, well," said Alan; and then in the same tone of childlike interest, "it has naething to do with the Seahorse, then?" he asked.

"With what?" says James.

"Or the lad that I have just kicked the bottom of behind yon windmill?" pursued Alan. "Hut, man! have done with your lees! I have Palliser's letter here in my pouch. You're by with it, James More. You can never show your face again with dacent folk."

James was taken all aback with it. He stood a second, motionless and white, then swelled with the living anger.

"Do you talk to me, you bastard?" he roared out.

"Ye glee'd swine!" cried Alan, and hit him a sounding buffet on the mouth, and the next wink of time their blades clashed together.

At the first sound of the bare steel I instinctively leaped back from the collision. The next I saw, James parried a thrust so nearly that I thought him killed; and it lowed up in my mind that this was the girl's father, and in a manner almost my own, and I drew and ran in to sever them.

"Keep back, Davie! Are ye daft! Damn ye, keep back!" roared Alan. "Your blood be on your ain heid then!"

I beat their blades down twice. I was knocked reeling against the wall; I was back again betwixt them. They took no heed of me, thrusting at each other like two furies. I can never think how I avoided being stabbed myself or stabbing one of these two Rodomonts, and the whole business turned about me like a piece of a dream; in the midst of which I heard a great cry from the stair, and Catriona sprang before her father. In the same moment the point of my sword encountered some thing yielding. It came back to me reddened. I saw the blood flow on the girl's kerchief, and stood sick.

"Will you be killing him before my eyes, and me his daughter after all!" she cried.

"My dear, I have done with him," said Alan, and went, and sat on a table, with his arms crossed and the sword naked in his hand.

Awhile she stood before the man, panting, with big eyes, then swung suddenly about and faced him.

"Begone!" was her word, "take your shame out of my sight; leave me with clean folk. I am a daughter of Alpin! Shame of the sons of Alpin, begone!"

It was said with so much passion as awoke me from the horror of my own bloodied sword. The two stood facing, she with the red stain on her kerchief, he white as a rag. I knew him well enough—I knew it must have pierced him in the quick place of his soul; but he betook himself to a bravado air.

"Why," says he, sheathing his sword, though still with a bright eye on Alan, "if this brawl is over I will but get my portmanteau—"

"There goes no pockmantie out of this place except with me," says Alan.

"Sir!" cries James.

"James More," says Alan, "this lady daughter of yours is to marry my friend Davie, upon the which account I let you pack with a hale carcase. But take you my advice of it and get that carcase out of harm's way or ower late. Little as you suppose it, there are leemits to my temper."

"Be damned, sir, but my money's there!" said James.

"I'm vexed about that, too," says Alan, with his funny face, "but now, ye see, it's mines." And then with more gravity, "Be you advised, James More, you leave this house."

James seemed to cast about for a moment in his mind; but it's to be thought he had enough of Alan's swordsmanship, for he suddenly put off his hat to us and (with a face like one of the damned) bade us farewell in a series. With which he was gone.

At the same time a spell was lifted from me.

"Catriona," I cried, "it was me—it was my sword. O, are you much hurt?"

"I know it, Davie, I am loving you for the pain of it; it was done defending that bad man, my father. See!" she said, and showed me a bleeding scratch, "see, you have made a man of me now. I will carry a wound like an

414

old soldier."

Joy that she should be so little hurt, and the love of her brave nature, supported me. I embraced her, I kissed the wound.

"And am I to be out of the kissing, me that never lost a chance?" says Alan; and putting me aside and taking Catriona by either shoulder, "My dear," he said, "you're a true daughter of Alpin. By all accounts, he was a very fine man, and he may weel be proud of you. If ever I was to get married, it's the marrow of you I would be seeking for a mother to my sons. And I bear's a king's name and speak the truth."

He said it with a serious heat of admiration that was honey to the girl, and through her, to me. It seemed to wipe us clean of all James More's disgraces. And the next moment he was just himself again.

"And now by your leave, my dawties," said he, "this is a' very bonny; but Alan Breck'll be a wee thing nearer to the gallows than he's caring for; and Dod! I think this is a grand place to be leaving."

The word recalled us to some wisdom. Alan ran upstairs and returned with our saddle-bags and James More's portmanteau; I picked up Catriona's bundle where she had dropped it on the stair; and we were setting forth out of that dangerous house, when Bazin stopped the way with cries and gesticulations. He had whipped under a table when the swords were drawn, but now he was as bold as a lion. There was his bill to be settled, there was a chair broken, Alan had sat among his dinner things, James More had fled.

"Here," I cried, "pay yourself," and flung him down some Lewie d'ors; for I thought it was no time to be accounting.

He sprang upon that money, and we passed him by, and ran forth into the open. Upon three sides of the house were seamen hasting and closing in; a little nearer to us James More waved his hat as if to hurry them; and right behind him, like some foolish person holding up his hands, were the sails of the windmill turning.

Alan gave but one glance, and laid himself down to run. He carried a great weight in James More's portmanteau; but I think he would as soon have lost his life as cast away that booty which was his revenge; and he ran so that I was distressed to follow him, and marvelled and exulted to see the girl bounding at my side.

As soon as we appeared, they cast off all disguise upon the other side; and the seamen pursued us with shouts and view-hullohs. We had a start of some two hundred yards, and they were but bandy-legged tarpaulins after all, that could not hope to better us at such an exercise. I suppose they were armed, but did not care to use their pistols on French ground. And as soon as I perceived that we not only held our advantage but drew a little away, I began to feel quite easy of the issue. For all which, it was a hot, brisk bit of work, so long as it lasted; Dunkirk was still far off; and when we popped over a knowe, and found a company of the garrison marching on the other side on some manœuvre, I could very well understand the word that Alan had.

He stopped running at once; and mopping at his brow, "They're a real bonny folk, the French nation," says he.

CONCLUSION

No sooner were we safe within the walls of Dunkirk than we held a very necessary council-of-war on our position. We had taken a daughter from her father at the sword's point; any judge would give her back to him at once, and by all likelihood clap me and Alan into jail; and though we had an argument upon our side in Captain Palliser's letter, neither Catriona nor I were very keen to be using it in public. Upon all accounts it seemed the most prudent to carry the girl to Paris to the hands of her own chieftain, Macgregor of Bohaldie, who would be very willing to help his kinswoman, on the one hand, and not at all anxious to dishonour James upon other.

We made but a slow journey of it up, for Catriona was not so good at the riding as the running, and had scarce sat in the saddle since the 'Forty-five. But we made it out at last, reached Paris early of a Sabbath morning, and made all speed, under Alan's guidance, to find Bohaldie. He was finely lodged, and lived in a good style, having a pension on the Scots Fund, as well as private means; greeted Catriona like one of his own house, and seemed

416

altogether very civil and discreet, but not particularly open. We asked of the news of James More. "Poor James!" said he, and shook his head and smiled, so that I thought he knew further than he meant to tell. Then we showed him Palliser's letter, and he drew a long face at that.

"Poor James!" said he again. "Well, there are worse folk than James More, too. But this is dreadful bad. Tut, tut, he must have forgot himself entirely! This is a most undesirable letter. But, for all that, gentlemen, I cannot see what we would want to make it public for. It's an ill bird that fouls his own nest, and we are all Scots folk and all Hieland."

Upon this we all agreed, save perhaps Alan; and still more upon the question of our marriage, which Bohaldie took in his own hands, as though there had been no such person as James More, and gave Catriona away with very pretty manners and agreeable compliments in French. It was not till all was over, and our healths drunk, that he told us James was in that city, whither he had preceded us some days, and where he now lay sick, and like to die. I thought I saw by my wife's face what way her inclination pointed.

"And let us go see him, then," said I.

"If it is your pleasure," said Catriona. These were early days.

He was lodged in the same quarter of the city with his chief, in a great house upon a corner; and we were guided up to the garret where he lay by the sound of Highland piping. It seemed he had just borrowed a set of them from Bohaldie to amuse his sickness; though he was no such hand as was his brother Rob, he made good music of the kind; and it was strange to observe the French folk crowding on the stairs, and some of them laughing. He lay propped in a pallet. The first look of him I saw he was upon his last business; and, doubtless, this was a strange place for him to die in. But even now I find I can scarce dwell upon his end with patience. Doubtless, Bohaldie had prepared him; he seemed to know we were married, complimented us on the event, and gave us a benediction like a patriarch.

"I have been never understood," said he. "I forgive you both without an afterthought;" after which he spoke for all the world in his old manner, was

417

so obliging as to play us a tune or two upon his pipes, and borrowed a small sum before I left.

I could not trace even a hint of shame in any part of his behaviour; but he was great upon forgiveness; it seemed always fresh to him. I think he forgave me every time we met; and when after some four days he passed away in a kind of odour of affectionate sanctity, I could have torn my hair out for exasperation. I had him buried; but what to put upon his tomb was quite beyond me, till at last I considered the date would look best alone.

I thought it wiser to resign all thoughts of Leyden, where we had appeared once as brother and sister, and it would certainly look strange to return in a new character. Scotland would be doing for us; and thither, after I had recovered that which I had left behind, we sailed in a Low Country ship.

And now, Miss Barbara Balfour (to set the ladies first), and Mr. Alan Balfour younger of Shaws, here is the story brought fairly to an end. A great many of the folk that took a part in it, you will find (if you think well) that you have seen and spoken with. Alison Hastie in Limekilns was the lass that rocked your cradle when you were too small to know of it, and walked abroad with you in the policy when you were bigger. That very fine great lady that is Miss Barbara's name-mamma is no other than the same Miss Grant that made so much a fool of David Balfour in the house of the Lord Advocate. And I wonder whether you remember a little, lean, lively gentleman in a scratch-wig and a wraprascal, that came to Shaws very late of a dark night, and whom you were awakened out of your beds and brought down to the dining-hall to be presented to, by the name of Mr. Jamieson? Or has Alan forgotten what he did at Mr. Jamieson's request—a most disloyal act—for which, by the letter of the law, he might be hanged—no less than drinking the king's health across the water? These were strange doings in a good Whig house! But Mr. Jamieson is a man privileged, and might set fire to my corn-barn; and the name they know him by now in France is the Chevalier Stewart.

As for Davie and Catriona, I shall watch you pretty close in the next days, and see if you are so bold as to be laughing at papa and mamma. It is

418

true we were not so wise as we might have been, and made a great deal of sorrow out of nothing; but you will find as you grow up that even the artful Miss Barbara, and even the valiant Mr. Alan, will be not so very much wiser than their parents. For the life of man upon this world of ours is a funny business. They talk of the angels weeping; but I think they must more often be holding their sides as they look on; and there was one thing I determined to do when I began this long story, and that was to tell out everything as it befell.

Footnotes

[1] Conspicuous.

[2] Country.

[3] The Fairies.

[4] Flatteries.

[5] Trust to.

[6] This must have reference to Dr. Cameron on his first visit.—D. B.

[7] Sweetheart.

[8] Child.

[9] Palm.

[10] Gallows.

[11] My Catechism.

[12] Now Prince's Street.

[13] A learned folklorist of my acquaintance hereby identifies Alan's air. It has been printed (it seems) in Campbell's Tales of the West Highlands, Vol. II., p. 91. Upon examination it would really seem as if Miss Grant's unrhymed doggrel (see Chapter V.) would fit with little humouring to the notes in question.

[14] A ball placed upon a little mound for convenience of striking.

[15] Patched shoes.

[16] Shoemaker.

[17] Tamson's mere—to go afoot.

[18] Beard.

[19] Ragged.

[20] Fine things.

[21] Catch.

[22] Victuals.

[23] Trust.

[24] Sea fog.

[25] Bashful.

[26] Rest.

About Author

Childhood and youth

Stevenson was born at 8 Howard Place, Edinburgh, Scotland on 13 November 1850 to Thomas Stevenson (1818–87), a leading lighthouse engineer, and his wife Margaret Isabella (born Balfour, 1829–97). He was christened Robert Lewis Balfour Stevenson. At about age 18, he changed the spelling of "Lewis" to "Louis", and he dropped "Balfour" in 1873.

Lighthouse design was the family's profession; Thomas's father (Robert's grandfather) was civil engineer Robert Stevenson, and Thomas's brothers (Robert's uncles) Alan and David were in the same field. Thomas's maternal grandfather Thomas Smith had been in the same profession. However, Robert's mother's family were gentry, tracing their lineage back to Alexander Balfour who had held the lands of Inchyra in Fife in the fifteenth century. His mother's father Lewis Balfour (1777–1860) was a minister of the Church of Scotland at nearby Colinton, and her siblings included physician George William Balfour and marine engineer James Balfour. Stevenson spent the greater part of his boyhood holidays in his maternal grandfather's house. "Now I often wonder what I inherited from this old minister," Stevenson wrote. "I must suppose, indeed, that he was fond of preaching sermons, and so am I, though I never heard it maintained that either of us loved to hear them."

Lewis Balfour and his daughter both had weak chests, so they often needed to stay in warmer climates for their health. Stevenson inherited a tendency to coughs and fevers, exacerbated when the family moved to a damp, chilly house at 1 Inverleith Terrace in 1851. The family moved again to the sunnier 17 Heriot Row when Stevenson was six years old, but the tendency to extreme sickness in winter remained with him until he was 11. Illness was a recurrent feature of his adult life and left him extraordinarily thin. Contemporaneous views were that he had tuberculosis, but more recent views are that it was bronchiectasis or even sarcoidosis.

Stevenson's parents were both devout Presbyterians, but the household was not strict in its adherence to Calvinist principles. His nurse Alison Cunningham (known as Cummy) was more fervently religious. Her mix of Calvinism and folk beliefs were an early source of nightmares for the child, and he showed a precocious concern for religion. But she also cared for him tenderly in illness, reading to him from John Bunyan and the Bible as he lay sick in bed and telling tales of the Covenanters. Stevenson recalled this time of sickness in "The Land of Counterpane" in A Child's Garden of Verses (1885), dedicating the book to his nurse.

Stevenson was an only child, both strange-looking and eccentric, and he found it hard to fit in when he was sent to a nearby school at age 6, a problem repeated at age 11 when he went on to the Edinburgh Academy; but he mixed well in lively games with his cousins in summer holidays at Colinton. His frequent illnesses often kept him away from his first school, so he was taught for long stretches by private tutors. He was a late reader, learning at age 7 or 8, but even before this he dictated stories to his mother and nurse, and he compulsively wrote stories throughout his childhood. His father was proud of this interest; he had also written stories in his spare time until his own father found them and told him to "give up such nonsense and mind your business." He paid for the printing of Robert's first publication at 16, entitled The Pentland Rising: A Page of History, 1666. It was an account of the Covenanters' rebellion which was published in 1866, the 200th anniversary of the event.

Education

In September 1857, Stevenson went to Mr Henderson's School in India Street, Edinburgh, but because of poor health stayed only a few weeks and did not return until October 1859. During his many absences he was taught by private tutors. In October 1861, he went to Edinburgh Academy, an independent school for boys, and stayed there sporadically for about fifteen months. In the autumn of 1863, he spent one term at an English boarding school at Spring Grove in Isleworth in Middlesex (now an urban area of West London). In October 1864, following an improvement to his health, he was sent to Robert Thomson's private school in Frederick Street, Edinburgh, where he remained until he went to university. In November 1867, Stevenson entered the University of Edinburgh to study engineering. He showed from the start no enthusiasm for his studies and devoted much energy to avoiding lectures. This time was more important for the friendships he made with other students in the Speculative Society (an exclusive debating club), particularly with Charles Baxter, who would become Stevenson's financial agent, and with a professor, Fleeming Jenkin, whose house staged amateur drama in which Stevenson took part, and whose biography he would later write. Perhaps most important at this point in his life was a cousin, Robert Alan Mowbray Stevenson (known as "Bob"), a lively and light-hearted young man who, instead of the family profession, had chosen to study art. Each year during vacations, Stevenson travelled to inspect the family's engineering works—to Anstruther and Wick in 1868, with his father on his official tour of Orkney and Shetland islands lighthouses in 1869, and for three weeks to the island of Erraid in 1870. He enjoyed the travels more for the material they gave for his writing than for any engineering interest. The voyage with his father pleased him because a similar journey of Walter Scott with Robert Stevenson had provided the inspiration for Scott's 1822 novel The Pirate. In April 1871, Stevenson notified his father of his decision to pursue a life of letters. Though the elder Stevenson was naturally disappointed, the surprise cannot have been great, and Stevenson's mother reported that he was "wonderfully resigned" to his son's choice. To provide some security, it was agreed that Stevenson should read Law (again at Edinburgh University) and be called to the Scottish bar. In his 1887 poetry collection Underwoods, Stevenson muses on his having turned from the family profession:

> Say not of me that weakly I declined
>
> The labours of my sires, and fled the sea,
>
> The towers we founded and the lamps we lit,
>
> To play at home with paper like a child.
>
> But rather say: In the afternoon of time

A strenuous family dusted from its hands

The sand of granite, and beholding far

Along the sounding coast its pyramids

And tall memorials catch the dying sun,

Smiled well content, and to this childish task

Around the fire addressed its evening hours.

In other respects too, Stevenson was moving away from his upbringing. His dress became more Bohemian; he already wore his hair long, but he now took to wearing a velveteen jacket and rarely attended parties in conventional evening dress. Within the limits of a strict allowance, he visited cheap pubs and brothels. More importantly, he had come to reject Christianity and declared himself an atheist. In January 1873, his father came across the constitution of the LJR (Liberty, Justice, Reverence) Club, of which Stevenson and his cousin Bob were members, which began: "Disregard everything our parents have taught us". Questioning his son about his beliefs, he discovered the truth, leading to a long period of dissension with both parents:

What a damned curse I am to my parents! As my father said "You have rendered my whole life a failure". As my mother said "This is the heaviest affliction that has ever befallen me". O Lord, what a pleasant thing it is to have damned the happiness of (probably) the only two people who care a damn about you in the world.

Early writing and travels

Stevenson was visiting a cousin in England in late 1873 when he met two people who became very important to him: Sidney Colvin and Fanny (Frances Jane) Sitwell. Sitwell was a 34-year-old woman with a son, who was separated from her husband. She attracted the devotion of many who met her, including Colvin, who married her in 1901. Stevenson was also drawn to her, and they kept up a warm correspondence over several years in which he wavered between the role of a suitor and a son (he addressed her as "Madonna"). Colvin became Stevenson's literary adviser and was the first editor of his letters after his death. He placed Stevenson's first paid contribution in The Portfolio, an essay entitled "Roads".

Stevenson was soon active in London literary life, becoming acquainted with many of the writers of the time, including Andrew Lang, Edmund Gosse, and Leslie Stephen, the editor of the Cornhill Magazine who took an interest in Stevenson's work. Stephen took Stevenson to visit a patient at the Edinburgh Infirmary named William Ernest Henley, an energetic and talkative man with a wooden leg. Henley became a close friend and occasional literary collaborator, until a quarrel broke up the friendship in 1888, and he is often considered to be the model for Long John Silver in Treasure Island.

Stevenson was sent to Menton on the French Riviera in November 1873 to recuperate after his health failed. He returned in better health in April 1874 and settled down to his studies, but he returned to France several times after that. He made long and frequent trips to the neighborhood of the Forest of Fontainebleau, staying at Barbizon, Grez-sur-Loing, and Nemours and becoming a member of the artists' colonies there. He also traveled to Paris to visit galleries and the theatres. He qualified for the Scottish bar in July 1875, and his father added a brass plate to the Heriot Row house reading "R.L. Stevenson, Advocate". His law studies did influence his books, but he never practised law; all his energies were spent in travel and writing. One of his journeys was a canoe voyage in Belgium and France with Sir Walter Simpson, a friend from the Speculative Society, a frequent travel companion, and the author of The Art of Golf (1887). This trip was the basis of his first travel book An Inland Voyage (1878).

Marriage

The canoe voyage with Simpson brought Stevenson to Grez in September 1876 where he met Fanny Van de Grift Osbourne (1840–1914), born in Indianapolis. She had married at age 17 and moved to Nevada to rejoin husband Samuel after his participation in the American Civil War. Their children were Isobel (or "Belle"), Lloyd, and Hervey (who died in 1875). But anger over her husband's infidelities led to a number of separations. In 1875, she had taken her children to France where she and Isobel studied art.

Stevenson returned to Britain shortly after this first meeting, but Fanny apparently remained in his thoughts, and he wrote the essay "On falling in love" for the Cornhill Magazine. They met again early in 1877 and became lovers. Stevenson spent much of the following year with her and her children in France. In August 1878, she returned to San Francisco and Stevenson remained in Europe, making the walking trip that formed the basis for Travels with a Donkey in the Cévennes (1879). But he set off to join her in August 1879, against the advice of his friends and without notifying his parents. He took second-class passage on the steamship Devonia, in part to save money but also to learn how others traveled and to increase the adventure of the journey. He then traveled overland by train from New York City to California. He later wrote about the experience in The Amateur Emigrant. It was good experience for his writing, but it broke his health.

He was near death when he arrived in Monterey, California, where some local ranchers nursed him back to health. He stayed for a time at the French Hotel located at 530 Houston Street, now a museum dedicated to his memory called the "Stevenson House". While there, he often dined "on the cuff," as he said, at a nearby restaurant run by Frenchman Jules Simoneau which stood at what is now Simoneau Plaza; several years later, he sent Simoneau an inscribed copy of his novel Strange Case of Dr Jekyll and Mr Hyde (1886), writing that it would be a stranger case still if Robert Louis Stevenson ever forgot Jules Simoneau. While in Monterey, he wrote an evocative article about "the Old Pacific Capital" of Monterey.

By December 1879, Stevenson had recovered his health enough to continue to San Francisco where he struggled "all alone on forty-five cents a day, and sometimes less, with quantities of hard work and many heavy thoughts," in an effort to support himself through his writing. But by the end of the winter, his health was broken again and he found himself at death's door. Fanny was now divorced and recovered from her own illness, and she came to his bedside and nursed him to recovery. "After a while," he wrote, "my spirit got up again in a divine frenzy, and has since kicked and spurred my vile body forward with great emphasis and success." When his father heard of his condition, he cabled him money to help him through this period.

Fanny and Robert were married in May 1880, although he said that he was "a mere complication of cough and bones, much fitter for an emblem of mortality than a bridegroom." He travelled with his new wife and her son Lloyd north of San Francisco to Napa Valley and spent a summer honeymoon at an abandoned mining camp on Mount Saint Helena. He wrote about this experience in The Silverado Squatters. He met Charles Warren Stoddard, co-editor of the Overland Monthly and author of South Sea Idylls, who urged Stevenson to travel to the South Pacific, an idea which returned to him many years later. In August 1880, he sailed with Fanny and Lloyd from New York to Britain and found his parents and his friend Sidney Colvin on the wharf at Liverpool, happy to see him return home. Gradually, his wife was able to patch up differences between father and son and make herself a part of the family through her charm and wit.

Attempted settlement in Europe and the US

Stevenson searched in vain between 1880 and 1887 for a residence suitable to his health. He spent his summers at various places in Scotland and England, including Westbourne, Dorset, a residential area in Bournemouth. It was during his time in Bournemouth that he wrote the story Strange Case of Dr Jekyll and Mr Hyde, naming the character Mr. Poole after the town of Poole which is situated next to Bournemouth. In Westbourne, he named his house Skerryvore after the tallest lighthouse in Scotland, which his uncle Alan had built (1838–44). In the wintertime, Stevenson travelled to France and lived at Davos Platz and the Chalet de Solitude at Hyères, where he was very happy for a time. "I have so many things to make life sweet for me," he wrote, "it seems a pity I cannot have that other one thing—health. But though you will be angry to hear it, I believe, for myself at least, what is is best." In spite of his ill health, he produced the bulk of his best-known work during these years. Treasure Island was published under the pseudonym "Captain George North" and became his first widely popular book; he wrote it during this time, along with Kidnapped, Strange Case of Dr Jekyll and Mr Hyde (which established his wider reputation), The Black Arrow: A Tale of the Two Roses, A Child's Garden of Verses, and Underwoods. He gave a copy of Kidnapped to his friend and frequent Skerryvore visitor Henry James.

His father died in 1887 and Stevenson felt free to follow the advice of his physician to try a complete change of climate, so he headed for Colorado with his mother and family. But after landing in New York, they decided to spend the winter in the Adirondacks at a cure cottage now known as Stevenson Cottage at Saranac Lake, New York. During the intensely cold winter, Stevenson wrote some of his best essays, including Pulvis et Umbra. He also began The Master of Ballantrae and lightheartedly planned a cruise to the southern Pacific Ocean for the following summer.

Politics

Stevenson believed in Conservatism for most of his life. His cousin and biographer Sir Graham Balfour said that "he probably throughout life would, if compelled to vote, have always supported the Conservative candidate." In 1866, Stevenson voted for Benjamin Disraeli, future Conservative Prime Minister of the United Kingdom, over Thomas Carlyle for the Lord Rectorship of the University of Edinburgh. During his college years, he briefly identified himself as a "red-hot socialist". He wrote at age 26: "I look back to the time when I was a Socialist with something like regret…. Now I know that in thus turning Conservative with years, I am going through the normal cycle of change and travelling in the common orbit of men's opinions."

Journey to the Pacific

In June 1888, Stevenson chartered the yacht Casco and set sail with his family from San Francisco. The vessel "plowed her path of snow across the empty deep, far from all track of commerce, far from any hand of help." The sea air and thrill of adventure for a time restored his health, and for nearly three years he wandered the eastern and central Pacific, stopping for extended stays at the Hawaiian Islands where he became a good friend of King Kalākaua. He befriended the king's niece Princess Victoria Kaiulani, who also had Scottish heritage. He spent time at the Gilbert Islands, Tahiti, New Zealand, and the Samoan Islands. During this period, he completed The Master of Ballantrae, composed two ballads based on the legends of the islanders, and wrote The Bottle Imp. He preserved the experience of these years in his various letters and in his In the South Seas (which was published posthumously). He made a voyage in 1889 with Lloyd on the trading schooner Equator, visiting Butaritari, Mariki, Apaiang, and Abemama in the Gilbert Islands. They spent several months on Abemama with tyrant-chief Tem Binoka, whom Stevenson described in In the South Seas.

Stevenson left Sydney on the Janet Nicoll in April 1890 for his third and final voyage among the South Seas islands. He intended to produce another book of travel writing to follow his earlier book In the South Seas, but it was his wife who eventually published her journal of their third voyage. (Fanny misnames the ship in her account The Cruise of the Janet Nichol.) A fellow passenger was Jack Buckland, whose stories of life as an island trader became the inspiration for the character of Tommy Hadden in The Wrecker (1892), which Stevenson and Lloyd Osbourne wrote together. Buckland visited the Stevensons at Vailima in 1894.

Last years

In 1890, Stevenson purchased a tract of about 400 acres (1.6 km²) in Upolu, an island in Samoa where he established himself on his estate in the village of Vailima after two aborted attempts to visit Scotland. He took the native name Tusitala (Samoan for "Teller of Tales"). His influence spread among the Samoans, who consulted him for advice, and he soon became involved in local politics. He was convinced that the European officials who had been appointed to rule the Samoans were incompetent, and he published A Footnote to History after many futile attempts to resolve the matter. This was such a stinging protest against existing conditions that it resulted in the recall of two officials, and Stevenson feared for a time that it would result in his own deportation. He wrote to Colvin, "I used to think meanly of the plumber; but how he shines beside the politician!"

He also found time to work at his writing, although he felt that "there was never any man had so many irons in the fire". He wrote The Beach of Falesa, Catriona (titled David Balfour in the US), The Ebb-Tide, and the Vailima Letters during this period.

Stevenson grew depressed and wondered if he had exhausted his creative vein, as he had been "overworked bitterly" and that the best he could write was "ditch-water". He even feared that he might again become a helpless invalid. He rebelled against this idea: "I wish to die in my boots; no more Land of Counterpane for me. To be drowned, to be shot, to be thrown from a horse — ay, to be hanged, rather than pass again through that slow dissolution." He then suddenly had a return of energy and he began work on Weir of Hermiston. "It's so good that it frightens me," he is reported to have exclaimed. He felt that this was the best work he had done.

On 3 December 1894, Stevenson was talking to his wife and straining to open a bottle of wine when he suddenly exclaimed, "What's that?", asked his wife "does my face look strange?", and collapsed. He died within a few hours, probably of a cerebral haemorrhage. He was 44 years old. The Samoans insisted on surrounding his body with a watch-guard during the night and on bearing him on their shoulders to nearby Mount Vaea, where they buried him on a spot overlooking the sea on land donated by British Acting Vice Consul Thomas Trood. Stevenson had always wanted his Requiem inscribed on his tomb:

Under the wide and starry sky,

Dig the grave and let me lie.

Glad did I live and gladly die,

And I laid me down with a will.

This be the verse you grave for me:

Here he lies where he longed to be;

Home is the sailor, home from sea,

And the hunter home from the hill.

Stevenson was loved by the Samoans, and his tombstone epigraph was translated to a Samoan song of grief. (Source: Wikipedia)